Out of Shadows

Susan Lewis is the bestselling author of twenty-one novels. She is also the author of *Just One More Day*, a moving memoir of her childhood in Bristol. She lives in France. Her website address is www.susanlewis.com

Acclaim for Susan Lewis

'Deliciously dramatic and positively oozing with tension, this is another wonderfully absorbing novel from the *Sunday Times* bestseller Susan Lewis . . . Expertly written to brew an atmosphere of foreboding, this story is an irresistible blend of intrigue and passion, and the consequences of secrets and betrayal' *Woman*

'A multi-faceted tear jerker' *heat*

'Spellbinding! . . . you just keep turning the pages, with the atmosphere growing more and more intense as the story leads to its dramatic climax' *Daily Mail*

'One of the best around' *Independent on Sunday*

'Mystery and romance *par excellence*' *Sun*

'We use the phrase honest truth too lightly: it should be reserved for books – deeply moving books – like this' Alan Coren

'Sad, happy, sensual and intriguing' *Woman's Own*

Susan
LEWIS

Out of the Shadows

arrow books

Published by Arrow Books 2009

2 4 6 8 10 9 7 5 3

Copyright © Susan Lewis 2008

Susan Lewis has asserted her right under the Copyright, Designs and Patents Act 1988 to be identified as the author of this work

First published in Great Britain in 2008 by
Arrow Books
Random House, 20 Vauxhall Bridge Road,
London SW1V 2SA

www.rbooks.co.uk

Addresses for companies within The Random House Group Limited can be found at: www.randomhouse.co.uk/offices.htm

The Random House Group Limited Reg. No. 954009

A CIP catalogue record for this book
is available from the British Library

ISBN 9780099492351

The Random House Group Limited supports The Forest Stewardship Council (FSC), the leading international forest certification organisation. All our titles that are printed on Greenpeace approved FSC certified paper carry the FSC logo. Our paper procurement policy can be found at:
www.rbooks.co.uk/environment

Typeset by Palimpsest Book Production Ltd,
Grangemouth, Stirlingshire
Printed and bound in Great Britain by CPI Bookmarque Ltd,
Croydon, CR0 4TD

To Susan S
From Susan L, Thank you

Acknowledgements

A huge thank you to Clare and Ian Blaskey whose beautiful home provided the inspiration and setting for the Larkspur Centre. Also for Clare's expert advice on all things equestrian. My sincere gratitude to Liz Garrett, Managing Director of Coty Prestige for her guidance through the corporate world of fragrance and beauty. Many, many thanks to Dr Chris Garrett for his invaluable medical advice. A huge thank you to Jenny Vigneau for the generous use – both fictional and real – of her Paris apartment.

My love and thanks to James Grafton Garrett for his unwavering support and patience and for being so utterly wonderful in every other way.

Lastly, my thanks go to Georgina Hawtrey-Woore, Kate Elton, Rob Waddington, Trish Slattery, David Parrish, Louise Campbell, Charlotte Bush, Averil Ashfield . . . a fantastic and formidable team without whom nothing would be possible.

Chapter One

'Choosing the wrong man is a bit like winning the lottery then finding out you've lost the ticket. The hopes, the dreams, the journey to the stars, are all the same. Then the truth hits and the disappointment is beyond crushing. For losing the ticket you want to shoot yourself. In his case, you want to shoot him.'

Susannah often talked this way to herself when she was stressed. It had started even before her shining light of a husband had short-circuited in magnificent fashion and been carted off to prison, but it had become more frequent now, mainly because she didn't have many people to talk to. 'Choosing the wrong man is like giving up on the golden opportunities life's throwing your way – except at the time you think he is the opportunity.' Or, 'Choosing the wrong man is a mistake you'll only make once – or so you like to think.' She'd never go there again though. She was as sure about that as she was about sitting here on the number 44 bus, surrounded by people who must surely have been sucked into a run of bad luck in their time, but she didn't want to know about them, any more than they did about her.

Actually, so far the day was going well. Not that anything wildly exciting had happened, or even mildly promising come to that, but that was fine, because nor had anything gone disastrously wrong. However, it was still only four o'clock and the post hadn't arrived before she'd left that morning.

Since barely a week went by now without another problem, or mishap, or unpayable bill landing on her doorstep like some grisly paving stone marking the road to all-out catastrophe, she rarely tempted fate by thinking she might be off its nasty little hook yet.

Wouldn't it be great if she could just throw in her hand and tell life she'd had enough, she wanted out of the game. Being dealt one bad card after another might be fun for the great god-banker in the sky, raking in her spirits as though they were high-stake chips – for her it was as though she'd used up all her credit and was now teetering over the void in six-inch heels. When she looked in the mirror she could see the energy draining out of her as though someone had pulled the plug. She could be one of those fast-motion films of flowers budding, blooming, then withering and dying. Her life was passing before her eyes. She was still only thirty-six, but felt closer to fifty, and probably even looked it, which was a disaster all of its own when what little success she'd once had was, at least in part, due to her looks.

Her tired now, but once exquisite, sloe eyes used to be known for their vivid aquamarine sparkle, thanks to a series of make-up ads in which they'd featured; and her full-lipped, dazzlingly white

2

smile had, for a while, earned her a certain amount of fame for its appearance in a toothpaste commercial. Her figure had managed its fifteen minutes too, modelling swimsuits and sun beds at a trade fair in Brighton. Not exactly the high spot of her career – in fact it had turned into one of the lowest when her employers for the week, and some of their clients, had assumed they could manhandle her as freely as the goods. It was not for this that she'd spent three years at the Webber Douglas Academy of Dramatic Art after her A levels instead of going to university, but she'd soon learned that promotional work paid well – when she could get it – and was something many unproven actresses did until they were discovered.

And she had been discovered, back then, because one day, like the proverbial knight in shining armour, Duncan Cates had ridden into her life and carried her off over the horizon into the world of her wildest dreams. As an up-and-coming young director, alive with charm and ambition, and over-flowing with talent, he'd already tasted the heady flavours of success with a West End triumph of a brand-new play. When he crossed Susannah's path he was casting a new production entitled *Blondes*, for which she was perfectly qualified with her long, silvery mane. However, the leading lady also needed to possess all the sensuous glamour *and* acting skill of a young Bardot. By the time Susannah had finished her audition Duncan had declared his search at an end and himself in love.

When *Blondes* first opened, in Bath, its reception wasn't exactly what its writer had hoped for, since the reviews were mixed, mostly bad for the

3

play, but full of praise for the director whose unusual staging and use of music had 'lifted the piece beyond the script's failings.' As for Susannah, the critics went into overdrive with their raves, gushing about her heart-wrenching delivery and the captivating, but tender, beauty 'that seemed to have a power all its own.'

After the tension of the build-up, Duncan's elation had soared past all sober limits. He was so high on success, and love, and cocaine that he'd insisted he and Susannah should celebrate by getting married that very week. As far as he was concerned they were Roger and Brigitte; Greta and Mauritz; Spencer and Katharine – any great love or mentor story from stage or screen would do. They were on their way to the top and nothing could stop them now.

During the following year their journey from being overnight sensations to the hottest properties on the market didn't go quite the way Duncan expected. In fact, it seemed to take an unscheduled detour down the one-hit-wonder street, which was so shocking to him that in his most bewildered moments he blamed Susannah. During his more lucid periods (when he was all coked up and raring to go) his zest for life and belief in them both remained as electrifying as ever. However, his growing dependency soon began to wreak its devastating havoc on his career, finances and looks, but most of all on his moods. If he couldn't get a fix he'd become maudlin and resentful and even, as time went on, angry and violent. Though he rarely raised a hand to Susannah, when things got really tough he did, and she often heard him threatening people on the phone. One night he came home with a bloodied face and cracked ribs and refused to say how he'd got them. It hardly mattered, because by then it was perfectly clear that his habit had become an all-out addiction, so it was doubtful he could remember the attack anyway, never mind who'd carried it out. He was no longer capable of holding down any kind of job, least of all one that demanded his creative talent. As for her, though she was still managing to cram auditions into a hectic schedule of waitressing, telemarketing and shelf-stacking, anything to make ends meet, no spectacular or well-paid parts were coming her way.

Then suddenly Susannah's star zoomed off on the ascent again. It was on her twenty-third birthday that her agent rang to say that Michael Grafton, one of the nation's leading TV producers, wanted to see her for a part in a major new drama serial.

'It's not a lead,' Dorothy told her, 'but apparently she's a key character, and the money's fantastic, so get yourself along there and wow the hell out of the man. This could prove the turning point for you, sweetie, and God knows you need one.'

Susannah put her heart and soul into the audition, wanting the part more than she'd ever wanted anything in her life. To her joy, even in the brief ten minutes that she was allowed to demonstrate her understanding of the role and how she would play it, she sensed that Michael Grafton was impressed. And it turned out she was right, because he cast her, but by the time the decision was made she was no longer in a position to accept the part. She was almost four months pregnant, meaning that she'd be giving birth around the same time as principal photography was due to begin.

So, with a grim and inexorable inevitability, her and Duncan's dreams of international fame, sprawling mansions and flashy cars materialised in the form of unemployment, Oyster cards and a three-up, two-down in Battersea. The struggle seemed endless. Months turned into years and things only got worse. The only real joy in her life was their daughter Neve, whom she adored, and who she was determined wouldn't be dragged down by her father's addiction. To his credit, even Duncan supported the idea of sending their daughter to private school when she was seven, and for a while he even managed to help pay for it. But things were soon back on the slide, and the depths he began sinking to following a high became so harrowing and frightening that Susannah frequently had to take Neve to her Aunt Lola's for fear of what he might do to them. Threats of murder and suicide became a regular refrain, and there seemed nothing he wouldn't stoop to to finance his habit. One night he even put a knife to Susannah's throat to try and get Neve's school fees out of her. That was when Susannah packed her bags for the last time and took Neve, who was by now close to ten, to live with Patsy, her best friend, and Neve's godmother.

Six months later Duncan was arrested and charged for his involvement in supplying dodgy amphetamines to a fifteen-year-old boy who'd overdosed and almost died. Happily the boy survived without brain damage, but this was the crime for which they were all now paying: Duncan in his prison cell, where he'd been for the past three years with another seven to go if he served his full time; Susannah, now back in the little terraced house with Neve, struggling to keep things together, and starting to fail – and Neve, who almost never mentioned her father. She even pretended not to mind that he didn't write, or use up one of his precious phone calls to find out how his family was managing.

Now, as Susannah stepped down off the bus into a huddle of impatient travellers, all waiting to get on, she tried to push aside the fear of mounting debts that was threatening to overwhelm her. Something would come good soon, she kept telling herself, some miracle or unexpected windfall would waft their way, because it just had to. However, she wasn't holding her breath.

It was typical February weather as she hurried along Battersea Bridge Road towards home, raining and cold, with small piles of slush clogging the gutters after a frenzied snowstorm at the weekend. For a precious few hours on Sunday afternoon, after the wind had died down, and everything was still looking picture-postcard and pristine, she and Neve had ventured over to Battersea Park to build a snowman, and make snow angels. To Neve's delight they'd ended up joining in a raucous snowball fight with some of their neighbours, but when it was over and the others took off to the warmth of the cafe for toasted sandwiches and steaming mugs of hot chocolate, Neve and Susannah had sat on a bench shivering as they drank cocoa from the flask they'd brought with them.

After popping into the local mart for some milk and apples, Susannah continued on down the main road, past the dismal grey council estate where she and Patsy had grown up, in one of the tower blocks, and where her beloved old aunt Lola who'd brought her up still lived – in one of the newer low-rise flats now. Her mind was darting about frantically, reaching for the scattered list of things she must do before leaving the house again at six.

She hated having to work at night, but without her job at the club she'd never be able to meet Neve's school fees even with the bursary they'd recently been awarded, and after all the uncertainty and upheaval Neve had been through during the worst times with Duncan, the last thing she needed was any more change in her life. She deserved the stability of the school she'd known for so long, every bit as much as she needed her friends. So Susannah was prepared to work all hours, and at all kinds of jobs, in order to make Neve's world as safe and secure as she possibly could, and to give her at least some of the luxuries and privileges other girls her age enjoyed. Not that Susannah had given up on her dream to act, but since having Neve she'd only been cast in a handful of low-budget commercials, apart from a few years ago when she'd won a second-lead role in an afternoon soap. It had died almost as soon as it hit the screen, but at least the money had helped get them over the crisis of the time, before they'd lurched on to the next.

Now she almost never heard from her agent, and even if she did, working so hard meant she had next to no time, or indeed energy, for auditions, let alone to take on a part. In her lowest moments, when she allowed herself to consider the career she might be having had everything not gone so disastrously wrong, the grief was as profound as if someone had died. And in a way this was so, because she was no longer the easy-going, vibrant young woman she used to be, full of optimism and *joie de vivre*, she was someone else now who was fast losing the battle to stay afloat.

Hearing her mobile ringing somewhere deep inside her bag, she began rummaging for it while rounding the corner into their terrace which curved off into a warren of similar terraces, where the houses were packed as tightly as teeth and were as uniform in their Victorian-ness as they were varied in their colours and decor. Though theirs was in desperate need of a fresh lick of paint, it was cosy and warm inside, and whilst not as splendidly updated as some on the street, it wasn't as grimly run-down as others. Anyway, it was home, which was all that mattered to Susannah, to have a roof over their heads that currently wasn't leaking or showing imminent signs of caving in, and she loved the place, in spite of the bathroom being downstairs off the kitchen, and the front door opening straight into the snug little sitting room.

Failing to find her phone in time, she gave up the search and had just reached the curve of the terrace when she spotted something outside her house that hadn't been there that morning. An irregular thump started in her chest. Either she wasn't seeing straight, and the For Sale was actually next door, or it was a mistake.

She walked on, and with each step she could feel herself turning hotter and more prickly with fear. The sign was definitely bolted to her front gate, but it must have been put there in error because in spite of being two months behind with her mortgage the building society would surely never put the place on the market so soon, or without warning her first.

Fishing out her mobile she pressed in the number on the board and was answered almost immediately by a cheery-sounding voice asking her to hold on for an operator unless she knew her party's extension, which she could key in right away. Next came a recording of Tchaikovsky's First, which she was still half-listening to as she let herself into the house and felt the warmth of the sitting room envelop her like a welcoming embrace. The gas bill at least was paid, as was the electricity – though not the council tax, or the water, or her credit cards . . .

After dropping her bag on the arm of a slightly tatty, but comfy and much-loved sofa that took up almost half the room, she hung her coat in the cupboard under the stairs and went into the kitchen where a round pine dining table dominated the space, and a lean-to conservatory allowed in plenty of light, except on a day like today.

'Hello, can I help you?' a plummy voice suddenly blurted on to the line.

'Oh, yes I hope so,' Susannah replied, starting to unload the washing machine. 'I seem to have acquired one of your For Sale signs by mistake . . .'

'Can you give me your name and address?'

After repeating her details, twice, she tried to insist again that an error had been made, but the woman at the other end was saying, 'Hang on, I'll see if I can find out what's happening.'

As she waited Susannah became aware of a very bad feeling creeping up on her. She tried reminding herself again that she wasn't far enough in arrears for a repossession to be in motion yet, but living in such fear of losing the house meant that she found it hard to be rational when something even remotely suggested it might happen. She took a breath, trying to still the panicky feelings, but they only seemed to get worse and she was soon frantically trying to work out what she'd do if she and Neve did find themselves out on the street. Obviously Lola would take them in, but not for long, because there were only two bedrooms in her aunt's tiny flat, and Neve was almost fourteen now. She had to have her own room, which she already had at Lola's, so Susannah would have to find somewhere else. Maybe a friend or colleague would be able to help out for a while, but what then? Pats would take them in with open arms, of course, were it not for the fact that she'd moved to Australia two years ago, creating a gap in Susannah's life that no one had ever come even close to filling. So Susannah just knew she was going to end up in some seedy government-run shelter until she managed to get back on her feet which might never happen, but even if it did, by then Neve would have had to change schools, and the possibility of ever putting a foot on the property ladder again would be as remote as finding herself a highly-paid acting job, which for most in her profession was already an oxymoron.

Forcing herself to sit down at the table, she tried to push past the paranoia and remember that she was still here, nothing bad had happened yet, nor was it going to. However, the louder and more strident Tchaikovsky's concerto became, the more lurid and horrifying her imaginings were turning. Everything was falling apart, her life was in pieces and no matter what she did she couldn't pull it together. Something had to change, radically, or she and Neve were going under. Even if the For Sale sign was a mistake, *and of course it was*, it was acting like a wake-up call, a stark and painful reminder of just how bad things really were.

'Mrs Cates?' another less plummy female voice asked. 'It's Heidi Jameson here. I have some good news. A young couple came in today and they're very keen to see the house tomorrow, if that's possible. They aren't in a chain, so we could have a nice quick sale on our hands.'

Feeling as though something had come unhinged in her head, allowing her nightmares to come spilling out into reality, Susannah said, 'I'm sorry, there's obviously some kind of confusion. My house isn't on the market. Maybe one of my neighbours . . .'

'You're Mrs Cates?'

'Yes, but I've never been in touch with your office, so I don't know how you've got my name, or how your board comes to be outside.'

There was a pause before the agent said, in a tone that was both dark and knowing, 'Oh dear. This isn't the kind of situation we like to become involved in, so perhaps you and your husband should talk this through some more and get back to us when you're *both* ready to sell.'

Turning very still, Susannah said, 'Are you . . . ? Are you saying my husband's been in touch with you?'

'He contacted us a few days ago, but listen, I'm sorry. This has obviously come as a bit of a shock to you, so . . .'

'Did he come into the office?' Susannah interrupted.

'I'm not sure. I didn't take the details myself.'

'Please will you check? It's important . . . I need to know if he was there in person.'

'Hold on.'

As she waited Susannah's inner rantings started again. If Duncan was out of prison this was the first she'd heard of it, and the horror of what it could mean was closing in on her like a choking black cloud. The house was in his name. She'd tried to get it changed, several times, but had never succeeded, so officially he was the owner and she was . . . what? A squatter? No, a tenant, surely, because she'd paid the mortgage for the past three years, and besides, she was his wife and Neve his daughter, which had to count for something. He wouldn't be allowed to sell from

13

under them, particularly when he'd virtually bankrupted and abandoned them three years ago.

'It seems,' the agent said, coming back on the line, 'that the instruction was taken over the phone, but one of my colleagues visited your home with Mr Cates yesterday to measure up and take photographs.'

Susannah fought back the panic. Duncan had been here? He'd actually set foot in this house and allowed an agent to take down particulars while he watched, knowing he was going to make his own daughter homeless . . .

'Hang on,' Heidi Jameson said, 'I'm just being told that it was actually the owner's brother who met my colleague at the house.'

The spinning in Susannah's head was stopped by a swell of fury. Now things were starting to make more sense. Duncan wasn't out of prison at all, but for some reason he was trying to stake a claim on the house and Hugh, the despicable two-headed snake that he was, was acting for him.

'Are you still there?' the agent prompted.

'Yes,' Susannah replied. 'Thank you . . . Uh, I'd be grateful if you could arrange for the board to be removed as soon as possible, and cancel any viewings. The house isn't for sale,' and after ringing off, she picked up the landline to call Hugh at his office in Limehouse.

As she waited to be put through, half-expecting to be cut off any minute, she carried on unloading the washing, while picturing him, Mr Slick and Slimy at his vast glossy desk overlooking the river, surrounded by all things sumptuous and decorative, right down to the telephonist who'd answered her call. His business was some kind of import–export enterprise, which to her mind fitted his shady character to a T. She'd always felt sure he'd been much more involved in Duncan's supply chain than the authorities had been able to prove, but even if they had he was so slippery he could make an eel look like Velcro.

'Susie,' he crowed, coming on to the line and making her cringe with the shortening of her name. 'Long time no hear. How are you? Still as gorgeous as ever, I'm sure. How could you be . . .'

'I don't know what the hell you're playing at,' she seethed furiously, 'but I've just taken this house off the market. And if you had even a shred of decency in your disgustingly rancid soul, which I happen to know you don't, you'd never have put it on in the first place.'

'Hey, don't shoot the messenger,' he responded breezily. 'I was just following instructions. Duncan needs the cash to get started again . . .'

'I don't care what he needs, and since he isn't even halfway through his sentence yet . . .'

'Correction, he's almost done. Or he could be. He's in front of the parole board at the end of the month and if it goes his way, we should have him back with us very soon thereafter.'

Trying to stop herself reeling, Susannah said, 'Even if that happens it doesn't change things. This house belongs to me and Neve . . .'

'Now you know that's not true, but hey, don't let's argue about it. If I were you I'd offer to buy him out. I'm not sure he'll accept half, but you can . . .'

'As far as I'm concerned he's not even entitled

to that,' she cut in scathingly, 'and if he as much as attempts to pull a stunt like this again I'll go straight to my lawyer. In fact, I'm going to do that anyway,' and banging down the phone, she stood over it, shaking badly as she tried to get her breath back. If only she had a lawyer, but on her budget she'd struggle to pay for the phone call, never mind the fees, so she had to find another way to deal with this. Were Neve not due home any minute she'd get in touch with Legal Aid right away, or the Child Support Agency, but she didn't want Neve walking in on the call, so it would have to go to the top of her to-do list in the morning.

It was a pity the messages on her answerphone couldn't wait that long too, but she'd learned the hard way that burying her head in the sand only made things worse, so abandoning the laundry for the moment, she obeyed the summons of the flashing red light and hit the playback button.

No more bad news please, she murmured as the first one began.

To her amazement it was from her agent, Dorothy. 'Hi, sweetie,' she chirruped, 'I'll try your mobile, but if I haven't caught up with you by the time you get this could you give me a quick bell? We're having a bit of a change-round in the office so I thought I should explain what's happening in person.'

Knowing that could only mean Dorothy was planning to drop her from her books, she quickly passed on to the next message, unable to deal with the final closing of that door yet.

'Hey, Susannah. It's me, Cathy. I've done a swap

16

with Felicity tonight, so I'll be passing your way around eight if you'd like a lift into work. Just text me yes or no, either way is cool.'

After sending a quick *yes please*, Susannah moved on to the next message, which turned out to be from the dentist whose reception she ran three mornings a week. He wanted to know if she could cover for the afternoon girl tomorrow and next Monday. Since he paid more than the architect whose filing she did twice a week, she immediately set about rejigging her schedule, which didn't present a problem, as it turned out, nor would it clash with the extra shifts she'd recently taken on cleaning a local school. The only difficulty was going to be staying awake, since her evening job meant she rarely got to bed before three on Thursdays, Fridays and Saturdays.

Hearing a key going into the front door she looked up as Neve came bursting in, all long blonde hair, and ruddy complexion thanks to the cold. Though still only thirteen she looked closer to sixteen, considered herself as grown-up as eighteen, and was already almost as tall as her mother. They were so alike that people often stopped in the street to stare. Or they used to, before Susannah's face had started to become ravaged by worry and fatigue.

'Hey, you're home already,' Neve cried, dumping her heavy bag at the foot of the stairs and unwinding her scarf. 'I thought you were going to be late.'

'That's tomorrow. Did Sasha's mother bring you home?'

'No, Ping, their housekeeper. She's such a crazy

17

driver, you should see her yelling at everyone on the road. Anyway, what's with the For Sale sign? Please don't tell me things have got that bad . . .'

'It's a mistake,' Susannah broke in.

'I thought so. Did you get my text about Barcelona?'

That was it, the rogue board was already forgotten. However, the next subject wasn't one Susannah could welcome in its place. 'Yes, I did,' she answered. 'How was your day?'

'Actually, fab. I had a text from Harry Gelson saying he thought I was really pretty. Isn't that amazing? Everyone's mad about him . . . Oh Mum, don't look at me like that. Just because you don't have boyfriends doesn't mean I shouldn't either.'

'There'll be plenty of time for that when you're older,' Susannah reminded her. 'At your age you need to concentrate on your studies.' Then with a playful smile, 'Tell me what you texted back.'

Grinning, Neve said, 'I told him I thought he was pretty too.'

With a laugh, Susannah hoisted up the basket of wet laundry to carry it into the bathroom, where they kept the tumble dryer. 'Do you have much homework?' she asked, as Neve jumped up the step into the kitchen and tore open the fridge.

'Oh God, tell me about it. I have this mega art project to get through and maths coming out of my ears. Am I staying at Lola's tonight, by the way?'

'Yes, so you should pack up whatever you need to take with you before we leave. She's got some nice lamb chops for tea, she tells me.'

18

Grabbing a carrot, Neve's eyes were sparkling with mischief as she turned round. 'It must be pension day,' she said, taking a bite. 'She always buys chops on pension days. Want me to go and put that in the dryer?'

'Yes please, but don't switch it on. I'll do that when I come home later.' She didn't have to explain that electricity was cheaper after midnight, Neve knew that already. 'How about a hug?' she asked, putting the basket down.

Having no problem obliging, Neve squeezed her mother hard, then gazed quizzically up into her eyes as Susannah cupped her face in her hands. Feeling a powerful surge of love and pride fill up her heart, Susannah reminded herself yet again that though she certainly hadn't struck lucky with Duncan, with Neve she was truly blessed.

'What's wrong?' Neve asked. 'I know something is. I can always tell with you.'

'I'm fine,' Susannah assured her, hoping she wouldn't mention Barcelona again, 'and you're too smart for your own good. Now, off you pop with the laundry while I go online to pay some bills.'

A few minutes later Neve was back with an empty basket which she dumped in front of the conservatory door, saying, 'Can you help me with my art project? I have to hand it in tomorrow . . . Oh, and Mrs Cluskey asked me today how you're getting on with the fashion show. Do you remember, you said you'd stage one for us again?'

Susannah was sitting at the computer, which was set up on a makeshift desk in a corner of the kitchen. On the screen in front of her was her bank account, which was looking so sickly it might already be too late for life support.

'Mum, are you listening?'

'Yes, of course. Sorry, yes, the fashion show. Actually the printer was playing up again this morning, so I might have to email the plans to you at school for you to print out there.'

Neve said nothing.

Sensing her tension, Susannah tried to ignore it.

'You haven't done anything, have you?' Neve accused.

'I thought you could present the ones we did last time. We can always update them as we go along.'

When Neve fell silent again Susannah turned to look at her, and felt her heart dissolve with guilt to see the disappointment in her eyes. 'I'm sorry,' she said softly, 'but we've still got more money going out than coming in, so I can't afford to take any time off to work on something new.'

'It's OK,' Neve said flatly. 'Actually, Mrs Cluskey said she'd be happy to take it over, if you want her to. I said I thought she probably should.'

Realising how crushed Neve was, since the last show they'd created together had been a spectacular success, Susannah tried not to feel even more guilt as she said, 'I'm sure it'll be different next year.'

'Whatever,' Neve shrugged, and having fetched her bag she hauled it on to the table and began taking out her books.

Knowing there was no more she could say,

Susannah returned to the computer and felt her stomach churn as she looked at the glaring minus sign in front of two thousand and forty-eight pounds. Still, at least a cheque for six hundred and eighty would go into her account tomorrow – her wages from the dentist. Though it might not make much of a dent in the debt itself, it would at least pull her back to the right side of her overdraft limit.

'Mum,' Neve said, a while later, 'I have to take the money in next week for Barcelona.'

Glad her back was turned so Neve couldn't see the way her eyes closed in despair, Susannah said, 'Remind me again how much it is.'

'Seven hundred pounds, but we've already paid a deposit of a hundred, so we only owe six.'

Only. Susannah took a breath. 'Why do we have to pay so soon, when the trip's not until July?' she asked.

'I think they have to book the flights now, or they'll get even more expensive.'

Susannah swallowed hard and tried not to see where this was going to end. She'd either have to tell Neve she couldn't go, or she'd have to take on more work at the club. It was an option she'd long resisted in spite of how much easier it might make her life – however, things were so bad now that maybe she couldn't afford the luxury of choice any longer. 'OK, I'll let you have a cheque on Monday,' she said, managing to keep her voice steady.

With a jubilant 'Yes!' Neve came to give her a hug. 'You know, I was really scared you were going to say I couldn't go,' she told her, 'but you've been working such a lot lately that I don't expect things are as bad any more, are they?'

'No, not really,' Susannah lied, quickly exiting the screen in front of her.

'So does that mean I can have something new to wear for Melinda's party next Saturday? Everyone's going shopping in the afternoon, and I've said I'll go too, but I don't want to if I can't buy anything. Oh and guess what, Mum, she's only inviting Jason Ricard. He is so fit. Well, you've seen him, and I really, really like him.'

'You're becoming boy-mad,' Susannah told her, getting up from her chair.

Undaunted, Neve ran on excitedly, 'Actually, I've seen this dress in Topshop. It doesn't cost very much. I think it was thirty-five, or it might have been forty-five, I'm not sure. Either way, that's not too much is it? At least it's not as much as the one Sasha's buying, because that's a hundred and thirty. If you ask me, I think it's a ridiculous price. I mean, it's a lovely dress, and she'll look gorgeous in it, but I bet it didn't cost more than ten or twenty quid to make. Anyway, I thought if I got the dress in Topshop I could wear your black over-the-knee boots . . .'

'But they're so old, Neve.'

'It doesn't matter. You've hardly worn them, and they're really cool, and we've still got those tights Lola won at bingo that we haven't opened yet. And Sasha said I could borrow the Butler and Wilson necklace she had for her birthday which is absolutely amazing.'

Loving her daughter more than ever for pretending not to mind that she didn't have anything like as much to spend as her friends, Susannah dropped a kiss on her head and went to fill up the kettle. It was the constant downside of keeping her at a school where just about everyone's parents, single or divorced, were awash with money, and privilege, and all manner of useful connections. Neve didn't even have her own laptop computer, instead she had to share a second-hand desktop with her mother. Nor could she boast an iPod, or the kind of swanky all-purpose mobile phone the rest of them carried around. As for make-up and clothes and all the other girlish fripperies that cluttered up her friends' spacious bedrooms, Neve's own little haven was such an embarrassing wasteland, as she'd once called it, that she rarely invited anyone up there.

'I know! Why don't we go shopping together on Saturday?' Neve pressed.

'I thought you wanted to go with your friends.'

'I do, but I get fed up with the way they keep asking my advice all the time. It's like they don't have minds of their own.'

'They want your opinion because they admire your sense of style.'

'Yeah, well,' Neve said, and turning back to her homework she let the subject drop, while Susannah's heart felt weighted with so much helplessness that she could only dread what might be waiting in the shadows of the next few days.

'It's not Neve's fault,' Susannah was saying later as Cathy drove them to Kensington. 'She can't help wanting what everyone else has, it's only normal for a girl her age. And she shouldn't have to do without.'

Having a teenage niece, and a sister who never stopped complaining about how expensive things were, Cathy was all sympathy as she pulled up at a red light. Apart from age, she and Susannah could hardly be more different, since Cathy was small and dark with round hazel eyes and a smile that, whilst lovely, was marred by a missing eye tooth. They'd first met several years ago during auditions for a play that had never got off the ground, and they'd stayed in touch, on and off, ever since, providing one another with the occasional opportunity for a gossip about the increasingly elusive world of mainstream showbiz.

It was through Cathy that Susannah had landed her job at the exclusive gentlemen's club in Kensington, not as a waitress like Cathy, or as a dancer, but behind the scenes, as a part-time office assistant. As far as Neve and Lola were concerned she was helping to run a trendy West End disco three nights a week, since she knew they'd think the worst if she told them where she was really going. Anyone would, and who could blame them when her circumstances were so straitened, but the truth was she'd never be able to face her family, or herself, if she were following the same path as Cathy and the other girls.

As the lights turned green Cathy drove on across the King's Road into Beaufort Street, where some of London's most expensive mansions were tucked away in the private enclaves of Chelsea Park Gardens. Susannah was vaguely registering them as they passed, knowing that at least two of

Neve's schoolfriends lived in these privileged surroundings. It wasn't that she aspired to such grandness herself, though she had to admit it would be nice, she simply wanted to make Neve feel less of a poor cousin, or a charity case, than she was right now.

'At risk of pointing out the obvious, yet again,' Cathy finally said, 'the answer's in your hands, Susie. You know very well that Henry would be more than happy to get you out of the office and into the bar, or one of the private dining rooms . . .'

'Don't let's go there,' Susannah interrupted, unable even to think about the option of topless-waitressing or nude-hostessing now she was coming so close to taking it. 'I'm not judging you for what you do, it's just not for me.'

Cathy didn't attempt to persuade her. They'd had this conversation too many times before for her not to know where it would end. Instead she said, 'Why don't you let me lend you the money for the Barcelona trip? You can pay me back when you have it. No rush.'

As gratitude tried to warm the hollow inside her, Susannah said, 'Thanks, but no, because I have no idea when that will be, and borrowing from friends is the surest way to lose them.' She didn't add that now Pats was no longer around she sometimes felt she didn't actually have any to lose, because it would hurt Cathy's feelings. Besides, it wasn't true. She did have friends, it was just that none of them was Pats.

'Well, the offer's there,' Cathy said. 'When are the next school fees due? Do you have them yet?'

'Mostly. I'm a couple of hundred short at the

moment, but by the time the bill comes in it'll be fine.'

Though Cathy's scepticism was almost palpable she said no more, simply continued to drive as Susannah took out her mobile to read an incoming text. It was from Neve, letting her know she'd borrowed ten pounds from Lola to top up her phone.

Susannah didn't bother asking what had happened to the ten pounds she'd given Neve three days ago for the very same reason. Those girls were texting one another morning, noon and night, so she knew already where the credit had gone – the only surprise was that it had lasted this long.

Twenty minutes later she followed Cathy into the club's brightly lit kitchens where the chef, Martin, and his staff were already hard at work. After the usual friendly and, in Cathy's case, flirtatious exchanges, Susannah took herself upstairs to the office where Henry, the manager, was sitting with his feet up on the desk, talking loudly into the phone. The room was large and dourly furnished with formidable leather sofas either side of a deep, shadowy fireplace, and a sombre Persian rug covering most of the dark oak floor. The computer, filing cabinets and her own small desk that she shared with the other part-time assistants were tucked neatly inside in a roomy niche, where another door led into the lobby of Henry's private residence.

Henry himself was a perpetually jovial individual, as short as he was round, and as avuncular as he was gay. He was popular with everyone, staff and clients alike, and Susannah was no exception.

'Hi, I'm glad you're early,' he said, putting the phone down. 'Teresa's rung in sick, so I was hoping you wouldn't mind running reception tonight. Don't worry, you can wear what you have on, it drives the punters wild anyway, seeing you all buttoned up like a schoolmarm, but if you've got any shoes to replace those passion-killers no one's going to be happier to see them than me.'

With a smile, Susannah went to open the drawer where she kept a pair of black stilettos for her forays into the club itself, and held them up for Henry to approve.

'Perfect,' he announced, 'and should you feel at all inclined to slip into Teresa's hostess corset and stockings . . . No? Not going to happen?'

Susannah was shaking her head.

'I had to try,' he sighed. 'Now, don't let me hold you up. We've got a busy night ahead. Both private dining rooms are booked out, and we're not taking any more reservations for the main restaurant. If any members turn up on spec wanting a table, they'll have to eat in the bar. Don't worry about the phones, all calls are going straight to messages, which I'll pick up every half-hour or so. You've done it all before, so you know the ropes. You can finish at midnight, if you like, or do the same as Teresa and swap with one of the other girls for a couple of hours and go and earn yourself some serious tips.'

Susannah's eyes twinkled in spite of the nervous churning inside her. 'Nice try,' she retorted, her usual response, 'but if you're letting me off at midnight I'll go home, thanks very much.' It helped to keep up the pretence for a while, that way if she decided she couldn't go through with the waitressing, or hostessing, no one would be any the wiser.

Since working reception meant checking coats and showing members and their guests to tables, she headed off to the girls' changing rooms first to make herself a little more presentable. Though she was wearing her regular uniform of black pencil-skirt and white shirt under a black V-neck sweater, she knew the sweater had to go, and the shirt needed to be open low enough to offer a glimpse of her bra. Thankful that she was wearing a fairly new white lacy one, she popped a few buttons, then borrowed some make-up and a necklace from Cathy, who was at her place in front of the mirror. She too was in uniform, which in her case consisted of a very short black flared skirt, hold-up stockings, a black bow tie and the same sort of stiletto heels as Susannah's.

After allowing one of the dancers to spray her with Chanel 19, and another to plait her hair, Susannah hurried off to reception where Henry was already greeting the first arrivals. It was a party of eight smartly suited businessmen who were down from Manchester for a three-day software conference. They'd reserved one of the private dining rooms, so after taking their coats she led them through the dimly lit bar to where Melanie, their hostess for the evening, was waiting to show them into the Edwards salon, as the small dining room was known. Since Melanie was wearing nothing more than a fully transparent body stocking with a smattering of sparkly sequins in strategic places, Susannah felt the frisson of male excitement the instant the men laid eyes on their hostess, and might have been amused by their typical first moments of embarrassment were she not feeling nauseous at the mere prospect of being in the same kind of costume later on.

Returning to reception she found Henry chatting with two regular members whom she promptly led through to the restaurant, where Elodie, the catering manager, in the same scant uniform as Cathy's and Melanie's, took over showing them to their table.

By the time midnight came round the club was packed and the first show was already under way. Susannah was still in reception, and though she'd been on the brink a hundred times of telling Henry that she was willing to work on after midnight, she still hadn't found the courage to say it. Nor would she, she realised, because no matter how dire her situation she simply didn't have what it took to strut around the place with next to no clothes on. For a while she'd considered the slightly less public arena of a private dining room, but being aware of what sometimes went on behind those particular closed doors she hadn't been able to face that either. As for exotic dancing, since she had neither the training nor the brazenness it took to exhibit herself that way, it wasn't an option. Which all went to show that the hope of solving her financial problems was as false as the charm she was having to exude in the face of lewd propositions.

Before abandoning her post she sent a message

to Henry's pager, and a few minutes later he emerged from the smoky darkness of the bar.

'Is it that time already?' he said, checking his watch. 'My, how it flies when you're enjoying yourself. You've done a great job, chuck. Just a shame you're not topping the bill at the end of the night.'

With her usual roll of the eyes, Susannah said, 'So who's replacing me? If she's ready to come now I might make the twelve-thirty night bus.'

'The what?' he protested. 'Didn't you rake in any tips tonight?'

'Of course. Almost fifty quid, actually.'

'Then get yourself a cab, for God's sake. You don't want to be messing around with buses at this time of night. It's freezing out there, and besides, it's not safe.'

'I'll be fine. I do it all the time.'

'I didn't know that. Well, it's not happening again. Whatever a taxi costs, I'll make it up to you in your next pay packet. Or,' he started to grin, 'you have the chance of swapping with Melanie in the Edwards salon, then Cathy can give you a lift home later. Mel's already earned herself a grand in tips tonight . . .'

Susannah's eyebrows rose. 'Yes, and doing what, exactly?'

'You know I don't ask that sort of question. All right, all right, I can see I'm wasting my breath again. Off you go. See you tomorrow, and thanks again for helping out here.'

Once in the minicab she'd ordered from the office, Susannah sat staring out at the passing streets, black and slick in the drizzly night, feeling jittery and vaguely disoriented to think of how close she'd come to abandoning her principles tonight. In truth, she wasn't even sure if they were really what was holding her back – maybe it was simply cowardice that was making her insides freeze at the thought of turning on the kind of performance Cathy and the others seemed to manage so effortlessly. Like most of them, Susannah called herself an actress – at least she used to – so why couldn't she just pretend she was playing a part? It didn't have to be real, she could even give herself another name, as though the role had been written for her. The club members would be crew, or fellow players, or even the critics of a weighty stage play. Then, whatever happened, her actions would be about art and interpretation, instead of shameful to the point of being unable to think of this any more.

Switching her thoughts to Neve and how she was going to break it to her that they couldn't afford the trip to Barcelona, she almost switched them back again. Nor was there going to be a shopping spree on Saturday. The dread of Neve's anger and disappointment when she heard this was already beginning to sink so deeply into Susannah's heart that she wanted to weep and rage with the sheer frustration of working so hard and never seeming to get anywhere. Something had to give, it just had to, but if it wasn't going to be her principles, or cowardice, or whatever her problem was with the one solution she had, she simply couldn't see what else was left.

Chapter Two

'No! It's not *fair*,' Neve raged furiously, tears starting down her cheeks as her frustration hit breaking point. 'You said I could go. Last night you promised to write a cheque, you even said when we were at Lola's that you'd bring it round for me this morning so I could take it to school today, then you didn't even bother to come.'

'I'm sorry. I overslept,' Susannah apologised, not wanting to admit that she'd decided to wait till this evening to break the bad news to Neve, rather than let her go off to school on top of the kind of row that was brewing now.

'But it means you lied,' Neve shouted. Her hands were bunched in fists at her sides, and her lovely face was contorting with impotence and fury. 'You said I could go. You even paid the deposit, and now you're changing your mind. Well, I won't let you. I'll borrow the money from Lola . . .'

'You know she doesn't have it,' Susannah broke in gently. Her own face was pale and tired, while inside she felt so wretched it was all she could do to stop herself crying too. 'I truly thought I'd have enough by now,' she said shakily. 'I swear to you, if I'd realised I wouldn't I'd never have said you could go, much less paid the deposit.'

'And that's supposed to make it better? Well it just makes it worse, because it means you're useless and you always let me down, even when you know how much something means to me. I suppose you're going to say next that I can't go shopping either, so I won't have anything new for the party . . . Oh my God, you are, aren't you? I can tell by the look on your face.'

'Neve, listen, please . . .'

'No, don't touch me. I hate you. We never have any money and it's all your fault. Why can't you get a proper job and be a lawyer, like Sasha's mum, or a stockbroker like Melinda's? Why do you have to be a bloody cleaner, or a receptionist, or a dumb actress who never even goes on auditions any more? It's so embarrassing.'

'Neve . . .'

'You don't know what it's like for me when people ask what my parents do. What am I supposed to say, that my dad's in prison and doesn't want to know us, and my mother's so broke that we don't ever even go out for meals, or do anything that other normal families do? *It's not fair.* Why am I the one who has to have *you* as a mother, and live in this stupid house that's not even as big as Sasha's front room? I hate it, and I hate you and I wish I'd never been born.'

As Neve charged up the stairs Susannah put her hands to her face and choked back a sob. Though she knew the eruption was long overdue, and that Neve didn't mean half of what she'd said, the words were cutting into her cruelly, making her feel even more desperate than she had before. How many more times was she going to tell herself that they couldn't go on like this? Saying it didn't make it happen, so she had to do something or she was going to end up driving Neve away.

After making herself a cup of tea she sat down at the table and once again racked her brains in search of an answer she might somehow have missed. As usual all her ideas ended up down dead-end streets, apart from the recollection that Dorothy had tried to get hold of her the day before. She felt a small flicker of hope in her chest, but it was quickly smothered by an inner voice telling her that if it had been about a job Dorothy would have rung back by now. No, the call had been about letting her go from the agency, so she had to ask herself if she really wanted to deal with the rejection right now? The answer was no, not at all, but like one of those trick candles that couldn't be blown out, the flame of hope suddenly flickered back up again. Maybe it *wasn't* bad news, because if Dorothy didn't want to represent her any more surely she'd have told her by letter, rather than put herself through the awkwardness of listening to Susannah plead with her to change her mind.

Picking up the phone, she made the call.

'Susannah, hi,' Dorothy's assistant, Ros, cried warmly when she realised who was calling. 'Yes, we were trying to reach you. Saatchi's were holding auditions today at the Connaught for some commercial, a breakfast cereal I think, and Dorothy thought you might like to go along. When you didn't ring back, we assumed you were out of town.'

Stunned by losing out on the possibility of earning as much as five thousand pounds for a couple of days' work, Susannah could only stare into the void that was yawning wider and wider in front of her. 'Is it too late?' she managed to ask. 'Are they interviewing again tomorrow?'

'No, the part's cast now. Linda Gooding got it, which we all expected, with her being married to the creative, but who knows, if they'd seen you they might have changed their minds.'

Not the way she was looking now, Susannah wanted to say, but managed not to. 'Why didn't Dorothy mention the casting in her message?' she asked. 'I'd have called back right away if she had.' Too late she realised that whatever Dorothy's call was about, she was supposed to jump to it when her agent rang. 'She only said she wanted to talk to me about rearranging the office.'

'Oh yes, she does, but she isn't here at the moment. It's nothing major, just that she's going into semi-retirement, so she won't be handling you personally any more. I think you're going to Samantha Walsh, but let Dorothy tell you about it. And the call for the commercial didn't come in until after she rang you yesterday. She was going to tell you when you rang back.'

Since kicking herself didn't even come close to what she wanted to do for allowing her fears to stall her, Susannah did the only thing she could and forced herself to let it go. There was no point getting angry and berating herself, it was too late now, she just had to make sure that the next time

35

her agent rang she didn't immediately assume the worst.

After putting the phone down she glanced up the stairs, wondering if she should go and talk to Neve yet. She could hear her crying, and had to swallow a lump in her own throat. This wasn't how it should be between them, arguing and hurting one another. She longed to pull Neve into her arms and make everything all right, the way she used to when she was little, but there was no kissing these wounds better, or putting a plaster over them until they healed.

Deciding to give her a while longer rather than risk the row erupting again, she went to set up the ironing board, wanting to get through at least half the pile before she and Neve walked over to Lola's for tea. After, she'd accompany Neve across Battersea Bridge to Sasha's house on Cheyne Walk, where she was spending the night. Unless Neve had changed her mind about going, now she was unable to shop tomorrow. She didn't usually back out through lack of funds, instead she gamely went along, advising and admiring, and not letting on how unhappy she was until she came home and cried on Lola's or Susannah's shoulders that she hadn't been able to buy anything herself.

With a horrible dryness in her throat Susannah plugged in the iron, and as she waited for it to heat up she stood looking at the phone. She was so desperate for someone to talk to, someone who'd understand what she was going through and be sympathetic, even if they couldn't really advise. Lola was wonderful, of course, but Susannah hadn't told her even the half of how bad things really were, she'd only worry and suffer all the same feelings of uselessness as Susannah and there was no point in that. The person she really longed for was Pats. OK, she might not have the answers, but Susannah had always felt stronger and safer when Pats was around. Since she'd left for Sydney it was as though a piece of Susannah had gone missing, and speaking on the phone never really filled the gap.

'It's only for a year,' Pats had assured her before she'd left. 'They want me to set up an office and run it until I find someone local to take my place.'

It was a career opportunity she couldn't refuse. As the marketing director of an American-based cosmetics firm, the assignment in Australia could project her right to the top if she made it work. And she was succeeding, there was no doubt about that, because Patsy's emails were full of the excitement of growing a new business in a city where her sister and brother-in-law lived, plus her niece and nephew, and now her parents, who'd emigrated six months ago to be near their family. So to think Pats would ever come back was just plain delusional, and Susannah certainly wasn't about to pour her troubles down the phone when Pats had felt bad enough about leaving her in the first place, with Duncan in prison and Uncle Fred, Lola's husband, only recently dead.

'We're past the worst of it,' Susannah remembered telling her. 'Fred's Alzheimer's means he hasn't been with us for a long time, so it's a bit of a blessing that he's finally let go, and with Duncan out of our lives things are bound to get better.'

Feeling her throat turn dry at the ludicrous but nonetheless unsettling attempt Duncan had made to sell the house, she tried comforting herself with the reassurance she'd received from the CSA when she'd called this morning. To her relief, she'd been told that he wouldn't be allowed to make her and Neve homeless. Moreover, he'd be liable for child support if he had any money, which actually was laughable given the circumstances, but she supposed it had to be said. Hugh, of course, was worth zillions, but she'd rather die than take any handouts from him, even if he were prepared to offer any, which he almost certainly wouldn't be. He'd never been generous with money, not even with his own niece. A simple card at Christmas with twenty quid inside, and nothing for her birthday, probably because he didn't have the faintest idea when it was.

After she'd pressed a fresh blouse for work that night, and some jeans and a top for Neve, she decided to leave the rest, because time was running short and she needed to try and make up with Neve before they went to Lola's.

The upstairs landing was so small that it took barely more than three steps to get from the top of the stairs to either of the bedroom doors. Her own was on the right, and Neve's was opposite, with a loo at right angles between them, and a tiny guest room opposite the stairs.

'Hi, can I come in?' she said, knocking as she pushed Neve's door open.

Neve was lying on her bed, facing the wall and clutching the tattered rag doll she'd had since she was a child. There were other cuddly toys piled up against the headboard, and along the wall. On the dressing table, under the window, was her carefully arranged collection of make-up and skin-care products, most of which had been sent over by Pats for birthdays and Christmas and any old time in between, because Pats was thoughtful and generous like that. The walls were covered in posters, mainly of boy bands or soap stars, but Beckham featured quite largely, along with Jose Mourinho whom Neve had put up for Susannah, though she'd admitted to quite liking him too, even if he was old.

Going to sit next to her, Susannah put a hand on her shoulder and felt her heart contract as Neve turned on to her back to look up at her. Neve never stayed angry for long and was probably already working out how to apologise, so making sure she got in first, Susannah smoothed the hair from her daughter's blotchy face, saying, 'I'm sorry. You know I'd do anything . . .'

'No, it's me who has to be sorry,' Neve interrupted, her voice thick and nasal. 'I shouldn't have said those horrible things . . . I didn't mean . . . You're the best mum in . . . the world.' As she started to cry again Susannah wrapped her tightly in her arms.

'Ssh,' she soothed, 'there's no need to be upset. It was all in the heat of the moment.'

'But it was horrible and you don't deserve anyone being mean to you, because you're never mean to anyone. And anyway, I don't care about that stupid trip. I'd rather stay here with you.'

Susannah bit her lip hard to stop herself crying.

'Maybe next year things will be different,' she said.

'It doesn't matter. All that's important is that we're together.' Then, pulling back to look into Susannah's eyes, 'You won't ever leave me, Mum, will you?' she asked, fear showing through the cracks of her bravery. 'You won't go away and not ever come back?'

'Oh Neve,' Susannah choked, knowing the insecurity was rooted in the way her father had abandoned her – and Pats too, if the truth be told. 'You're the most important thing in the world to me. I'd never leave you, you know that.'

Sniffing, Neve said, 'Are you sure?'

'Of course I'm sure.'

Neve's bloodshot eyes were still on her mother's. 'You might not be as rich as everyone else's mum,' she said, touching Susannah's face, 'but you're ten times more beautiful and special and easy to talk to and I'd never swap you for anyone.'

Summoning a wavery smile, Susannah said, 'Well I'm glad about that, because I'd certainly never swap you.'

'We'll be all right,' Neve said, her eyes widening earnestly.

'Of course we will. We're just having an expensive time right now, with so many bills coming in. I'm really sorry I've had to let you down about the trip and the shopping tomorrow, but one of these days . . .'

'Mum, it's OK. I can always borrow something of Sasha's for the party. We're the same size and for me it'll feel like something new.'

Wondering if it were possible for her heart to ache any more, Susannah hugged her again. 'I swear,' she said, 'that once we're through this bad patch, I'll make it up to you somehow.'

'You don't have to. I know how hard you're working, and one of these days, when I've left school and been to university, I'm going to get a job and earn shedloads of money so we never have to go without anything again.'

Though touched by the promise, Susannah felt troubled by the way Neve seemed to be taking the onus on herself to provide. It told her that Neve was starting to lose faith in her ever being able to make things right, and at Neve's age she shouldn't have to be thinking that way at all, much less worrying herself so much about her mother.

'I don't want you to be unhappy,' Neve said.

'I'm not,' Susannah lied.

'I know you are, but I've had this brilliant idea. It came to me a couple of weeks ago and I really think it could work.'

Susannah regarded her warily.

'It's to do with us and how we can become rich, or less poor anyway, and make you happy, but it's my secret, for now. I'll let you know what it is when I'm ready to.'

And if that wasn't enough to make her uneasy, Susannah was thinking as she hugged her again, she couldn't imagine what was.

It was almost four in the morning by the time Cathy dropped Susannah home after a crazy evening at the club. Just like the night before, both private rooms had been booked out, as had the restaurant and bar. Since it was Friday there had been two shows, neither of which Susannah had watched, but that wasn't unusual, because she rarely did. Besides, the stage wasn't visible from inside the private room where she'd just spent the past three hours as a nude hostess, weaving amongst groping hands, squirming off laps and pretending the whole thing was a highly erotic tease that she was enjoying as much as the diners.

During the journey back through the dark, damp streets of Kensington, then Chelsea, she and Cathy hadn't spoken much. They were both tired and there wasn't really much to say, though Cathy kept glancing at Susannah, wanting to say something, she just couldn't find the right words. In the end, when Susannah got out of the car Cathy only said, 'Try to get some sleep. Things might not look so bad in the morning.'

Knowing they were going to look a hundred times worse, Susannah thanked her for the lift, then turned in through her front gate. The For Sale sign was still there, jutting up with attitude, as though proud of the fact that it remained yet another problem still unresolved.

After letting herself into the house she went to the bathroom and started to fill the bath. It might relax her a little to soak in some of the therapeutic oils Pats had sent at Christmas. Taking one of the bottles she emptied it into the cascade and stood watching the yellow liquid swirling around in the steaming water, constantly changing shape like the thoughts inside her as it got caught in the rushing current of bubbles and steam. Then, returning to the kitchen, she put on the kettle to make some tea.

As she waited for the water to boil, she sat down at the table with her hands and knees pressed tightly together. Her eyes were heavy with fatigue and stared at nothing. There were no specific thoughts in her head, only vague whispers of what needed to be done tomorrow, or today as it already was. She had to be up by nine for her cleaning job at the school. It was a three-hour shift with other women who were probably no better off than she was, yet somehow they seemed to manage. Or did they? Who knew what went on in other people's lives, what secrets they might be hiding, or what lies they might tell?

She needed to create a lie of her own now, for Neve, who would be sure to ask, when her mother turned up unexpectedly at Sasha's at lunchtime, where the money to buy something new for the party had suddenly come from. Then the confusion over how they could now afford the trip to Barcelona would follow. She'd say she'd taken an advance on her wages. That was easy enough to believe, for both Lola and Neve, so yes, that was definitely what she would say. They didn't need to know the truth, the burden of that was hers to bear, along with the terrible fear that she'd just embarked on the beginning of the end.

'Still no answer,' Neve said, clicking off her mobile, 'but she was working late last night, so she's probably still asleep. Or she might be at the school already.'

'Remind me which disco she runs,' Sasha said, yawning as she turned on her laptop.

'It's called Moonshine.'

'Oh yeah, that's right.' Sasha yawned again. 'You know, I think it's really cool having a mum who runs a disco. Wish mine did.'

Neve's smile was faint.

'Honestly, the way mine nags,' Sasha went on with feeling. 'Ugh!' Then, switching her attention to the computer, 'OK, we're connected. Shall I check my messages first, or do you want to?'

'I don't mind waiting,' Neve answered, going to sit cross-legged on the bed she'd slept in, which was one of two facing each other across a room that had a plasma TV with Sky Plus, DVD recorder/player, three different game consoles, a video iPod and two docking stations, an electronic keyboard, and a humungous wardrobe so packed full of clothes it was hard to get the doors shut. Also, there was an amazing dressing table that ran the whole width of one wall and was covered in all kinds of make-up and beauty stuff, from Chanel, to Bobbi Brown, to Lancôme. Sasha even had her own bathroom with twin washbasins and a steam shower she could actually lie down in, like a sauna.

'Are you girls decent?' a voice called from the landing. 'I've brought your breakfast, but someone needs to open the door.'

'Coming,' Neve shouted, jumping up and slipping into one of Sasha's robes.

'Here we are,' Sasha's dad declared, entering with a tray. 'Muesli, toast and croissants. Oh, and orange juice. Did you sleep all right, the two of you?'

'Fine, thank you,' Neve answered, quickly clearing a space for him to put the tray down on the end of Sasha's bed.

'Where's Mum?' Sasha asked, glancing over her shoulder.

'She had to go into the office, and it's Ping's day off, so I'm your slave for this morning, but this is your lot I'm afraid, because I'm off to the gym in half an hour, and I've got a stack of work to catch up on later.'

'You're supposed to be helping us with our maths homework this morning,' Sasha reminded him.

'So I am. OK, let's meet in the kitchen at eleven. Will that suit?'

'Perfect. You can go now.'

Neve bubbled with laughter as Mr Phipps gave her a wink, then grabbing Sasha by the shoulders he rubbed her cheek with his unshaven chin.

'Get off me,' Sasha protested, trying to push him away. 'You're horrible and scratchy and it *hurts*.'

Loving the way they pretended to fight, Neve laughed with delight as Mr Phipps scooped Sasha up in his arms, carried her to the bed and dumped her there. He was always full of fun, unlike Sasha's mother, who took herself, and life, much more seriously, but as a lawyer Neve supposed she would, while as the head of some Internet music thing Mr Phipps was really cool.

After he'd gone Sasha began tucking into some muesli, while Neve went online to check her emails. 'Oh my God, there's one from Jason,' she cried excitedly.

Sasha sprang forward. 'What does it say?'

Neve's heart was beating fast. 'He's definitely going to Melinda's party tonight, and wants to know if I'll be there too.'

'No. Don't answer straight away,' Sasha cautioned as Neve started to type a reply. 'You don't want to seem too keen.'

'Definitely not,' Neve cried, taking her fingers off the keys as though they'd started to burn. 'My God, what was I thinking.'

'Anyway, Harry Gelson's going to be there too, so you need to make up your mind which one you want.'

Neve's head fell back. 'What am I going to do?' she groaned. 'I like them both.'

'That's the trouble with looking like you,' Sasha told her, 'you get all the boys. It must be such a pain.'

Neve turned to look at her. 'Yeah, and like you're really ugly! I don't think so.'

Sasha grinned, showing her braces, and made Neve squeal as she crossed her eyes. Though she was never going to be as striking as Neve with her mousy hair and pale complexion, when she was made up and wearing all her trendy gear, as far as Neve was concerned Sasha was seriously hot.

'I'll bet that's Melinda,' Sasha declared as her mobile started to ring. 'I'll tell her to come over as soon as she's ready. Check who's online in case there's anyone we want to talk to.'

As Sasha answered the phone Neve turned back to the computer, and a few minutes later, as Sasha ended the call, she left the desk to go and fetch some juice.

'I should try Mum again,' she said, putting the glass down.

'You've already left a message,' Sasha reminded her. 'She'll call when she wakes up, or goes on a break.'

Neve nodded. 'Yeah, I suppose so. It's just we had a bit of a row before she went to work last night . . .' She shrugged. Then, returning her attention to the computer, 'I just checked to see if there was anything from *you know who*.'

Sasha took a moment, then, realising who Neve meant, her eyes grew round. 'Well?' she prompted.

Neve shook her head. 'Nothing,' she said.

Sasha pulled a face. 'So what's going to happen if you do hear back?'

'I don't know. I haven't worked that bit out yet. Oh, here she is,' Neve cried, grabbing her mobile as it rang. 'Hi, Mum, I've been trying to get you.'

'I'm sorry, my phone was turned off. Is everything OK?'

'Yeah, cool. We're just having breakfast. How was last night?'

'Fine. I didn't get back till late. What time are you going shopping?'

'About one, I think.'

'Good. I'll try to get over there before that to give you some money. You deserve to have something new for tonight. Will you and Sasha be staying over at Melinda's?'

'Yes. How come you suddenly changed your mind?'

'I just did. Now, I'd better go or I'll have someone on my case. Give my love to Sasha, and don't forget to call Lola to say good morning.'

47

As she rang off Neve's delight started to take on some awkward angles.

'What's wrong?' Sasha asked.

'I don't know,' Neve answered. 'She sounded as though she'd been crying. You know, all like bunged up.'

'Maybe she's got a cold.'

Neve's eyes flicked to hers. 'Yeah, maybe,' she said, and feeling an embarrassing tightness in her throat she turned away. She had to do something to make her mum happy, and she was trying, but it wasn't really working out. At least not yet. Maybe she just needed to give it a bit more time.

Lola's adorable old face, with her all-seeing grey eyes and random feathery lines, was showing all the concern Susannah was afraid of as she watched Susannah come into the kitchen. Though Susannah smiled brightly, her aunt's expression didn't change.

'What is it?' Lola asked bluntly. 'And before you say nothing, I know you too well, so you might as well come out with it.'

'I'm just tired,' Susannah replied, starting to unpack the shopping she'd picked up on the way back from her cleaning job.

'Well, I know that, and who wouldn't be, working all the hours you do, then having to get up again at seven. What time did you get home last night?'

'Late, but I'll have a nap this afternoon before I go in later.' Though the very idea of setting foot over the club's threshold again was making her insides shrink, somehow she'd have to make herself do it.

Seeming to let it go for the moment, Lola opened the fridge to put away the milk Susannah was passing her. 'So Neve's staying at Melinda's tonight?' she queried.

'There's a party, so I said she could. We'll be here for lunch tomorrow though, if that's all right.'

Lola looked amazed. 'I should think so,' she retorted. 'Where else would you go for your Sunday roast?'

Smiling, Susannah walked round the small Formica table to embrace her. 'Even if we had somewhere else to go we wouldn't want to be anywhere but here,' she assured her.

Lola held her for a moment, patting her back, much as she had when her niece was a child. It was almost Susannah's undoing, but fortunately before the tears could surface Lola let her go. 'Now, what's happened to that ironing you were supposed to be bringing over?' she demanded, going to put the kettle on.

'I'll bring it tomorrow and we can do it between us,' Susannah replied. Then after a pause, and trying to make it sound casual, 'Did Neve mention anything after I left last night about the row we'd had before we came round?'

'Yes, as a matter of fact, she did. She was feeling a bit ashamed of herself, she said, because she'd come out with some hurtful things. I told her as long as she'd apologised and tried to think before she spoke next time, then it would all be forgotten.'

'Did she tell you it was about the Barcelona trip?'

'Yes, but she doesn't mind not going, she said.' Lola's expression showed that she hadn't believed a word of it. 'It's a pity, but we all have to cut our cloth . . .'

'Actually, I've changed my mind,' Susannah blurted, knowing she had to get this out sooner rather than later. 'I think she should go, so I'm going to borrow the money.'

Lola's eyes narrowed.

'I thought I'd take it from her school fees.'

Lola could hardly have looked more disapproving. 'That sounds like the start of a very slippery slope,' she said darkly.

Afraid she was already on one that was a thousand times worse, Susannah turned away. 'She's got to have some privileges,' she said. 'God knows she already misses out on enough.'

'But how are you going to pay it back?'

'I just will, so stop worrying. Now tell me how much I owe you. I know Neve borrowed ten pounds for her phone. Is there anything else?'

'No, that's it.'

'What about her lottery ticket? She's bound to have bought one, she always does.'

'We went halves, but I won't make you cough for fifty p.'

'Well here it is anyway.' She put a ten-pound note and a two-pound coin on the table. 'Now she's in credit.'

With a roll of her eyes Lola set about making some tea. By the time she carried two cups into the sitting room Susannah was already there, standing in front of the gas fire, flicking through a photograph album she'd found on the sofa with a faraway smile on her face.

'What's this doing out?' she asked, enjoying the pleasing flood of nostalgia as she turned the pages. 'I haven't seen any of these photos in years.'

'Neve wanted to look at them,' Lola answered, sinking down in her favourite wingback chair. 'She loves hearing about what you were like and what you were doing when you were her age.'

Smiling as she remembered how she used to plague Lola to tell her about her own mother, Susannah continued to leaf through the album, but she was hardly registering the photos any more. She was wondering, pointlessly, how different her life might have been had her parents and younger brother not been killed in a car crash when she was five years old. It wasn't that she'd ever lacked for love, because no parents could have been more doting than Lola and Fred, but the question often arose in her mind, what would she be doing now if her parents had lived? Where, and who, might she be?

She hadn't gone with them the day of the accident. They were going on the yearly Christmas trip to Longleat, but she'd had to stay behind with Lola and Fred, because she'd had chicken-pox. Jonathan was only three at the time, but he'd understood what a very special treat he was in for, going to see Father Christmas and lots of real animals, and riding on a train through a grotto. He'd been so excited before leaving that Susannah, angry and frustrated by having to stay at home, had slapped him. Even now, over thirty years later, she could still see his little face crumpling as he started to cry, and hear her mother's voice telling her sharply that there would be no Christmas presents for her if she didn't mend her ways. Then she'd cried too and her father had come to comfort her, the way he always did, because he couldn't bear to see his little angel upset.

She knew it was absurd to still be feeling so guilty about hitting her brother, but she did. She hadn't even said sorry before they'd left. It was why she'd never allow the sun to set on an argument now, nor would Lola or Neve. They both knew that not making up with Jonathan and her mother had proved the most difficult part of the loss for Susannah to overcome. Though she rarely mentioned it now, hardly a day passed when she didn't think of her family, and wonder how close they might all have become. It was the reason she'd never wanted Neve to be an only child, as though, in some way, having two would recreate the world that she and Jonathan had been denied. And Neve herself longed for siblings, but Duncan had never been the right father, and the chances of finding anyone else now felt even more remote than the place she'd have to go to in her head tonight when she stepped out of her clothes at the club.

Chapter Three

It was Tuesday lunchtime, and Susannah had just popped home after a morning's filing at the architect's office before going on to the dentist's reception at two. Today her lunch was going to consist of some delicious parsnip soup Lola had made on Sunday, and a chunk of crusty bread. She might even spread on some butter, since gaining weight had become a requirement lately, rather than a fear. However, she only had to think of her body, and how she was exposing it now, for her appetite to shrivel inside a ball of shame.

Putting the soup on to heat anyway, she went to start up the computer, intending to carry out a job search in the vain hope of discovering something that might, by some miracle, replace her income from the club. It was a bit like sending a note to Santa, she thought despondently, you could always ask, but the chances of receiving were about as likely as the fat fellow himself wriggling down the chimney on Christmas Eve.

She was as far as the Google home page when the phone started to ring, and the soup to boil over. Dashing to the stove she quickly lowered the gas and grabbed the receiver, saying, 'Hello, Susannah Cates speaking.'

'Ah, I'm so glad it's you. I was afraid I might get the machine. How are you?' the voice at the other end asked, laughingly.

Realising who it was, Susannah lost her voice in a powerful rush of emotion. 'Pats!' she gasped. 'Oh God, it's so wonderful to hear you. How are you? I'm sorry I haven't called, but . . .'

'Don't worry, we've both been busy, and email's fine – up to a point. I needed to hear you, though – and to see you.'

Susannah hardly dared to hope. 'Does that mean you're coming over?' she cried, unable to imagine any more welcome news.

'Actually, what it means is if you go to the front door, I'm standing right outside.'

Susannah's heart contracted as a deluge of tears surged to her eyes – and without wasting another instant she ran across the sitting room to tear open the door, almost afraid this was a dream. 'Oh my God, oh my God,' she sobbed as Patsy opened her arms. 'You don't know how happy I am to see you.'

'Mm, you look it,' Patsy commented drily as she hugged her hard, though tears of happiness were swamping her own lively green eyes. Her auburn hair was wayward and short and framed her elfin face like autumn leaves, while the rest of her, all wrapped up in fake winter furs and long leather boots, was as slender and elegant as any self-respecting cosmetic executive ought to be. In their day she and Susannah had been quite a twosome, though Pats was under no illusions:

when it came to real beauty, Susannah was in a class of her own.

'When did you get here?' Susannah demanded, holding her back to get a good look at her. 'And why didn't you tell me you were coming?'

'Well, it was all a bit last-minute, and I was going to send an email, but then I took it into my head to surprise you.'

'You've certainly succeeded in that,' Susannah assured her, cupping Patsy's beloved face in her hands. 'Look at you. You're more gorgeous than ever – and so . . . *sophisticated*. Australia obviously suits you.'

Patsy's warm eyes filled with irony as she said, 'Maybe, but I'm not sure I suit it any more. However, that's for later. Right now, it would be great to come in out of the cold, and if you have the time, let's open some champagne.'

Loving the idea, but grimacing as she stood aside, Susannah said, 'I'm sorry, I'm all out of champagne, and I don't have any wine either.'

'You surely don't think I came empty-handed,' Patsy chided, swinging a large bag off her shoulder as she stepped into the sitting room. 'Oh heaven, warmth – and memories. This is such a welcoming house, you know. I've always loved it, apart from when Duncan was here, so why are you selling?'

'I'm not,' Susannah answered, closing the door. 'The sign's being removed this afternoon, apparently, but that's something else for later. Let me take your coat. It's amazing. Did you get it in Sydney?'

'I did, and if you like it you can have it.'

Susannah's eyes rounded. 'No, I didn't mean . . .'

'I know you didn't, but I have another that's almost the same, so consider that one an early birthday present – or belated, whichever, as we're kind of midway. Now, I'm afraid this bottle isn't as cold as it should be, but it'll have to do. Glasses in the same place?'

Laughing and hugging the coat to her, Susannah watched her beloved friend sail on into the kitchen, where she proceeded to carry on as though she'd never been away.

'When did you get here?' Susannah asked, following her in. 'And where are you staying?'

'I arrived at the crack of eggs this morning and went straight to the Ritz.' Patsy's eyes were dancing as she slanted them Susannah's way. 'My only excuse is that it's close to the London office, and they booked me in,' she apologised.

Susannah's tone was droll as she said, 'Then I won't ask if you'd like to stay here, but you know you're very welcome. How long are you going to be in London?'

'A couple of weeks. Then I'm off to Paris which, I trust you'll be very happy to hear, is where I'm going to be based from the beginning of next month.'

Susannah's eyes dilated with disbelief, and joy. It might not be London, but it was a hell of a lot closer than Sydney, and practically in the same time zone as the UK. 'That is the most fantastic news I've had since I can't remember when,' she declared, meaning it. 'Is it a promotion?'

Patsy grinned, and after filling two glasses she handed one to Susannah, saying, 'It's OK, you don't have to curtsy, but, my darling, you are looking at the new Executive Vice President for Bryce Beauty Europe.'

Susannah stared at her in stunned admiration. 'You're amazing,' she told her with feeling, 'whoever thought your business degree was going to pay off like this?'

'And my French,' Patsy reminded her, 'which is just as vital now I'm going to be working in France. The company might be American, but everything over there is done in French – apart from job titles – and it's going to be interesting to see how they react to having a foreigner *and* a female as a boss, because, apparently, there's a solid glass ceiling in the French houses that no woman ever gets through.'

'They won't know what's hit them,' Susannah murmured humorously.

'We'll see. It's typical of Claudia Bryce to smash through social mores, of course. She's made a career out of it, and I'm very lucky to have met her when mine was just starting out, which is all thanks to you, as we know, because you were the one who introduced us, sixteen years ago, when you were promoting her new range of eye make-up. So here's to you and Claudia and being back in Europe.'

'And to you too,' Susannah added warmly, clinking her glass, and wondering if this was really happening – or wise, when she hadn't eaten yet today and had to go to work in an hour. But what the hell, and knocking her drink back she laughed delightedly as Patsy grabbed the bottle for a refill.

'You took a risk coming unannounced,' Susannah told her, as the champagne fizzed over on to her fingers. 'I only popped home to use the computer.'

'Confession number one, I've just come from Lola's so I knew you were here when you rang to tell her what you were doing.' Her eyes narrowed slightly. 'She also brought me up to speed with everything that's been happening with you, most of which doesn't seem to have made your emails.' Her frown deepened. 'Why on earth didn't you tell me you've been finding things so hard? You know very well I'd have helped out.'

With defiance Susannah said, 'Whatever Lola's told you, she's exaggerating, and anyway, I sure as heck wasn't going to load my emails up with sob stories, especially when you're doing so well. I've got my pride, you know.' Then, remembering how little she had left since she'd shed it along with her clothes, her spark faded. 'Actually, I'm not sure I have any more,' she corrected, 'but don't let's get into that.'

'No, let's,' Pats insisted, and pulled out a chair to sit at the table. 'Lola's set me the task of finding out what's on your mind, because she's certain something is and she's worried. And before you go any further you're going to let me give you the money for Neve's school trip so you can pay back what you've borrowed from her school fees.'

Susannah's expression turned mutinous. 'Lola shouldn't have told you about that, and anyway, it's not a problem . . .'

'Yes it is, because Lola's right. Once you start dipping into those funds there's no knowing

58

where it might end, and the last thing we want is Neve's education to suffer. As her godmother it's my responsibility to see that it doesn't . . . No, don't argue. I haven't forgotten the time you bailed me out when I was broke and you and Duncan were flush . . .'

'That was years ago, and for about fifty quid, as I recall.'

'It's all relative, and anyway, as your best friend I am not going to let you stitch yourself in a fix you can't get out of.'

Not sure whether she wanted to laugh or cry, Susannah said, 'I think I'm already there – not that I can't get out of it, but I . . .' Her voice trailed off as she thought of what she'd done. There wasn't another soul in the world she'd admit it to, and she wasn't even sure she could to Pats.

'Come on, nothing can be that bad,' Pats prompted when she stalled. 'And you know me, I'm unshockable.'

Susannah's smile was faint as her eyes went down. Her throat suddenly felt constricted, and dry, as though trying to keep the words in, because once they were out there it would all be real, and somehow she'd have to face it herself. 'Last week,' she began, still staring at her drink as though her disgrace was at the other side of it, somewhere hazy and unreachable, 'Neve and I had a row and . . . No.' She shook her head. 'It doesn't have anything to do with her, apart from trying to make sure she has everything she needs – or that her friends have . . .' She took a breath and tried again. 'The opportunity has always been there for me to . . . The other girls do it, well, it's their job, they know what's expected of them and they're fine with it. I . . . Well, I was certain it was something I'd never be able to do . . .'

'Can I take it we're talking about the club you work at?' Patsy interjected softly.

Susannah nodded. 'But then I did,' she blurted. 'Last Friday. I guess I hit rock bottom, or I panicked, or . . . I don't really know what was going through my head, I just had this feeling that the world was collapsing around me, and that if I didn't do something to make some money right away it would all be over. Neve would have to change schools, we'd lose the house, Lola would be so stressed it would make her ill . . . Everything was crowding in on me, and I was so tired and . . .' She swallowed hard, and bunched her hands more tightly together. 'The answer was right there in front of me. It wasn't even that difficult in the end, because all I had to do was act. It didn't have to be me, so . . . it wasn't. It was someone else who went into a private dining room to serve food and drinks to a bunch of half-drunk American lawyers. I gave myself another name, Trudie, and when they touched me I giggled and squirmed, because that's what Trudie would do. She was a game girl who didn't mind too much about being groped, but she drew the line at anything below the waist. If she'd been prepared to . . . Well, she could have earned up to a thousand pounds in tips. As it was, she earned four hundred on Friday, and another five hundred on Saturday. One man offered her *two thousand pounds*, cash, if she'd go back to his hotel room for the night. She . . . It seemed . . . It was so much money and if I could have stayed as Trudie . . . But the mask was starting to crack by then. I was becoming me again, and I just wanted to get out of there. I was horrified enough by what I'd done, and when I found myself being tempted . . . I kept thinking that this was just the beginning, that Trudie might start taking over, like some horrible alter ego, and maybe next time she would go to a hotel room. The money's so easy, it's all in cash, and things have become so tight . . .'

At last her eyes came up to Patsy's, dark with misery and shame. 'That's how low I've sunk,' she said, attempting a smile. 'That's the kind of use I'm now putting my training to. I'm hiding behind a fictitious character to . . .'

'Stop,' Patsy broke in. 'Anyone would think you'd committed some terrible crime, when all you did was let a few blokes see you naked . . .'

'Topless.'

'Even less shocking. It's happening all the time, my darling, on beaches, in magazines . . .'

'But I let them touch me.'

'Come on, we've all done things we've regretted in the morning, and someone grabbing your boobs is pretty low down the scale of curl up and die.'

'It might not seem major to you, but for me it was like I'd crossed some invisible line and . . .'

'OK, I understand that's not who you are, or what you wanted to do, I'm just trying to help you put it in some perspective. You did what you felt you had to at the time, but think of it this way, when it came right down to it, you resisted the big bucks.'

'But what about the next time? That's what's really scaring me.'

'There won't be a next time. When are you due to go in again?'

'Thursday. I've already told Henry that I'll be in the office the entire time, though. I dare not put myself in the way of that kind of temptation again, because if something else comes up for Neve, or another unexpected bill drops on to the mat . . .'

'No more. It's done, finished, you won't be doing it again, so put it behind you. I'm going to give you the money for Neve's trip, and if anything unexpected does turn up, I'll take care of it. No, I don't want any arguments. You know very well you'd do the same for me if our situations were reversed . . .'

'But borrowing from friends, Pats . . .'

'Who said anything about borrowing?' Her hand went up as Susannah started to protest again. 'OK, so now that's sorted, you should be in some credit after last weekend's tips. Personally, I'd blow it all on a night out, or an amazing new outfit, or a weekend in a spa, because frankly you look as though you could do with all three.'

Susannah smiled and shook her head fondly. 'Since when did you become my fairy godmother, Patsy Lovell?' she challenged.

'Actually, I'm Neve's, so now we've started on the road to sorting you out, tell me how she is. Her emails are about as informative as yours, now I know the truth.'

'She's great. A bit teenagerish at times, which is only to be expected, but she's doing really well at school, and you wait till you see her. She's so grown-up it's almost scary. Sometimes when I look at her I can hardly believe this gangly, gorgeous young creature is my baby. She's getting into boys, big-time, these days, and music, and partying, and make-up and all the things we loved at her age.'

Smiling at the memories, Patsy said, 'Does she ever see Duncan now?'

Susannah shook her head. 'Never. He made it clear when his sentence started that he didn't want us to go to the prison, and I didn't argue because frankly I never wanted her exposed to that kind of environment.'

Since she'd never had any fondness for Duncan, Patsy was happy to dismiss him for the time being. 'It would be good for her to have some kind of male figure in her life though, wouldn't it?' she ventured.

Susannah's smile was crooked as she said, 'I'm in no hurry to go down that road again, thank you very much. Once was more than enough.'

'So there's no one on the scene?'

'Absolutely not, but even if I wanted someone, which I *really* don't, I'm working just about every hour God sends so there's no time anyway. In fact, I have to leave soon to be at the dentist's office, but we haven't talked about you at all yet so I think we should change the subject now.'

Patsy looked surprised. 'I've got my promotion, I'm back in Europe and I've got two fancy coats. I think that about covers it,' she declared.

Susannah smiled. 'Yeah, right. Come on, I know you, there's bound to be some kind of scandal or hot new passion you're holding back. How are your parents, by the way? What do they think about you leaving Australia?'

Patsy pulled the kind of face that had always

made Susannah laugh. 'Right now, I think they're pretty relieved I'm no longer on the same side of the planet,' she confessed. 'There was a bit of a scene before I left, that got in the papers. It was a tad embarrassing, I must admit.'

Susannah's eyes lit with amusement. 'Go on,' she prompted.

Patsy threw out her hands. 'What was I supposed to do? The man betrayed me so he had it coming.'

'Oh my God, what happened? No, hang on, first of all, who are we talking about?'

'Mike, the one with the boatyard. Remember, I started seeing him just after I arrived?'

'Of course, but you stopped mentioning him after a while, so I thought he was history.'

'Well he is now, and the relationship was always a bit on/off, frankly more on for me and off for him, which was why I stopped talking about him in my emails. I didn't want to come across as one of those saddos addicted to unrequited love, because we already know that's who I am and I wanted you to think I'd had some rehab that had worked.'

'You are so *not* a saddo addicted to unrequited love,' Susannah cried with a laugh.

Patsy winked. 'Anyway, we actually started hotting up for a while, and he even got round to talking about marriage and kids. Can you believe it? *Marriage and kids.* So there was me thinking this is it, I've finally met Mr Right – pity it's going to mean giving up my ambition for one of the top jobs, but can't see him moving to Europe, or the States, when the furthest he's ever made it out of

Sydney is a couple of miles offshore to show off one of his boats. However, in its own little way, it was all making sense. My parents were living half an hour away, my sister, brother-in-law, niece and nephew, even closer. Sydney's a paradise. So if he did get round to actually popping the question I decided my answer would be yeah, OK Mike, I'll marry you, glad to, mate, just name the day and I'll buy me frock. So what did he do? He pops the question all right, just not to me.'

Susannah's laugh at the Aussie accent froze.

'It turns out he's been seeing this other Sheila – seriously, that's her name – who's dumb, fat and *forty-six*! OK, she probably wouldn't describe herself that way, but I swear I've never felt so humiliated.'

'I can imagine. Not to mention heartbroken?'

'Oh, don't get me started. Buckets! Sobbing morning, noon and night. Redefined the meaning of pathetic. I turned into a stalker. I swear it. I started following them around the place, and ringing them up in the middle of the night. Then I heard he was about to take out some kind of restraining order on me, and that was it! I lost it completely. Next day I went to his boatyard when I knew she'd be there too, and I took a gun.'

Susannah choked on her champagne.

'It wasn't real, obviously, but they didn't know that. I'm telling you, it was worth spending the night in a police cell just to see their faces.'

Susannah burst out laughing. 'You spent the night in a police cell!' she cried incredulously. 'Oh God, Pats, I've missed you so much.'

Patsy's eyebrows rose. 'With any luck my parents

will feel the same way in a year or two,' she responded. 'As it stands, they're keen for everyone to forget they have a madwoman for a daughter. Whereas my darling boss, Claudia, insists she couldn't be more thrilled, because she was ready to whisk me out of there anyway. So, here I am, jet-lagged, jettisoned, and . . . give me another J . . .'

Susannah thought quickly. 'Just in time,' she told her.

Patsy gave a clap of delight. 'Brilliant, but if I'd come a week ago you might not have those dark shadows round your eyes and be tearing yourself apart the way you are.'

'The way I'm seeing it is, you might have come a week later, then I really would be in a mess. What matters is that you're here now, and though I have absolutely no intention of letting you pay my way, I will gladly accept your offer to finance Neve's trip. Now, I'm really sorry, but I have to love you and leave you or I'll be late for work. Can we get together this evening? I'm not working and Neve's at home, but you've probably got all kinds of things arranged.'

'Yeah, like going back to Lola's until you finish,' Patsy told her. 'Don't worry, I'll think of something to put her mind at rest about you without giving her the real spill, but there's no point me going back over the river when I don't have to, and when I *love* being in her little flat. It's such a trip – straight down memory lane. Or would you like me to go and pick up Neve from school? I can go by taxi, or limousine if you think she'd like it.'

Laughing as she got to her feet, Susannah said, 'I'm sure she'd love it, but she has a dance lesson on Tuesdays, then she goes to her friend Melinda's to do some homework before coming back here for six, by which time I'm usually home, because I finish at five thirty and it's a twenty-minute walk from the dentist's. You see, it works, after a fashion, but only thanks to Lola, because if I'm ever late, or things change last minute, she's less than five minutes away.'

Patsy nodded understandingly. 'We all need a Lola in our lives. We couldn't survive without them.'

'Tell her that. She likes to feel needed.'

'Don't we all. Now tell me again what time you'll be back. I thought I'd take you all for dinner tonight – if I can stay awake that long,' she added with a yawn.

'Before I go,' Neve was saying as she packed her homework into her bag, 'can I check my emails again? I can't do it at home, because Mum'll be there by the time I get back.'

'Feel free,' Melinda replied, waving her towards the computer. 'Did you watch last night's *Hollyoaks*, by the way? I really reckon she's going to top herself, don't you?'

Because of the similar fears she'd been having about her mother, Neve quickly shook her head. 'No, she'll get him back,' she replied confidently. 'She's bound to, because . . .' Her eyes suddenly widened as a new screen popped up in front of her. 'Oh my God,' she cried. 'Guess who's online.'

Melinda immediately sat up, her pretty freckled

face paling with excitement. 'Don't tell me. It's him,' she said, riveted to the edge of the bed.

'If you're talking about Jack, then yes. And he's going to know you're logged on now, so do you want to chat with him?'

Melinda shrank back. 'No way, he's got to chat with me first. Anyway, it's you he's interested in, not me.'

Neve gawped at her incredulously. 'He so is not! It was you he kept dancing and hanging out with at the party. If your parents hadn't been around I bet anything he'd have snogged you.'

Melinda's head dropped back in ecstasy. 'Can you imagine?' she growled with longing. 'Oh my God, he is so fit. I am just going to die if he ever asks me out.'

'That'll make you a lot of fun,' Neve commented, typing in a password to access the new Hotmail account she'd set up a couple of weeks ago. 'I just want to see if there are any messages,' she said, 'then I'll be out of here and you can chat with Jack to your heart's content. But don't forget to save it, so me and Sasha can read it later.'

Coming to stand behind her, Melinda gazed rapturously at the name in the top right-hand corner of the screen. 'Do you reckon I should ask him if he . . .'

'Oh my God! Oh my God!' Neve suddenly gulped. 'There's a message.'

Melinda looked mystified until, realising what Neve was talking about, her dark eyes bulged with intrigue. 'What does it say?' she urged. 'Quick, go on the website and find out what's there.'

A few minutes later, after reading a lengthy email on the Friends Reunited web page, Neve and Melinda turned to stare at one another in amazement.

'That is seriously spooky,' Melinda whispered, as though the sender might be able to hear. 'What are you going to do?'

'I don't know,' Neve whispered back.

'You'll have to tell your mum.'

'Are you insane?'

'But that's why . . .' Melinda broke off as the jingle of contact trilled from the computer, and her hands flew to her cheeks as Jack Fitzsimmons's IM came up.

Hey, how are you doing?

'Oh my God, what shall I say?' Melinda cried.

With a roll of her eyes Neve vacated the chair for her to sit down. 'Try telling him you're dead hot for him, and you want him to be your first snog with tongues,' she suggested.

Melinda gave a snort of laughter. 'Yeah, right, I'm really going to do that. Shall I say something like, I'm cool, how are you?'

Neve was winding a long woolly scarf round her neck. 'No way,' she replied. 'He's going to think you're a real slag if you come on to him like that.'

Melinda's mouth dropped open, then realising Neve was joking she threw a pen at her, saying, 'It's all right for you, I don't even know how to snog at first base, never mind with tongues.'

'Sad,' Neve retorted, putting on her coat. 'Get Sasha to show you. According to Barry Goldsmith she had his tonsils for dinner the other night.

69

Anyway, I've got to run or I'll be late. See you at school tomorrow. Double geography first thing, yuk!'

After shouting a goodbye to Melinda's mother Neve tugged open the heavy front door and ventured out into the sleeting rain. It was freezing and dark and her bag was seriously heavy. If only her mum had a car, she was thinking, she could come and pick her up. It didn't have to be a Mercedes like Sasha's mum's, or a four-wheel drive like Melinda's, it didn't even have to be especially new or flash, just as long as it went, and had a heater that worked. They'd be at home in no time, all snug in front of the little gas fire, where they'd stay till bedtime, eating their tea, doing homework and watching TV all cuddled up under a blanket to keep out the cold.

Still, at least it wasn't far from the humungous houses near the park round to their terrace, and the email she'd just received was making her feel all excited and optimistic in a way she hadn't for ages. She was a bit confused too, because she had to decide what to do next, and that wasn't going to be easy now he'd come straight back saying he wanted to see her. Before she agreed she needed to ask him all kinds of things. In fact she'd start making a list as soon as she got home, and maybe she should also get him to send some pictures. Except he might feel a bit offended if she did that, or think it was a bit weird when she was already supposed to know what he looked like. Actually, she did, and he was seriously drop-dead, but that was then, and this was now, and for all she knew he might have morphed into some disgusting fat slob with bad breath and twitchy eyes since the photos she'd seen were taken.

She'd just reached their front gate and was taking out her keys when her mobile started to ring. Seeing it was her mother, she opened the front door, saying, 'Hi, I'm here.'

'Where?' Susannah said.

'Hello,' Neve laughed as Susannah appeared in the kitchen doorway.

Laughing too, Susannah rang off, saying, 'Don't worry, I wasn't checking up on you. I just wanted to let you know that there's a surprise waiting for you that I think you're going to like.'

Neve dropped her bag and quickly unwound her scarf. 'So, bring it on,' she demanded, looking round the sitting room.

Susannah moved aside to let Patsy step into the doorway. 'Here it is,' Patsy declared. 'And if you dare to look disappointed . . .'

'Oh my God! Pats!' Neve shrieked incredulously. 'When did you get here? Oh my God, this is so fantastic. I can't believe it.'

'Crikey,' Patsy laughed, staggering as she caught her in a crushing embrace. 'You're not as small as you were, but it's wonderful to see you. If I'd known I was going to get such a fantastic welcome I'd have come sooner.'

'No, now is absolutely perfect,' Neve assured her. 'It's like . . . You just don't know . . . Oh my God.'

Susannah was laughing, and loving how genuinely thrilled Neve was to see her godmother. 'We're going out to celebrate tonight,' she told her. 'Lola's coming too, so you'd better run upstairs to change out of that uniform.'

Neve was round-eyed with amazement. 'This is like the best thing in the entire world,' she declared, still looking at Pats. Then turning to Susannah she put her arms round her, saying, 'I love you so much. You are the best mum in the universe so I know you're going to let me wear your black jeans and fur gilet tonight.'

'In which case,' Susannah said, 'you won't mind if I wear your purple polo neck and pink glittery scarf.'

Neve looked stricken. 'But I was going to wear that top with the jeans, and the scarf.'

Susannah glanced at Pats with twinkling eyes. 'OK, I suppose Cinderella will just have to go in rags again,' she said, 'but at least I have a new coat to cover them up. Wait till you see it,' she told Neve, 'it's to die for, but before you even think about asking, no, you cannot wear it.'

Laughing, Patsy went to the phone. 'I'll call a taxi to come and pick us up,' she said. 'Chutney Mary's suit you?' she asked Neve. 'I've already reserved.'

'Oh, that is only my and Lola's absolute favourite,' Neve gushed. 'We went there for her birthday last year, didn't we Mum? But it's so expensive we could only have a starter each.'

Pinching her cheeks, which were crimson with excitement, Susannah pressed a kiss to her forehead, saying, 'I've already showered, so the bathroom's all yours. I'm going upstairs to get changed.'

Neve waited for the sound of Susannah's floorboards creaking overhead, then closing the kitchen door she whispered to Patsy, 'I have to talk to you.

It's really important. Oh my God, this is so amazing that you should be here, but I can't tell you anything now. If Mum should find out she'll go ballistic.'

Intrigued, Patsy said, 'Do I get some kind of a clue?'

'No! Not yet. I can't. We have to sort out a time . . . I'll give you my mobile number and we can arrange to meet without Mum being there.' She was already jotting it down, and handing the scrap of paper to Patsy, she said, 'Promise me you'll call so we can set something up.'

As amused as she was intrigued, Patsy said, 'Believe me, there's no way I'm denying myself the satisfaction of finding out what this is about. Expect my call first thing tomorrow.'

Chapter Four

True to her word Patsy called Neve the following day, later than she'd intended, thanks to a jet-lag oversleep, so she had to leave a message for Neve to call back.

It was ten thirty when her mobile rang. 'I'm between lessons,' Neve said hurriedly, 'so my phone's not supposed to be on. When can you make it?'

'What about Friday evening, while Mum's at work?' Patsy suggested. 'I can't make it any sooner, I'm afraid, because I've got meetings and dinners I have to go to.'

'Friday's fine,' Neve assured her. 'Can you come to the house?'

'Of course, or you can come here. I thought you might like to spend a night at the Ritz.'

Neve groaned with pleasure. 'I'd absolutely love to,' she told her. 'But do you have a computer there, because we're going to need one?'

'Of course,' Pats replied, her eyes shining with amusement. 'I'll send a taxi to pick you up at seven. You'll be at Lola's, yes?'

'That's right. Oh, Pats, this is so exciting I can hardly wait.'

After putting the phone down Patsy ordered coffee from room service, checked to make sure there were no more messages, then dragged herself into the shower, before starting on the emails that had come in overnight.

An hour later, feeling far more refreshed than a near sleepless night should have allowed, she was striding into the London office for a meeting that was scheduled to run straight through lunch and on into the afternoon. In the event, it didn't finish until after six, which left her less than an hour to dash back to the hotel and change for a party to celebrate the launch of a new fragrance. So much for having a break before taking up her post in Paris, but it was useful catching up with everyone in London, and fun, since she knew most of the team well, and liked them a lot, particularly Anita Shayfer the MD.

'You're going to love it in Paris,' Anita told her during a brief break in mingling during the party, 'but you'll have your work cut out trying to break through all that chauvinism. I'm especially interested to see how Frank Delacourt reacts. Everyone thought he was the hot favourite for your position.'

'Mm, I believe he was,' Patsy responded, 'but Claudia tells me he turned it down.'

Anita seemed surprised. 'So he was offered it?' she said. 'How interesting.'

'Isn't it? Do you have any idea why he'd back off?'

Anita shook her head. 'I wouldn't like to say. Frank's . . . Well, he's an unusual man. You've never met him, have you?'

Patsy shook her head. 'So what's he like?'

Anita's eyes were starting to shine. 'Let's put it this way,' she said, 'he's nothing like your archetypal Frenchman, either in looks or manner. As for the job, he's got his own personal style which is . . . well, as I said before, unusual, and from what I can make out he commands the kind of loyalty the rest of us can only dream about.'

Patsy waited for her to go on. 'You have to give me more than that,' she protested.

Anita was close to laughing. 'No, I don't think I will,' she decided, and with an airy little wave she went off to mingle again.

Over the next two days Patsy's schedule remained hectic, making her thankful she'd gone to surprise Susannah the instant she arrived, or heaven only knew when she'd have managed to fit it in. Seeing her again, and feeling their bond reasserting itself so immediately, had been every bit as wonderful, and emotional, as she'd expected. However, the shock of finding her looking so gaunt and unhappy was still reverberating through Patsy's conscience as though she were in some way to blame. She'd never felt good about leaving England when she had, and now, discovering what a drastic downturn Susannah's fortunes had taken, she was determined to do whatever she could to change their direction. Helping out financially, particularly with Neve, was a good place to start, if only to prevent a repeat of the disastrous decision Susannah had taken last weekend. It made Patsy almost breathless to think of how far that might have gone had she not come back when she did, but fortunately it seemed someone up there had got his timing right for once. Not a chap generally to be relied upon, in her opinion, but then show her one who was – in fact, don't, because unless he was gay, her father, or dead, he'd inevitably turn out to be a sex-change. For a fleeting moment she wondered if that was the unusual part of Frank Delacourt, then put it out of her mind.

It was extraordinary, she was thinking, as she waited for Neve to arrive on Friday evening, how adept both she and Susannah had proved over the years at choosing the wrong man. Though it had to be said, Duncan was in a class of his own when it came to worthless individuals. Pats had never liked him from the get-go, but Susannah, young, bedazzled and dying to slap on the grease-paint, had been swept away by his charm, which even Pats had to admit he'd had plenty of till the drugs took hold. Such a waste of a talent! Though to Patsy's mind he'd never had as much of that as he'd tried to make out. She was more inclined to consider him a fake, a *blagueur*, in fact a pretty pathetic sort of specimen, particularly when it came to taking care of his family.

Still, it was behind them now, and though she continued to despise the man, she had little fear of him inflicting his loathsome self on them again should he actually manage to get out. He had neither the decency nor the courage it took to try, he only had the barefaced audacity to instruct his slimeball of a brother to put Susannah's house on the market. Well, he'd never stood a hope in hell of getting away with that, which he presumably knew by now, and if he didn't Patsy would have no problem finding a very good lawyer to hammer the message home in ways he wouldn't be able to misunderstand.

However, all that was for another time, should it prove necessary. What mattered this evening – and always – was his daughter, who had just arrived at the hotel and was on her way up.

Pats was standing at the door as Neve stepped out of the lift, looking overawed and rapt, and so like Susannah that it gave Pats a bit of jolt. 'Darling,' she said, opening her arms, 'you should have let the porter bring up your bag.'

'It's fine,' Neve replied, coming to embrace her. 'This place is amazing, isn't it? I mean, a bit OTT on all the gilt and curly-wurly antique stuff, but hey, am I complaining?'

Laughing, Pats caught hold of her hand and led her into the sitting room of her suite, where the sumptuous draperies, curly-wurly antique furniture, silk walls and Persian carpets made it a haven of luxury and prestige. 'There's an extra bedroom and bathroom, just for you,' she told her, 'but if you're nervous about staying on your own I'll get them to put an extra bed in my room. Now, what would you like to drink? There's Coke, orange juice, lemonade . . . You name it. If it's not here, we'll have it sent up.'

Still seeming slightly overwhelmed, Neve began unbuttoning the coat Pats had given Susannah. 'Can I have wine?' she asked. 'Mum lets me sometimes, half a glass with soda.'

'Coming right up,' Pats replied, her voice wavering on a surge of affection. She'd always adored Neve and seeing how fast she was growing up was making her feel quite emotional, and anxious that she might never have any children of her own. 'Tell you what,' she said, 'tomorrow, instead of me taking you home, why don't we get Mum to come here and the three of us can spend the weekend together?'

Neve's eyes lit up. 'Oh, she'd so love that,' she answered warmly. 'She hardly ever goes out, so coming somewhere like this would be a mega treat.'

Patsy's eyes softened as she cupped Neve's face in one hand. 'You really love her, don't you?' she said tenderly.

Neve's eyebrows rose in surprise. 'Well, yeah, she's my mum, so it kind of follows.' Then, seeming to realise more was required, 'Actually, yeah, she's really cool. At least, I think so, apart from when she's on my case about something, or in the bathroom when I want to go in there.'

With a smile, Pats pressed a kiss to her forehead and went to fix their drinks. 'Here's to you and Mum, and all of us being back together,' she said, when they were both holding spritzers.

'Cool,' Neve said with a grin, and clinking her glass she took a tiny sip and put it down on the glass-topped table. 'So I expect you want to know what I need to talk to you about,' she said, dropping to her knees on a fur rug in front of the fireplace. 'Where's your computer, by the way? Is it here?'

'It's on the desk next door.'

'And you can access the Internet?'

'Of course.'

'Great, because we'll need to.'

Patsy sat down on one of the Louis Quinze chairs. 'OK, I'm all ears,' she informed her, 'please don't keep me in suspense a moment longer.'

Neve took a gulp of wine, as though to jump-start her courage, then said, 'OK, here goes. I've done something that you might think is really crazy, or you might not. I don't know, but the thing is . . . Well, I've been really worried about Mum for ages now. She never has any fun, or anything, and she's always broke, even though she works really hard. I know it's my fault, because she wants to keep me at the same school, so I thought if I could do something for her that might help make things easier . . . This is going to seem seriously random now, I know, but you've got to see it this way . . . Mum's really sad inside. She tries to hide it, but I can tell . . .' She swallowed as tears suddenly filled her eyes. 'She's afraid that things might never get better, and that she'll keep letting me down all the time, and I don't help because I get all angry and uptight when I can't have the things I want. So anyway, I thought if she could meet someone with loads of money . . . Well, not just money, obviously, because he'd have to be kind and good-looking and really love her, which is the most important, but you know her, what's not to love?'

Realising she was supposed to give an answer, Patsy said, 'Absolutely nothing. It would be a good idea if she loved him too though, wouldn't it?'

'That's exactly what I thought, and then I remembered there used to be someone, before she met Dad. She's told me about him a few times, and you must know him because you all went to school together. Alan Cunningham?'

Patsy's eyes grew wide.

'You remember him?'

'Of course.'

'He was Mum's first love, right?'

'Right, but it was a long time ago. We haven't heard from him in years.'

'I know, but I've been asking Lola about him, well, about all of you actually, so's not to make her suspicious, and she showed me pictures . . . She said really nice things about him, and when I saw his photo . . . Pats, he was seriously fit.'

Patsy looked puzzled. 'He was in the football team,' she agreed.

'No, I mean fit as in drop-dead gorgeous.'

'Oh yes, he was definitely that. All the girls fancied him, including yours truly, but he only ever had eyes for Mum.' A certain understanding was starting to creep up on her. 'What have you done?' she asked, carefully. 'Don't tell me you've found him, after all this time?'

Neve's eyes were shining as she nodded. 'Yes, I have,' she answered. 'I went on to Friends Reunited a couple of weeks ago and on Tuesday he got in touch.'

Patsy shook her head in wonder and affection. 'Ordinarily I might have a bit of a problem with dredging up people from the past,' she said, 'but in Alan's case . . . Where is he? What's he doing? The last I heard he was in Manchester, or was it Liverpool, but that was way back. He must be married, surely.'

'I don't know, I haven't asked. I just went on

the website, pretending to be Mum, to find out if he might be out there somewhere and still interested, and I got this message back. That's why we need the computer, so I can go online and show you.'

'Take me to it,' Patsy commanded, getting to her feet. 'My God, you're amazing, Neve Cates. Remind me, if I ever have a daughter, she has to learn the ropes from you.'

Minutes later they were connected to Neve's private mail on Friends Reunited and reading Alan Cunningham's message.

Susannah, what a wonderful surprise. To be honest, I'm not quite sure what to make of it, because the last person I expected to find when I made an idle browse of the FR website was you. It was my first visit, and I only went on because my life changed rather dramatically a few months ago (if we meet, and I hope we do, I'll tell you all about it) but it meant that I decided to leave Manchester, where I've been since university, to return to London. Finding myself alone in a place I'd once known so well, I thought I'd go online to see if I could contact any of the old crowd from school. I didn't even dare to hope to find a message from you, but there it was, and so many memories came flooding back . . .

You won't know this, but sixteen years ago, when I finished my studies, I came to find you hoping to restart our relationship. How arrogant was that, when I just took off after we'd finished our A levels, promising to keep in touch, and only managing it for a few months before university life suckered me into its specious web? Anyway, I got my comeuppance when I discovered that you'd met a very glamorous director and were madly in love. So, with my tail between my legs, I took the job I'd been offered in Manchester, and moved into the flat I'd imagined sharing with you.

My God, that was all such a long time ago. It seems really odd talking about it now, as if it happened yesterday. So much water has gone under the bridge for both of us. I've no idea if you're still with the director chap, but I guess not, or you wouldn't have left a message for me on FR.

Patsy sighed, and realising where she was in the text, Neve said, 'He sounds really cool, doesn't he?'

Nodding, Patsy read on.

I'd love to meet up, if only to have a drink and a laugh about old times. I'm going to put my mobile number below, so you can ring any time. In case you didn't know, I got my psychology degree, so that's my profession these days. I mention it because if you don't get an answer straight away, it could be because I'm mid-session. Whatever, I'll definitely call back, so please leave a message.

Love Alan

PS, if you're still in touch with Pats, please send her my love. And if dear Lola and Fred are still with us, please send to them too.

Patsy sat back so abruptly that she banged into Neve. 'I'm sorry,' she said, putting a hand to her mouth. 'It's just so . . . It's really getting to me. Straight down memory lane without passing go.'

Laughing, Neve put her hands on Patsy's shoulders. 'He's a really nice guy, isn't he?' she said. 'You can tell, by the way he writes.'

Sniffing, Patsy said, 'It's making me wonder about my old flame, Jamie Stone, and what he might be up to these days. On second thoughts, I'd rather have a drink. Bring me wine, and lots of it.'

Obediently Neve ran into the sitting room, topped up Patsy's glass, and took it back to the study. By the time she returned Patsy had read the message again.

'OK,' she said, having herself under better control now, 'what we need to decide is how to proceed from here. Evidently he thinks you're your mother, so the question is, do we come clean to him that it's us, or do we tell Mum and let her take over from here?'

'Oh Pats, I knew you'd have the answer,' Neve cried, throwing her arms around her.

'That was a question,' Patsy said, bewildered by the sudden gush of praise.

'Yes, but you're saying us, and getting involved, and I knew you would. So what shall we do?'

'Let me think about it,' Patsy said, sipping her wine.

Neve waited.

Patsy continued to think. 'We know from this,' she said, nodding towards the screen, 'that his life has changed dramatically, but we need to know what that means. After all, your father's life changed dramatically, and look what it meant for him. Sorry, but you get my point.'

'It can't be as bad as that,' Neve responded, 'because he's obviously not banged up.'

Patsy spluttered with laughter. 'True,' she conceded, 'but you don't need me to tell you what a difficult time Mum's had of it, so we need to be ultra-protective.'

'Exactly, but you used to know him and if you ask me he sounds like he needs a friend, and so does Mum. OK, you're here now, but you're going off to Paris soon, and anyway, it's not the same thing.'

'Not at all,' Patsy agreed, wondering if she could ask Neve to take her love life in hand. 'You know what I think?' she said, decisively. 'I think we should go downstairs to that ludicrously posh dining room and brainstorm this over lobster and foie gras.'

Neve's eyes boggled. 'Never had either,' she responded, 'but I'm game for anything, so lead the way.'

'OK, here's what I think,' Patsy declared, after a smartly uniformed waiter had finished serving them a terrine of ham hock with foie gras. 'We need to find out, first and foremost, if Alan's married, because if he is, he stays buried in history.'

'Do you think he'd have answered if he was?' Neve asked, trying not to stare at the people on the next table, because she was sure one of them was Heidi Klum, the supermodel.

'Yes, it's her,' Patsy confirmed, 'but try to stay focused, there's a love. To answer your question, anything's possible, so before we mention anything to Mum about her blast from the past we need to be sure. How's your terrine?'

'Fantastic. I could live on it. I don't suppose they'd let me take some home for Lola?'

With a laugh Patsy said, 'I'm not sure they do doggy bags here, but tell you what, we'll pick up some foie gras from the Caviar House in the morning. It's just along the road. Now, what we need to focus on next is our reply to Alan's email asking him some direct questions, such as his marital status, if he has any children, exactly where he's living – London's a big place – and how rich he is.'

Neve choked. 'You're not seriously going to ask him that?' she gulped.

'Maybe not in so many words, but it's important to find out, don't you think? Anyway, if he's a professional psychologist he should have a decent enough income, presuming he has clients, and his email indicates he has.'

'I think we should ask for a photograph too,' Neve suggested. 'OK, he was dead fit all those years ago, but for all we know he might be really fat by now, or have lost all his hair, or his teeth.'

Laughing, Patsy said, 'Good idea. I wonder if we should send one of Mum.'

'No, not until we've seen what he's like first. We don't want him getting all excited about seeing her, then have to tell him he's a muppet so he needs to forget it.'

Laughing again, Patsy finished up her starter and reached for her wine. 'So, let's move this on a stage,' she said. 'Presuming he does still have hair and teeth, and is suitably solvent, at what point do we fess up that it's us and not Mum sending the emails? Or should we make a clean breast of it to her first, and let her decide how to go forward?'

Neve chewed a large mouthful of olive bread as she pondered. 'I think,' she eventually replied, 'that we should make that decision after we've heard back from him.' Then, appearing slightly less confident, 'Do you think she's going to be angry when she finds out? She's always telling me that she never wants to get involved with anyone again.'

'Oh, everyone says that when they've been hurt,' Patsy broke in dismissively. 'They never mean it, unless they're me, of course, because I am definitely never going down that road again. It's like being a hitch-hiker who keeps getting chucked out miles from where you want to be. It takes too long to find your way back, and even when you do you're in a terrible mess. Mum's different. She's got much more to offer where a relationship's concerned, and she and Alan were always very close when we were young. Did you know he was her first? Oh God, listen to me. I shouldn't be telling you things like that . . .'

'It's all right, I already know. She told me herself.'

Patsy was impressed. 'How thoroughly modern of her. What else has she told you about him?'

'Not much else actually. The subject only came up because we were talking about a girl in my class who got pregnant.'

'At thirteen!' Patsy cried.

'Actually she's fourteen, but I know you're going to say that's still too young.'

'Well, it is.' Then, seeming less sure, 'Isn't it?'

Neve shrugged. 'Legally speaking, but loads of girls my age are doing it. I don't mean getting pregnant, I mean having sex. It's no big deal.'

Patsy was watching her closely. 'So are you?' she dared to venture.

Apparently unfazed, Neve said, 'I haven't gone all the way yet, but I've snogged a few boys and done some other stuff. You know.'

Afraid she might know, and not really wanting it spelled out, Patsy said, 'Have you told Mum how far you've gone?'

'Oh yeah. I tell her everything. She's really easy to talk to, but she doesn't open up much herself. Or not to me, because she's afraid it'll upset me. I suppose that's normal though, isn't it?'

Patsy nodded. Yes, she guessed it was. 'Do you have a special boyfriend?' she asked.

'Not at the moment. There are a couple I like, but I'm not actually going out with anyone. What about you? Mum told me about the Mike thing. He sounds a real waste of space.'

With a sigh, Patsy said, 'Sad, but true. In fact I was only reflecting earlier that when it comes to choosing the wrong men your mother and I are in a league of our own. Having said that, she did get it right once, with Alan, so provided he proves to be as dashing and eligible as he sounds, and definitely was back then, I think, my darling, you can feel proud of the way you're trying to help turn her life around.'

Neve's cheeks glowed pink with pleasure, and as she looked at her lovely young face Patsy could only wonder why it had taken her this long to realise that it wasn't just a partner for her mother Neve wanted, it was a father for herself.

*   *   *

'There's nothing I'd love more than to come and spend a weekend at the Ritz,' Susannah assured Neve on the phone the following morning, 'but once I've finished at the school I've got a thousand things to do before I go to work tonight...'

'Oh Mum, *please*. This place is amazing, you'll love it, and we're really close to Bond Street so we can go shopping and have lunch at Nicole Farhi. I know she's a designer, but apparently there's a restaurant downstairs in her shop. And Pats is going to arrange for us to have our hair cut and blow-dried in a salon where all the celebrities go, and even highlighted if we want...'

'Neve, will you put Patsy on the line please,' Susannah broke in, tucking the phone under her chin to begin drying her breakfast dishes.

Neve let out a groan of protest. 'You're going to tell her I have to come home, aren't you?' she demanded belligerently. 'It's not fair. Why do you always have to spoil things? Just because *you* hate having a nice time...'

'Don't be ridiculous. Now, let me speak to Patsy please.'

'I'm not coming home.'

'Did you hear me say you have to?'

A moment later Pats came on the line with a cheery good morning.

In spite of her throbbing head Susannah managed a smile. 'I take it you two are having a ball,' she commented.

'Something like that. You're not joining us?'

'I can't. Apart from everything else on my plate, Lola was sounding a bit breathless when I rang just now, so I'm going round there when

I've finished at the school to check up on her. Don't tell Neve, she'll only worry, and she deserves to have a nice weekend if you're sure you're up for it.'

'Of course I am. She's great company, and who else have I got to spoil, apart from you two? Why don't you just come along to the hairdressers?'

With a grateful smile Susannah said, 'I know my hair's not looking as good as it could, but truly I'm quite capable of doing it myself, when I have time, and the hairdresser on Lavender Hill does a very good cut for less than ten quid.'

'Susannah, will you just ease up for . . .'

'I'm not arguing about this, Pats. I know you mean well, and I really appreciate it, but I want to hang on to what's left of my pride, and besides, it's my responsibility to get us through this bad patch.'

'As your daughter is standing right next to me I'll let you get away with that,' Patsy told her sharply, 'but be assured I'll come back to it if you try spinning that nonsense again.'

'I'm sure you will, but my answer will always be the same, you can treat Neve to all the hair-cuts, lunches and fancy hotels you like, she's your god-daughter and you have that right, but . . .'

'Didn't you just hear me say ease up? Now tell me, how was last night?'

'If you're asking did I keep my clothes on, the answer's yes.'

'Good. So why are you sounding so irritable?'

'Just tired, and wishing I didn't have to go in again tonight.'

'Then let me cover what you'd lose in wages.'

'No! Now, I don't want to end up falling out with you, so I'm going to ring off before you start trying to wave your magic wand again. Just remind Neve that she still has homework to do, so she should be back here by four at the latest tomorrow.'

After allowing Pats the rich retort she expected, Susannah put the phone down and went into the bathroom to turn on the shower. Whilst waiting for the hot water to come through she took a couple of Nurofen, then stood watching the mirror cloud around her pallid reflection. It was like watching herself fade into oblivion, which was exactly where she'd like to be heading, she was so achy and tired.

An hour later, she was carrying a bundle of sheets down the stairs when the letter box flapped open and the post sailed through. Since this was never her favourite moment of the day, she was about to pretend it hadn't happened yet, when she recognised the markings, and handwriting, on one of the envelopes, and felt her heart stand still.

Dropping the laundry she picked up the letter and sat down on the bottom stair, wanting to rip it to shreds rather than find out what Duncan had to say. However, slotting a finger under the flap she tore it open and started to read.

Dear Susannah, I know you're probably wishing I was dead rather than littering your doorstep with letters . . .

How right he was.

. . . but my boat hasn't turned up for the Styx just yet, so I'm still on the same bank as you, so to speak. This means that when I finally get out of here – and

I'm hoping it's now going to be sooner rather than later – I will need some kind of capital to get started again.

When I asked Hugh to talk to an estate agent about selling the house, it wasn't to put it on the market right away, it was only to get an idea of what it might be worth if we did decide to sell. Unfortunately, he misunderstood, and that's why the For Sale sign appeared out of the blue.

Knowing full well he was trying to cover his tracks, in case this serious tactical error ever went before a judge, she felt her bile starting to rise.

I'm sorry for the shock it must have given you. You know I would never want to cause you any more distress than I already have. There have been times when I've considered asking you to forgive me, but I guess we're a long way past that now, so I'm resigned to the fact that I must make a new life for myself when I come out.

The last thing I want is to try and force you and Neve to move house, particularly as you're close to Lola where you are, which I know is important to you. Also, the mortgage repayments are quite low for a house that's been valued at half a million quid. (Who'd ever have thought our part of Battersea would become so desirable when we first moved in there?)

Anyway, what I'm getting round to is the fact that since the house is in my name, technically speaking, it belongs to me. Obviously, as Neve's father, it's my duty to provide a home for her, and I want to do that, so what I'm proposing is that you increase the mortgage to give me my share (I'm only asking for fifty per cent, which after the original mortgage is paid off should be around two hundred grand) and that way you can stay where you are. I hope you think that's reasonable. If not, please let me have your thoughts so we can start trying to find an answer that will give us both what we need.

As for custody of Neve, I don't intend to fight you for that — I'm not foolish enough to think I'd win, unless she wanted to come to me, of course — but I would like to have some visiting rights.

In your dreams, Susannah seethed angrily.

I guess she's old enough now to decide for herself whether or not she wants to see me, so I'll write to her once I know whether or not my application for parole has been successful.

OK, I think I've covered everything I set out to, apart from the fact that if I am released it's my intention to start again in Scotland. It's where I was born, as you know, and I have the possibility of working with a new theatre company that's just started up in Glasgow. Wish me luck, because, as you know, I've been a bit down on it these last few years.

Duncan

As Susannah's fingers closed around the single page she could only wish it was Duncan himself she was screwing into a tight piece of rubbish that she could toss, burn or crush underfoot like a cockroach. How bitterly she rued the day she'd met that man; how impossible it was to imagine she'd ever loved someone she now despised with every fibre of her being. Merely to think of his connection to Neve made her feel murderous, and if he seriously believed he was ever going anywhere near his daughter again, then he'd better start applying for a frontal lobotomy because he had to be out of his mind.

* * *

93

'Oh my God!' Neve squealed excitedly that evening. 'He's come back to us already, *and* he's sent a picture.'

Patsy came running in from the bathroom, still zipping up her jeans. 'Let me see,' she demanded. 'What's he like these days? Hair weave? Dentures? Nasal piercings?'

Neve's jaw dropped as she opened the JPEG, while Patsy came to a standstill and blinked at the screen.

Neve looked up at her.

Patsy looked down at Neve and together they started to grin.

'He is seriously good-looking, isn't he?' Neve commented. 'I mean for someone his age.'

Patsy shot her a withering glance. 'I'll remind you of that when you're thirty-six,' she retorted. 'You're right though, he's wearing disgustingly well.'

Neve turned back to study her mother's first boyfriend again, and felt her heart trip with excitement. 'He looks a bit like Beckham, don't you think?' she said eagerly. 'I mean his hair's longer, but it's fair, and he's got really kind eyes. Do you reckon he's as tall?'

'Probably, unless he's shrunk since he was eighteen.' Shaking her head in admiration for how well he'd kept himself together, Patsy said, 'Well, I don't think we've got any problem about taking this to the next stage, have we?'

'Which is?'

Patsy thought about it. 'Have you read his message yet?'

'Oh no, I forgot about that.'

'And who says looks don't count?' Patsy laughed as Neve quickly clicked back to the email and enlarged it to full screen.

Dear Susannah,

To say I was delighted to hear back from you so soon is something of an understatement, and please don't feel the need to apologise for asking so many questions. I don't blame you for being cautious, particularly now I know how badly Duncan Cates let you down. It pains me a great deal to think of all you've had to suffer because of him, and I can only feel glad that he is out of your life now. At least as far as he can be, given that he's Neve's father.

I'd love to hear more about your daughter. If she looks at all like you then I know already she's very beautiful. It saddens me to say that I have no children of my own. When I married, just over seven years ago, it was to a woman who was quite a bit older than me and who already had two daughters and a son. As one of them was nearly a teenager by then, and the others weren't far behind, I didn't have the joy of being present at their births, or of watching them grow. Please don't get me wrong, they brought a great deal of happiness to my life anyway, enriching it in ways I won't have to explain to you as a parent, but I still carry the hope that one day I'll have a son or daughter of my own.

You might wonder why my marriage broke up, and to some extent I'm still asking myself the same question. I guess Helen and I just stopped loving one another. Not in a bitter or angry way, it was simply a fact we both became aware of about a year ago, and after talking it through we decided we should part. That's making it sound a lot easier than it actually was, because the trauma of the break-up was hard for us all, particularly the children. In the end, after talking it over with Helen, I decided to leave Manchester and start a new life back in London, in the hope that they might also be able to begin again if I was no longer around.

I'm living in Clapham now, close to the common, and my practice is in Bayswater, where I took over the clients of a colleague who was wanting to retire. You asked for news of my parents: sadly my father's suffering with Alzheimer's these days so he's had to be moved into permanent care, and my mother passed on just over ten years ago. My brother Grant is in Yorkshire with his wife and three children.

I hope this thumbnail is informative enough for the time being. Obviously I'll be happy to go into more detail if you'd like me to. I'm going to dare to suggest that might happen over coffee, or even dinner should you feel up to braving it. If nothing else, we can talk about the old days, and have a few laughs about who we were and the kind of things we got up to then.

Alan.

PS: I'm attaching a photo as you requested, but I'm going to confess here and now that it was taken about two years ago by my stepson, who's hoping to become a professional photographer. Judging by how good he's managed to make me look, I think he's in with a chance!

As she finished reading Patsy was smiling all over her face. 'He's very loquacious, isn't he?' she remarked admiringly.

'What does that mean?' Neve asked.

'Chatty. Not holding back, but then, given his profession, I think it's probably safe to assume that he's over his hang-ups, if he ever had any, and is by now fully in touch with all sides of himself, including the feminine. Neve,' she went on, cupping Neve's face in her hands, 'you are a genius, my love. I always used to think your mother and Alan Cunningham were made for each other, everyone did, and now, thanks to you, they're about to find one another again.'

Neve was beaming with pride. 'So how do we make it happen?' she said, thinking of the brother in Yorkshire, with three children. She'd never had cousins before, or an uncle – at least not one who made much of an effort to remember he had a niece.

Patsy pulled a face. 'Good question,' she replied. 'Off the top of my head, I think we need to confess to him first that we're behind this.'

Neve didn't look so certain. 'But think how embarrassed and disappointed he'll be. He really thinks he's writing to Mum, so he's going to feel totally set up.'

'Mm,' Patsy grunted, and carried on thinking. Suddenly her eyes lit up. 'I know what we're going to do,' she declared, starting to rummage around the desk. 'Where's my diary?'

Spotting it on the floor, Neve grabbed it and handed it over.

'OK, it's your mother we need to work on,' Patsy said decisively, flicking through the pages, 'so we need to sort out when we can . . . Oh hell, looking at this I don't have a free evening now till Friday.'

'Mum works at the disco on Fridays.'

'Blast. Actually, I might be able to get out of this dinner on Wednesday. Yes, I'm sure I can. Will she be at home then?'

Neve nodded. 'She usually is on Wednesdays. Why, what are we going to do?'

Patsy grinned. 'All you have to do, my darling, is be there. The rest you can leave to me.'

Neve looked uncertain. 'What about Alan? He'll be expecting an answer, so are we going to send one?'

Patsy turned to the screen and stared thoughtfully at the email. 'Let's wait until we come back from seeing *Joseph*,' she said. 'I should have things a bit clearer in my mind by then.'

Delighted to leave the big decisions to Pats, Neve threw her arms round her neck. 'Do you know what I really love about you?' she said.

'Oh, do tell,' Patsy encouraged.

'It's that you don't treat me like a child.'

Patsy looked amazed. 'You're nearly fourteen,' she reminded her. 'I knew *everything* by the time I was your age. It's only now that I'm stupid.'

With a bubble of laughter Neve skipped off to her own room, full of what a fantastic time she was having, especially now she was getting something right for her mum. And everything Pats had bought her today would suit Mum too, so she wasn't really missing out, or not all that much, and once she got together with Alan again, everything was going to be even better than she'd dared to imagine.

Chapter Five

'What on earth's all this?' Susannah cried in amazement as she carried armfuls of heavy shopping in through the front door to find the sitting room transformed into a beauty salon.

'Come in, come in, it's freezing out there,' Neve urged, pushing the door closed and grasping one of the carrier bags.

'Where did you get all this?' Susannah demanded, gazing in bewilderment at the extraordinary assortment of cosmetics, brushes, shampoos and body lotions covering the coffee table, floor and sofa. 'As if I need to ask. Is she here?'

'In the kitchen!' Patsy shouted. 'Be right with you, just don't come in here.'

'Take off your coat and sit down,' Neve instructed, clearing a space at the fireside end of the sofa. 'I'll unload the shopping, you just make yourself comfortable.'

Susannah's eyes were wide with curiosity as she followed orders, guessing she was about to be treated to some kind of makeover, and totally in love with the idea. It was so long since she'd last been pampered with such a luxury that her skin was already tingling with anticipation. 'Is this your doing?' she asked, as Neve disappeared into the kitchen.

'Both of us,' Neve called back. 'Would you like a glass of wine? We have white or red, or champagne if you prefer.'

Laughing in amazement, Susannah said, 'I'll have white, thank you. What are you doing in there, Patsy Lovell?'

'You'll find out soon enough,' Patsy replied, checking her watch as she came into the sitting room. 'OK, it's five thirty now. The facialist is due at six, the hair colourist at seven and the masseuse at nine. Dinner's being delivered at seven thirty – I hope sushi's OK – and tomorrow you have an appointment with one of our top hair stylists for a cut and blow-dry. He couldn't make it this evening, which is why you're being highlighted first. Now, before everything gets under way . . . Ah, here's my able-bodied assistant with our wine – thank you Neve – we need to tell you that there is a purpose to all this. Cheers.'

'Cheers,' Susannah responded, raising her glass. 'Do you have soda in yours?' she asked Neve.

'Yeah, yeah. When do I ever not?'

Susannah turned back to Pats, who was making room for herself in the far corner of the sofa.

'Right,' Pats began, settling herself down. 'Neve and I have some news for you that we think, *hope*, you're going to like. Actually I know you will, but it's going to be a bit of a surprise, so brace yourself, and don't say anything until you've given it a chance to sink in. OK?'

Susannah's eyes were simmering with intrigue

as they moved to Neve. 'OK,' she promised, unable to imagine where this was going, but loving how excited Neve was looking.

'Good. I wanted Neve to be the one to tell you,' Patsy continued, 'because it was her idea, but she's insisted I . . .'

'No, it's OK, actually I don't mind telling her now,' Neve jumped in.

Patsy immediately sat back to give her the floor.

Neve put down her drink and looked at her mother. 'Pats has helped me arrange all this,' she said, waving her arms to indicate the beauty treatments, 'because you've got a date on Saturday night and we know you'll want to look your best when you see him.'

Susannah's smile dropped.

Neve glanced anxiously at Pats, who gave her a nod of encouragement. 'It's with your old boyfriend, Alan Cunningham,' Neve told her hesitantly. 'We've been in touch with him and he's living back in London now . . .'

'Hang on, hang on,' Susannah interrupted. 'What do you mean you've been in touch with him? How?'

Neve's eyes made another worried trip to Pats.

'It's OK,' Pats said softly. 'Just tell her how it happened.'

Swallowing, Neve looked at her mother again. 'I went on to the Friends Reunited website,' she confessed, 'and left a message saying you . . .' Her voice faltered as her cheeks started to flame. 'I thought he was someone you'd like to see again,' she said, 'so I . . .' She took a quick breath. 'I pretended to be you . . . No, don't be mad,' she cried as Susannah's eyes darkened. 'You're always so unhappy and you never go out anywhere, or see anyone, so I did it to try and cheer you up. Pats thought it was a really good idea, didn't you?' she added desperately.

'I did and still do,' Patsy confirmed. 'And remember, Susannah, you agreed not to say anything until you'd allowed it to sink in.'

'But you can't play God with my life like this,' Susannah protested. 'If I'd wanted to be in touch with Alan Cunningham, I'd have done it myself.'

'No you wouldn't,' Neve objected. 'You never do anything to try and meet anyone and it's not normal.'

'What I do or don't do is my concern,' Susannah told her, 'and as for using the Internet to track him down . . . You know how I feel about those social-networking sites. They can be dangerous for a girl your age . . .'

'Before you go any further,' Patsy jumped in, 'why don't you try being a little appreciative of how much your happiness means to your daughter?'

'Yeah,' Neve came in belligerently.

'She contacted Alan with the very best intentions,' Pats went on, 'and as soon as I knew about it I supported her all the way. It's a brilliant idea, because it's high time this sackcloth and ashes existence was kicked into touch. So do yourself a favour and get down off that high horse before it throws you, and go and read Alan's emails. They're all set up on the computer, and you'll find a recent photograph of him ready to open too.

If you're still not interested by the time you've finished, then you have my word on it that we'll call the whole thing off.'

'No we won't!' Neve protested, but quickly backed down as Patsy threw her a warning look.

Not sure how to refuse without getting into an argument or appearing unreasonably churlish, Susannah took her drink into the kitchen and sat down in front of the computer. It was all starting to feel slightly unreal, because if the truth be told she'd been thinking about Alan quite a lot lately, wondering where he might be living, and how life was treating him . . .

'Before you begin,' Patsy called after her, 'bear in mind that he thinks he's writing to you.'

For the next few minutes Susannah scrolled through the emails, feeling herself floating back through time, while her emotions ran the gamut of nostalgia, pleasure, surprise and even anger. 'You told him about Duncan!' she shouted, her insides clenching with embarrassment.

'Why not?' Neve retorted, coming into the kitchen. 'It's not your fault he's in prison, is it? So why should you feel it's something you have to hide? And I thought we should be honest, right upfront.'

Though Susannah was still staring at the screen she didn't fail to register the 'we', and finally started to realise what this was meaning for Neve. She wanted a father every bit as much as she wanted to stop worrying about her mother. Feeling a lump rising in her throat she continued to read, aware of being less angry now, and even a little intrigued. *Saturday night works fine for me,* he'd written in his most recent email. *I'd be happy to come and pick you up, or we can meet somewhere, whichever you'd prefer.*

Without uttering a word she clicked on the JPEG and her eyes widened as her heart started to beat faster. If it were possible, he was even more attractive now than when she'd last seen him.

'Pats and I reckon he looks like Beckham,' Neve piped up.

Not quite able to see the resemblance herself, Susannah couldn't help going back to the first email and reading it again.

'So what do you think?' Neve prompted when she'd finished. 'Are you interested? Will you go?'

Taking a breath, Susannah got up from the chair and went to refill her glass.

'Please say yes,' Neve begged. 'Please, please, please.'

At last Susannah smiled. 'If I could, I would,' she responded, 'but you know I work on Saturdays . . .'

'You can call in sick.'

'Or resign,' Pats suggested. 'Oh come on, you two were always made for one another, life just got in the way for a while. Now, thanks to your amazingly perspicacious daughter, it's all getting back on track.'

'What does that mean?' Neve demanded.

'That you're brilliantly insightful,' Pats informed her. 'And now she's getting over the shock, I rather think your mother's inclined to agree.'

Starting to blush, Susannah said, 'I think you've got some ridiculously high hopes pinned on this. We'll probably hate one another.'

'Just give it a chance,' Neve implored.

With a sigh Susannah said, 'OK, I'll think about it.'

Pats was shaking her head. 'The date's already made and your makeover is about to begin, so by the time Saturday evening comes around you, my darling, will be our very own Cinderella on her way to the ball. Which means,' she went on playfully, 'that you don't get to escape my magic wand after all.'

For Susannah, the next few days passed in the kind of nervous anticipation she hadn't experienced since . . . Well, since she was a teenager going on a first date with Alan Cunningham. So many doubts and insecurities kept cropping up that she lost count of how many times she came close to cancelling. Then all kinds of memories would come flooding back and it would start to seem as though no time at all had passed, and she was still that young, vibrantly carefree girl, full of dreams and bursting with all the joy life had to offer. She'd felt blessed then in a way she could only marvel at now, taking everything so completely for granted, as though it were her right, even her destiny, to be happy and fulfilled. Had anyone told her at the time that she'd only reach the fringes as an actress, or that she and Alan would end up drifting apart, she'd never have believed them. Why would she, when everything had felt so magically possible – and when for three whole years, since their first awkward kiss at the age of fifteen, she and Alan had been virtually inseparable?

Now, as she spent just about every waking moment either dreading, or longing for the weekend to arrive, she had to wonder who was more excited, since Neve was bursting with it. It was as though she was going on the date herself, she was so full of what Susannah should wear, and say, and even think during the build-up, and the evening itself.

'If he doesn't ask to see you again on Sunday, don't start getting negative and telling yourself he's not really interested,' Neve cautioned, blithely unaware, or simply not caring, how many times she'd already said it. 'He'll probably just be playing it cool, not wanting to seem too keen at the beginning.'

Highly amused, Susannah's usual response was, 'And what should I do if he does want to meet up again on Sunday? I mean, I don't want to appear too eager, do I?'

'No, definitely not, but I think, seeing as you knew each other before, it's probably all right to have a second date the next day. I'll ask Pats what she thinks, shall I?'

Pats, of course, was brimming with as much advice and even more opinions than Neve, and Lola wasn't backward in weighing in with the occasional offering of encouragement, or caution either.

'He's bound to have changed a bit over the years,' she warned on the Friday evening, before Susannah left the flat to go to work, 'so try to remember that you have too. You're not kids any more, you've both had experiences, and he might well have had his fair share of knocks too. Sounds to me like he has, if his family broke up.'

'Exactly,' Neve chimed in, 'so don't only talk about yourself. Remember to ask about him too.'

Stifling a laugh, Susannah planted a kiss on Neve's forehead, then another on Lola's, and disappeared into her old bedroom, now Neve's, to get changed for work. As she closed the door she found herself recalling the countless hours she'd spent in this very room, putting on make-up and choosing what to wear to meet her great heart-throb. She could almost see herself sitting at the scallop-shaped dressing table with its rosy drapes and bracketed mirrors – long gone now – pulling a brush through her hair, and talking to her reflection so she'd know what she looked like when she talked to him, or laughed at what he was saying, or pouted at some kind of tease.

By the time she went back out into the hall Neve and Lola were washing up in the kitchen, and still, apparently, chatting about Alan.

'He is so drop-dead,' Neve was saying as she took a soapy dish from Lola. 'I swear, if he was my age, or I was his, I'd be like, oh my God.'

'Really?' Lola responded drily. 'Then you'd have it bad.'

'Oh yeah, I would,' Neve replied seriously. 'You really liked him, didn't you? You know, when he was going out with Mum before?'

'There was nothing not to like about him. He was always very polite, but he had a wicked sort of charm, as I recall. He used to come round here, calling for your mother who was never ready on time, so he'd sit in there chatting away with Fred about football and cricket. They got on like a house on fire, those two. Then your mother used to come breezing out of her bedroom, pretending to be surprised to see him, and off they'd go, arm in arm across the estate like they were straight out of *West Side Story*, was what Fred used to say.' She gave a dreamy sort of sigh, and stood gazing out of the window as though she could see Susannah and Alan out there now. 'Yes, we always had a soft spot for that young man,' she said. 'We were nearly as upset as your mother when he went off to university. She missed him like billy-o the first few months he was gone. They used to be on the phone to one another nearly every night, and she went up there to see him a couple of times. Oh, the tears when she came back. We had a job to know what to do with her. But then time went on and she got caught up in her classes at Webber Douglas and I suppose he must have been busy up there at university, and gradually they stopped being in touch.'

Neve's eyes were full of the tragedy as she said, 'So you're really happy they're seeing one another again?'

Lola gave her a wink. 'Yes, I think you did the right thing,' she assured her, having read the need for approval. 'It's high time your mother started living again, so it's lucky she has you to remind her that she's not getting any younger.'

Charming, Susannah thought to herself.

'She's looking fantastic though, isn't she?' Neve declared enthusiastically. 'You'd never think she was as old as thirty-six. I reckon she looks much younger, especially since Patsy's people went to work on her.'

'It's certainly good to see her lovely hair with

a bit of a shine on it again, and those dark shadows gone from her eyes, even if they are only being covered up by make-up.'

Having no more time to eavesdrop, Susannah picked up her coat and bag and after kissing them goodbye, and instructing them not to stay up all night partying because she knew what they were like, she went off to meet Cathy for her lift into work.

How wonderful it would be, she was reflecting as she all but floated across the estate in the rain, if tonight could turn into her last at the club. She knew thinking this way made her as guilty as Pats, Lola and Neve of setting her hopes too high and allowing her imagination to run away with her, but it was so long since she'd dared to feel optimistic about anything that she wasn't going to dash herself down yet. Why should she, when life was perfectly capable of crushing her dreams all by itself? Besides, Alan's emails had given her no reason to be fearful, or even in any way doubtful, so for tonight, at least, and tomorrow, why not let her hopes soar to the moon and the stars, maybe even to the same dizzying heights as Neve's had apparently achieved?

It was eight o'clock on Saturday evening and Susannah was so strung out that she managed to slap Neve's hand far more sharply than she'd intended, as Neve tried to fuss with her collar.

'That hurt!' Neve complained.

'I'm sorry, but you're getting on my nerves,' Susannah told her, turning to the full-length mirror for yet another inspection of how she looked. 'This is fine,' she declared firmly, in an attempt to convince herself. 'Or do you think I should wear my hair up?'

'No!' Patsy and Neve chorused. 'It looks gorgeous hanging loosely like that,' Patsy assured her. 'It's how he'll remember you.'

Susannah continued checking her appearance, turning from side to side, assessing the caramel silk trouser suit she'd finally decided on with a pale cream camisole underneath. It was a huge treat to be wearing heels for a date as well, because Alan had always been taller than her, while Duncan was an inch shorter and hadn't appreciated being towered over whenever she put on stilettos.

'You definitely think this is better than the orange and black dress?' she said.

'It's perfect,' Patsy told her, 'and anyway, you haven't got time to change again. The taxi'll be here any minute.'

'What bag are you taking?' Neve asked, going to rummage through the wardrobe shelves.

'What about the little gold purse we found at the boot sale?' Susannah suggested.

'Oh yeah, brilliant. I'll go and get it.'

As Neve dashed off to her own room Susannah rolled her eyes. 'I should have known it would find its way in there,' she commented, turning back to the mirror and looking decidedly undecided again as she regarded her reflection. 'You don't think this is too formal?'

'It's lovely and shimmery and shows off your fabulous figure to perfection,' Patsy said firmly. Then with a twinkle, 'I wonder what sort of state he's getting himself into now? Do you reckon he'll be worrying about whether his undies match his shirt, or if his wallet's big enough to impress you?'

With a choke of laughter, Susannah took the gold beaded bag Neve brought in and checked inside. 'What's this?' she said, pulling out a small photograph of Neve.

Blushing and shrugging, Neve said, 'I just thought you might want to show him, you know, if he asks about me, or anything.'

Feeling her heart tighten with love, Susannah tucked the photo away again and hugged Neve to her. 'I'm sure he will ask about you,' she told her, realising again how much this was meaning for Neve. 'And if he doesn't I'll tell him anyway.'

Embarrassed, but happy, Neve said, 'It'll be a good topic to get on to if things start to turn a bit boring.'

Susannah's laugh was swallowed by a wave of nerves as a car pulled up outside, only to drive off again.

'Do you have any condoms?' Neve wanted to know.

Susannah's shock dissolved in an unsteady chuckle. 'I'm not sleeping with him on the first night,' she protested, as Patsy cherished the moment.

'Yeah, but you should still take some, just in case,' Neve told her. 'We don't want you ending up pregnant, do we?' She looked at Pats. 'Or maybe we do.'

Patsy nodded, seeming to think it a fine idea.

'Will you behave?' Susannah chided. 'We're just having dinner, as old friends, and I might, *might*, invite him in for coffee when he brings me home. Now, which lipstick?'

'This one,' Neve said, fishing a slim tube of honey-coloured gloss from the selection Pats had brought with her.

'She's got a good eye,' Patsy commented as Susannah applied it.

Susannah might have responded had her voice not been swallowed into a gulf of trepidation as someone knocked on the door.

'That'll be the taxi,' Patsy announced, and leaving Susannah to dab on some perfume and give a last flick and brush to her hair, she went off to answer it.

'OK, Cinderella,' she grinned a few minutes later, as Susannah came down the stairs wearing the fur and leather coat she'd given her, and managing to look both radiant and terrified, 'your carriage awaits. It's already paid for, so no need to worry about that, and you've got the number should you need picking up. But that is not going to happen, because he's bound to bring you home.'

'Exactly,' Neve agreed. 'Your mobile's in your bag in case you feel the urge to nip to the loo and let us know how it's going, and I've put some breath freshener in too. Not that you need it, but if you have something with garlic in you don't want to asphyxiate him into the sack.'

'She's good,' Patsy laughed.

'Don't encourage her,' Susannah responded. Then, taking a deep breath, 'OK, I'm going,' she declared, as though about to leap out of a plane into free fall. 'If it's a disaster I'll get the taxi to bring me straight to Lola's to fill you in, otherwise I'll come back here and see you in the morning.'

After hugging her and wishing her luck, Pats told her to say hi from her, and stood at the front door with Neve watching Susannah sink into the back of a silver Mercedes. As it pulled away they both laughed at the way they teared up as they blew kisses and waved her off into the night.

It was a little after eight thirty when Susannah walked into the candlelit restaurant on Northcote Road, where a sonorous tenor was adding his own special flavour to the Italian surroundings and piquant aroma of *peperoncino* and roasting garlic. The place was almost full already, and noisy, but in a convivial sort of way that made it seem as inviting as the maître d' who materialised to take her coat.

When she turned round again, her heart gave an unsteady beat and her cheeks flooded with heat as she spotted someone winding his way through the tables with his eyes fixed on hers. She felt suddenly breathless and shaky, and then such a surge of happiness that she started to laugh. This man might look older and more distinguished than the Alan she'd known, but the mop of fair hair and roguish twinkle in his warm brown eyes had hardly changed at all.

'Susannah,' he said, his tone weighted with affection and humour. 'You're even more beautiful than I remembered, and I felt sure that wouldn't be possible.'

'Then let's hope they don't turn up the lights,'

she said, only half jokingly. 'You're looking extremely good yourself.'

His eyebrows rose comically, and taking her hand he kissed her gently on the cheek, before gesturing for her to go ahead of him to the table.

'Will you have a glass of champagne?' he offered, as the maître d' seated them. 'A Kir royale, maybe?'

'That sounds wonderful, thank you.' She put her purse on the table and realised she felt slightly intoxicated already.

After giving the order, he turned back to her and his eyes were gently mocking as he said, 'I'm tempted to pinch myself, just to make sure this isn't a dream.'

'I have to admit, it's feeling a bit strange to me too,' she agreed. 'It's like I know you, but I don't, or not who you are now. You seem so . . . so . . .'

'Old?' he suggested. 'Grey? Grown-up?'

Laughing, she said, 'Actually yes, grown-up, but assured and . . . relaxed, I suppose.'

'You wouldn't have said that if you'd seen me an hour ago,' he promised wryly.

With a smile, she pulled herself back from the easy flirtation they were sinking into and said, 'Before we go any further, there's a confession I have to make. I hope you're not going to be angry, but it wasn't me who went on to the Friends Reunited website trying to find you, it was my daughter, Neve, meddling in my life as she usually does.' She was gazing directly into his eyes. 'In this instance, I'm glad she did,' she told him shyly.

He was frowning curiously. 'Then I should probably say that I am too, but let me get this straight.

114

She pretended to be you? Does that mean *all* of your emails were written by her?'

Susannah pulled a face. 'I'm afraid so – and Patsy, it has to be said.'

Surprised, but clearly amused, he said, 'I might have known Patsy Lovell would feature in there somewhere. So you two are still friends? You don't know how good it feels to hear that. How is she these days? No, let that wait, carry on telling me about Neve. I know from the emails you're supposed to have sent that she's almost fourteen, not much younger than you were when we first met. Is she like you?'

Susannah nodded as she dug into her bag. 'Quite a bit,' she said, passing the photograph over.

His eyes softened as he gazed down at the picture. 'This could almost be you,' he told her. 'She's lovely.'

Blushing with pride, Susannah took the photograph back and put it away again.

'So can I take it you're now familiar with what you're supposed to have said in the emails?' he asked, his eyes full of humour.

With a laugh she said, 'I am, but believe me, I'd never have told you half as much as they decided to, especially when it came to Duncan being sent to prison and how hard I've been finding it since. I wanted to brain them when I read all that.'

His eyes were still laughing, but his tone was serious as he said, 'I was really sorry to hear that things haven't been going so well for you. Actually, I was surprised too, because the last I heard you were getting quite a bit of acting work, but I guess you've given that up now.'

'More like it's given me up, but even if something came my way I'd have to turn it down, because the hours would be bound to clash with Neve's schooling. As it is, Lola has to help out quite a bit, particularly when I'm working at night. Neve generally stays with her then, which suits them both quite well, because Lola loves the company, and Neve can get away with all sorts of things with Lola that she never would at home.'

'And Fred?' he asked.

Susannah swallowed. 'He died two years ago.'

He looked genuinely sorry. 'I was afraid you might say that. He was a great old guy. I used to enjoy my chats with him when I came calling for you. How did Lola take his passing?'

'Harder than you'd ever get her to admit. You might remember how she was never comfortable discussing her feelings. "They're there," she always says, "they don't have to be shouted about to make them any bigger."'

Smiling, he said, 'I can almost hear her. She had a way with her though, didn't she? She was always really good at making us kids feel a bit pleased with ourselves. I used to think I was the bee's knees after I'd had a chat with her.'

'I'm glad you remember her so fondly, because that's certainly how she remembers you. In fact, she and Neve have hardly talked about anything else these past few days. You're quite their hero.'

He gave a shout of laughter, but she could tell he was pleased. 'What are they doing tonight?' he asked.

'Pats is taking them to the private screening of a movie yet to be released, because our Pats is very well connected these days.'

'Really?' He sat back as the waiter brought their champagne.

After setting the glasses on the table the waiter recited a list of the evening's specials, then stood aside as a colleague offered an assortment of breads, and yet another laid down the menus and wine list.

When finally they were alone again Alan picked up his glass, and looking into her eyes he said, 'So what shall we drink to?'

Feeling a leap in her pulse, she put her head to one side as she gave it some thought. 'I know, how about making up for lost time?' she suggested, and then immediately blushed for how forward that might sound.

Seeming to read her thoughts, he arched an eyebrow as he touched his glass to hers. 'Sounds a great toast to me,' he said. 'So, here's to making up for lost time.'

As they drank she could feel her head spinning, as much with relief as with a rising sense of elation. This was turning out to be so easy and uncomplicated, and was even starting to feel right in a way nothing had in too long.

'Can I ask,' he said, when they put their glasses down, 'why you chose this particular restaurant for tonight?'

Remembering, she grimaced as she said, 'Actually, it's one of Neve's favourites. We always come here, or Chutney Mary's, when we have something to celebrate, so when you offered to let me choose where we should meet, I'm afraid she insisted it had to be this place. Do you mind? Does that spoil it?'

'No, not at all. I was just wondering if you'd been here before, and if there were any particular memories attached. Clearly there are, if you come for special occasions.'

'None of which include Duncan,' she told him, in case that was what he was thinking. 'We only found this place after he'd . . . gone his separate way.'

His eyes darkened slightly. 'It must have been a very difficult time for you when all that happened,' he said. 'The shock of the arrest, then the court hearing and the sentence.'

Her eyes dropped to her glass as she picked it up and took a sip. As far as she was concerned Duncan's presence wasn't welcome at the table, but Alan had sounded so empathetic and non-judgemental that she was on the brink of admitting how she'd really felt at the time. However, it wasn't a suitable subject for this evening, and finally becoming mindful of Neve's warning before she'd left that she shouldn't rattle on too much about herself, she injected some mischief into her smile as she said, 'You're obviously an expert at drawing people out, but I'm going to resist it for now, because I want to hear all about you.'

Appearing surprised, he said, 'I think I told you more or less everything in my emails.'

'Maybe, but not in any great detail. I was sorry to hear about your parents, especially your father. It must have been very hard to make the decision to put him in a home.'

'Yes and no. He'd reached a point where it was virtually impossible for my aunt to take care of him any longer, but he's not far away. She sees him every week, and I go too, but not quite as often as that.'

'Does he know you?'

'Not really. He thinks I'm his brother who died about twenty years ago.'

'Your uncle Jim. I remember him. We went to the funeral together.'

'Of course. On the motorbike and my father was furious. He said it showed a lack of respect, roaring up to the church on two wheels wearing leathers.'

Smiling at the memory, Susannah said, 'You had a dreadful row with him later, as I recall, and you didn't speak for ages after. Two whole days, I think it was.'

His eyes were twinkling. 'And you were appalled, because you'd never allow the sun to set on an argument. It was one of the things I used to love about you, but I think I took advantage of it too, because I knew you'd always apologise first.'

'You were shameless the way you exploited my good nature,' she informed him tartly. 'It used to make me so mad the way you did that.'

Grinning, he said, 'I promise, if we ever fall out again, I'll be the first to say sorry. Now, before we start getting lost down memory lane, I think we should decide what we're going to eat.'

Since she knew the menu quite well Susannah didn't take long to choose a rocket salad with Parmesan shavings and lobster risotto with truffle oil, while he finally opted for the antipasti followed by a traditional Neapolitan lasagne. Then he selected a fruity aglianico wine which neither of them had tried before.

Once the waiter had taken the orders Susannah drank more champagne, then said, 'OK, I'm not being sidetracked any more, I want to know all about your life in Manchester, most particularly about your wife and stepchildren.'

His eyes went down as his fingers linked around the stem of his glass. 'To be honest,' he said, 'I made light of it in the email, because the truth is, it's still a little painful. Not the actual break-up of the marriage, but having to leave the children. I really miss them, but they're not mine, so unfortunately I have no rights.'

'Do you mean your wife won't let you see them?'

He took a deep breath before answering. 'Helen is a wonderful woman whom I still love in many ways,' he said, 'but her approach to life can be very black and white. Now we're no longer together she thinks it's best for the children if they focus on building a relationship with her new partner and try to forget me.'

Susannah's eyes rounded with shock. 'But that's not only short-sighted, it's cruel,' she protested. 'Children can't just switch their emotions on and off like they were battery-operated, and you took care of them for over seven years. She can't pretend that didn't happen. How do the children feel about losing contact with you?'

'Actually, they're not terribly happy about it either, but their mother is their mother, so she gets to make the decisions. Obviously I've tried discussing it with her, but she's adamant her way is the right one, which I wouldn't argue with if the children supported her. However, I certainly don't want to be the cause of a rift between them, so it's best that I do things her way – at least for now.'

Susannah was incredulous. 'I can't believe a mother would do that to her own children,' she said. 'How old are they?'

'Robin's almost seventeen – he's the one who wants to be a photographer. Julia's fifteen now, and Kim will be fourteen next month.'

'So the girls are virtually the same age as Neve? What happened to their real father? Surely she doesn't stop them seeing him too?'

'He died of cancer when Kim was six years old.'

'Oh, how sad. Do they remember him?'

'Robin and Julia have quite a few memories, Kim less so, and Helen has done more or less the same with him as she did with me. She never talks about him, though I think she used to, before I came on the scene, but then his photographs were all packed up and anything that used to belong to him disappeared from the house. I only know that because Robin told me. I never saw any of it myself.'

'She sounds a very . . . controlling sort of woman.'

'Yes, I guess she is in some ways, but I keep reminding myself that it won't be long before the children are old enough to make up their own minds about who they have in their lives. I'm ever hopeful they'll still want to know me then.'

Susannah's eyes were full of sympathy as she sat back for the waiter to deliver their starters.

'Don't worry, it'll be all right,' Alan told her as they began to eat. 'Seeing you again is what matters tonight.'

Regarding him tenderly, she said, 'Lola was clever enough to remind me before I came that you've probably had your share of knocks.'

His eyebrows went up in a philosophical way. 'Life doesn't happen without them,' he remarked. 'If it did, I for one would be out of a job.'

Smiling at the irony of that, she said, 'I suppose I always imagined someone in your profession to have it all worked out, or you'd have a way of dealing with life's challenges that allowed you to rise above the pain so you didn't end up being all screwed up by it. That's a pretty naive assumption, wouldn't you say?'

'But a common one. In actual fact we shrinks are some of the nuttiest people on the planet, but please don't tell anyone, it's not something any of us want to get out.'

Laughing, and remembering how much she used to love his sense of humour, she carried on eating as the wine waiter held up a bottle for him to approve, before opening it.

The rest of the meal seemed to pass far too quickly as they meandered down the avenues of their past lives, reminding one another of events long forgotten, and sometimes laughing so hard that Susannah could barely catch her breath. His expression was so dry as he watched her that it inevitably set her off all over again, until he was no longer able to keep a straight face himself.

They were the last to leave the restaurant, and Susannah waited in the doorway while he ran round the corner to get the car. It turned out to be a black BMW that she knew right away was going to impress the heck out of Neve. More importantly though, Neve was going to adore him, and though she knew it was boastful to think it, she felt confident he'd adore her too.

'I can't tell you how much I've enjoyed seeing you again,' he said, as they drove through the lamplit streets of Battersea. 'In some ways it feels as though we've never been apart, which I suppose is a bit of a corny thing to say, but I'm afraid it's the best I can do.'

'It's a lovely thing to say,' she assured him, 'and it's how I feel too.'

He glanced at her in his gently self-mocking way. 'If I hadn't been such an ass all those years ago things might have turned out very differently,' he said, 'but I left it too late to come back and find you. You'd already met Duncan, and I knew I'd never be able to offer you what he could when he'd already cast you in one of his plays.'

Thinking back to that time, she said, 'The only good thing ever to come out of that marriage was Neve, and I wouldn't be without her, so it would be wrong to regret it. I'd like it all to be over now though.'

'Does that mean you're not divorced?'

'Not yet. Don't ask me why. I suppose I couldn't quite bring myself to dump that on him as well when he went away. As soon as he comes out though, I intend to put it in motion.'

'Do you have any idea when that's likely to be?'

'I'm afraid it might be quite soon. He's applied

for parole, so he could be roaming free by the end of the month.'

He threw her a quick look. 'How do you feel about that?'

'Frankly, sick, because I have a feeling he's going to ask to see Neve. I don't think she'll want to, but I hate the idea of her even having to make a decision.' Suddenly realising how similar this was sounding to his own situation, she added quickly, 'Please don't think I'll stand in her way if she wants to. It's just that he truly hasn't been a good father . . .'

'It's OK,' he assured her. 'I'm not making comparisons. The circumstances are very different, but I have to admit I'm already feeling quite protective towards Neve, possibly because if everything had gone according to plan twenty years ago, she could be mine.'

Feeling a swell of wine-fuelled emotion rise up in her, Susannah said, 'Frankly, she'd be a very lucky girl if she were.'

He smiled and put a hand over hers. 'Thank you for that,' he said. 'It means a great deal.' Then, after glancing at her, 'As I think I said in one of my emails, one of my big regrets is that I've never had a child of my own.'

Lifting her eyes from their hands, Susannah said, 'I can't wait for you to meet Neve. I have a feeling you two are going to get along very well together.'

Chapter Six

'So come on, what happened? Where is he?' Neve cried, jumping on to Susannah's bed the next morning to wake her up.

'Oh God. Who let you in?' Susannah grumbled, trying to push her off. 'What time is it?'

'Nearly ten o'clock and we're going off our heads waiting to find out how it went. So come on, cough! Every last detail.'

As the memories came flooding back, Susannah felt her heart expand warmly through her chest. 'I swear, you are the world's most precocious child,' she told Neve, trying to sit up. 'And what's this, for heaven's sake?'

'A bag of croissants. It's OK, Pats,' she shouted. 'The coast is clear, she's on her own and she's got a nightie on. Have you?' she said, pulling back the duvet.

'Yes I have,' Susannah retorted, grabbing the duvet back. 'Now will you get off me, please, you're heavy.'

'I want to know what happened,' Neve insisted, rolling on to the other side of the bed. 'Didn't he stay the night?'

'Evidently not, and will you stop asking personal questions.'

'I'm the one who set this up, so I have a right to know. Did you snog him when he brought you home?'

'I'm not answering that.'

'Mum! I'm your best friend, we're supposed to tell one another everything.'

'No. *She's* my best friend,' Susannah informed her as Patsy came into the room. '*You* are too nosy for your own good, so go and heat up those croissants and put some coffee on, please.'

'This could be my future we're talking about,' Neve protested.

Susannah looked at Pats in dismay. 'What do I do with her?'

'If I were you, I'd just give up and answer her,' Patsy advised.

Delighted, Neve sat cross-legged at the end of the bed facing her mother.

Laughing as she looked at her, Susannah said, 'OK, it was a fabulous evening, virtually as though no time at all had gone by. I can't remember when I last felt so relaxed with a man . . . And yes we kissed, but only outside, in the car.'

Neve's eyes turned incredulous. 'Didn't you invite him in?' she demanded. 'For heaven's sake.' Then to Pats, 'She is so out of practice.'

'I didn't want to appear too eager,' Susannah explained, 'but you'll no doubt be thrilled to hear that he's coming round later to take us all out for lunch.'

'*Yes!*'

'That includes you, Pats,' Susannah went on,

'and Lola, obviously, which'll save her conjuring up one of her roasts this evening.'

'He's taking us all?' Patsy murmured. 'Is he insane?'

Sparkling with laughter, Susannah said, 'Oh come on, it's not as though he doesn't know us, except Neve, of course, and we can always protect him from her.'

'Oh, thanks very much,' Neve retorted. 'Like I'm a liability, or something?'

'Embarrassment,' Susannah corrected. 'Or you could be, so *please* don't start asking him to adopt you, or marry me, or . . .'

'Like as if!' Neve cried. 'I'm the one who has experience with men, remember?'

'I'm so glad you don't know how that sounds,' Susannah told her.

As Neve opened her mouth to respond, Patsy quickly clapped a hand over it saying, 'Enough. Time to go and heat those croissants, I think.'

'But that's not fair,' Neve grumbled as she got off the bed. 'If it weren't for me last night wouldn't even have happened, so why . . .'

'Will you stop complaining,' Susannah chipped in. 'You're going to meet him later, so what more do you want?'

'*Details*,' Neve reminded her as she went through the door.

'That's a two-way street,' Susannah called after her.

Neve was back. 'I tell you everything,' she retorted.

'Really? Then what a boring life you must lead.'

In spite of herself Neve had to laugh, and still

trying to think of a suitable riposte she went off downstairs to turn on the oven.

'So it was good,' Patsy said, taking over Neve's spot on the bed.

Susannah was glowing. 'Frankly, that would be an understatement,' she confessed. 'He's so . . . Well, like he used to be, but funnier, more sophisticated . . . I can't wait for you to see him again. You can make it today, I hope.'

'Are you kidding? I'd cancel my own wedding rather than miss it.'

Laughing, and stretching as a shiver of happiness coasted through her, Susannah said, 'I know I've only seen him once, but I already have such a good feeling about this. It's like something that was out of kilter has just clicked back into place.'

Unsurprised, but no less delighted, Patsy gave a sigh of rapture. 'Did he talk much about what he's been doing all these years?' she asked.

'A bit. He's had quite a difficult time of it lately, mainly through the break-up of his marriage, but I'll tell you about that later. What matters is that he's back here in London, trying to make a go of things again.'

'And the timing could hardly be more perfect. There you are, both of you, needing to rebuild your lives, and up pops fate, God, the Universe, call it what you like – actually, Neve might be a good name – to sort things out so you can do it together. Amazing, but I guess that's how great things happen, by all the elements turning up in the right place at the right time.'

Experiencing another surge of elation, Susannah

said, with no little irony, 'You don't think we're getting a bit ahead of ourselves here?'

Patsy gave a blink of surprise. 'How's that possible, when you're already twenty years behind?'

By the time Alan came to pick them up, with Lola already comfortably ensconced in the front seat of the BMW, Susannah's happiness had grown to such a peak that she simply couldn't stop smiling. One look at him told her that he was in much the same state, and as they embraced, kissing briefly on the lips, she could almost feel Neve's excitement bubbling out of control.

'Here she is,' Susannah said, her throat tightening with pride as she turned to make the introduction, 'the infamous meddler.'

Neve's blue eyes were alight with eagerness as she looked up at Alan, and with her hair loose like her mother's, and her lips shimmering with the same pink gloss, she looked almost as radiant.

'I think architect of our reunion suits you better than infamous meddler,' Alan told her affectionately, shaking her hand, 'and I have a feeling I'm going to be long in your debt for coming up with the design.'

Beaming delightedly, Neve looked for a moment as though she might throw her arms around him, but in the end she only said, 'Cool.'

Laughing and showing no such reticence, Patsy came forward and embraced him warmly. 'It's great to see you again,' she told him. 'And I think you're extremely brave taking us all on at once, particularly when we know how raucous Lola can get after a couple of glasses.'

'I heard that,' Lola retorted from inside the car. 'And it only takes one to get my pecker up.'

'Please tell me she didn't just say that,' Susannah muttered, turning away as the others started to laugh. 'No!' she said quickly as Neve appeared about to respond. 'Whatever's on the tip of your tongue, swallow it.'

Neve's mischievous eyes went to Alan, who was clearly enjoying himself immensely.

'OK,' he said, gesturing for everyone to start piling into the back seat, 'I've booked a table for one at the Rose and Crown in Kew.'

'What about the rest of us?' Patsy quipped as she got in first.

'She's such a wag,' Susannah chided, giving her a shove.

'I want to go in the middle,' Neve insisted.

Half an hour later they were pulling up alongside the pub on Kew Green so Lola could get out to save her walking too far – and once the others were out too Neve quickly hopped into the front seat saying, 'Can I come with you while you park?'

Clearly delighted, he said, 'Of course. Seat belt on. Do you know this area at all?'

'Not really,' she answered, giving her mother a cheeky little wave as they pulled away. 'We came here once with the school, to look around the Gardens, but it was ages and ages ago. About a year, I think.'

'Oh, ages,' he agreed, suppressing a smile. 'I thought, as the weather's not too bad today, we might take Lola for a stroll through the Gardens after lunch.'

'Oh, she'd love that, but we should have brought her chair.'

'It's in the boot,' he told her. 'I used it to get her across the estate when I picked her up.'

'Oh, yeah of course. I bet she was really pleased to see you, wasn't she? She says really nice things about you.'

With a laugh, he said, 'Are you trying to make me blush, young lady?'

Reddening herself, she said, 'I mean it. She does.'

'Ah, there's someone pulling away,' he said, glancing up ahead, 'we can probably squeeze in there.'

After the car was parked they started back towards the green, walking side by side in a slightly awkward, but pleasurable silence, until Neve shyly took his arm as they crossed the busy road.

'Mum told me that you don't see your stepchildren any more,' she dared to venture as they reached the other side and she let go again. 'That's a real shame. I expect you miss them, don't you?'

'Yes, I do,' he admitted.

'Do you think your wife might end up changing her mind?'

He inhaled deeply before saying, 'I'd like to think so, but she isn't showing much sign of it yet, I'm afraid.'

'You'll keep trying though?'

'Of course.' He glanced down at her and smiled fondly. 'I hear you don't see your father,' he said. 'That's a great shame too.'

She shrugged. 'He was into drugs and stuff before he went away, so it's best I don't see him really.'

'Don't you miss him?'

'No. Well, I suppose I did a bit at first, but he was always out of it, and shouting at Mum, or passing out like he was in a coma. It wasn't very nice, so actually I was quite glad when he went away.' She stole a quick look up at him, and receiving a playful smile, she said, 'It's kind of funny, isn't it, that you don't see your children, and I don't see my dad. It's like, perhaps we can fill the empty spaces for one another. You know, if you and Mum do get together. Do you think you will?'

Unable to stifle a laugh as he imagined Susannah's face if she could hear this conversation, he said, 'It's certainly my hope.'

Sounding a little sheepish now, she said, 'I suppose I shouldn't have said that, should I? Please don't tell her, or she'll get all embarrassed and mad with me.'

'Don't worry, it'll be our secret.'

With a big smile she looked up at him again. 'I'm really glad I decided to go on to Friends Reunited. Mum would never have done it on her own.'

'I'm glad you did too,' he said, and picking up her arm he tucked it back through his as though to seal their promising new friendship.

By the time they'd finished lunch the sun had broken through the clouds, making a visit to Kew Gardens a must.

'It'll give you lot a chance to walk off some of that wine you managed to get through,' Lola chided, throwing a wink at Neve.

'Apart from Alan,' Neve piped up defensively, 'because he's driving.'

Patsy was about to deliver one of her famous retorts when she lost it to a hiccup, making them all laugh.

'I'll go and get your chair from the car,' Alan told Lola, as Susannah lowered her aunt on to a bench in front of the pub. 'Coming?' he said to Neve.

Brightening and blushing, she needed no persuading, and emboldened by her own share of the wine she linked his arm as soon as they set off across the green.

'Is anyone else getting the impression she's developing a crush?' Patsy wondered idly, as she slumped down next to Lola and lifted her face to the sun.

Susannah's eyes were glowing as she watched Neve and Alan. 'He's wonderful with her, isn't he?' she said, giving Lola a hug from behind.

Patting her hands, as her own eyes shone, Lola said, 'It's about time your luck changed, my girl. His too, from what he's been telling us.'

'It's really touching that he still carries pictures of his stepchildren, don't you think?' Susannah commented, going to sit next to Patsy.

'They're lovely-looking,' Patsy replied. 'The boy's a bit spotty, but he can't help that I suppose. I wonder what the wife's like.'

Susannah stifled a yawn. 'You mean, apart from unreasonable?'

'Well, look at it this way,' Lola said, 'would you want him popping up to Manchester all the time to see them? Or them coming down here, taking up his weekends? I know it all sounds like it could be happy families, but it might turn out to be a lot less complicated like this.'

Susannah's eyes went to Patsy and they both arched their eyebrows in a comical sort of way. 'Best not say that to Alan,' Susannah cautioned.

'As if I would,' Lola retorted, fumbling in her bag for a tissue. 'The other thing is,' she went on, 'Neve might think she wants a couple of sisters and a brother, but if they're not on the scene she'll get Alan all to herself – and if today's anything to go by, she'll be quite happy about that.'

'I wonder how she'd take it if you had another child?' Patsy mused.

Susannah gave a choke of laughter. 'This is our second date,' she protested, 'give us a chance, will you? And in case you'd forgotten, we're both still married.'

'I think Neve would be all right with a baby,' Lola commented ruminatively. 'It would be having to share with someone her own age she might find difficult.'

'Let's just hope she doesn't mind sharing him with me,' Susannah joked. 'Imagine having to take her everywhere with us.'

With a laugh Patsy said, 'You know the more I think about it, the better the timing seems to get for this, because Neve's right on the brink of breaking free now. Once she's over the novelty of having a man around she'll stop worrying about you and become wholly focused on herself and making a life of her own, the way kids do at her age. And you won't miss her quite so much, or feel so inclined to tie her to you, if you've got Alan in your life.'

Susannah was regarding her incredulously. 'You know, I just love the way you seem to have everything all worked out,' she said drily.

'It's not my doing,' Patsy claimed innocently. 'It's all down to fate, and my stunningly brilliant god-daughter, of course. Actually, it seems perfectly obvious to me that you're being given a second chance – both of you – to do things the way you were supposed to twenty years ago. So count yourself lucky, not everyone gets a second crack at the right guy, and he always was right for you. Wasn't he, Lola?'

'No doubt about it,' Lola agreed. 'So now, the question I'm asking myself is, who are we going to find for you?'

Patsy's eyes glittered a warning. 'Don't even think about dredging up any dead wood from my past,' she implored. 'The only one I can think about without going into an uber-cringe is Jamie Stone, and the last I heard he'd finally come out of the closet. So you see what a knack I had of finding the right one.'

'There were others,' Susannah reminded her.

'Yes, and *please* let them stay washed up on other people's shores. I am so happy being single I'd marry myself if I could.'

Laughing, Susannah said, 'I bet there's some gorgeous Frenchman waiting for you in Paris, divorced or heading that way . . . What's his name again, the one you were telling us about?'

Patsy wrinkled her nose. 'You mean Frank – pronounced *Fronk* – Delacourt? As far as I can make out he's a bit of a weirdo, so you're barking up the wrong tree with him. Anyway, I swear it doesn't matter what kind of package they come in, when you get the wrapping off they're all the same on the inside, egotistical bastards with more hang-ups than a coat rail and less integrity than a slug.'

Susannah was still pondering the issue. 'I think I'll ask Alan if he knows anyone,' she said.

Patsy turned to Lola in amazement. 'Did she hear a word I just said?'

'What was that?' Lola asked.

'You're ganging up on me,' Patsy objected. 'Please read my lips. I do not want to get involved with anyone, ever again . . .'

'No, it's definitely your turn to find the right one,' Susannah said, making it sound not only reasonable, but inevitable.

'Listen, I know you mean well, but I'm deadly serious. In *my* experience men never turn out to be who they say are at the outset, and by the time you find out you've been had, it's way too late.'

Gazing off towards the church where Alan and Neve were just about to vanish from sight, Susannah said, 'That was absolutely true of Duncan, but in Alan's case we know he's who he says he is, so we don't need to be worried that he's trying to deceive us.'

'There are always exceptions,' Patsy conceded, 'and I'm prepared to accept that Alan is very prob-ably one. However, we've only heard his version of why his marriage broke up, and if his wife's refusing to let him see the children, you have to wonder, is she really as stubborn as he's saying, or is she using them to punish him for something he hasn't got round to telling us yet?'

* * *

Alan's expression was both amused and hurt as Susannah repeated Patsy's question about his wife. 'I wonder if I should try to come up with something dastardly, just to satisfy her,' he responded, closing the front door and following Susannah into the kitchen. 'If I don't she might start thinking I'm too dull for her best friend.'

'Oh no, please don't start pandering to her wronged-woman paranoia, it's bad enough already. Anyway, I promise you she wasn't serious. She just likes to add a little intrigue where it hasn't managed to find its own way in. Would you like tea? Or something stronger?'

'Tea sounds good,' he said, leaning against the sink and folding his arms. Then, with a half-laugh, 'I hope she doesn't start sharing her doubts with Neve, because I should hate anything to . . .'

'She wouldn't,' Susannah assured him. 'She's well aware of how impressionable teenage girls are, so she wouldn't dream of doing anything to spoil the great start you and my incorrigible daughter seem to have got off to. Besides, like I said, she didn't mean anything by it, and I only mentioned it because I thought it would make you laugh. I can see now that it was pretty insensitive, so I'm sorry. I wish I'd thought first.'

Smiling as he regarded her dismay, he said, 'No, I'm the one who should be apologising. Helen's behaviour is as big a mystery to me as it is to everyone else. In my case though, I have the frustration, and dare I say pain, of it too, so my sense of humour often tends to fail when the subject comes up.'

Going to stand in front of him, Susannah took

his hands in hers. 'There is no funny side to it,' she told him earnestly, 'so please forgive my stupidity, and if she'd had any idea it would upset you so much I know Pats would be saying sorry too – before taking me aside to give me the kind of earbashing I deserve for repeating it.'

His eyes were full of amusement as he gazed into hers and put a hand to her face. 'All you deserve is to be cared for and loved,' he told her softly.

Her eyes went down as her throat tightened with feeling.

'This has been a wonderful day,' he whispered. 'From the way Lola welcomed me so warmly when I picked her up, to spending time with you and Pats again, to meeting Neve who's a very beautiful young lady and an absolute credit to you . . .' His voice grew huskier as his fingers spread out over her cheek. 'I want to give you the perfect end to a perfect day,' he said, 'but I know Neve's going to be home in the next hour or so . . .'

Susannah raised her eyes back to his. Her pulse was shaky and her voice barely audible as she said, 'We can always take her school things over to Lola's.'

His gaze seemed to deepen, and tilting her face towards him, he kissed her tenderly on the mouth. 'I don't want to rush you,' he said, his lips still touching hers.

Having to swallow first, she said, 'It's not as though we've never done it before.'

He smiled and kissed her again. 'If I stay the night I'll have to leave early in the morning to go home and change for work. Is that OK?'

'Of course it is.'

Pulling her into his arms he kissed her more firmly, holding her against him and making her feel desired in a way she hadn't in so long.

'Would you like me to take Neve's things over?' he offered after a while.

'Would you mind?' she said, not wanting to presume, but also glad for the chance to prepare. Then with a mischievous twinkle, 'I'll be waiting when you get back – and mine is the first door on the right.'

It took him a moment, then remembering the time he'd crept into Lola and Fred's one night and ended up stumbling into the coat cupboard and crashing over the vacuum cleaner, he laughed and kissed her again.

After the front door closed behind him Susannah quickly picked up the phone to let Lola know he was on his way and to warn Neve not to say anything crass.

'Like as if,' Neve protested. 'And what happens if you haven't put everything in my bag? How am I going to get it?'

'Text what you need and I'll bring it first thing in the morning.'

'OK, but this is really gross, I hope you know that. You're my mother, I'm not supposed to know about your love life.'

'Hang on, wasn't it *you* telling me to take condoms with me last night?'

'See, I told you you'd need them. Have you got any?'

'Mind your own business. Is Pats still there?'

'Yep. I'll put her on. Good luck, and if you can't make it, fake it.'

Blinking, Susannah said, 'You're not supposed to say things like that to me.'

'Bye! Here's Pats.'

A moment later Patsy's voice came down the line saying, 'I get the impression a big event is about to take place.'

'I'm starting to consider selling tickets,' Susannah quipped. 'Anyway, I just wanted to warn you not to say anything else about his wife and only knowing his side of the story. I mentioned it just now and he got quite . . . Well, not upset, exactly, more concerned that you'd think that.'

There was a moment before Patsy said, 'You amaze me sometimes, Susannah. Why on earth did you tell him what I'd said, when it was only *en passant* . . . In fact, I'd completely forgotten it until you just brought it up again. And as for thinking I'd say it to him . . .'

'I'm sorry. Of course you wouldn't. I don't know what I'm thinking. I guess it's nerves.'

Patsy's tone was a little gentler as she said, 'It's OK, but if you do think it's an issue . . .'

'No, I don't. His wife might tell the story in a different way to him, but I have no problem believing him. Do you?'

'No, none at all.'

'So that's all right then.'

'It would seem so.'

Aware of how tense she suddenly was, Susannah took a deep breath and let it go slowly. 'I feel completely foolish now,' she said, 'not only for telling him, but for bringing it up again with you.'

Laughing, Patsy said, 'That's the trouble with

romance, it makes fools of us all, but the important thing is to enjoy it anyway.'

Susannah laughed and shivered, and after a hurried goodbye she ran upstairs for a quick tidy round and to light some candles, before diving into the shower.

Half an hour later a moody jazz sound was drifting from her old CD player, and her bedroom was bathed in a soft amber glow that undulated gently around the walls. She sat expectantly, anxiously, on the edge of the bed, listening to the front door opening and closing, followed by the tread of Alan's footsteps on the stairs. Her heart was thudding with so much anticipation that she could barely breathe, and when he came into the room, seeming so large and masculine in her very feminine domain, she gave a gasp that she tried to cover with a laugh.

Coming to sit beside her on the bed, he took the wine glass she was holding and put it on the nightstand. 'There's a lot I'd like to say to you right now,' he told her, letting his eyes roam over her lovely face, 'but when I look at you, sitting here like this, I start finding it hard to believe it's real. Am I dreaming? Will I wake up in a minute and find myself back in a world where you were a memory and I was the fool who'd let you go?'

Putting her arms tentatively round his neck, she pressed her mouth to his. 'Did that feel real?' she asked huskily.

He nodded, his eyes holding lovingly to hers. Pulling her closer, he kissed her with a growing passion that seemed to wrap itself around them as though binding them in a world that contained only desire.

Their lovemaking was tender and fulfilling, and as fluid as a well-practised dance. He seemed to know her in ways she barely even knew herself, his fingers and lips arousing her and playing with her, making her gasp and moan, his body covering hers and moving with her as though it might be one with her. She felt an intimacy with him that only a shared past could bring, and connected to him in ways that went beyond words. At the peak of their lovemaking he held her as she soared, urging her higher and still higher until she was dizzied and breathless and couldn't take any more.

'Are you OK?' he asked, several minutes after his own release.

'Mm, I think so,' she murmured, and they smiled into one another's eyes.

Her heart was still racing, her skin remained alive with sensation, and as she looked at him she felt as though she was losing herself in the depths of their shared emotions.

'I don't know what happens from here,' he whispered, the shadows on his face moving and darkening in the flickering light, 'but whatever it is, I want us to be together.'

'So do I,' she answered. 'Yes, so do I.'

Chapter Seven

Over the following weeks, as her relationship with Alan renewed and deepened, Susannah could feel an aura of happiness settling around her as though it were a tangible, even a visible force. She saw it reflected in the eyes of people who smiled at her in the street, or sat next to her on buses. It was as though she was reaching a place inside them that had sat too long in darkness, lighting it up with her own inner radiance. She felt the way she always used to, full of confidence and kindness, unfearful of life and enthusiastic about the future – and at times so exhilarated that she might erupt with joy.

'Haven't seen your feet on the ground for a while,' Lola would cheerfully grumble every now and again.

'He's the best thing that ever happened to us,' Neve kept gushing, so often that even Susannah wanted to gag her.

'If you could see the difference between the way you look now, and how you were three weeks ago,' Patsy declared, on a brief visit from Paris, 'you'd swear you'd been exorcised. It's like the lights have come back on . . . Actually, you're making me feel so emotional I might cry.'

Patsy relocating to Paris had been the only dark spot, but at least her job called for her to be in London two or three times a month, and they were able to catch up on the phone most days. Susannah was always full of Alan, and how he was trying to persuade her to give up her job at the club (strictly office-only now) and let him make up the money she'd lose – an offer she'd so far refused.

From Patsy's end the chat was mainly about how hostile she was finding her French colleagues, with the surprising, and curious, exception of Frank, pronounced *Fronk*, who, according to Patsy's wry observation, had to be seen to be believed.

'No, he's definitely *not* good-looking,' she cried, when Susannah asked, 'but OK, I have to give credit where it's due, he has this smile that's . . . Well, let's put it this way, they could save on bills if they plugged him into the Eiffel Tower.'

With a splutter of laughter, Susannah said, 'What's he like otherwise? Tall, short, fat, thin? Charming, rude, fastidious, flirtatious?'

'Let me see. Neither tall nor short – about five ten, I guess. Pot belly, partly bald, apart from his seriously scary eyebrows that are like a pair of pubic outcrops with a life all their own. Charm would certainly top the list of his attributes, though he has a pretty unique brand of it. Rude wouldn't feature at all, because he's polite to a fault; I'd call him dedicated rather than fastidious, and if he tries flirting with me one more time I'm going to slap him.'

Laughing again, Susannah said, 'I can't wait to meet him.'

'Don't hold your breath.'

'What about life outside the office?'

'Still non-existent, apart from work-related events. I'm just not finding the time to go exploring, or shopping, or do any other kind of socialising. Besides, I don't really know anyone yet, and from what I can tell, the French don't do things quite the way we do. They're incredibly formal, and everyone here, at the office, is so distant with me they might as well be in Sydney once the working day is over. Anyway, I'm sure it'll get better, and once I've managed to find a place of my own and move out of Claudia's apartment, I'll be able to do some entertaining. I don't want you to wait that long, though. Please come for a weekend, just as soon as you can.'

As soon as Susannah mentioned the invitation to Alan he was all for it. 'Just say the word and I'll book the flights,' he told her, 'unless you'd rather go by train.'

Susannah didn't mind how she got there, but as she still couldn't afford to give up her job at the club, a wonderful romantic break in Paris wasn't on the cards just yet. At least not for her. Neve, on the other hand, was bursting to go, and even suggested that Alan should take her instead, an idea he didn't seem wholly averse to. However, Susannah drew the line at such overindulgence. He was spoiling Neve enough already, having bought her an iPod *and* a laptop computer, not to mention the extremely expensive birthday dinner at the Ivy so Neve could star-spot and boast to her friends about who she'd seen.

In fact, he was slotting so easily into their lives that it soon became hard to imagine how they'd ever managed to get along without him. He'd started taking care of all the little jobs around the house and Lola's flat that Susannah couldn't manage, and insisted on paying the grocery bills on the grounds that he ate with them far more often than he did at home. He even drove Neve to and from school when it fitted in with his schedule.

For Susannah it was simply wonderful having someone ringing or texting to ask what she wanted to do for dinner, or where they should spend the night, her place or his? His house was in a small, leafy terrace just off Clapham West Side, and was at least twice the size of her own, with two large Victorian bay windows at the front, a cellar underneath and a walled-in patio and garden at the back. Most of the interior had been modernised before he'd bought it, so the attic was already a fourth bedroom with its own shower room, while the master en suite was straight out of a design magazine with its walk-in closets, jacuzzi bath and recessed lighting. On the whole though, the place was sparsely furnished, with no more than a two-seater sofa and a high-backed armchair to fill up the large sitting room, and the brand-new SieMatic kitchen still lacked a table for the breakfast area, as well as all kinds of knick-knacks to make it feel lived-in. The house was, he insisted, Susannah's to do as she pleased with, and already they'd been on several shopping trips to start transforming it into a place that felt more like home.

It was during their sixth week together, close to the end of April, that Susannah received a call from her agent to say that Michael Grafton, the producer who'd wanted to cast her in a series a long time ago, was asking to see her again for a part in a new soap he was backing.

'The auditions are next week,' Dorothy told her, breaking the good news from her semi-retirement in the country, 'and I think you could be in with a chance, given that he's asked for you personally. He's got Marlene Wyndham exec-producing it – the fearsome little termagant who's had more success with soaps than Procter & Gamble. So it's probably her you'll have to convince, but I'm told he'll be there too, so do whatever it takes to keep him on your side. Samantha's biking the script round as soon as it arrives.'

For the first time in Susannah couldn't remember how long, it wasn't Neve or Lola she called right away to share the good news, it was Alan.

It took him a moment to understand what she was saying, she was so excited, but after realising what it was, and how much it meant to her, he managed to sound every bit as thrilled as she was as he said, 'This is fantastic. We have to celebrate. I'll bring some champagne home . . .'

'I haven't got it yet,' she protested.

147

'But you will,' he insisted. 'How could they turn you down? Do you know anything about it yet? What the series is? What kind of part you're up for?'

'Apparently a script is on its way, so I should know more then. Dorothy thinks it's probably quite a good role, so I might find myself in more than one episode, which would be brilliant.'

'It certainly would,' he agreed. 'And I have another surprise for you, but it'll have to wait until tonight, I'm afraid, because I want to see your face when I tell you what I have in mind.'

Lola was in no doubt, when Susannah called her, that Alan was going to propose.

'But we're both still married,' Susannah laughed, 'so it can't be that.'

'Why not? You don't have to do it right away, it'll be like a pledge. No, that's what it is, and I hope you're going to say yes.'

'If I am he'll be the first to know,' Susannah retorted. 'So what do you think about my other news? I'm up for an audition. Isn't that amazing?'

'It certainly will be if you get it, and I'm sure you will. Have you told Neve yet?'

'No, her phone's off while she's in class, so I sent a text asking her to call as soon as she could. Alan's picking her up later, but he's on his honour not to say anything, because I want to tell her myself.'

'She'll be as cock-a-hoop as you are,' Lola said knowingly, 'which will be no bad thing, because she's been a bit down lately, don't you think?'

Startled, Susannah said, 'She seems fine to me. Why do you say that?'

'I don't know, really. I suppose it could be all the time she's spending on that computer now Alan's got us connected up with this broadband number. I'm not convinced it's a good thing, all this Internet stuff. She needs to be having real chats with real people, the way she always used to.'

'You mean like when you used to tell her she had too much to say for herself?'

'Yes, like then. Anyway, it's probably just the novelty of the thing at the moment. Once it wears off she'll be back to her normal self, all full of it again. Any news from Pats lately?'

'Yes, she's coming over next Monday and Tuesday, so keep the evenings free. She wants to take us all out for a meal on one of them.'

'Oh, my admirers will be disappointed when I let them down.'

Laughing at the dryness of her tone, Susannah rang off and went back to work, filing the architect's drawings and correspondence. It was hard concentrating with her mind running off in so many directions, but it was the upcoming audition that was preoccupying her the most. It had been so long since she'd last acted that she was already starting to feel the turmoil of nerves, so heaven only knew what kind of state she'd be in by the time it came round.

'You'll be fine,' Alan assured her when she rang him again. She was on her way home by now, sitting at the back of the bus absently watching the world go by.

'I wonder if there's some kind of refresher course I could do between now and then,' she pondered.

'Even if there is, I'm sure you won't need it.'

'Maybe I should call some old actor friends to ask if they'll come and run lines with me. I wonder how many I'll have. I hope I'm in more than one scene, then I won't be as likely to find myself on the cutting-room floor.'

'I think you're worrying too much. It'll all work out just fine, you wait and see. And like it or not, I'm bringing home some champagne.'

'No don't, it's tempting fate . . .'

'Hang on, we might have something else to celebrate, so the decision's made. I'm outside the school now, waiting for Neve, so we shouldn't be much longer. Are you on your way to your place, or mine?'

'Mine, and my stop's coming up, so I'll see you in about half an hour.'

It was actually closer to an hour before the front door opened and Neve came in, shouted, 'Hi Mum,' and ran straight up the stairs.

'Is everything OK?' Susannah asked Alan as he hung his coat up. 'I was starting to worry.'

He looked surprised, until, remembering the delay, he said, 'Oh yes, Neve wanted to stop off at a friend's house to pick up some things, then there was an accident on Battersea Bridge which held us up for a while. I should have rung, sorry.'

She smiled as he kissed her, and wanting to prolong the feel of his arms around her she sank against him, resting her head on his shoulder. 'How was your day?' she asked.

'Oh, fairly normal, if you could apply such an epithet to my line of work. Half a dozen patients and lunch with my lawyer.'

'Business or pleasure?'

'A bit of both. There are still a few things being tied up in Manchester that we needed to go over. Mostly though, we talked about cricket and you, and how my life's got back on track since we met up again.'

Smiling happily, she said, 'Was he pleased for you?'

'He certainly sounded it, but I did get a few of the old clichés about not going too fast, there's plenty of time, don't rush things.'

Concern showed in her eyes. 'Do you think that's what we're doing?'

'We're doing what feels right for us,' he replied, smoothing the hair back from her face, 'and that's all that matters.'

She nodded, and went up on tiptoe to kiss him. 'How was Neve on the way home?' she asked, going back to the meal she was preparing. 'Lola thinks she's seemed a bit down lately. Does she to you?'

Looking slightly baffled, he shook his head. 'She seems fine to me. Full of chat, mostly into her mobile phone, or otherwise plugged into her iPod.'

'Do you think she spends too much time online? That must be where she is now, and she barely said hello when she came in. Maybe she's making contact with someone she doesn't want us to know about.'

'If she is then we need to find out. When did you girls last have a heart-to-heart?'

Realising she couldn't remember, Susannah felt a pang of guilt strike her. 'I should try and have a chat with her tonight,' she said. 'Did she mention how much homework she has?'

'Quite a bit, apparently, but I'm sure she'll want to hear your news.'

Brightening, Susannah said, 'Of course, and I still haven't heard yours yet – and actually I've got more of my own that came in the mail, but that can definitely wait. So, what's the surprise you mentioned earlier?'

Sitting her down at the table, he took her hands in his as he said, 'I know you don't want to give up working at the club because of how much it pays you, and you've already turned down my offer to make up what you'd lose in wages, so I've been thinking . . . Why don't you come and live with me, and let this place out? The rent should more than cover what you earn at the club, and if you do get the acting job, well, who knows how rich you might turn out to be.'

Laughing, and loving him more than ever, she squeezed his hands tightly, and went to sit on his lap. 'I think that's the most irresistible proposition I've ever received,' she told him huskily, 'because I'd love to come and live with you in your wonderful house on your cherry-blossom street. I just have to be certain that you are including Neve.'

With an incredulous laugh he said, 'I'm sorry, I thought that went without saying. Of course it includes her. In fact, she's already staked a claim on the top bedroom.'

Susannah blinked in surprise. 'You discussed it with Neve before me?' she said, certain she must have it wrong.

'Not discussed, just mentioned. I wanted to sound her out on the idea, because I knew if she wasn't up for it, you wouldn't be either.'

Seeing the sense in that, she hugged him again, saying, 'I'm sure she didn't even hesitate, she's so crazy about you, but now I have to tell you what came in the mail today, because it could affect things where this house is concerned. Certainly where Neve is concerned.'

Having fetched a letter from her bag Susannah handed it to him, saying, 'It's from Duncan. He's being released at the end of next week and he wants to talk about taking his share of the equity in the house. He also wants to see Neve.'

Alan's face was grim as he unfolded the letter and began to read. By the time he'd finished he still wasn't looking pleased. 'As far as this place is concerned,' he said, 'he might not be entitled to anything, or at least not as much as he thinks, but we won't know for sure until you've spoken to the CSA again to find out how much you can claim in back maintenance. As for seeing Neve . . .' He inhaled deeply and looked at the letter again. 'You'll have to let her decide what she wants to do,' he said. 'Though I can't say *I'd* be thrilled to have him as part of our lives, if Neve feels otherwise then it wouldn't be right to stand in her way.'

Later, when Susannah put it to Neve, her lip immediately curled. 'No way do I want to see him,' she snorted, slumping down on her bed and picking up a magazine. 'He hasn't wanted anything to do with us since he went away, so if he thinks he can just come waltzing back into our lives now, he is *so* wrong. I hate him for how unhappy he made you, and now, just when things are going right for you, he's got to turn up and try to spoil it all.'

'Listen, whatever's gone on between me and Dad, he's still your father, so if you do want to . . .'

'I just said I don't,' Neve snapped, 'so let's change the subject, shall we? What's this surprise you texted me about earlier?'

'That can wait. I'd rather find out what's on your mind.'

'Who said anything was?'

'I can tell, so why don't we talk about it and see if we can get it sorted.'

'Actually, we can't, and anyway there's nothing. I'm just tired, and it's the time of the month.'

'Are you having problems at school? Is someone bullying you?'

'*Mum*, will you stop going on. I just told you, it's the time of the month so I'm feeling a bit stressed. OK?'

Susannah regarded her carefully. 'Does it have anything to do with who you're spending so much time online chatting to?'

Neve slapped down the magazine. 'I'm chatting to my friends when I go online,' she said tightly. 'What's wrong with that? Now will you please stop getting at me.' Her voice faltered at the end and as she started to cry Susannah pulled her into her arms.

'Come on, what is it?' she said gently. 'Whatever it is, we can make it all right.'

'No we can't,' Neve sobbed. 'It's all a mess and

it's my fault and I wish I didn't love you so much because then I could hate you.'

With a laugh, Susannah said, 'Why on earth would you want to do that?'

'I don't, I'm just saying.'

Lifting her chin up, Susannah looked into her eyes and started pulling faces until finally Neve laughed.

'I promise it's the time of the month,' she said, wrapping her arms around Susannah. 'You know I get a bit weird when it happens. It'll be fine by tomorrow. So will you please tell me now what your surprise is. Alan said it's fantastic, but he wouldn't even give me a clue what it might be.'

'That's because I wanted to tell you myself.' Her eyes shone as she said, 'I've got an audition next week for a new drama series and they asked specially to see me, so Dorothy thinks I'm in with a good chance.'

Neve's jaw dropped as her eyes filled with joy. 'That's amazing,' she cried, flinging her arms round Susannah again. 'You'll get it, I know you will, and then you'll be rich and famous and everyone will love you, but you'll be my mum so I'll love you the most.'

'In which case, life will be utterly perfect, because Alan's just told me about wanting us to move in with him and I've said yes, that we'd love to. I take it that was the right answer?'

Neve's arms were still round her, so she squeezed hard as she said, 'Yes, of course it was. Definitely. It'll be really great to live there, and it's only a short bus ride from Lola so we can still go and see her all the time. Can't we? And some of my friends live down that way, so I'll be near them, which is great too.'

Smiling at the tears on her cheeks as she pulled back to look at her, Susannah said, 'Things really seem to be working out for us at last, don't they, and it's all thanks to you for finding Alan.'

Neve's mouth trembled as more tears threatened. 'He's really special, isn't he?' she said. 'At first I was scared that he might not like me, or he'd want to have you all to himself, but he never makes me feel as though I'm in the way.'

'Because you're not,' Susannah assured her.

Neve swallowed. 'I just wish . . .'

'What do you wish?'

'I was going to say that he was my dad, but I don't think I really mean that. Or I do, but . . . Oh, I don't know. It's just fantastic that he's turned out to be so . . . I don't know, like he is.'

Hugging her hard, Susannah said, 'It hasn't been easy for you, growing up without a dad, but that's going to change now. We'll be a real family, the way you've always wanted.'

'Lola, hi, it's Pats. How are you?'

'Oh, I'm lovely, dear, thank you,' Lola replied from her end. 'How are you? Susannah says you're working very hard over there.'

Patsy spun away from her computer. 'Tell me about it,' she said, gazing out of her glassed-in office past the open-plan arrangement of the rest of the executive floor to where the directors of finance, marketing and beauty appeared to be in some kind of conspiratorial huddle. 'It's great until I come unstuck with my French, but let's not get into that. I had a message earlier from Susannah asking me to call, but I can't find her. She's not there, I suppose?'

'No, she's gone for an acting lesson – or coaching, is what she calls it. She's quite anxious about this audition next Wednesday so Alan's paying for someone to help her brush up a bit.'

'That's kind of him. Has she got the script yet? She was still waiting for it to arrive the last time we spoke.'

'Yes, but apparently it's not from the actual series. It's just some scenes they want her to play with a couple of other people they're interviewing at the same time. The real scripts are still being revised, her agent said.'

'Sounds as though they don't want anything going public until they're ready,' Patsy commented, watching the conspirators get into a lift, then turning her chair so she was gazing out across the glistening grey rooftops of Paris. 'So any idea when I can reach her?'

'Probably not till tomorrow, unless you manage to catch her on her way to the club later.'

'OK. Is Neve with you tonight?'

'She will be later. Alan's taken her and a couple of her friends to the pictures, then they're going on for a pizza after. You should have seen her going out of here earlier. All done up like a dog's dinner, she was, like she was off to some fancy-dress do from the sixties. They're wearing their skirts so short again these days, makes me feel perished just to look at them, especially with the weather turning nippy. And how Alan puts up with all that bloomin' giggling and squealing, I'll never know. He's a saint if you ask me.'

'He'll be used to it, having two stepdaughters,' Patsy laughed, returning to her computer screen. 'So how come you didn't go with them?'

'Oh, I had one of me turns earlier, so Susannah said I had to stay home and put me feet up. You know what she's like when she starts laying down the law . . . Oh, before I forget, I had a postcard from your mother this morning. She wanted to know if you was managing to stay out of trouble over here, and said I had to keep you away from red wine, men and guns.'

Patsy groaned. 'Don't you just love her?'

Chuckling, Lola said, 'I expect you'll tell me the story one of these days. I hear you're coming over again on Monday.'

'Yes, but I can't make dinner till Tuesday, which is one of the reasons I'm trying to get hold of Susannah. She might want an early night before her audition.'

'I'm sure she will, but the rest of us will still be up for it. I want to hear some more of your stories about Paris and this bloke who keeps waving at you with his eyebrows. You had me laughing for days over that the last time we spoke.'

'Yes, he's a pretty unique sort of character,' Patsy muttered, keeping her back resolutely turned to the dividing glass wall that separated her own office from Frank's next door. 'Right now I can feel him ogling me through the window partition that keeps him apart from the right-minded world. He calls it an executive suite, so to humour him, I do too.'

158

With a choke of laughter, Lola said, 'I wouldn't half like to see him. You make him sound a real picture . . . Oh, hang on, I think that's my mobile ringing. It has to be Susannah. She got it for me so she could get through when Neve started using my phone all the time. Or it'll be Neve, asking me to record something. Or it might be Alan . . .'

'If you answered it you'd find out,' Patsy said drily.

'I would if I knew where the bloomin' thing was, but it'll stop ringing before I get there so I'll say a proper goodbye to you before I go off on the hunt. Any message for Susannah?'

'Just let her know about next Tuesday, and tell Neve I've got samples of a new lip-gloss range for her to try out. I'll bring them with me when I come.'

As she rang off Patsy returned to her computer, continuing to ignore the scrutiny she could feel emanating through the glass wall like heat. If the man weren't so excellent in his role as senior vice president, and so popular with the staff, she might be trying to find a way to let him go by now, because he was turning into a menace with his strange behaviour and impossibly thick skin. No matter how withering or abrupt she was with him, he never seemed to get the message, or even to take offence. On the contrary, he almost seemed to welcome her rebuffs, which had made her wonder on occasion if he was trying to turn her into some kind of laughing stock. The theory might have held up if he'd ever teased or flirted with her in front of other people, but he never did. Nor, if the truth be told, did he strike her as someone who'd be so devious or cruel as to try and hurt a colleague that way. In fact, underneath the ludicrous humour and bizarre physique, she'd already detected a hint of a golden heart. Well, there had to be some reason why everyone liked him so much, and it certainly wouldn't be for his fashion sense.

Anyway, she was far too busy to be dwelling on the oddities of her most senior executive right now, particularly when the final pitch from a new advertising agency was about to begin in the second-floor boardroom. At this stage it required her approval, so she couldn't hang about any longer waiting for a return call from the VP Commercial concerning the appalling figures that had just come in. Evidently the man was in no hurry to explain the downturn to her, but if he thought she was going to hand the situation to *Fronk* to deal with, he was gravely mistaken.

'Patreesha,' Frank said, appearing in her doorway, 'are you ready to go down now? I think they are waiting for us.'

'Of course,' she replied, and reaching for the pile of things her secretary had prepared for her to take with her she got to her feet. 'Have you seen the report from Alain Savier?' she asked.

'I 'ave, and it is not good. We will discuss it later, per'aps, before you speak with him?'

As she nodded she forced herself to look at him and just as she expected, it was as though the eye contact acted as a switch, because he instantly lit up with one of his dazzling grins. In spite of her efforts not to, she had to admit that his smile truly did turn him into an attractive man – apart from the eyebrows, of course – and he presumably knew it, which was why he played on it the way he did. However, the rest of him was a disaster, because he was heavy, hirsute – excluding the top of his head – and today he was all decked out in a flowery Versace suit with matching wing-collar shirt and a stripy tie. He couldn't have looked more comical if he'd come as Bozo the Clown. Were it anyone else she'd feel certain he wasn't serious about such a get-up, but looking at him now, eyeing her in a way that was presumably meant to make him irresistible, she could only presume he was.

'It's a joke, right?' she said, as they started along the corridor that ran through the middle of the semi-open-plan offices to the lifts at the far end.

'*Comment?*' he replied, apparently not understanding.

'The suit,' she explained.

'Ah, you like!' he cried happily. '*C'est un cadeau* from Donatella for when we go to the Prix Goncourt last year. I tell myself, this morning, when I take 'im from the closet that 'e will work 'is magic on Patreesha in a way that will make her beautiful green eyes shine. And you see, I am right.'

Patsy took a breath, but had to let it go in a laugh, because there was nothing she could say about his suit, or his belief, that would come even close to crushing him; she'd already learned he was made of rubber where her putdowns were concerned. So instead she changed the subject to the upcoming meeting, and kept her eyes trained on the stunning view of the Eiffel Tower as the lift glided down the exterior of the seven-storey building. She loved this city, there was no doubt about that, but the people, *Fronk* in particular, were presenting the strangest kind of challenge and, as yet, she didn't have a clue how to handle it.

Chapter Eight

'Susannah Cates? Would you like to come through please?' The lanky young lad who'd introduced himself earlier as Ben, the casting assistant, looked up from his clipboard and gave her a busy, but friendly smile.

Casting an anxious glance at the other hopefuls in the waiting area, Susannah rose to her feet, clutching her script tightly and hitching her bag higher over her shoulder. To say she was nervous would be to lend understatement a whole new depth of meaning, but she somehow managed a winning smile as she took the first few fateful steps towards the auditioning room that several others had already passed into that morning. So far none had come out again. Which meant, of course, that there was another exit, but in her absurdly over-wrought imagination the inner sanctum of this West End hotel suite was swallowing up actors like the plant in *Little Shop of Horrors*, and regurgitating them into the dreaded purgatory of 'waiting for a call back that might never come'.

Standing aside for her to pass, Ben closed the double doors behind him, and sighed as his mobile phone started to bleep.

'Go on,' he whispered to Susannah, 'they won't bite.' Then, in a louder voice, 'Susannah Cates, everyone. She's reading for the part of Penelope.'

The room was large, plushly carpeted and draped, but unfurnished, apart from a long white linen-covered table where the casting panel was seated, most of whom looked up as she approached. She could only pray that she didn't appear – or act – as uptight as she was feeling, because right now the butterflies in her stomach might be wearing hard hats and hobnail boots, they were knocking about so wildly. The only face she recognised was Michael Grafton's, who was sitting at one end of the table, slightly apart from the others. He was every bit as striking as she remembered, with a presence that seemed to dominate the room in spite of his casual appearance with one elbow hooked over the back of his chair, and one foot resting on the other knee. His hair was longish and dark, slightly greying now, and his hooded eyes with their piercingly intense gaze might have made him appear stern to the point of hostile, were it not for the friendliness of his smile.

'Hello Susannah,' he said, his voice deep and welcoming, 'it's good to see you again. Thank you for coming along today.'

'Thank you for asking me,' she replied, somehow managing to sound far steadier than she felt.

His eyes remained on hers for a moment, as though he might say more, or perhaps he was reassessing his decision to call her. in, then he turned to the others and began introducing them.

By the time he'd finished the only name she remembered was Marlene Wyndham's, who turned out to be a diminutive, slightly sour-looking woman seated at the centre of the group, and who was glaring at Susannah as though she'd barged into the session uninvited. The others, fortunately, appeared far less formidable, and the fact that only their titles – casting director, two producers, series deviser – had registered, might have unnerved her more if Dorothy hadn't reminded her again last night that it was Marlene Wyndham she needed to impress.

'Rumour has it Michael Grafton's given her total carte blanche with the series,' Dorothy had warned, 'which probably means she has a veto on the casting. Have you learned the lines?'

'Of course. I can recite them in my sleep and play them with every emotion in the spectrum.'

'So would you recommend Guy Phelps as a coach?'

'Definitely, if I get the part. If I don't, he's still pretty good.'

She'd have given almost anything for Guy to be with her now, coaxing the very best out of her, but the moment had finally arrived for her to do this alone, and she could only wish that it wasn't meaning so much – perhaps then she wouldn't be feeling that this was the last chance she was ever going to get to prove herself.

'Please, sit down.' Marlene nodded towards a small table and chair at the centre of the room where there was a script, notepad, pen and a glass of water.

With a bizarre sense of taking the stand in a courtroom trial for her life, Susannah did as she was told, all the time trying her level best to look relaxed.

Clearly she wasn't succeeding because the next thing Marlene barked at her was, 'Relax! We're simply going to run through a few questions to begin with.' Before she got any further Michael Grafton claimed her attention, and whatever they were discussing seemed to involve Susannah, because a couple of the others threw an occasional glance her way.

Certain they were about to ask her to leave, Susannah sat very still, her nails digging into her palms as she tried to keep herself calm. Then Marlene Wyndham turned back to her, asking abruptly, 'Have you ever ridden a horse?'

Susannah swallowed. Starting with a negative answer was bad news indeed, but she could hardly lie. Or should she? Some would. 'No,' she replied.

Marlene made a note, then said, 'How do you feel about horses? Are you afraid of them?'

Susannah was aware of an uncomfortable heat rising inside her. 'I don't think so. To be honest, I haven't come into very much contact with them.'

Another note. 'Do you have any physical disabilities that might prevent you from riding?'

'None that I know of.' This part clearly depended on being adept in the saddle, so it was with a surge of misery that Susannah realised she was already wasting everyone's time.

'Do you know Derbyshire at all?' Marlene went on. 'Most specifically the dales.'

Susannah shook her head. Yet another negative.

'I'm afraid not,' she answered. 'I'd love to though,' she added, and felt so pathetically unctuous that she immediately wished she hadn't.

'Can I ask about your family commitments?' Marlene continued. 'Are you married? Do you have children?'

'My husband and I aren't together any more,' Susannah replied, certain that if they knew about Duncan any remaining chance she had of being cast would go up in a puff of smoke. 'I have a fourteen-year-old daughter.'

'I see.' Marlene's tone seemed to suggest that the negative pile had increased yet again. She glanced down at her notes, then said, 'This series is going to be shot entirely on location in the Derbyshire dales. If you get the part you'll be required to ride a horse and to spend quite a lot of time away from home. Would either of these situations present a problem for you?'

Susannah took a breath. 'Not at all,' she said, and immediately winced as she remembered she'd just admitted that she couldn't ride, so there was problem number one right off the bat. Problem two, she and Alan were about to move in together. Problem three, Neve would have to stay at Lola's for most of the week, which could be too much for Lola at her age. 'Obviously I'd have to take riding lessons,' she heard herself adding, 'but I could find a stables straight away . . . I'm not sure when you intend to start shooting, but hopefully I'd be reasonably competent by then.'

'The beginning of June,' Marlene told her, showing no sign of being impressed by Susannah's willingness to learn. 'What about your daughter?

Who's going to take care of her if you're not around?'

'My aunt,' Susannah answered quickly. 'Neve often stays with her anyway. She lives quite close.'

Marlene nodded and turned to the man next to her. Apparently this was a signal for him to take over, because he sat forward, resting his chin on his hands as he regarded Susannah with a warmth that went a little way towards melting the icy veins Marlene had left her with.

'In case you need reminding,' he said, in a mellifluous Welsh lilt, 'I'm Donald Davidson, the series deviser. We'll be screen-testing you some-time next week, should you pass this part of the audition, but before we see what you've made of the script we sent you I have a few questions I need to ask. The role of Penelope is going to call for some nudity. Would you have a problem with that?'

Susannah tried to swallow, but her throat had turned dry. 'No, not at all,' she lied. 'I mean, provided it isn't too explicit.' Her eyes went invol-untarily to Michael Grafton, but his head was down, showing that he was only listening, not watching.

'Don't worry, it'll all be done in the best possible taste,' Donald Davidson assured her with a twinkle.

As the others smiled at the Kenny Everett line, so did she, but inside she was already panicking. What if they asked her to undress now? She wouldn't do it. She just couldn't.

'The programme has an eight-thirty transmission time,' Donald Davidson went on, 'so hopefully that'll help to set your mind at rest regarding how explicit the scenes will be. The real issue will be on set. Naturally it'll be closed to all non-vital personnel while the more intimate scenes are being shot, but you will still be in full view of the director, camera and sound operators, and, of course, whoever you're playing the scene with.'

Wondering if she'd have come for the interview if she'd been aware of this before, she said, 'Is it possible to know a bit more about the character? How old she is? What makes her tick?'

'She's about your age, beautiful, but not terribly bright. Her passion is horses. She's had some success showing, and keeps her prize horses at the Larkspur stables, which is where the series is based. It's not a huge part, but her scenes during the first four episodes are crucial to setting up one of the lead characters and what he's about.'

'I see. And is she . . . Does she disappear after the first four episodes?'

'At the moment, yes, but there's always a chance she'll come back, so don't give up on her yet.'

As Susannah smiled Marlene said, 'While she is appearing, she'll be in enough scenes to make her presence on set necessary two, possibly three, days a week.'

Susannah nodded. Hopefully neither Alan nor Neve would mind too much about that. At least it wasn't five or six.

'OK, I think we've covered the basics for now,' Marlene said. 'Perhaps we could see you playing the lines we sent. Ben will speak the other part,' she added, waving the casting assistant forward.

As Susannah got to her feet she was wretchedly

aware of never having felt less like performing, and noticing Michael Grafton speaking to the person next to him was, for some reason, making her more self-conscious than ever.

Realising she had to let go of herself completely or she'd never get through this, she put her head down and closed her eyes. After a few seconds she began to feel Jackie Drake, the character she and her coach had been rehearsing in every conceivable way for the past five days, emerging through the mists to take on a clarity that finally eclipsed Susannah.

'OK, I'd like to see you play it like a victim to begin with,' Marlene instructed. 'Someone who's been kicked about by life and the people around her, and instead of showing strength and rising above it, she's become frail and sorry for herself. A bit of a whiner, or a whipped puppy.'

Nodding understanding, Susannah/Jackie-the-victim turned to Ben, who was leaning against her small table, holding the script. Their eyes met in a silent agreement to begin.

'Oh God, not you again,' Ben started, in a sneery voice.

'Yes, it's me,' she said tremulously. 'I hope you don't mind. I needed some water.'

'Help yourself. You know where the tap is.'

Jackie-the-victim mimed filling a glass. 'How much longer are you going to wait?' she asked, casting him a whipped-puppy glance.

'As long as it takes. What's it to you?'

'Nothing. I mean, I can't help worrying about you, sitting here all alone. If you'd like some company . . .'

'Go to bed, you're getting on my nerves.'

Susannah had just drawn breath to carry on when Marlene said, 'OK, that's enough. Try it in a bored, superior way now.'

A moment later Jackie-the-superior started to yawn as Ben launched into the scene again. This time they completed it before Marlene said, 'OK, angry, impassioned.'

Jackie-the-impassioned surged to the surface and her eyes flashed wildly as she turned them to Ben. To her surprise Ben gave a whimper as he cowered, and suddenly the unthinkable happened: his mouth began to tremble, and as Susannah realised he was about to laugh she felt herself starting to lose it too. A moment later they were both gasping uncontrollably.

'I'm sorry,' Susannah gulped, desperately trying to straighten her face, but to her horror Marlene's scowl was only making it worse. Ben was almost beside himself, whooping as though the most hilarious event on earth had just occurred, and the more he fought his hysteria the worse it was becoming for them both.

Putting her head down, Susannah covered her face with her hands. She took a breath, but it shot out in a gale of mirth. She couldn't believe she was doing this right in the middle of an audition, but as horrifying as it was, she couldn't stop.

Finally Marlene sent Ben out of the room and Alex, one of the producers, got up to take his place.

Jackie-the-impassioned was ready to go again.

'Oh God, not you again,' Alex sneered.

'Yes, it's me,' she seethed. 'I hope you don't *mind*, but I needed some . . .' She could go no further. She was going to laugh again, and now Alex was right on the brink too.

'I'm so sorry,' Susannah cried, dabbing her eyes. 'I don't know why . . . I'm . . . Oh God, perhaps I'd better leave. I . . .'

'You're doing fine,' Michael Grafton told her evenly.

When she dared to look at him she saw straight away that he was having trouble containing himself too, and so was everyone else – with the exception of Marlene.

'Honestly, I wanted to die,' she told Alan later, when he came to Covent Garden to take her for lunch. 'Everyone was falling apart, though God knows why, and that bloody woman kept glaring at me like some Victorian schoolmarm, making it a thousand times worse. If she'd laughed too I swear I'd have been able to stop, but her face didn't even crack.'

'So how have you left it?' he asked, standing aside for her to go down the steps to Joe Allen's ahead of him.

'God knows. If it's up to her I won't even make it as far as the screen test, that much was plain to see. Michael Grafton was a bit more encouraging as I left, though. He told me not to worry, everyone corpses sometime in their lives – but why did it have to happen to me in an *audition*?'

Apparently amused by it himself, Alan said, 'Well, at least they'll remember you, and people like to laugh. It's got to be better than making them cringe, or tear their hair out, or fall asleep. Table for three, Cunningham,' he told the receptionist who came to greet them.

172

'Three?' Susannah said, turning to him in surprise.

'Patsy just called. She's taking a later train back to Paris, so she's going to join us.'

Susannah's eyes lit up. 'Fantastic. It was horrible missing out on the dinner last night, so this'll make up for it.'

After they were seated and had checked the menus which were chalked up on huge boards around the walls, Alan poured them both some water from the bottle he'd ordered and touched his glass to hers. 'Cheers,' he said, 'here's to corpsing and still getting a screen test. When will you know?'

'Next week, apparently, but I honestly don't think I should hold my breath. Apart from totally cocking it up at the end, I need to be able to ride a horse, and the closest I remember ever being to one was taking Neve to a Changing of the Guard when she was five.'

'Won't they provide lessons?'

'If the part were big enough I'm sure they would, but it's only four episodes, so they won't go to the expense.'

'You never know. Did you find out any more about the actual programme yet? I know Dorothy told you it was supposed to be quite upscale and lavish, but what does that mean exactly?'

'It's set in a riding stables – or equestrian centre, was how one of them put it – so it sounds as though they're trying to distance themselves from the "working-class" type soaps that are all over the screen. The problem is, it's being shot in Derbyshire, so I'd have to be away for at least part of the week. On the other hand, it's only for a month, so that should be OK, provided Neve doesn't mind staying with Lola.'

He was nodding gravely. 'Perhaps they could both come and stay at the house every now and again to give Lola a bit of a break and let me take over some of the fussing and cooking,' he said.

'I'm sure they'd love that, considering how much you spoil them already. Ah, here's Pats. In here,' she cried, waving through one of the brick arches.

'So how did it go?' Pats immediately demanded as she embraced her. 'Don't tell me, you blew them away.'

'Wait till you hear,' Alan warned drily as she turned to hug him.

Quickly Susannah described again the embarrassment of how the audition had ended, while Alan ordered some wine.

'I was just saying when you arrived,' Susannah went on, 'that there's not much going for me really, I can't ride, it's all being shot in Derbyshire, and apparently there's some nudity required.'

Alan's face darkened. 'You didn't mention that,' he said. 'What kind of nudity?'

Susannah almost laughed. 'I think there's only one kind, isn't there? But it's going out before nine, so they won't be allowed to actually show anything. I guess what they're after is bare backs and legs, which'll mean having to be undressed in front of the crew.'

Alan looked at Patsy. 'I'm not sure I like the sound of that,' he said.

174

Patsy pulled a face. 'Models spend half their time in the nude for photo shoots,' she told him, 'but you never see the naughty bits in the end result.'

'Which is fine for them, but the idea of Susannah exposing herself on a film set full of men . . .'

'Excuse me, since when did I disappear?' Susannah interrupted. 'Stop talking about me as if I weren't here, and let's be reasonable about this. No one is less happy about being undressed in public than I am, and since I almost certainly won't get the part after this morning's debacle, I think we might as well let the subject drop.'

Patsy regarded her closely. 'Are you going to mind very much if you don't get it?' she asked.

Susannah had to nod. 'Just to do *something* would be wonderful,' she admitted, feeling her heart churning with disappointment already, 'but to be in a brand-new series at a time when the ratings are almost bound to be high . . . It could easily lead to other parts, and before you know it my career might be taking off again.'

'So what you're saying,' Alan came in, 'is that if you do get it, you'll agree to the nudity, even though you don't want to do it?'

'I'd have to,' Susannah told him, 'or they wouldn't take me, and it's not as though it won't be discreet or . . .'

'I'm sorry, but I fail to see what's discreet about being on a bed, or in a barn, or wherever you're supposed to be, with no clothes on.'

'Oh, come on, you're being deliberately difficult,' Susannah protested. 'The set will be closed, meaning only essential crew will be there, and a

175

dresser's bound to be on hand with a robe as soon as the camera stops.'

He looked at Patsy again. 'Am I being hopelessly Victorian about this?' he asked her. 'I am, aren't I?'

Patsy nodded.

'It's just the thought of anyone else seeing you the way only I should,' he said to Susannah, 'well, frankly, I don't like it, but . . .' he threw out his hands, 'far be it from me to stand in the way of your comeback. If that's how it has to be, then that's how it has to be, just please don't try and tell me that those men won't be turned on by seeing you in the nude, because they're not dead, and I'm not stupid. And if any one of them tries to lay a finger on you, make sure you tell them I can be pretty lethal when my dander is up.'

Laughing, Susannah put a hand on his arm. 'You're stumbling into some pretty dreadful double entendres, so let's do as I said and forget it for now.'

He was laughing too as he squeezed her hand. 'I know when I'm beaten,' he said, 'so OK, let's talk about something else, such as a date for you and Neve to move in? I thought the weekend after next would give you time to pack and sort out what furniture you might want to bring with you.'

Blinking rapidly, Susannah glanced at Patsy and shrugged as she laughed. 'Why not that soon?' she said. 'Because if I do, by some miracle, get the part, we'd at least have had some time to settle in before I start. However, we still need to sort out what's going to happen to my house, and we won't have a clear idea about that until I've spoken to Duncan.'

'Have you arranged to see him yet?' Patsy asked.

Susannah pulled a face. 'Sunday at his brother's,' she replied.

Patsy turned to Alan. 'Are you going too?'

'We're still discussing that,' he answered. 'I want to, in case he starts putting on pressure, but Susannah thinks my presence could inflame things.'

'Well, I guess you both have a point, but if Duncan's going to have his slimy brother there, I think Alan should go with you,' Pats said to Susannah. 'Ah, great, here's our wine,' she said as the waiter set the glasses down. 'OK, let's drink a toast to Lady Godiva,' she announced mischievously once they were all holding their glasses.

Susannah wrinkled her nose.

'Horsewoman, nudity, long blonde hair,' Patsy expanded.

Susannah groaned. 'Very funny. Actually, I think we should drink to Michael Grafton, because if I've still got any chance of getting that part, I know it'll be thanks to him.'

'Because he thinks you're a good actress, or because he wants to see you with nothing on?' Alan enquired mildly.

Susannah flushed.

'I'm sorry,' he jumped in hastily. 'That came out totally the wrong way. It was supposed to be a joke . . . Pats, help me out here. She's really mad and I'm starting to get scared.'

At that Susannah had to laugh, and after

allowing him to give her a quick kiss of apology she turned to Pats, as Pats said, 'OK, I have to ask about Neve. I had a text from her earlier telling me that the samples I gave her were brilliant and she's already tried some and it was really embarrassing. So, is anyone able to explain that?'

Susannah was at a loss, but Alan was starting to look amused.

'I think I can,' he said. 'I woke up around one o'clock this morning thinking I heard a noise downstairs so I went down to investigate, and lo and behold, there was her ladyship, in the bath, trying out some of the bubbly stuff you'd given her.'

'Didn't she have the door closed?' Susannah said, aghast. 'She's got to get used to having a man around.'

'It was almost closed,' he assured her, 'but because I saw the light on I blundered straight in, expecting to find a burglar having a pee, or trying to make good his escape. I never dreamt I'd be confronted by a little nymphet having a soak. So I don't mind telling you, she's not the only one who was embarrassed.'

As they all laughed, Patsy's mobile started to ring, and seeing it was *Fronk* she said, 'Believe me, until you've met this man you don't know the meaning of embarrassing,' and excusing herself she took the phone outside in the hope of achieving better reception.

'I'm really sorry about Neve,' Susannah said, slipping a hand into Alan's. 'I'll have a word with her and tell her to take better care next time.'

'If I were you I'd just leave it,' he advised. 'It was obviously an accident, so it's best forgotten.'

It was Sunday afternoon and Susannah was sitting in the passenger seat of Alan's car, staring up at one of the swanky apartment blocks that comprised the ultra-modern and uber-rich residences of London's Canary Wharf. It was many years since she'd last been here, and given the choice she'd never have come again, but she'd decided it was important to show Duncan – and Hugh, since he was the one pulling the strings – that she wasn't afraid to face them. She had right on her side – a truism that bolstered her considerably – and it was time they found out that they'd be making a big mistake if they thought they could intimidate her over the house or indeed anything else.

'It'll be fine,' Neve assured her, leaning her elbows on the backs of the two front seats. 'Alan and I will be here, in the car, if you want to make a quick getaway – just don't jump because we didn't bring a trampoline.'

'That wasn't funny,' Susannah told her.

'Only because you're uptight – not that I'm blaming you. If it was my husband and he'd behaved the way Dad has, I'd want to take out a contract on him, but we can't afford it, so we have to do it this way.'

Blinking, Susannah said, 'Are you my daughter?' not entirely sure she was joking.

Alan squeezed her hand. 'I'm still willing to come in with you,' he said softly. 'Just say the word and we can park the car and madam here . . .'

'Oh *thanks*,' Neve snorted, sitting back in her seat and folding her arms. 'I've got to be parked now, have I?'

'Neve, you're not helping,' Susannah told her. 'This is not about . . .' Realising what she was about to say, she stopped and glanced at Alan.

'*Me?*' Neve finished for her. 'Hello, but I think it is.'

'Please stop,' Susannah said. 'I'm tired after working last night, uptight as you said, and I can't think straight while you're behaving like this.'

'So it's my fault . . .'

'Neve,' Alan said gently, 'we can have a chat after Mum's gone in, let's give her our support now.'

Susannah's eyes returned to where the sun was glinting off the windows, about twenty-four floors up. If anyone were watching it would be impossible to make out who was in the car that had drawn up in the street below, unless they had binoculars, which knowing Hugh, he probably did.

'OK, here goes,' she said, and opening the car door she got out in a surge of resolve.

'Good luck,' Alan said.

Neve remained silent, clearly still sulking because she'd been told off, though Susannah sensed that on a much deeper level she had all kinds of issues incubating away about her father, which was why Susannah was allowing her some slack today.

Reaching the large plate-glass doors of the block she found Hugh's buzzer and gave it a short, sharp blast. As she waited she turned back towards the car, vaguely registering the flowery scent of blossom as it swept down from the nearby trees as though to sweeten the acrid mix of salty river-bank debris and traffic fumes. She noticed Neve had moved from the back to the passenger seat, and gave a small wave in return as Alan held up a hand of encouragement.

Suddenly the doors clicked and shifted, and began sliding apart to allow her entry into a marble lobby where a security guard was stationed behind a wave-like counter top. He barely looked up as she passed, apparently far too engrossed in the match he was watching to be interested in guests who'd been given access from someone within.

The rise to the twenty-fourth floor was swift and seemed almost motionless, which added to the surreal sense of performing a walk-through with no lines or action, only moves to various positions.

She found Hugh's front door ajar, so stepped through and instantly baulked at the familiar scent of his aftershave mingling with marijuana that tried to tug her back through the years.

'We're in here,' Hugh shouted, apparently hearing her footsteps clip on the marble floor.

Passing three doors that she knew were bedrooms, she walked down the hall into a sitting room where wall-to-wall picture windows offered a magnificent view of the river, right along to Tower Bridge. Standing in front of them was a short, wiry figure that she knew to be Duncan, but with the light behind him she was unable to make out his features right away.

'Susie,' he said, coming forward to hug her.

She flinched at the name and stepped back from the embrace. Now he was visible she could see his prison pallor, grey and pinched, and how all the vibrancy and charm had been drained from his once confident smile. His eyes were puffy and shadowed, and deeply lined, and his posture seemed awkward, almost diminished, as though he'd withdrawn into himself, like a mollusc into a shell.

'How are you?' he asked, coming no closer.

'Fine. Don't you think it would have been wiser to take a pass on the drugs today?' she said bitterly.

His eyes went to his brother in an accusatory way. 'I'm clean,' he told her.

'Susie, gorgeous as ever,' Hugh gushed, coming out from behind the bar to try his own luck at embracing her.

Her hands went up, and he stopped, apparently more amused than offended by the contempt in her eyes.

'Shall we sit down?' Duncan suggested, making a jerky sort of gesture towards one of the sofas.

Staying on her feet, Susannah said, 'Why does your brother have to be here? Aren't you capable of speaking for yourself?'

'Oh come on,' Hugh said affably, 'you know very well what a softie he is. If I don't protect his interests he's going to end up with nothing.'

Susannah's upper lip curled. 'Maybe you don't consider his daughter one of his interests, but I do,' she said scathingly. 'Now either make yourself scarce, or I'm walking out of here and we'll let the proper authorities, and *lawyers*, deal with it all.'

'Susie, he's only trying to help,' Duncan said gently. 'I'm still getting used to being out . . .'

'Oh grow up,' she snapped. 'You might have paid for your drug crime, but you haven't even begun to pay for how grossly you've neglected your daughter. I can sue you for back maintenance, I suppose you realise that? So whatever money you might make in the future, you'll always be in debt to me and Neve . . .'

'Susie, if you're so hell-bent on involving bureaucrats and barristers, what are you doing here?' Hugh enquired pleasantly.

'I'm here,' she fumed, keeping her eyes on Duncan, 'to tell you that I am prepared to forgo any claim on whatever income you might make in the years ahead if you will agree to do the same regarding the house. Sign it over to me, and we'll be quits.'

'Hang on,' Hugh chipped in with a spurious laugh, 'that house is worth half a million quid, you can't expect him to just walk away from that.'

'Correction, it's worth closer to four hundred thousand, and if I'm forced to sell and give half to him after the mortgage is paid off, with the way the market is now I'll never be able to buy anywhere else in the same area, and that's where Neve needs to be.'

'But it's his house, so he has to have something out of it.'

'Neve's also his daughter, and I'm getting sick of repeating myself. Now, you either accept my offer, Duncan, or I'll leave.'

'What about,' Duncan said, with a nervous glance at Hugh, 'if or when you do sell, I get something out of it then? OK, maybe not fifty per cent . . .'

'Dunc, stop. Let me handle this,' Hugh interrupted. 'You can't turn your back on a hundred and fifty K plus . . .'

'I'm not trying to . . .'

Speaking over him, Hugh said to Susannah, 'What about this new boyfriend of yours? He doesn't seem short of a few bob, so you're hardly on the breadline, are you?'

Susannah's eyes narrowed with loathing. 'You've been spying on me,' she spat furiously. 'I didn't think it was possible for you to sink any lower . . .'

'It's my duty, as Duncan's older brother, to protect his assets . . .'

'If you're so concerned about your *duty* why don't *you* do something to help him get started again? Why do you have to make him come after us . . .'

'We're getting off the boyfriend,' he interrupted, 'and we need an answer about what part he's playing in your life, because you can't have it all ways, Susie. Rich boyfriend, Duncan's house . . .'

'He's not rich, nor does he have any responsibility, financial or otherwise, where Neve is concerned. That belongs exclusively to her father, much as he'd obviously like to shirk it.' Turning to Duncan, she said, 'As for giving you something when I do sell, I'm prepared to consider it, but instead of settling on a percentage now, why don't we agree to discuss it when, if, it happens?'

Duncan shrugged. 'I guess that sounds reasonable.'

184

'Which is why you're standing there like a sack of old spuds,' Hugh told him crossly. 'That house is in your name . . .'

'Thank you for reminding me,' Susannah cut in. 'I need my name on those deeds,' she said to Duncan, 'so I'll get the relevant paperwork drawn up and send it to you. Will you be here? Or somewhere in Scotland?'

'I'm getting the sleeper to Glasgow tomorrow night,' he told her. 'I have to report to my probation officer on Wednesday morning so I can't hang around in London.'

So he'd already set things up for himself north of the border, which could hardly be better news as far as Susannah was concerned, though once again there he went, turning his back on Neve. 'Do you have an address yet?' she asked coldly.

'I'm staying with friends close to the centre until I can find a place to rent.'

'Which is why you need . . .'

'*Shut up*, Hugh,' Susannah hissed. 'You're like a stuck record. So, Duncan, if you can let me have an address for these friends . . .'

Having taken a square of white paper from a fancy notepad stand on the coffee table, Duncan jotted it down while Hugh muttered and growled in annoyance. Susannah ignored him, and once she had the slip of paper in her hand she said, 'Thank you. I think that's everything. I hope things work out for you in Scotland.'

Duncan swallowed nervously as she started to turn away. 'How's Neve?' he suddenly blurted.

Surprised, but liking him better for asking, she said, 'She's fine.'

'Will you tell her . . .' He took a breath and wiped a hand over his face. 'I couldn't let her come to the prison,' he said. 'It's no place for a girl her age, and I didn't want her to see me like that.'

'No, I didn't want her to either, but you could have phoned, or written.'

'Then she might have wanted to see me, and I wouldn't have known how to refuse. Will you try to explain that to her?'

'I already have.'

'It's not that I don't care. I want her to know that I'll always be there for her, if she needs me.'

Deciding there was no point challenging him on that, she gave him a half smile and prepared to leave.

'Will you tell her?' he pressed. 'I want her to understand that now I'm out things can be different. We can try to rebuild our relationship.'

'While you're in Scotland and she's here in London?'

He flushed at her sarcasm. 'She can come to visit, as soon as I have a place.'

Seeing no point in worsening his misery, she said, 'I'll tell her,' and once again she started to leave.

'Your boyfriend,' he went on quickly. 'Does she like him? Do they get on together?'

'Yes, they do,' she answered, keeping her back to him.

'It's just that . . . I don't want some stranger barging their way into her life.'

'Oh for heaven's sake,' she snapped, turning around. 'He's not a stranger. In fact, he's already

186

been more of a father to her than you ever managed, but in your case that wouldn't be difficult when your priority was always the next fix.'

Flushing, he said, 'She's still my daughter, and despite what you say I care about her . . .'

'Then you've got a funny way of showing it. And you can't expect to walk back into her life now because it happens to suit you. She's just finding some stability after years of paternal neglect.'

'With a man who's . . .'

'It's Alan Cunningham, who I was with before I met you, but of course, you already know that,' she added with a withering look at Hugh.

'Yes, that's what's bothering me,' Duncan replied.

Too taken aback to be annoyed, she said, 'What do you mean by that? You've never even met him.'

'I have. Once. Twenty-odd years ago, when he came looking for you. Something happened that you didn't need to know about then, but perhaps you do now. You might remember how I was attacked one night, in Richmond?'

Her eyes widened.

'It was him. He beat me up and threatened to kill me if I didn't stay away from you. A few days later some of Hugh's people sorted him out and he went . . .'

'You're lying,' Susannah told him. 'Alan's never been violent in his life, so this is something *he's* put you up to,' she seethed, jabbing a finger towards Hugh. 'I don't know what your game is,' she spat, 'and I don't want to know, but I will tell you this: I've known Alan Cunningham since I was a child, and he has more integrity in his left foot than you'll ever have . . .'

'I'm not lying,' Duncan cut in.

'Whether you are or not, I could hardly care less. It's history and so are you. I'll have my solicitor contact you about the deeds,' and turning on her heel she marched out of the flat.

A few minutes later as she crossed the pavement in front of the building, she became aware of a strange light-headedness coming over her. It took a while for her to realise that it was relief and achievement, and a sense of finally being set free. The nightmare of the last few years was at last drawing to a close; the two men she'd just left behind with their crimes and corruption were no longer a part of her life, and need never be again. She kept on going, walking faster and faster as though moving from the past towards the future, where Alan was already getting out of the car to meet her.

'How did it go?' he asked, folding her into his arms.

'I think I got a result, of sorts,' she answered. Then, tilting her face up, she smiled as he kissed her. 'How's Neve?' she asked softly. 'Did she calm down a bit after I'd gone?'

'Stop talking about me, I can hear you,' Neve warned, climbing out of the passenger side of the car. 'I suppose I have to get in the back again now.'

'You suppose right,' Susannah told her. 'Does anyone feel like a coffee, because I certainly do?'

Alan looked around to get his bearings. 'I believe there are a few cafes the other side of those town houses, next to the river,' he said. 'Come on, I'll drive round to see if we can park any closer.'

After finding a space they began strolling along the towpath towards a rank of cafes and restaurants where an assortment of tables and colourful parasols was spread over cobbled terraces and grassy banks.

'So, what did he have to say?' Neve finally ventured, slipping between them in order to link both their arms.

'Not much, actually,' Susannah replied, 'but he's agreed not to try and force us to sell the house, and . . . he'd like to try and rebuild his relationship with you.'

'Ugh! No way!' Neve cried in disgust. 'I don't want anything to do with him.'

'Maybe not now, but he wants you to know that if you do ever need him, he'll be there for you.'

As Alan glanced at her Neve said, 'Oh, you mean like he has been since he went down? Great. I'll have to remember that, except, of course, one little problem, I don't actually know where he lives.'

'He gave me an address.'

'And that would be where?'

'Glasgow.'

'Oh, just round the corner then. Wicked. Remind me never to go.'

They wandered on in silence, passing several other families who were taking advantage of the warm spring sunshine, until finding a free table outside an Italian coffee bar, Susannah and Alan sat down while Neve went off to the Ladies.

'I don't know how to make this any easier for her,' Susannah said with a sigh. 'All this attitude . . .

She's obviously feeling angry and rejected, and who can blame her? He's still her father, no matter what he's done. What did she say while I was gone?'

'Not a great deal, but if I was reading her correctly, I think she'd rather focus on us becoming a family now than dwell on where he's supposed to fit into her life. She seems to think that seeing him will just start complicating things, and to a degree she's right, because it probably would.'

Susannah looked across the table at him, and found herself smiling at the kindness and concern in his eyes. Then, remembering Duncan's accusation, a teasing humour crept into her tone as she said, 'He told me you beat him up once.'

Alan gave a slow blink of astonishment. '*I* beat *him* up,' he repeated incredulously. 'That's rich, when it was the other way round, and three against one, I might add. I put up a fight, but I still ended up in hospital for the night.'

Having expected him to deny it, Susannah's face dropped. 'I had no idea about any of this,' she protested. 'Why have you never mentioned it?'

He shrugged. 'I guess because it was a long time ago, and back then, once I realised he could offer you the kind of world you wanted, there was no point me throwing down the gauntlet for a rematch. Anyway, I wasn't exactly proud of being on the losing end, but I think we should drop the subject now, because Neve's on her way back and she doesn't really need to know I got duffed up by her father twenty years ago. Apart from not doing much for my pride, it won't help things between them at all.'

With a smile, Susannah put a hand to his face and leaned forward to kiss him. 'You're a wonderful man,' she murmured softly. 'Did I ever tell you that?'

'Mum, you are so *embarrassing*,' Neve hissed, coming up behind her. 'Just stop, will you, or I'm going to leave.'

With twinkly eyes Susannah sat back in her chair, and as Alan gave their order to a waiter she started refocusing her thoughts on the screen test she still hadn't quite given up hope of being offered. Neve, on the other hand, seemed to plunge into some fairly black thoughts given the frown that pleated itself between her eyes, and for once, not even Alan was able to coax her out of her sulk. If anything, he ended up making it worse, because she suddenly jumped up from the table and flounced off in a huff to go and wait by the car.

As she vanished along the towpath Susannah looked at Alan, but he only shook his head in despair, clearly as confounded as she was by the mercurial shifts in Neve's moods.

Chapter Nine

'You haven't got a clue what it's like,' Neve was complaining with an anguished wail that loaded the words with frustration. 'She's my mother, for God's sake, and I love her more than anything, so it's not fair that this should be happening. I mean, it's not my fault, is it? I didn't ask for any of it.'

Sasha's expression was a picture of required sympathy. 'Do you reckon he knows?' she asked kindly.

'Are you *insane*?' Neve cried. 'Of course he doesn't *know*. I can hardly tell him, can I? Anyway, actually, I think he might.'

Sasha blinked. 'You just said he didn't.'

'I mean, I think he can tell. Oh God,' Neve groaned, letting her head fall back as misery engulfed her. 'I'm getting like I don't want to go home, because I can't stand to see them kissing, or even holding hands, and we're moving into his house next weekend . . . What am I going to do? Sash, this is so bad. Did I tell you what happened last week, when I was having a bath? Oh my God, it was like . . .'

'You mean when he walked in?'

'Yeah. He must have seen everything . . . He had to have, because I was just getting out, and I didn't realise he was there at first until he passed me a towel.' She started to giggle as she groaned again. 'It was wicked the way he just said "Sorry," then turned around and walked out. I wanted to die, I swear it, but it was kind of cool as well, like in a way he was letting me know that . . . you know.'

Sasha looked puzzled and shook her head.

Neve shrugged self-consciously. 'I don't know. It doesn't matter. It's hard putting it into words, but . . . Do you swear you won't repeat a word of what I'm about to tell you now, to anyone? Not even Melinda.'

'On my father's life,' Sasha vowed, which was as solemn a promise as she could offer, because she was mad about her dad.

'Well, the thing is,' Neve whispered, in case someone might be listening outside Sasha's door, 'I really think he likes me too. I mean, don't get me wrong, it's not that he's said anything, or anything, but he's really, really nice to me, and he always treats me like an equal, not like I'm a kid. And I feel so chilled when I'm with him, you know, like . . . Well, sometimes it's a bit like we're a couple, because he lets me hold his arm when we walk along together, and he never seems to mind when it's just me and him going somewhere, you know, the times Mum can't make it. Oh God, Sash, what am I going to do?' she said desperately. 'If she ever found out . . . But there's nothing to find out. I mean, it's not as if anything's happened, and it's not my fault he saw me with no clothes on, is it?'

Sasha shook her head loyally. Then, after a pause, 'So what *are* you going to do?' she asked breathlessly.

Neve shrugged. 'There's nothing I can do, is there, except move into his house at the weekend with Mum, and thank God my room's far enough away from theirs so I can't hear them. That would just be like . . . Oh, I would hate it so much, but it's all my own fault, because I'm the one who got in touch with him, and Mum's really happy now, which is what I wanted, so I'll just have to be the one who's miserable.'

Sasha regarded her gravely. 'It must be hell,' she murmured sympathetically.

Neve nodded.

They sat in mournful silence for a while, then Sasha said, 'What would you do if you found out he really did fancy you?'

Neve's breath caught on the jolt in her heart. 'Don't even say it,' she gasped, pressing a hand to her chest. 'It would be the most amazing thing, but it would be majorly terrible.' Her face transformed itself into an expression of romantic longing. 'I keep thinking about kissing him,' she confessed, 'but it's never going to happen, is it? It can't, so I might as well try to forget him, but how am I going to do that when we're living under the same roof? Oh Sash, it's all so horrible and such a mess . . .'

'Is that your phone or mine?' Sasha said, as a mobile started to bleep with a text.

'Mine, I think.' Neve picked up hers and as she read the message her eyes grew wider and wider. 'Oh my God, my mum's only got a screen test,' she cried excitedly. 'That is so brilliant. I have to call her,' and seconds later she was connected to Susannah saying, 'Mum, I got your text. You must be so pleased.'

'I am,' Susannah laughed joyously, 'and stunned and shocked and scared out of my wits, but it's fantastic, isn't it? I've actually been shortlisted, so I must still be in with a bit of a chance.'

'You'll get it,' Neve told her confidently. 'It doesn't matter that you can't ride a horse, you'll learn, or they'll use a double or something. So when is it?'

'Wednesday afternoon, at the London studios. Alan can't take me because he's working, but he's offered to pay for a cab. Isn't that generous? He's so good to us, I already can't imagine how we ever managed without him.'

'He's the best,' Neve assured her, while looking dolefully at Sasha.

'What time are you coming home?' Susannah asked. 'I thought we should get on with some packing tonight. There's a lot to do before the weekend.'

'I'm just finishing my homework so I won't be long. Is Alan staying with us?'

'No, he's at a conference somewhere in Kent today, and he won't be back till late, so he's going straight home. I know what you're going to say, the place feels a bit empty without him now, doesn't it?'

'Yes,' Neve agreed. 'I really love it when he's there.'

'Well, luckily he loves it when you're there too, because I'd have a real problem on my hands if he didn't. Anyway, I want to tell Lola and Pats about Wednesday so I'm going to ring off now.'

'OK. Tell Lola I'll be calling in on my way past to pick up some stuff. Love you,' and clicking off the line she let out a howl of frustration as she kicked her feet up and down on the bed. 'It's not fair, Sash, but it's brilliant and wicked and oh my God, I can't believe my life is so amazing and horrible all at the same time. What am I going to do? You have to tell me, or I'll end up going mental.'

During the build-up to the screen test it didn't once occur to Susannah that Michael Grafton might not be there to watch, so when she turned up at the London studios on Wednesday afternoon to find out he wasn't coming, her disappointment virtually eclipsed her nerves. She suddenly felt like a tightrope walker whose rope had just gone slack, or more pertinently a horse set to pass the post without a rider. No matter how well she did, she needed Michael's support, or his colleagues were going to push her aside in favour of their own personal favourites. She wasn't even sure it helped to learn that Marlene Wyndham wouldn't be putting in an appearance either, except actually it did, because of course they were going to watch the tests later. And once she'd managed to get a more sensible grip on herself it didn't take long for her to begin feeling the buzz of being around a place where TV was made. The hustle and bustle was electric as floor managers, technicians, production assistants, any number of people, whizzed through reception with stopwatches, clipboards and walkie-talkies, while lights blinked to red behind the receptionist to show a programme had either gone on air, or was being recorded.

She soon learned from Plum, another casting assistant (Susannah couldn't help feeling relieved that Ben wasn't around, after the last fiasco), that Jane Fullerton, a well-known drama director who'd already been hired for the opening episodes of the series, was in charge of the screen tests. No costumes were required, she was told, or props, and what make-up was needed would be applied by professionals in the studio's make-up rooms.

As she sat in the chair having her eyes darkened and cheeks blushed, she could feel herself becoming higher and higher on her surroundings. Photographs from top-rated programmes were all over the walls, talkback from a production gallery was coming from some speakers somewhere, the ubiquitous smell of greasepaint was all over the place. She was absorbing it all like oxygen and feeling the charge running through her like adrenalin. It felt so right to be here, as though she was finally on the right train travelling in the direction she should always have been going. She wasn't allowing herself to focus on failure, it was only on a subliminal level that she knew she simply wouldn't be able to bear it if she suddenly found herself abandoned at a station again, watching the last carriages disappear along the track with another actress in a seat that could have been hers.

The scene she was to play was a fairly straightforward two-hander from episode three of the series, apparently, and had been biked round to her on Monday, so by now she knew it entirely by heart.

'George Bremell's being tested for the other part,' Dorothy had informed her over the phone. 'I'm sure you're not too young to remember him.'

'Are you kidding?' Susannah cried. 'But why's he auditioning? Don't they just offer parts to someone like him?'

'Usually, but in dear George's case they need to be sure he can remember his lines long enough to make starting the camera worthwhile. He had a drink problem a few years back that, so they say, addled his brain and put his looks through a mangle. He's supposed to be on the wagon now, and the right side of a face job, so if he can prove himself he'll be one of the leads and you'll be a lucky girl, because most of Penelope's scenes are with him and even when drunk he was always an absolute sweetheart.'

'So I take it he's the one Penelope's supposed to be sleeping with?'

'Indeed, but not because she has the hots for him, remember. She's doing it to get back at his extremely beautiful, much younger, and fiendishly scheming wife, was how it was described to me. In fact, I've now learned that the series is more or less centred around the wife, but you won't meet anyone who's up for that part when you go on Wednesday, because Wednesday's all about Penelope and Jerome, the character George is hoping to play.'

When Susannah's call to the studio finally came her insides dissolved into chaos, and she wasn't sure whether she felt buoyed, or more nervous than ever, when all four make-up artists embraced her for good luck and whispered that they hoped she got it over the other actresses who'd already gone through. It was wonderful to feel them rooting for her, but maybe they were saying the same to everyone.

As she followed a floor assistant from the make-up rooms, along a narrow corridor, then across a cluttered scene dock and in through the heavy fire doors of a small, undressed studio, she was focusing intensely on the little she now knew about her character, Penelope. She was clearly an angry and vengeful person, peevish and possibly very unattractively jealous. So there was quite a bit to play with there. Did she have a soft centre of any kind? If so, it wasn't evident in the scene that she'd been sent. However, she'd been told at the original audition that Penelope wasn't terribly bright, which gave her a slightly vulnerable and sympathetic edge, Susannah decided.

The next thirty minutes passed in what seemed like a heartbeat, as George Bremell, a portly, middle-aged Lothario who'd clearly already done a fine job of winning over the director and crew, encountered no problem at all adding Susannah to his conquests. With his fulsome moustache and wickedly twinkling eyes, she found him as mischievous and charismatic as he always seemed in chat shows, and he turned out to be so generous and respectful of her efforts, in spite of her lowly status, that she wanted to hug him over and over for how much confidence he gave her.

'I promise you,' she told Pats later, on her way

home in a cab, 'if I get this part it'll be totally down to him. I've never come across an actor with so little ego and so much talent. If he weren't gay and sixty I swear I'd be in love with him already. In fact, scrub that, because I think I am anyway.'

'So he's definitely off the booze?'

'All I can tell you is that there was no problem about him remembering his lines today, which was what everyone was afraid of, and he's still incredibly attractive in spite of the pouchy eyes and swollen veins, so I'm not convinced he's actually had any surgery. Honestly, going in front of a camera with him was like being able to dance without knowing the steps. He just leads you through it, and before you know what's happening you're taking your bows and everything's perfect and you're still not quite sure how you did it.'

With a smile in her voice Patsy said, 'OK, so if you're the totty, did you find out who's up for the part of his wife?'

'Oh yes. Apparently it's between Angelica Crush and Frances Emery.'

'Never heard of either. Have you?'

'Absolutely. They're both around forty-five, maybe fifty, stunning in very different ways, and amazingly talented. I certainly wouldn't want to be in the position of having to choose between them, because they've both been sensational in just about everything I've seen them in.'

'But they weren't there today?'

'No. Today was the B list, apart from George, which means I got to meet the other contenders for Penelope, which was *interesting*. George insists that none of them stands a chance and I'm bound to get it, but for all I know he said the same to them. Actually, I kind of know one of them. Polly Grace. We did a commercial together aeons ago. She didn't remember me, or she pretended not to, anyway. Apparently she's the real hot favourite for Penelope.'

'Ah, but does she have Michael Grafton's backing?'

Experiencing a renewed fluttering of nerves, Susannah said, 'We're not even sure I do, and he wasn't there today, which really threw me at first, because it was like getting all dressed up for a show and finding the audience hasn't turned up. It seemed a bit pointless going on for a while, but thankfully I got over it, and thanks to George – and Jane the director, who was lovely too – the day turned out to be a lot of fun.'

'So what's next?'

At that Susannah almost groaned. 'Any number of sleepless nights, because apparently the final decisions might not be taken for at least another two weeks, maybe even a month.'

'*What?* They can't keep people in suspense that long. What if you get cast in something else?'

'In my case I doubt that's going to happen, but if it did, I'd have to take whichever was offered first.'

'Mm, I guess so. Oh, one last question before I have to go, do I take it the clothes stayed on for the screen test?'

Chuckling, Susannah said, 'Absolutely, so my conscience will be clear when I report back to Alan. Now, before you rush off, when are you coming over again?'

'Actually, I thought I might hop on a train this weekend to give you a hand with the move. If I don't I'll only end up spending it at the office, or flat-hunting on my own, or having dinner with *Fronk* which is . . .'

'You mean he's asked you out?'

'He never stops asking me out, lunch, dinner, even breakfast yesterday, and no matter what language I say it in, he doesn't seem able to get his head round the concept of *no*.'

'The poor guy's obviously smitten, and he sounds so lovely and irresistible . . .'

'That would *not* be him.'

Laughing, Susannah said, 'OK, then speaking selfishly it would be fantastic if you did come over. Alan's hiring a van and a couple of lads from Lola's estate are going to help shift the bigger things, but I'd really appreciate some backup with everything else. Neve'll be around, obviously, complete with stroppy moods and bone-crushing spurts of affection. Honestly, I never know where I am with her these days, but I guess she's going full throttle into puberty now.'

'I take it she's still happy about the move?'

'Oh, she can hardly wait. Or that was this morning's take on it, by now she could have done a complete one eighty again. I think she'll miss our little house though. Actually, we both will.'

'Which reminds me, if you're still intending to rent it out, there's a young girl here who's moving over to our London office in June so she's going to need somewhere to live. I'm not sure what her budget is, but shall I put her in touch?'

'Definitely. If she's coming with a recommendation from my best mate, I can hardly wish for more. I might even offer a better deal.'

'Have you told Duncan you're letting it?'

'Not yet, but he still owes me half of all the mortgage payments I've made, so I don't think he'll shout too loudly once I remind him of that. Oh, I think this is Alan trying to get through, and I'm almost at Lola's now, so I'll have to love you and leave you. Don't be too hard on *Fronk* – if nothing else, he's clearly got great taste if he's fallen for you.'

As she put the phone down at her end Patsy was wincing inwardly, determined not to look in *Fronk*'s direction. All the time she'd been speaking she'd been aware of his moody brown eyes gazing through the glass partition at her, and *franchement* if he didn't let up soon she was going in there to belt him one. Better still, she might call maintenance to have the window bricked up, his door too, if she could only get away with it. The man was certifiably weird, though she clearly remained alone in thinking so, because everyone else insisted on treating him as though he were some kind of rock idol, or sporting hero. It wouldn't even surprise her very much if, when the lift doors opened in the morning and he came swaggering down the concourse in yet another outrageous get-up, the girls in the offices either side suddenly leapt on to their chairs screaming hysterically and bombarding him with their knicks. She could just see him, pocketing a pair of little white frillies like a handkerchief, then producing them with a flourish in the middle of a meeting with a major client to blow his nose. And would he blush, or excuse himself, or quickly stuff them out of sight hoping no one had noticed? Would he hell! He'd undoubtedly bellow with laughter and hold them up for all to see, with some outrageous comment like, 'Can you imagine the little derrière that belongs in these?' Or – and she turned cold at the thought – he'd just as likely toss them across the table saying, 'Patreesha, I think these must be yours.'

'Patreesha, I hope I am not interrupting.'

Starting, and feeling her cheeks burn, she looked up from her computer and instantly wanted to bounce him back out of the door just for coming in, never mind for how pleased he appeared with having made her blush. 'No, you aren't interrupting,' she told him smoothly. 'What can I do for you?'

That had to be the singularly most stupid question she could have asked someone like him, because right on cue, his appalling eyebrows went into some kind of ritual mating dance, and though he wasn't swivelling his hips or clicking his fingers, he somehow managed to give the impression he was. 'Oh, I think you can do very much for me,' he told her in his most suggestive drawl. 'I have very big hard for you.'

She blinked in shock, until she realised he'd actually said 'heart'. At least she hoped he had, and anyway, it wasn't all that much better. 'I have to tell you, *Fronk*,' she said tartly, 'you are absolutely without equal when it comes to being the world's *worst* flirt.'

'Ah, thank you,' he purred. 'I am very flattered you think so. And you, Patreesha, are sweeter to me than all of our fragrances and all of the flowers that make them.'

'Oh God, pass me a bucket,' she groaned, almost serious about wanting to puke.

'*Un bouquet*? For you, naturally,' he promised.

'A bucket!' she corrected. '*Un seau.*'

He gave a jolt of surprise. 'But why do you need a boo-kette?' he asked solicitously.

'To be sick in.'

'You are unwell? Please let me help you. Tell me what I have to do.'

Knowing he was deliberately misunderstanding her, she said, 'Getting lost would be a good start.' Realising that for him, that would be quite likely to read as a come-on, she asked, crisply, 'What did you want to see me about?'

'Ah yes. I have some good news,' he announced. 'Madame La Comtesse du Petits-Louvens is very interested to speak with us about carrying our Fleuriste range of products in her 'ealth clubs.'

In spite of her inbuilt resistance to him, Patsy was suitably impressed. 'Excellent,' she responded, not having the faintest idea who Madame La Comtesse was, but all potential new clients were welcome. 'Where are the clubs? And how many are there?'

'They are many in the United States, but here in France they are two, here in Paris, and three in the south – St Tropez, Cannes and Monte Carlo. They are very exclusive. Only for the very rich people, which is why she is interested in our most prestige range. She 'as been using it herself, apparently, and she is very impressed. Naturally, I 'ave halready give her many samples.'

'And you've set up a meeting?'

'She will call me when she is returned from New York, which her secretary says is in two weeks. This will give us time to put together a very good package for a total body range which is her biggest interest. We are also invited to spend some time, as her guests, at the Thermes des Marins in Monte Carlo. This spa use only products of the sea, *comme suggère son nom*, so she would like us to relax and enjoy in this very special place while we formulate our ideas for the spas she have in the US and the rest of Europe. So, I have taken the liberty to book us a room at the very famous Hotel Hermitage.'

Patsy stared at him, dumbfounded.

'For two nights,' he added.

His nerve was so breathtaking that she still couldn't think what to say. In the end, all she managed was, 'I'm going to London this weekend.'

'Ah.' Then, throwing out his hands in his typically French way, 'But it is all very simple, we will go the weekend after. And now that is settled I will return to my desk.'

'No, no,' she cried, almost reaching across her desk to grab him. 'What do you mean *a* room? I think that's supposed to be *two* rooms, isn't it?'

'No,' he replied affably. 'We only need one.'

She regarded him fiercely, until she remembered he liked it. 'Frank, you're going too far,' she informed him. 'Clearly we can't turn down the comtesse's generous invitation, but I have no intention whatsoever of turning it into a dirty weekend with *you*. So either reserve another room, or I'll get my secretary to do it, or I'll . . . I'll . . . fire you.'

He grinned.

She closed her eyes helplessly. 'Just go,' she said, 'before I end up doing something I regret – and don't even think about double-entendring that or you're toast, and I mean it.'

She should have known that would set off the eyebrows again, so she quickly covered her face with her hands and stayed that way until she heard her door close.

To her relief, when she looked up, he really had left, and when she dared to peek next door she discovered he wasn't there either. Thank God. With any luck the next time she saw him would be out the window as he hurtled past en route from the top of the Eiffel Tower. The cheek of him. The sheer bloody impudence, not to mention conceit. How dare he book her into the same room as him? Apart from being gobsmackingly presumptuous, it was downright disrespectful and took wishful thinking to stratospheric levels.

It was only as she returned to her computer that it started to dawn on her that the whole thing was probably a wind-up, and he was no doubt down the corridor somewhere now chortling away with his chums at her expense. She felt both dismayed and embarrassed – and angry that being the butt of his joke seemed to be bothering her more than the fact that the comtesse and her health spas probably didn't even exist. If only she could remember the woman's name she'd be able to check her out online, but she couldn't and she sure as heck wasn't going to give him the satisfaction of asking. No, she was simply going to carry on now as though the past ten minutes hadn't happened, leaving it up to him to persuade her that a business/leisure trip to Monte Carlo was not only genuine, but worth making, even if it did mean having to put up with him for an entire weekend.

Chapter Ten

Though the big move from Battersea to Clapham didn't go off without the occasional hitch, at least the weather remained good, and the two helpers from Lola's estate proved themselves worth every penny of the generous tip Alan insisted on paying them before they left.

From the beginning Pats had declared herself in charge of the move out, while Susannah directed events at Alan's house, and Alan himself drove the van back and forth with Neve and the lads. Though Susannah realised that Neve's outrageous flirting with the boys was an attempt to make Alan jealous or protective, all it seemed to earn her was Patsy's amusement, her mother's occasional irritation, and two new admirers whom she neither fancied nor wanted. As for Alan, apart from the odd jokey look he cast Susannah's or Patsy's way, he seemed to take it all in his stride.

It was a day of many mixed emotions for them all, not to mention strenuous effort, so by the time six o'clock came round they were exhausted and ravenous, and quietly elated that everything seemed to have ended up where it should be –

until Susannah received a text from Neve informing her she'd been left behind at the house in Battersea.

'It's a good job she can't see us laughing,' Susannah said, as Alan put the phone down and Pats took off to answer a ring on the doorbell. 'I thought she was here, upstairs in her room.'

'So did I,' he agreed. 'Do you want me to go and get her?'

'No, it's OK, I will. I need to do a final check anyway. Do you mind if I take the car?'

'Of course not. The keys should be on my desk in the study, if no one's moved them. I'll get some refreshments set up here. Who's at the door, can you see?'

Looking down the hall Susannah's eyes widened with surprise to see Pats coming towards her with a magnum of champagne and a large foil dish of handmade canapés. 'What's all this?' she laughed, as Pat sailed past to set it all down on the table.

'You know me,' Pats replied airily, 'prepared for every occasion, and I believe this is one we should be celebrating. *Oui ou non?*'

Exchanging glances, Alan and Susannah agreed that indeed it was, and eager to restore their energy with a glass of bubbly before the day went any further, even if it meant leaving Neve on her own a while longer, they began rummaging for plates and champagne flutes, while Pats set about popping the cork.

'OK,' Pats announced, when they were each holding a fizzing glass, 'here's to you two and many happy, healthy and hugely successful years in this wonderful house. May God bless her and all who sleep in her.'

Echoing the toast, Susannah and Alan clinked glasses, and gave murmurs of pleasure as they took their first sip.

'Right, I guess I'd better go and rescue the abandoned one,' Susannah declared, reluctantly putting her drink down before she coasted over the limit. 'Just make sure there's some of that left when I get back.'

For a Saturday evening the traffic was fairly light, so it didn't take much more than five minutes to reach the old house, which was already, she thought with some sadness, starting to look a little forlorn.

'Oh, it's you,' Neve said snippily, as Susannah let herself in the front door.

'Were you expecting someone else?' Susannah asked, a disingenuous question if ever there was one, since she knew full well that Neve had hoped Alan would come.

Neve only shrugged and turned to pick up a heavy box of her belongings to carry out to the car.

'That should have gone in the van,' Susannah told her, taking it and putting it down on the stairs.

'Yeah, well it didn't, did it, because obviously only your stuff matters.'

Having started towards the kitchen Susannah stopped and turned back, her expression tinged with impatience.

'What now?' Neve demanded belligerently.

Biting back her exasperation, Susannah put her hands on Neve's shoulders and looked directly into her eyes. It didn't surprise her to see a lot of confusion there behind the hostility, but it did, as it turned out, help to soften her. 'Moves are always stressful,' she said, 'so don't let's fall out. We've got . . .'

'I'm not rowing,' Neve butted in. 'I'm just . . .' She took a breath that shuddered slightly as she turned her head away.

Deciding to tackle the immediate issue first, Susannah said, 'You're upset about leaving this house, aren't you?'

After a beat Neve nodded and gave a watery sniff. 'I really thought I wanted to go,' she said brokenly, 'and I do, but . . .'

'It's OK,' Susannah said, pulling her into an embrace. 'This is the only home you've ever known, apart from Lola's of course, so it's natural that you're finding it hard to say goodbye.'

As the tears started to roll from Neve's eyes she turned to look around the room. There was only the bare minimum of furniture now – the dear old sofa, a small coffee table, and a bookcase that was attached to the wall. Everything else, all the little knick-knacks that had made it theirs, had gone. 'It looks really sad, doesn't it?' she said, her voice barely making it past the knot in her throat. 'I feel like it's going to be lonely without us.' As she turned her face into Susannah's shoulder, Susannah found herself struggling with a few tears of her own.

'Do you think we'll ever live here again?' Neve asked, looking up at her with eyes that made her seem so very young.

With a sigh Susannah said, 'I don't suppose it's likely.'

Swallowing hard, Neve turned away and went to slump down on the sofa. 'I hope the girl from Patsy's office takes good care of it, if she decides to move in,' she said, smoothing a hand over the worn fabric of the cushions.

'So do I,' Susannah responded. 'I'm sure she will.'

Neve's eyes went back to her mother. 'You know what makes this house really special?' she said. 'It's that for a lot of the time it was just you and me living here. We might not ever be on our own again now.'

Susannah smiled. 'If we were that would mean Alan was no longer with us, and I don't think either of us wants that, do we?'

Neve shook her head. 'No.' Then, after a pause, 'I really like him, Mum.'

'I know you do,' Susannah said, and going to sit with her she slid an arm round her shoulders.

Leaning in to her, Neve said, 'Do you think I'll be able to come and watch you filming, if you do get the part?'

Realising how all over the place her young mind was, Susannah pressed a kiss to her head as she said, 'I'd have to ask, but I hope so.' Then, taking the phone from her pocket as it started to ring, she looked at the number and clicked on. 'Hi, yes we're on our way,' she told Alan, and clicked off again. 'They're wondering where we are,' she said gently. 'Are you ready to go?'

Though Neve's eyes welled up again she managed a nod, and getting to her feet she went to pick up her box.

'Leave it,' Susannah said. 'I'll bring it. You go and sit in the car.'

After Neve had gone Susannah wandered upstairs into each of the rooms, checking to make sure nothing had been left behind, and taking one last look around. Though in many ways she was more than ready to move on, being on the brink of so much change was making her feel a little more anxious than excited right now. It was hard to trust life after her early dreams had been crushed so brutally, and when she'd spent so long being afraid that no happiness or light was ever going to steal its way out of the shadows. The fact that it finally had was comforting and encouraging, particularly when she knew that she was loved now in a way she never had been with Duncan. However, being certain about the decision to leave here didn't make it any the less poignant or momentous now it was upon her, nor would it ever make her anything but grateful to this little house for the warmth and shelter it had provided during the most difficult years.

An hour later, after the entire bottle of champagne had been consumed, and pizzas were on order, Alan went out to the car with Neve to help bring in her box, while Susannah and Patsy began sorting through bedding and towels for that night.

'There's only a single bed in the guest room at the moment,' Susannah apologised, as they set up separate piles, 'we've got a king-size on order, but . . .'

'A single's great,' Pats assured her. 'It'll make me feel young again. Where do you want these? They look new.' She was holding up a pile of pink fluffy towels that were encased in tissue.

'They're for Neve,' Susannah told her. 'There's a cupboard in her shower room, so if you can take them up there, maybe you could manage some of her spare bedding too. What she needs for tonight is already on her bed, it just has to be made up.'

'I'll do it while I'm there,' Patsy said, and leaving Susannah to deal with what was left, she dropped her own sheets in the guest room on her way past, then carried the rest up to Neve's private loft apartment, as Neve had decided to call it.

Though this wasn't the first time Pats had been up here, she still couldn't help feeling excited on Neve's behalf as she stepped into the chaos of boxes and bags, and thought of how wonderful it must be to have so much space after the tiny room she'd had before. The silk-padded head of her new double bed was centred against the triangle of the far wall, with two large Velux windows over it that allowed sunlight to flood in during the day, and stars to shine through at night. Alan had already hired a carpenter to transform the eaves into an area containing a desk with built-in shelves and drawers on one side, and a wall-to-wall hanging and storage place for her clothes on the other. Having her own bathroom was going to be a real treat for her too, no longer having to trot all the way downstairs to shower, or clean her teeth, or simply go to the loo.

Pats was in the middle of loading up the cupboard when she heard voices next door in the bedroom. Realising Alan and Neve had come up with the box, she was about to call out to them when she heard Neve giggle in a way that gave her a moment's pause.

'Is this really all mine?' Neve was saying playfully.

'You know it is,' Alan replied. 'And you deserve it. I just hope you don't get lonely up here.'

'If I do, will you come to visit?' Neve asked, and Pats could almost see her winding a finger round her hair while glancing up at him in a shamelessly coquettish way.

Alan's reply was drowned by the sound of her mobile ringing, and grabbing it from her pocket she sailed nonchalantly into the bedroom, stopping in feigned astonishment as she saw them. 'Hi,' she said into her phone, appearing amused by their double take.

'Patreesha. It is *Fronk*.'

Of course. Who else would it be? 'How lovely to hear you,' she responded with a warmth that was totally misplaced, 'I was going to call you.' What was she saying? This was *Fronk* she was talking to.

'You were? For what reason?' he asked.

Giving Neve and Alan a wave she began descending the stairs. 'No reason,' she hissed into the phone.

'Good. I like that you feel free to call any time . . .'

'Don't read anything into it,' she snapped. 'What do you want?'

'To know if you would prefer your room to have a sea view, or to overlook the gardens . . .'

'Where are *you* going to be?'

'I have chosen a sea view. It is more romantic, I think.'

'Just put me in the furthest room from you –

but make sure it has a sea view too. I have to go now. Goodbye.'

As she clicked off Susannah came to the bottom of the stairs, saying, 'I'm looking for a John Lewis box that has plates in.'

'I'm sure Alan's already got some,' Patsy responded, turning off her phone as she followed her back into the kitchen.

'Of course, I just thought it would be nice to have more. We're OK for our pizzas. The table's all set.' She turned round and treated Pats to a spontaneous embrace. 'I'm so glad you're here. It makes everything feel . . . I don't know, right, I suppose. Yes,' she decided, 'right.'

'Good, I'm glad,' Patsy said, hugging her back, 'because there's nothing like right to put wrong in its place.' And if she actually knew what she meant by that she might be madly impressed with herself, but she guessed, in the grand scheme of things, it wasn't all that important.

Glancing back along the hall as she heard Alan coming downstairs and going into his study, she said, 'Looks like you're in for some interesting times ahead, with Neve's crush getting up momentum.'

'Oh, God, tell me about it,' Susannah groaned. 'Half the time I don't know whether to pity her or punish her. You saw what she was like today, showing off and coming on to those boys like some oversexed slapper. Ugh, don't let's go there again, it makes me cringe just to think of it. I don't know how Alan manages to stay so patient with her, but I guess if anyone knows how to handle her, it's him.'

'So have you discussed it with him?'

'Not at any length, because we've all been so busy lately, but I managed to ask him the other night if he was worried, or embarrassed, by it . . . Ah, here are the plates!'

'And he said?' Patsy prompted.

Susannah looked up from the box she was lifting on to a counter top. 'Oh yes,' she said, remembering where they were, 'he said considering the situation with her father over the last few years, which has been all about rejection and abandonment, it's not really surprising that she's throwing herself at someone the same age as Duncan, especially someone who's involved with her mother. It's like she doesn't trust me to hold on to him after I messed up with Duncan, so on a subconscious level she's assuming the responsibility herself by employing all the ammunition in her little cannon to make sure we don't lose out again.'

After giving it some thought, Patsy could see how that made sense. 'So once she's confident that your relationship with Alan is settled,' she said, 'she'll let go and get on with her own life?'

'Apparently. And if you ask me it can't happen soon enough, because competing with my own daughter for the same man definitely isn't my idea of fun.'

With a laugh, Patsy said, 'Poor Neve. Who'd be her age again, huh? Come to think of it, who'd be ours when you're me and you've got the abominable *Fronk* to contend with? But please don't let's go there. He's insane and I'm absolutely starving, and if that's not the pizza boy at the front door I'm going to beat up whoever it is just for getting my hopes up.'

'I don't want it there!' Neve snapped. 'I preferred it over there, where *I* put it in the first place.'

'I'm sorry,' Susannah said, taking the photograph of her and Neve back to where she'd found it, on a shelf in a small niche on the far side of the room. 'It's just you always used to keep it next to your bed.'

'Yeah, well I don't want to now. I see enough of you as it is, without having to wake up looking at you.'

Susannah's eyebrows rose. 'Charming,' she commented. 'Now where do you want these?' She was holding up a small box of cuddly animals that Neve had kept since she was a baby.

'I don't know yet,' Neve answered irritably. 'Anyway, I can do it. I don't need your help.'

'I'll remind you of that the next time you ask for it. Oh Neve, you didn't bring all those old magazines! What do you want to keep them for?'

Neve's eyes flashed. 'It's my bedroom, so I get to say what goes in it – and *who*, so if you don't mind, I'd like you to go back downstairs and get out of my space.'

Planting her hands on her hips, Susannah said, 'What on earth's eating you? You've been grumpy ever since you got up this morning. I thought you were excited about being here.'

'I *am*. It's just you, keeping on all the time and invading my *private* apartment.'

With a sigh, Susannah threw down her duster and said, 'OK, suit yourself, but I don't want you up here chatting on the phone, or messing about on the computer, when there's still a lot to be done – here and downstairs.'

'Yeah, yeah, blah, blah. What time's Alan coming back?'

'Any minute I should think. He's only gone to get Lola.' Then, finally realising what this was really about, she rolled her eyes in despair. 'You're sulking because I wouldn't let you go with him,' she stated. 'Neve, I . . .'

'*Shut up*,' Neve seethed. 'That is *not* true and you should apologise right now for saying it.'

Accepting that she hadn't handled it well, Susannah said, 'OK, I'm sorry, but you've got to start getting a better grip on yourself . . .' Then, as Neve's eyes flashed again, 'OK, this is annoying mother on her way out, but she'll be back in half an hour to check on progress, so make sure there is some.'

'Nag, nag,' Neve muttered as Susannah walked out of the door.

Letting it slide over her, Susannah continued down the stairs to the landing, where Alan had stacked several boxes ready to be unloaded. Deciding to get at least some of them out of the way she began carrying them into the master bedroom, where the bed hadn't yet been made that morning, and piles of her clothes still needed to be hung in the closets. It was a wonderfully light and airy room, with high ceilings, a deep bay window and a marble fireplace where real flames flickered over a pebble bowl at the touch of a switch. The real *pièce de résistance*, however, was the en suite bathroom where a vast jacuzzi bath, multi-head shower and twin washbowls carved into a pale-coloured limestone surface made it a place in which Susannah would spend most of her time, if only she could.

After dumping the boxes and collecting the water glasses from each side of the bed, she carried on downstairs to find Pats performing miracles in the kitchen.

'It smells delicious,' Susannah informed her, inhaling the mouth-watering aroma of roasting pork with a fig and apricot stuffing. 'Neve's just thrown me out of her *private* apartment,' she went on, going to fetch the phone as it started to ring, 'but I'm hoping she'll cheer up when her friends come over this afternoon to see her new room. Hello,' she said into the receiver. Then, after a beat, 'Hello?'

Still no reply.

Tucking the phone under her chin as she opened the fridge, she said, 'You'll have to speak up, whoever you are, because I can't hear you.'

A moment later a monotone told her that the line had gone dead.

'Must have been a wrong number,' she said, plonking the phone back on its base. 'Have you peeled the carrots yet?'

'Done. I'll put them in with the pork towards the end,' Pats answered, giving her parboiled potatoes a shake before dusting them in flour. 'Does everyone like sprouts? I thought I'd do them Nigella's way if you have some Marsala.'

'You get Nigella in Oz?'

'We get everything in Oz, even twits who cook.'

Smiling, Susannah turned round to look at her. 'Are you missing it at all?' she asked.

Surprised by the question, Patsy tilted her head to one side as she thought. 'Actually, less than I expected to,' she replied, 'but that's probably because I've been so busy.'

'Enjoying Paris?'

'How can you not enjoy Paris? I'll be happier when I have my own place though. Staying at Claudia's is great, naturally, given its location and how luxurious it is, but it's not mine, and now my stuff has turned up from Sydney I'd like to start looking around for somewhere to buy. How I'm ever going to find the time when I'm in Rome for two nights this week, Madrid the next and Berlin the week after, is another story, but hey, I'm hardly in a position to complain. Now, back to the Marsala wine. Do you have any?'

'I doubt it, but I'll call Alan to ask him to pick some up on his way back. Ah, that might be him now, unless it's our mystery caller again. Hello?'

'Hi darling, it's me,' Alan told her. 'We should be there in a couple of minutes, but I've just had a call from a patient in crisis, so I'm afraid I'll have to drop Lola off and go straight out again.'

'Oh no,' Susannah groaned. 'How long will you be?'

'Hard to tell, but obviously I'll try to get back in time for lunch.'

'What's the matter with her? Him?'

'Him. You know I can't really discuss it, but he has a severe depression, so it's not something I can put off till tomorrow. We're outside the house now, so I'll bring Lola in first.'

Ringing off, Susannah filled Pats in as she went along the hall to open the front door. Seeing Lola coming through the gate performed its usual trick of bringing a smile to her face, while Lola's rheumy blue eyes twinkled with pleasure. 'Are you OK?' Susannah asked, going to hug her.

'Of course,' Lola assured her. 'Bit breathless after me jog round the park, and aerobics class, but nothing a spot of lunch won't sort out.'

Laughing, Susannah hugged her again, then let her move on to Pats, who was standing at the door, while she walked back to the car with Alan. 'Where do you have to go?' she asked. 'To the office?'

He nodded and opened the driver's door. 'My phone will be off while I'm in session,' he said, 'but I'll call as soon as I'm free to let you know I'm on my way back.'

'Great. I hope it goes OK. I think he might have called here, actually, because someone rang just before you did.'

He stopped. 'What did they say?' he asked.

'Nothing. Whoever it was just hung up. Do all your patients have your home number?'

'Only those who need it,' and kissing her briefly he got into the car and started the engine.

As he drove down the street Susannah stood watching him, trying not to feel fed up that he'd been called out on their first Sunday at the house. It wasn't that she expected him to ignore a patient in distress, but all the same, she couldn't help hoping it wouldn't turn into a regular occurrence.

'Where's Alan gone?' Neve demanded, as Susannah closed the front door behind her.

Susannah looked up to see her sauntering down the stairs, all long skinny legs and bare midriff with a jewel glittering in her navel. 'He has to go and see a patient,' she answered.

'On a Sunday?'

'People don't cheer up or get over their problems according to the day of the week,' Susannah replied, more tersely than she'd intended. 'He's going to try to get back in time for lunch. Is Sasha joining us?'

'No, she's coming after. And Melinda, but Janey Munroe just rang and asked if I wanted to meet her at Scoffers on Battersea Rise for a coffee. I thought I'd go if there's time.'

'Fine, if your room's up together. If it's not, well, I guess it's your friends you want to impress this afternoon . . . Go and say hello to Lola before you leave.'

After doing as she was told, with a lot more bounce for Lola than she was managing for her mother, Neve took off to meet her friend, while Patsy checked the joint and turned down the oven.

'Does Alan often get called out at weekends?' Pats asked, wiping her hands on a towel as Susannah started to make a sauce.

'This is the first time I've known it,' Susannah replied, 'but obviously it happens.' Then with a sigh, 'I hope we're not going to cause too much disruption in his life.'

'I wouldn't worry too much about that,' Patsy said, with a wink towards Lola. 'Remember he had three stepchildren before, so you and Neve are probably going to seem pretty tame by comparison.'

Susannah laughed. 'You're right,' she said, 'though I'm not sure I'd describe my daughter as tame. Quite the reverse half the time.'

'Whatever. Behaviour's his thing,' Pats reminded her.

Susannah frowned as she nodded. 'He seemed quite worried about the guy he's going to see.'

'Whoever he is, he was letting off some steam when he rang,' Lola informed them. 'I couldn't make out what he was saying, but he sounded pretty desperate, poor chap. Alan had a job calming him down.'

'It can't be easy,' Pats murmured, 'having to deal with people's inner demons all the time. I know he's trained for it, but he must get some real weirdos turning up at times. Oh God, talk about right on cue,' she groaned and laughed, checking the ID on her mobile as it bleeped with a text. *Rooms and flights reserved for next Sat. Sea view as requested. F.*

She blinked in surprise. 'For once a sensible message,' she commented as she clicked off. 'I just hope this jaunt turns out to be on the level, because if it's not I'll brain the fool. Except he's not a fool, because he has a brilliant business mind, which is all he has going for him.'

'And we would be talking about . . . *Fronk*?' Susannah ventured.

'Who else?'

Chuckling, Lola said, 'He's still after you then?'

'I've no idea what he's up to,' Patsy told her, 'he has a wavelength all of his own.'

Susannah was watching her closely. 'Are you sure you don't fancy him?' she asked teasingly.

Patsy's eyes bulged as she gulped with the sheer horror of it. 'Don't even think it, never mind say it,' she protested. 'Even if he were the last man on earth I'd still rather have cellulite. The man's a menace the way he goes about the place flirting like a vampire bat on Viagra. And I'm telling you this now, if he tries anything on when we're in Monte Carlo he's going to find out the hard way that yours truly is nothing like the French fluffies he's so obviously used to.'

'Which could be why he's so interested in you,' Susannah suggested. 'You're a challenge.'

Patsy recoiled at the mere thought of it. 'Let's change the subject,' she demanded. 'I have enough of him during the week, so I don't need him turning up at the weekend, even in conversation. Now, what I want to know is if you're going to contact your agent tomorrow to find out if there's any news yet?'

Susannah immediately blanched as a storm of nerves broke out inside her. 'She'll get in touch with me as soon as she has some,' she replied.

'OK. But you're giving up working at the club anyway?'

'I am. My last night is next Friday. Sandrine, from your office, is coming to see the house on Tuesday, did she tell you?'

Patsy shook her head. 'No, but I think you'll like her. She can seem a bit flighty at times, but actually she's very reliable and her English, as you've no doubt gathered, is pretty spot on. OK, let's get these roasters in now and start peeling some sprouts. I'm sure this won't be up to your standard, Lola, but I'm doing my best.'

By one thirty the meal was close to ready, so Susannah sent a text to Neve telling her to come home right away, and another to Alan letting him know they'd keep his warm until he got there.

Ten minutes later, as Pats was lifting the joint from the oven, Neve sailed in through the front door shouting, 'I'm back. It smells fantastic whatever it is.'

'Sounds like the mood might have improved,' Susannah commented under her breath.

'So Alan's still not back?' Neve asked, coming into the kitchen.

'Not yet, but we've laid him a place, just in case. You're there, next to him. Lola, you stay where you are at the end, Pats and I can go either side of you.'

'Has he called?' Neve wanted to know as she went to wash her hands at the sink.

'No,' Susannah replied, 'but he will, as soon as he can.' Her eyes went to Patsy's and she shook her head in dismay.

'So how's the boyfriend scene?' Patsy asked, starting to carve the pork as Neve took her place. 'Anyone I should know about?'

Neve shrugged. 'Not really. I don't want any potatoes, thank you. Where did Alan go? Back to the office?' she asked Susannah.

'Yes, now please, give it a rest.'

Neve's eyes narrowed. 'Oh, excuse me for breathing,' she snapped. 'I was only asking . . .'

'The same thing, over and over,' Susannah interrupted. 'He'll be back soon, I'm sure. Now Pats has gone to a lot of trouble, so let's try to eat our lunch without falling out.'

Looking very much as though she didn't even want to try, Neve blazed her a glare and reached for the gravy. She didn't speak again for the rest of the meal, and when it was over she took herself off to her room.

'Thank goodness for that,' Susannah sighed, starting to clear the plates. 'It's like having a ticking bomb at the table that can't make up its mind how much time it has left.'

'Shame there's no word from Alan yet,' Lola commented, putting down her napkin. 'That was a delicious lunch, Pats, and it's never the same if it doesn't get eaten right away.'

In the end it was almost six o'clock when he finally rang to say he was on his way home. 'I'm sorry,' he said, sounding exhausted, 'the poor guy has some serious issues, but I think he's in the right hands now. It just took some time to get him there. Has Pats left yet?'

'About an hour ago,' Susannah told him. 'She had to get the train. Lola's still here, waiting to be taken home.'

'Of course. I'll do it as soon as I get there. I should warn you though, I'm looking a bit of a mess. The guy thumped me at one point, so I've got a lovely shiner in the making.'

'He *hit* you? Oh my God, are you all right?'

'I'm fine. One of the hazards of the job, I'm afraid, though fortunately it's rare.'

'Thank goodness for that,' she replied.

It wasn't until several minutes after she'd rung off that she found herself remembering the altercation he'd once got into with Duncan. However, the two events were hardly connected, so by the time she'd returned to her unpacking she'd already forgotten it again.

Chapter Eleven

It was early on Wednesday afternoon, just after she'd wheeled Lola over to bingo, that Susannah received a call from her agent telling her that the role of Penelope had gone to Polly Grace.

Susannah's disappointment was so crushing that she couldn't stop tears springing to her eyes and almost stepped off the kerb in front of a speeding van, she was so upset. The blare of the driver's horn brought her back to her senses, but was so angry and loud that she could no longer hear what Dorothy was saying. But what did it matter? She'd only be spouting the usual platitudes of comfort, expressing how sorry she was and telling her not to give up because something else was probably right around the corner.

'So, congratulations, my dear,' were the next words she heard Dorothy uttering, 'a leading role in a major new series. A bit more than you were expecting, mm?'

Susannah stopped walking. 'But you just said I didn't get the part.'

'Of Penelope, that's right, because they want to offer you Marianne.'

Shock sent a giant wave through her heart. 'You

mean . . . ?' No, it couldn't be . . . but that was what Dorothy had just said. 'I'm not sure I . . . You mean, Marianne the wife?' she asked.

With an amused tut of exasperation Dorothy said, 'That's right. She's the major character in the series, with her much older and rather stupid husband, who's going to be played by George Bremell. So even more good news, yes?'

'Yes,' Susannah murmured. She was still so stunned that she was becoming oblivious to the traffic streaming by, the sun blazing down on her, the other pedestrians who were swerving to go round her, even where she was going. She was being swept from the mundane reality of Battersea into a dream world that she wanted so badly she hardly dared allow herself to believe her own ears.

'Are you still there?' Dorothy asked.

Susannah tried to answer, but lost it in a sudden sob of emotion. 'Oh my God,' she finally managed, pressing a hand to her mouth. 'Are you serious? You're not . . .'

'Would I joke about something like this?'

'But why? How? No one ever mentioned . . . I didn't even know her name until you just told me.'

'It's all news to me too, sweetie, but what matters is that they've clearly had a major rethink. Or maybe they were testing you for both parts all along and didn't want to get your hopes up about Marianne. Whichever, this is the break all actors dream of, and very few ever achieve, so your star is on the ascent, my love. This is going to make you famous, and a whole lot richer than you are now – though let's face it, that wouldn't be hard.'

Susannah's elation was building to such a pitch that she could barely contain it. This was beyond anything she'd dared hope for, and yet everything she'd ever wanted. 'What – what do I do now?' she asked, putting out a hand for her bus. *A bus.* She was getting on a bus to Clapham, going to work at a dentist's reception. For some reason that suddenly felt less real than becoming the lead in a major new drama.

'I'll know more later,' Dorothy answered, 'but before you find yourself inundated, let me get in first and take you to lunch to celebrate. Friday ends my last full week at the agency . . .'

'You can't leave now,' Susannah protested.

'I'll still be coming in two days a week, and I'll be at the end of the phone if you need me, but Samantha's much younger and hungrier than this old banger who's been round the block way too many times, so you'll be in far more capable hands. I'll invite her along for lunch too. Meanwhile, my only instruction for you is to start resigning from all those dreadful little jobs of yours.'

'Of course,' Susannah replied, hardly even thinking about it as she climbed aboard the bus. 'But what about the riding issue? If Marianne owns the stables . . .'

'I'm sure they've got it all worked out, so don't worry yourself about it now. Apparently we'll have a script by Friday, and I believe Michael Grafton's going to be contacting you personally. He asked for your number, anyway.'

Susannah's euphoria foundered on more

surprise, then suddenly surged with such force that she almost kissed the driver just for accepting her bus pass. 'Does that mean it was him who rang to tell you I'd got the part?' she asked, wending her way to the back.

'Actually no, it was the casting director. Michael rang straight after. He also asked me to pass on his congratulations, which this is me duly doing.'

'Oh my God, Dorothy, I don't know what to say,' she laughed as she sank into a seat. 'This is so fantastic I can hardly take it in. Never, in my wildest dreams . . .' She took a breath. 'I'm sorry, I'm trying not to gush and make a fool of myself. I need to think straight. What do I need to ask?'

Dorothy's tone was full of fondness as she said, 'Don't worry about that now. There's plenty of time to . . .'

'What else do you know about the character?' Susannah blurted. 'Isn't she supposed to be a bitch? Does she have children? Oh God, does she have to take off her . . .' Remembering where she was, 'Does she have to do the same things as Penelope?'

'You mean undress, no idea, but my guess is yes, because I can't see them not utilising all your wonderful assets. Now listen, you need some time to digest it all, so I'm going to ring off, because I have a doctor's appointment I need to get to. But I'll call again later and we can have another chat then.'

After saying goodbye Susannah sat holding the phone so tightly it might have been a lifeline, or a vessel of good luck that would evaporate if she let go for a moment. She bubbled with laughter as she thought of it as a lamp, since that would make Dorothy a genie. Then so much emotion began trying to spill out of her that she buried her face in her hands. She dared not make a call yet. If she did, she'd end up making a public spectacle of herself by shrieking or sobbing with joy.

Finally her stop came and as she skipped down on to the pavement she caught the eye of an old lady passing by. Unable to stop herself, she said, 'I've just been cast in a major new series.'

The woman looked startled, then apparently catching Susannah's euphoria, she started to smile. 'That's marvellous news, my dear,' she said. 'Congratulations.'

'Thank you,' Susannah said, squeezing her hands. 'Thank you so much.'

As the old lady walked on Susannah turned towards the dentist's office, floating on air. Then she called Alan's number. Even if she couldn't reach him, she had to tell him the news. With any luck it might bolster his spirits a little, because he'd been quite down since Sunday, when he'd finally returned home with his bruised eye, and so wrung out that he'd brushed her and Neve's fussing aside and gone straight upstairs for a relaxing soak in the bath.

Finding herself being diverted to his voicemail, she was about to blurt out a message when she decided to wait until she could tell him in person. She wanted to see his reaction, then hug him and dance round and round in circles and break out the champagne.

Next she tried Neve, knowing she'd be in class, but this time she left a message telling her to ring the instant she could to hear some unbelievably fantastic news. Of course Neve would think she'd got the part of Penelope, and Susannah could hardly wait to hear what she had to say when she found out what was really on offer.

Next was Lola, but her mobile would be off too while she was playing bingo, so hanging the expense she called Pats.

'Oh my God!' Patsy cried in a gush of amazement. 'That is so fantastic. I wish I was there, I want to shriek and jump up and down with you. I might even have to go and hug *Fronk*. On second thoughts . . . Susannah, I'm so proud of you. You must have done a spectacular audition if they dumped the minor role on someone else and cast you in the lead. It's incredible, and no less than you deserve. Have you told Alan yet?'

'No, you're the first one I've been able to get hold of. Honestly, I can hardly catch my breath it all feels so unreal, and when I think of everything that has to happen now . . . I'll presumably have to have riding lessons, and costume fittings . . . Oh my God, I've just realised it's probably going to mean being in Derbyshire for the whole week instead of just a couple of days. I don't think Alan's going to like that too much.'

'He'll be fine about it,' Patsy assured her. 'He understands how much it means to you. Neve, on the other hand, might present a bit of a problem, because she'll have to stay with Lola while you're away and now she's got that lovely big bedroom . . .'

'Oh hell, I hadn't thought of that.' Susannah's elation was starting to deflate. 'She's bound to want to stay put, and knowing Alan he'll say it's OK, but I can't inflict her on him like that. No, she'll have to go to Lola, or I can't take the job.' Despair was rapidly clouding her joy, because she couldn't ask Lola to have Neve any more than she already did, it wasn't fair at her age. So did this mean she wouldn't be able to take the part?

'Why don't you let Lola speak for herself?' Pats suggested.

When Lola did her snort of disgust at being considered too old it was so typically Lola that it made Susannah laugh and hug her. 'I'm not that decrepit yet,' her aunt informed her, 'and our girl's practically a grown-up. She doesn't take that much looking after any more.'

'But she's become very wilful lately,' Susannah reminded her, 'and you know how soft you are with her.'

'Not so soft that I'd let any harm come to her, so stop worrying about me, and think about how you're going to persuade her to give up that lovely new bedroom five nights a week, because that's going to be your biggest problem, if you ask me.'

However, to Susannah's amazement it didn't prove anywhere near as difficult as she'd feared, because Neve was so excited by the prospect of having a famous mother that apparently no sacrifice was too great. Not even the precious private apartment.

'I'll still have it at weekends,' she declared, 'and like you said, on the days you're not working, if you're back in London I can stay there then. So no, it's cool.' Then, with a beaming smile that melted away all the clouds of the past couple of weeks, she threw out her arms. 'My famous mum,' she laughed, and squealing with delight she squeezed Susannah with all her might.

Alan's response to the news was another surprise, but not in the way Susannah had hoped for, because though she hadn't expected him to be thrilled by the idea of her being away all week, she hadn't imagined him putting up such a fight.

'Yes, it's fantastic news for *you*,' he cried, putting down the glass of champagne she'd handed him as he'd come through the door, 'but what about *us* as a couple? Or doesn't that count now you've got fame in your sights?'

'Don't put it like that. It's not about fame . . .'

'Then what?'

'It's about what I do, who I am. This is the biggest role I've ever been offered, or am ever likely to be offered.'

'But the timing . . .'

'Isn't brilliant, I know, but I promise you our relationship matters to me every bit as much as it does to you. Finding you again has been the best thing that's ever happened to me, but I still have my dreams, and right now they're being handed to me . . .'

'By another man,' he cut in sharply. 'Don't you think we've been down this road before?'

Confused, she said, 'What other man?'

'Michael Grafton, who else? You said yourself you'd only get the part if he supported you, and now here you are with nothing less than the lead. So please excuse me if I'm finding his motives a little worrisome.'

'For heaven's sake, I hardly even know him. I've met him twice . . .'

'But he's clearly remembered you all these years, and now here he is, putting your name in lights. I can't help wondering if he'll be exacting any kind of payment for his patronage.'

The slap to his face was so hard that it knocked him back a step and shocked her almost as much as it did him.

'I'm sorry,' she gasped, 'but that was totally uncalled for.'

'You're right,' he admitted, rubbing his cheek. 'It wasn't what I meant. It came out wrong . . . I guess I'm uptight because we haven't even been living together a week, and you're already talking about spending at least eighty per cent of your time somewhere else.'

'Not because I don't want to be with you. I'd give anything for the programme to be based in London so I could come home every night, but I don't have any say in it.'

'I understand that,' he said, 'but please try to see where I'm coming from, will you? I lost you once to a low-life director, what kind of chance am I going to stand against a hotshot producer?'

'It's not like that, and you're not going to lose me to anyone. I'll be here every weekend, and during the week if I'm not needed . . . Look, right now it's impossible to say how it's all going to unfold, because I haven't even received a script yet, or a call from anyone on the series, so let's stop getting ourselves worked up and at least allow ourselves a glass of champagne.'

As she embraced him he pressed a kiss to her

hair and reached for his glass. 'I guess we should toast your success,' he said flatly.

Regarding him with dismay she picked up her drink too.

'Am I right in thinking you've taken the part without actually knowing what kind of character you'll be playing?' he asked, without making a toast. 'I mean, does she get up to the same kind of tricks as the other one?'

'I don't know yet.'

'But if she does, you're happy to do it?'

'Not happy, no, but everyone has elements of their jobs they don't like. Even you.'

With a turbulent sigh that seemed to draw on an equal measure of restraint, he said, 'Yes, even me.' For a moment his thoughts seemed to go elsewhere, then coming back on track, he said, 'That's why, when I come home . . . I was imagining relaxing with you, and Neve, making you the focus of my world. Now all I have to look forward to is an empty house again.'

Understanding why he was seeing it that way, and suspecting that she might too were she in his shoes, she said, 'We'll probably find it's nothing like we're expecting. I could end up with whole weeks off at a time . . .'

'Would you turn it down if I asked you?' he demanded abruptly.

She started and her face froze as a stirring of alarm broke loose inside her. Please God, he didn't really want her to answer that.

'Forget it,' he said. 'Of course I won't ask you. I, of all people, know how disastrous it can be to a relationship to try and come between someone and their dreams. I just hope you can appreciate why I'm so anxious about yours.'

'I promise you, there's no need to be,' she assured him, going to wrap her arms around him again. 'I wish I knew how to convince you of that right now, but you'll see, over time, that I have absolutely no intention of letting anything or anyone come between us. Particularly not a married man.'

He frowned in confusion. 'Michael Grafton's married?' he said.

She nodded and smiled. 'To Rita Gingell, the novelist.'

'I see.' After absorbing the information he said, 'Well, I have to admit that does make me feel a little better.'

'Good, I'm glad. Now, why don't you go and do whatever you need to before dinner, and I'll start getting things under way.' She didn't feel good about lying to him, but for all she knew Michael Grafton and Rita Gingell might have got back together since their highly publicised break-up a couple of years ago. If they hadn't, well, Alan would find out soon enough that Michael's interest in her was purely professional, as was hers in him.

The following morning as Alan walked through the reception area that he shared with two other doctors, one of medicine, the other of psychology, his secretary looked up from her desk and smiled warmly as she said good morning.

'It's good to see you back,' he told her. 'How was Tenerife?'

'Wonderful,' she replied, her deeply tanned and lined features showing how pleased she was to be asked. 'My husband had a bit of a tummy for a couple of days, but nothing new there.'

The drollness of her tone made Alan smile, and he was about to walk on when she said, 'I've just been checking the machine. Did your brother-in-law manage to get hold of you in the end? He left a few messages, I think it must have been on Sunday. He sounded quite stressed again.'

Keeping his tone light he said, 'Yes, he reached me at home, thanks, and I've seen him since. He's receiving proper treatment now, but if he rings again, put him straight through, will you? There's no reason why you should have to deal with him.'

'OK, but what if you're in session? Shall I still put him on?'

'Certainly, if he starts becoming abusive. What was he saying in his messages? Do you still have them?'

A look of discomfort came into her eyes. 'No, I don't,' she admitted, 'and I think I'd rather not repeat it.'

Understanding completely, he said, 'I'm sorry you had to hear it. I take it it was as bad as the last time he rang?'

She nodded.

'Then it's good that you erased it. I wouldn't want it falling into the wrong hands – apart from the damage it could do him, it wouldn't do me much good either.'

'If you ask me, he should . . .'

'Let's just try and forget it,' he interrupted

gently, 'and remember, if he asks for my home address you mustn't give it to him. I don't want him bothering Susannah and Neve, and the same goes for Helen, my estranged wife. I wouldn't want her being hurt by her brother's accusations, any more than I'd want her believing or repeating them.'

'Of course,' she said, still looking worried.

Going back to her desk, he said, 'It's me he's angry with, but if you're feeling insecure and want to involve the police . . . They're already aware of what happened before I left Manchester, but if it would make you feel better to speak to someone . . .'

'No, it's fine,' she told him. 'It's not me I'm bothered about, it's you. To have something like this . . .'

'I can handle it,' he assured her. 'Just make sure to let me know if it becomes too much for you.'

After he'd walked into his office Janet turned to one of her colleagues at a nearby desk, who'd clearly been listening to the exchange.

'What do the messages say?' the other secretary whispered.

Deciding it had to remain confidential for the sake of such a kind and understanding man, Janet merely shook her head and went back to her computer. She didn't really think Dr Cunningham's brother-in-law was going to kill him, any more than Dr Cunningham was likely to have committed the horrible crime he was being accused of, but it was best not to make it the subject of gossip. And it was a good job Dr Cunningham had been to the police already, she decided, because they needed to know when this sort of thing was going on, especially when it could ruin a good man's reputation. And there was no doubt in Janet's mind that Dr Cunningham was a very good man with a reputation that was fully deserved.

Chapter Twelve

'EasyJet!' Patsy exclaimed as the taxi pulled up outside Orly airport in the teeming rain. 'You've booked us on . . .'

'I will sign thank you,' Frank informed the driver. 'Patreesha, perhaps you run fast into terminal. I will bring your bag.'

Annoyed at being ordered around, but not wanting to get wet, Pats poked her umbrella out of the door, shot it up and made a quick dash into the airport building.

By the time Frank came to find her she was waiting in a zigzag line between two orange tapes leading up to the check-in desk, and wondering how she could send him to the back of the queue so they might board in different groups and therefore avoid sitting together.

'Your bag is very heavy,' he commented as he joined her, raindrops running like pearls over the top of his bald head, and into the inky black fuzz of the hair that surrounded it.

'It's full of samples,' she informed him.

He seemed surprised. 'But why? I have already send them by courier to save us carrying. They will arrive yesterday at the hotel.'

Patsy cast him as nasty a look as she could muster. 'You might have thought to tell me,' she retorted.

'I am very sorry, but is no problem, because I am happy to carry the bag.' Then, eyeing the queue in dismay, 'Pity is not possible to check in online for this flight, but things are moving I suppose. I could, how you say, murder for a coffee?'

'Looking at you, I could do it for much less,' she muttered, and promptly had to turn away because he laughed and she very nearly did too.

'Have you been to Monte Carlo before?' he asked chattily, when they were finally settled at a cafe close to the departure gate.

She lifted her frothy cappuccino, and took a sip. 'No, this will be my first time,' she replied. 'How about you? No, don't tell me, some wizened old biddy is blind and dumb enough to have you as her gigolo, so you go every weekend.'

His expression was a pastiche of hurt. 'She is not so old,' he informed her gravely, 'but I admit she has few problems with the eyes.'

Not entirely sure if he was joking, she continued drinking her coffee, wondering whether to get out her laptop now, or wait till they were on the plane.

'So, this is your first time in Monte Carlo,' he mused, sipping his espresso.

'Yes, but before you start offering to show me around, this is . . .'

He blinked in amazement. '*Quelle idée merveilleuse*,' he said. 'Why did I not think of it myself?'

'Think of what?' she said, worried when he stopped.

'Think of showing you around,' he replied. 'There is much to see, and we cannot be all the time having body massage and facial scrubs. I will speak with the concierge as soon as we arrive.'

'Don't worry. If there's time for any sightseeing, I'm quite capable of going alone.'

He simply shrugged and downed the rest of his coffee. 'I think I am to get on the plane now,' he informed her, standing up. 'I will take your heavy bag with me.'

'What?' she demanded in confusion.

'I am in the Speeding Boarding group,' he explained. 'It is a service you must book online, but it is not an expense I expect the company to pay for, so I pay for it myself.'

Patsy looked down at her own boarding card. Group C. Right in the middle of the scrum, that would end her up near the back of the plane. Great!

When she finally edged her way on to the aircraft, between an enormous woman who'd already trodden on her twice, and a man with chronic halitosis, it was to find Frank comfortably ensconced in a window seat, two rows back from the front, a copy of *Le Monde* in his lap, and a stewardess kneeling on the middle seat in front, clearly basking in his flirtatious attention.

'Ah, she is here,' he said, spotting Patsy's contemptuous look approaching.

A poor excuse for Miss France turned around, still batting her eyes, but managing to smile a cheery welcome as she said to Patsy, 'We have been saving a place for you. Welcome on board.'

Realising how churlish and childish she'd look

if she refused to sit down – besides which, she needed her laptop which was in the locker above him – Patsy thanked the trolley dolly and slipped into the aisle seat.

'I am afraid we have a full flight this morning,' the stewardess told her, 'so please could you move into the middle, next to your husband?'

Patsy's head spun round to Frank. He appeared all innocence, and since, at a push, it might be considered a reasonable assumption, she decided not to give him the satisfaction of rising to it.

'I'd like to spend the flight discussing Alain Savier's report on retail sales in France,' she informed him, once she was settled next to him with her laptop. 'He assured me it would be on your desk by the end of the day yesterday, so I'm hoping it was.'

'I am 'appy to tell you that it was, complete with the analysis you requested when we last spoke on the matter. I spend many hours with it already, and I think this flight is presenting a very good opportunity to put our heads together.'

Patsy braced herself for the suggestive wink, or eyebrow waggle, or worse, some kind of nudge, but when she looked at him he only treated her to a surprised sort of smile.

'This is what you would like, yes?' he enquired. 'For us to put our heads together?'

Ignoring what she felt sure was artifice, she said, 'Does this mean when I next go online I can expect to find an email containing the necessary data to start formulating a plan?'

'I would hope so,' he answered. 'I send it late last night, so there is no reason for it not to be

246

there. Meantime, I have all that we require right here on my laptop.'

Registering the fact that he'd been working while she was at a party hosted by *Paris Match*, she said, 'I'm impressed by your dedication, and now, *Fronk*, I have a question for you.'

Appearing both pleased and intrigued, he produced his most affable smile as an encouragement for her to continue.

'It's something I've been wondering for a while,' she began, already regretting getting into this, but apparently she was going to anyway, 'why didn't you take my job when Claudia offered it to you? You're obviously more than qualified, you've got the support of everyone in the Paris office, so it's not making any sense to me that you should have turned it down.'

To her amazement he laughed. 'Patreesha, I believe you think I am hiding a wicked secret,' he teased.

Because she did, she reddened slightly and turned away, saying, 'Forget it. You obviously have your reasons, and as I'm extremely happy to be in Paris – most of the time – provided you don't try to undermine me . . .'

'Do you know me to do this?' he interrupted, sounding concerned.

She gave him a sidelong look. 'Actually, no, but we both know you could, if you wanted to . . .'

'I can assure you, Patreesha, that I do not want to. I am most content with the position I have, and as the senior vice president *de Paris* I will do everything in my power to make things work for you and for the company. Already, everyone they like and respect you . . .'

'Then they have a funny way of showing it,' she said tartly, 'but let's not get into it. I'd much rather discuss these figures.'

'As you wish,' he conceded graciously, and opened up his own laptop so they could begin.

By the time the plane was preparing to touch down in Nice they'd managed to pass just over an hour in extremely useful debate on how to address the problem of sluggish retail sales. A full and workable strategy would eventually be drawn up by the executive team as a whole, but it was important, if she was to head the meeting, that she went into it not only prepared, but with some proposals for a solution.

'This is a very beautiful approach to an airport,' Frank informed her, looking out of the window as he closed his computer. 'We are flying very low all along the Côte d'Azur. You see.' Pulling back against his headrest, he pointed her to the landscape and as she leaned forward, careful to keep a distance in case he pounced, she soon found herself hypnotised by the dream-like view of sparkling blue sea and spectacular mountains that rose up behind some of the world's most exclusive bays.

'We have down there now the famous bay of Cannes,' he explained, as the plane's shadow glided over the glittering water like a dolphin. 'In the middle of summer the sea here is very much full of yachts belonging to the super-rich people of the world. Ah, you will see, at the end of the Croisette – this is the road that goes in a curve and is lined with palm trees, yes?'

Patsy nodded.

'This building at the end is the Palais des Festivals,' he told her, 'which is where they have the famous film festival in May each year, and where we also go for our annual show in October. You have never been to this show?'

Patsy shook her head. 'I wasn't senior enough until my last year in Europe, and then I had to cancel my trip at the last minute thanks to an attack of appendicitis.'

'Oh, that is too bad,' he sympathised. 'A very painful thing, and had it not happened we might have met sooner, because I have been each year for the past seven. Ah, here we are passing over the Cap d'Antibes, with the very chic and *very* expensive Hotel du Cap at the end. It is beautiful setting, no, surrounded by blue sea. I have been there few times for dinner at the restaurant Eden Roc. I can recommend for the view, but there are better restaurants on the Côte d'Azur.'

Patsy's eyebrows rose. 'You seem to know this area quite well,' she commented.

'This is because I used to spend my summers here at a place called Roquebrune, which is further along the coast, closer to the border with Italy. I do not come so often any more, which is sad, but things change, life moves on. Very soon now we will land in Nice, which is where I am at university for one year, before I go to study in the States.'

Finding herself more interested in this little *Fronk*-biog than she wanted to admit, Patsy said, 'I didn't realise you'd studied in America.'

'*Si*. At Berkeley in California, but this is a long

time ago.' He drew back to give her a clear view of the landing as the plane seemed to skim over the surface of the sea and only just manage to reach dry land before its wheels touched down.

'*Bienvenue au Côte d'Azur*,' Frank said warmly. 'I hope you will have a very pleasant stay, but please remain in your seat until the plane has come to a standstill in case anything fall out of overhead locker.'

Laughing at his impersonation of a flight attendant, Patsy was just feeling as though she might start warming to him when he said, 'This is a very beautiful place for all the beautiful people so you, Patreesha, are going to fit very well in here.'

Slicing him one of her more dangerous looks, she leaned forward to pick up her handbag, making ready to turn on her mobile phone.

In the event they were through the terminal and in the back of a taxi heading towards Nice *Centre* and the Promenade des Anglais before she finally got round to checking both her emails and text messages. Next to her Frank was listening to his voicemails, when his phone started to ring. After checking who it was he clicked on. '*Si, chérie. J'écoute.*'

Though Patsy didn't want to listen to a personal call from a woman – presuming *chérie* was *chérie* and not *chéri* – it was hard not to when he was a mere two feet away.

'Yes, the flight has just arrived,' he was saying in French. 'The weather is very good here, yes. A little cold inland, they say on the forecast, but sunny and warm on the coast . . . *Oh la la, chéri(e)*, I told you yesterday that I will not be back until . . . I am sorry, you will have to . . . I am listening, but you are not. OK, I'm going to end this call now. Goodbye,' and true to his word he cut the connection.

Not wanting to be accused of eavesdropping Patsy gave the appearance of being engrossed in her messages, while dying to ask what all that had been about. She couldn't think how to, though, without giving the impression she was interested in his private life, which she most definitely was not. At least not usually, but in this instance she had to admit she wouldn't mind knowing if *chérie* did have an e at the end, and if so, was *chérie* aware that he was on the French Riviera with another woman, who was his boss, of course, therefore definitely not a *chérie*, but another woman all the same.

'I know you are wondering,' he said after a while, 'so I will tell you that was my wife, but not to worry, she is divorcing me.'

As Patsy's cheeks flushed, her insides performed a peculiar lurch of shock. 'Then I can only compliment her good sense,' she snapped pettily, and to her annoyance he laughed.

A moment later her own phone bleeped with an incoming text.

So much to tell. Call when you can. Hope Riviera is gorgeous. Love Sx PS How are you getting on with Frank?

Trying to ignore fact he's alive, never mind here, Pats texted back. *Riviera stunning.*

And it was, even more so than she'd expected with its dazzling vista of sun-drenched sea, so blue and inviting it was making her toes tingle with the urge to dip them. In the distance the Alps slumbered and swelled like watchful beings, while the pebbled beaches stretched out lazily across the bays, like exotic cats relaxing in the sun. It was no wonder the rich and famous had chosen it as one of their playgrounds, everything about it seemed to exude privilege and glamour, from the massive ocean-going yachts in the marinas, to the grand, glossy hotels, to the palm-lined boulevards where the world was strolling, jogging, cycling, roller skating and even kick-boxing its way through the day.

For the rest of the journey, which lasted about forty minutes, she continued to ignore Frank as she absorbed herself in the sensuous surroundings. She could hear him sending texts and emails, tutting and chuckling and occasionally sighing, fragments of noise washing up like flotsam on her private shores. She wanted to ask him to shut up, but judged it wiser not to engage with him again until forced – which happened when they entered the Principality and began winding through a labyrinth of towering apartment blocks and stunning belle époque villas. At first she could hardly believe how many exclusive car showrooms and international banks were co-existing in such close proximity. The entire place reeked of money in a way she'd never come across before. She found herself wondering about the indigenous people and how their lives blended with the rarefied existence of the tax exiles, indeed if they blended at all. There was probably some invisible barrier that no one with less than thirty, forty, fifty million was allowed to pass, except to clean or cook or garden or chauffeur. She tried to imagine what she'd do if she had a hundred mil in the bank, and had just got round to purchasing her second yacht complete with onboard cinema, jeep, jet skis and helipad when they rounded a sharp bend in the road and the view that unfolded before her virtually took her breath away.

'Wow,' she murmured, gazing down across the sloping sculpture gardens and frothing fountains to where the world-famous casino sat in all its baroque splendour, at the far end of the *place*. The green copper cupolas and rococo turrets glinted like jewels on a gloriously bedecked grande dame, while the shining balustrades and brazen cherubs could be the carriages and retinue in close attendance. She could only imagine the elegant salons and legendary gaming rooms behind the famous facade, and the exclusive clientele that frequented them, but it wasn't too difficult for she'd seen it all many times in films.

'This casino, he is designed by the same person who design the Opera House in Paris,' Frank informed her, sounding as proud as if the architect were an ancestor of his. 'His name was Charles Garnier. He was my great-great-great-uncle on the side of my mother.'

Patsy turned to him sharply, certain he was mocking her, but he appeared to be genuine. However, there was never any telling with Frank, especially when he employed his eyebrows to embellish his story the way he was now.

Turning back as they skirted the edge of the gardens, she watched the casino coming into full view, along with another iconic landmark of Monte

Carlo, the Hotel de Paris. Uniformed valets and doormen were stationed outside to escort their visitors through every step from the car into the lobby, and she couldn't help wondering why Frank hadn't booked them in there.

'Oh, this is because I have memories of times I spend there that I do not enjoy,' he answered when she asked. 'And also because this hotel is *un peu fatigué* now. A little dismal on the inside, very formal and how you say, a little sombre?'

Patsy nodded.

'Whereas the Hotel Hermitage,' he went on, 'well, you will see, because we are now turning the corner, *et . . . voilà.'*

As he fanned out his hands Pats looked up ahead and felt herself starting to smile at the sheer romance of the exquisite white palace in front of them, glinting and sparkling in the midday sun, with sentries of starburst palms and flowering trees. Everything was gleaming like a wet painting in a frame of clear blue Mediterranean sky. 'This is stunning,' she murmured, as the taxi drove across the road and around the gardens to the front doors.

A host of staff was waiting to greet them, one to open the car door, another to stand aside as they entered the hotel, and another to bring in the bags. While Frank went to check them in Pats stood in the middle of the lobby, gazing up at the exquisitely frescoed ceiling and beautiful Tissot-style paintings on the walls. For all she knew they could be as genuine as the pale-coloured marble of the floors and pillars, or the elaborate sprays of fresh flowers that adorned every niche and occasional table.

254

'OK,' Frank said, rubbing his hands in a businesslike manner as he joined her. 'Our first massage is at two, so can I suggest that we freshen up after the flight, and meet back here in half an hour to go over to the spa?'

'But it's only midday,' she protested. 'Why would we want to go so early?'

'To have lunch, of course. There is a very good restaurant on their terrace that will serve us a light meal before we begin the process of destressing and relaxing.'

She nodded slowly. 'OK,' she agreed. Eating lunch with him might be marginally more agreeable than lunching alone, so why not?

'Half an hour it is,' he said, and gesturing for her to go ahead into the lift he surprised her by pressing a button, then stepping out again.

'Where are you going?' she demanded.

'To check that our samples are here,' he replied.

'I don't know my room number,' she shouted, as the doors began closing.

'*Comment?*' he shouted back.

Quickly she fumbled for the button to reopen the doors, but it was too late, they were closed and the lift was starting to rise.

Taking out her mobile she pressed in his number. 'Where am I going?' she demanded when he answered.

'Ah, *si*. Second floor, room seven hundred and thirty.'

'And where are you?'

'Me? I will be next door in seven hundred and thirty-two, but you will be very pleased to hear that there is a private door to connect . . .'

Cutting him off, she stepped out of the lift on the wrong floor and startled an old couple as she made an about turn with a noise that could have been a growl or a laugh, even she wasn't entirely sure which.

'I swear to you,' she was saying to Susannah ten minutes later while pulling open a set of French doors in her luxury room to take a look outside, 'I'm either going to belt that man, or sack him before this weekend's out. He's completely . . . Oh my God, you should see this,' she murmured, as she stepped on to an ornate balcony that overlooked the marina, and a glittering expanse of sea that was so vivid and close she could almost reach out and touch it. 'You have to come here when you're one of the rich and famous,' she told Susannah, meaning it. 'It has to be seen to be believed.'

'I have no problem with that,' Susannah responded. 'Are you meeting the Comtesse de Whatsit while you're there?'

'Du Petits-Louvens,' Patsy supplied, her heart still melting in the beauty of the view. 'No, she's in New York. This is a complimentary weekend for me and *Fronk* – though why the Comtesse should be so generous when she's the customer and we're the supplier, I've no idea. Or when the spa here isn't on the list of those she needs new products for.'

'And you're sure she actually exists?' Susannah prompted. 'It's not some wildly romantic ruse on *Fronk's* part to win you over?'

'Don't worry, I've checked her out, and there's

no question she's who he says she is. I've even had an email from her giving me an idea of the kind of package she's hoping for, so it's all above board.'

'Oh, can you hang on a second, someone's at the door with a parcel I need to sign for.'

As she waited, Patsy's eyes drank in the scenery, up over the mountain that seemed to be tumbling into the town, then back down to the sea where she followed the progress of a flashy white yacht as it slid back towards its mooring. She wondered about the people on board, where they came from and how they'd made their money. How fantastic it would be if she could just trot down there and ask, better still if she could have a look round all those decks and staterooms. Her curious gaze moved on across the bay to where the Grimaldi palace seemed to be melding into an outcrop of rock, home to Prince Albert of Monaco and his stupendously elite little family. It must be quite something waking up to their view every morning, she reflected, looking back to the marina. She imagined them standing at one of the palace windows, or on a balcony as she was now, yawning and stretching as they surveyed it all. It was a bit like being in opposite boxes at the theatre, she decided, though there wouldn't be many stages in the world that could boast the kind of props this one had, when most of them were multimillion-dollar yachts and top-of-the-range Ferraris.

'Back with you,' Susannah said. 'So where were we? Ah yes, the comtesse and *Fronk*. Any idea how he made contact with her in the first place?'

'No, but it's an interesting question, because from what I can make out he seems to have all sorts of amazing connections. I even heard him telling someone the other night that he was going to the Elysée Palace for drinks, but knowing him he was saying it to try and get some kind of rise out of me, which needless to say didn't work.'

'Why? You should ask, maybe he'd invite you along. It would be quite something to have drinks with the *Président de la République*, wouldn't it?'

'Let's put it this way, it would be an improvement on spending a weekend in Monte Carlo with a nutter in Spandex shorts and a sequinned vest.'

'You're not serious,' Susannah choked.

'I wouldn't put it past him, because there's no knowing what he'll turn up in next. Actually, to tell you the truth, I don't understand why he came here. I mean, it's not very masculine, is it, being pummelled and pampered in all kinds of perfumed oils and seawater scrubs?'

'I can't believe you just said that,' Susannah replied.

With a laugh Patsy tore herself from the view and turned back into the room, where the contents of her overnight bag were spilling over the summery blue bedspread like little islands of frivolity in a tropical sea. 'Oh, by the way, he's married,' she said, 'but apparently his supremely sensible wife is divorcing him, presumably on the grounds of him being mad.'

Susannah gave another cry of laughter. 'Does he have any children?' she asked.

'No idea. Honestly, I dare not ask about his private life or he'll take it as some kind of green light, and the last thing I need is him thinking I'm interested in him.'

'But you are.'

'I am *not*.'

'Then why do we spend so much time talking about him?'

Patsy blinked. 'Let's change the subject immediately,' she said forcefully. 'I'm almost done telling you how this place is gorgeous beyond reason. The sun is streaming into my room like it has nowhere else to go, and if I ignore the sound of traffic below I could probably hear nothing more than seagulls and waves. If that isn't bliss, I don't know what is. Now, tell me what's happening your end?'

'You're asking me to follow that!' Susannah protested.

'This is all smoke and mirrors – or diamonds and dreamland. Give me the real stuff. Have you seen a script yet?'

'Yes, as a matter of fact, and I know I *have* to say this, but it's really good. I'm still trying to get myself to accept that I'm playing Marianne, because her name's all over every page. It's such a trip. She's really feisty and awful, and so mad about horses that I'm actually starting to get hooked myself. They're arranging for me to have riding lessons, but I'm not sure where or when, someone's getting back to me on Monday about that. The costume designer's been in touch; she's coming to take my measurements later today, and we're going on a shopping trip next week. Marlene Wyndham sent flowers to congratulate me and to say how pleased she was to welcome me on board – very unexpected, so doubly appreciated.'

'What about Michael Grafton? Have you heard from him yet?'

'Actually, no. I thought I might have, seeing as he got my number from Dorothy, but I guess he's busy and if Marlene's going to be running the show I suppose there's no real reason for him to be in touch.'

'And how's Alan dealing with it now? Still uptight and nervous, or is he starting to settle down a bit?'

'Hard to tell really, but he's doing his best to be supportive, and you have to love him for that when you can understand why he's not thrilled. Who would be when their new live-in partner's about to disappear for most of the week, every week? And the other thing he won't have realised yet is how much I'm going to be in the public eye. Not just as Marianne, but as myself, because I received an email this morning . . . Pats, you should see it. What's not on the list for interviews and photo shoots over the next few weeks isn't worth doing anyway, though whether or not they'll get that much interest remains to be seen. My head's still spinning with it, and if I think about it too much I start feeling sick, because it's terrifying. On the other hand, I can't wait to get going.'

'What about Neve?'

'My darling daughter is so beside herself about it all you'd think it was happening to her, and more than half the time I wish it was.'

'She's going to absolutely love having a famous

mum,' Patsy smiled fondly. 'What girl her age wouldn't, but she's so generous in her spirit and she loves you so much . . . It's no wonder she's over the moon. And I'm sure, once Alan's had some time to get used to it, he'll be equally happy to have a famous wife. Where is he now?'

'Would you believe, playing golf with one of his colleagues – and, wait for this, madam has gone with him to caddy.'

Patsy gave an incredulous laugh. 'Neve?' she said.

'I know, I still can't quite get my head round it either, but off they went at eight o'clock this morning, all clubs and balls, as she so delicately put it. I'm not sure Alan's partner was terribly thrilled when he realised she was tagging along, but he seemed to take it well enough when she jumped into the back seat of his car.'

Patsy was about to respond when she heard someone in the next room, and spun round to eye the connecting door. 'Well, I guess the important thing is that she feels wanted, and accepted,' she said, 'especially now you're going to be away a lot.'

'Exactly what Alan thinks. It'll probably make handling her crush a little more complicated, he reckons, because he doesn't want to encourage it, but at the same time the last thing we need is her feeling rejected, or shut out in any way.'

'I can't imagine you'd . . .' Patsy broke off as the handle of the connecting door started to move downwards. 'Hang on,' she said tartly, 'I'll be right back,' and dropping the phone on the bed she stormed across the room and grabbed

261

the wiggling lever. 'What do you want?' she shouted.

'Ah, Patreesha, I was just making certain the lock is closed in case you tried to walk in on me.'

She gave a gasp of outrage that lost itself in a laugh. 'In your dreams,' she told him. 'Now go away, *allez-vous en*,' and marching back to the phone she said, 'That man is utterly impossible. He actually seems to think I'm going to storm his bastille or something. What a fantasist!'

'I really love the sound of him,' Susannah told her. 'I just want to know when we'll get to meet him.'

'You *won't*! There is absolutely nothing going on between us and never will be, so you're as delusional as he is if you think anything else.'

'OK, I believe you, even if you do protest too much. Now, I'm going to love you and leave you, because I have to go and pick Lola up from the hairdressers. Call again as soon as you can. A vicarious trip to Monte Carlo is better than none at all, and so far, I have to say, I'm having a pretty marvellous time.'

Unable not to laugh, Patsy rang off, and after refreshing her make-up and changing into a pair of pale linen shorts and a T-shirt that turned out to be semi-transparent, she changed again, then went downstairs to meet Frank in the lobby, as arranged. Never mind that they were right next door to one another, the only room she was going to share with him this weekend was the lift – and if that too could be avoided, so much the better.

* * *

'Mum, it's me,' Neve cried down the line. 'Alan asked me to ring and let you know that we won't be back for lunch, OK?'

'I guess so,' Susannah replied, engrossed in the contract that had been hand-delivered while she was talking to Pats.

'We probably won't be home till gone four,' Neve continued. 'He's teaching me how to play and it's really cool. He says I'm quite good already.'

'Really,' Susannah said. Her head was swimming with the figures in front of her. Was someone seriously going to pay her that much for doing something she'd willingly do for nothing if they asked?

'I don't think you'd enjoy it much though,' Neve told her. 'It's not really your thing.'

'No, I can't imagine it would be,' Susannah agreed, turning the page and wanting to whoop with joy simply to see her name at the top of that one too.

'Oh well, I suppose I'd better ring off. Alan's waiting for me in the car. We're going to some pub he knows that's not very far from here.'

'OK, have a lovely time the two of you,' Susannah said. 'I'll probably be out when you get back, but I'll see you this evening. Maybe we can all do something together.'

'Maybe. I'll have to see what Alan says. He might be quite tired after we've been out all day.'

Finally tuning in to Neve, Susannah raised an amused eyebrow at the proprietorial tone, and said, 'Did Sasha get hold of you? She rang about half an hour ago.'

'Yeah, she did. She wants me to go round there

263

tonight, but I'm not sure yet. I said I'd ring her later. Anyway, I'd better go. Love you.'

'Love you too,' Susannah said, and putting the phone down she concentrated again on her contract, wanting to absorb every last detail as though only by doing so could she make any of it start to feel real.

'You know, *Fronk*, I'm really glad you're here,' Patsy murmured drowsily, 'or I might be in danger of thinking I'd died and gone to heaven.'

On the lounger next to her Frank smiled and kept his eyes closed, mainly because they were weighted with sea-mineral-infused cucumber slices.

Whether he was wearing them for effect, or because he was undergoing some kind of beauty routine, Patsy had no idea. Nor would she ask. She was happy simply to lie out on this glorious sun terrace, listening to the gentle slap of the spa's pool coming through the open doors, and inhaling the heady aroma of fresh sea air mixing with the fruity flavours of her cocktail.

She couldn't remember when she'd last felt so relaxed, or so thoroughly and unspeakably pure. Colonic irrigation wasn't a treatment she'd ever imagined herself going in for before today, and she wasn't sure she would again, but feeling this squeaky clean, inside and out, couldn't be a bad thing. Whether or not *Fronk* had taken the plunge, so to speak, she hadn't a clue, and would very much like to keep it that way.

Experiencing a moment's irritation as someone on a nearby lounger broke the tranquillity with a cough, she raised her head for a pinch-herself moment. Yes, she really was on a sun-drenched terrace overlooking the world-famous port of Monaco, all wrapped up in a plush white terry robe, and with a matching velvety towel turbaned around her head. *Fronk*, with his cucumber accessories and complimentary spa slippers, was in similar garb, as were most of their compatriots, with the exception of the Cindy Crawford and Naomi Campbell look-alikes who kept parading up and down in nothing more than a thong.

'These one-piece bikinis are for sale in the shop if you would like one too,' Frank had offered when they'd first sauntered out on to the terrace.

Patsy had sliced him a look that might have thinned down his cucumbers, had he been wearing them then.

'You would look very beautiful in one, I am sure,' he told her earnestly.

She'd been about to say, 'Why don't you get one for yourself?' when she'd wisely stopped herself, for knowing him he would. Even now the thought of him prancing around the terrace in little more than an eyepatch-sized groin coverage on the end of a gold chain was making her uneasy, so she dismissed the scary image and began to wonder instead about dinner. She'd already decided she was going to eat on the restaurant terrace, and maybe she'd have a drink at the bar first, or perhaps she'd wander down to the port for an aperitif. She still wasn't sure about the Casino later. She'd never been a gambler, but to be right next to it and not go in . . .

'Ah, is it that time already?' Frank murmured sleepily.

Since he hadn't moved a muscle, Patsy said, 'No, much later.'

When he laughed his dazzling white teeth made his five o'clock shadow look even darker, or was it the other way round?

'Maybe we should go to get dressed for the evening,' he said, lifting a cucumber to have a peer out. 'I have booked a taxi for seven to take us over to Monaco.'

Not sure which issue to address first, the dinner, the taxi or the destination, she heard herself say, 'I thought we were in Monaco.'

'Ah, maybe you do not realise that the Principality is in four *quartiers*,' he said helpfully. 'Monaco-Ville, the old town, where is the palace; Monte Carlo, where is the Casino; La Condamine which have its own harbour; and Fontvieille, which is the newest *quartier* and was built on land reclaimed from the sea.'

'Really,' she remarked, actually quite interested to know that.

'So this evening we go to Monaco for to have dinner with some of my friends. They invite us to their home and they are very much looking forward to meeting you. I have not seen them for a long while, so it will be a happy reunion I am sure. Albert I was at school with, and Caroline I met later when we were all studying in the United States.'

Patsy became very still, not sure whether to go with this or not. In the end, she said, 'Are you telling me that you are friends with the Monégasque royal family?'

266

He merely smiled.

Reaching over she plucked off his cucumbers and said, 'You're winding me up again.'

'I guess, unless you come, you will never know,' he responded.

Infuriated, she stuffed the cucumbers in his drink and rose to her feet.

'I know it's a wind-up,' she said to Susannah on the phone when she got back to her room, 'but what if it isn't?'

'Either way, I'm sure you'll have a great time.'

Patsy drew breath to argue before realising she agreed.

'You're in Monte Carlo, for heaven's sake. Lighten up and enjoy it.'

'I am enjoying it, or I would be if that twit wasn't with me.'

'Rubbish, he's making it for you, and if you weren't so stubborn you'd not only realise it, you'd be able to admit it.'

'OK, subject change coming up: what are *you* doing this evening?'

'Well, Lola and I are going to hit the dizzy highs of Battersea bingo, but I don't want you to start getting envious. I know it's going to be hard having to stay there and go to dinner at the palace, but someone has to do it.'

With a chuckle, Patsy said, 'Where are Neve and Alan?'

'One's at Sasha's, the other's gone into the office.'

'On a Saturday night?'

'Apparently. I spoke to him a few minutes ago. He's sounding pretty fed up about it, but it's a patient he inherited from the previous guy, he says, so he doesn't want to let him down this early in their relationship.'

'No, I can see that wouldn't be a good idea. What time does he expect to be back?'

'About nine, I think. He'll collect Neve on the way.'

Patsy nodded and said nothing.

'Hello? Are you still there?' Susannah asked.

'Still here. So, what am I going to wear?'

'What did you take?'

'Nothing suitable for a palace, that's for sure.' Then, 'How can *Fronk* know the royal family? It has to be a wind-up.'

'Well, like he said, you won't know unless you go. So, *mon amie, je vous souhais un très bon appétit, et une merveilleuse soirée.*'

'I'd forgotten you speak French.'

'Nothing like as well as you do, but I comfort myself with the fact that you went to degree level while I dropped out at A. Anyway, Lola's about to serve us up some tea before we go, and she's asking if you'll send her love to Albert and Caroline.'

'I'm glad you're all having so much fun at my expense.'

'Which isn't nearly as much as you're having, you just haven't realised it yet. But you will. *Bonne chance.*'

As the line went dead Patsy clicked off too, and though she remained convinced Frank was playing some kind of game, she began dressing for dinner anyway. Actually, she was starting to hope that it would turn out to be a hoax, because as gorgeous as her little black Gucci number was with its accompanying Manolos, she'd had both for over two years now, so they weren't only out of date, they were also getting a tad low on lustre. Besides which, she'd never have chosen an outfit with such a daring neckline or so short a skirt for a royal rendezvous. This made her wonder what they were doing in her bag anyway, when there was only supposed to be Frank for company, but there was no time to go there.

With a final dab of Prestige Dix-Huit and a last critical glance in the mirror, she left her room and took the lift down to the lobby, determined to meet him there rather than let him anywhere near an open door to her room.

'*Ah, comme tu es belle, chérie,*' he gushed when he saw her coming towards him.

'I am not your *chérie,*' she muttered through the smile she kept up for the benefit of anyone watching, 'nor have I given you permission to *tutoyer* me.'

'I want only to admire you and make you feel like a princess,' he responded smoothly.

She arched an eyebrow. 'I think one per evening is enough, don't you?' she retorted chippily.

His eyes twinkled as he said, 'In my heart, it will only be you.'

'Oh, get me out of here before I throw up.'

'You need the boo-kette?' he asked solicitously.

Ignoring him, she turned towards the door and hoped no one was watching as she went into a little skid on the marble floor. Fortunately she righted herself before Frank could leap to her aid, but when she put out a hand to open the glass door as she marched towards it she found only air and sailed straight through with unnecessary speed.

'If you're laughing,' she muttered threateningly as Frank came up beside her.

'Would I?' he responded, sounding as though he was about to burst with mirth.

The drive from Monte Carlo to Monaco-Ville took less than twenty minutes, most of which she spent enjoying the sights that ranged from wizened old ladies on spindly heels with big hennaed hair and cute little dogs, to a gold-encrusted Aston Martin, to the inevitable girthy old git with a stick of eye candy on one arm and a Rolex Oyster on the other.

It was towards the end of the journey that she ventured to ask Frank, very casually, how he'd managed to interest the Comtesse du Petits-Louvens in their products.

'But it was she who approach me,' he told her, with one of his Gallic shrugs. 'She call me on the telephone one day and say, *Fronk*, I want to freshen up my spas and you are the one to do it.'

Patsy threw him a dubious look. How had he managed to make that sound smutty, or was it her own dirty mind? Whatever, such a call out of the blue didn't seem very likely to her, but since they were just pulling into a very glossy cobbled square *right in front of the Grimaldi palace*, now wasn't the time to take it any further.

'Oh no!' Neve shrieked into her mobile. 'That is too major. Are you serious?'

'I swear,' Susannah laughed from her end. 'She

just texted me to say they were right outside the palace, about to go in.'

'Oh my God.' Neve turned boggle-eyed to Sasha. 'My godmother is only about to have dinner with Prince Albert of Monaco,' she informed her.

'Who?' Sasha asked. She wasn't in a good mood.

'So where are *you*?' Neve asked Susannah.

'Outside the bingo,' and registering the absurdity of the contrast they both burst out laughing. 'I'd better go back in,' Susannah said. 'Lola's taking care of my card. I just had to call and let you know. I can hardly wait to talk to Pats in the morning. Anyway, see you later.'

As the line went dead Neve rang off too, and turned her glittering eyes back to Sasha. 'This is so amazing,' she declared. 'My mother's about to become famous and my godmother's in Monaco dining with *royalty*.'

'Yeah, and my dad knows Robbie Williams,' Sasha retorted, 'it still doesn't mean Ricky Shawton wants to go out with me, or that you're ever going to get anywhere with you-know-who.'

Neve stiffened.

'Are you seriously going to have golf lessons?' Sasha sneered sulkily as she flopped back on the bed. 'It sounds mega boring, if you ask me.'

'It's not when you're there,' Neve told her. 'It was really cool, being out in all that fresh air and nature . . .'

'Do you think I should send Ricky a text inviting him to the next Robbie concert? My dad can always get tickets . . .'

'No way. You've got no idea when there's going to be one, and it'll look desperate, Sash.

Whatever else we are, we must not look desperate, remember?'

Sasha nodded woefully and reached for her Coke. 'So what are you going to do?' she asked, the straw still in her mouth.

Though Neve knew very well what she was talking about she pretended not to, until collapsing into the sheer hopelessness of it all, she wailed, 'I don't know. I've never felt like this before. It's awful, Sash. I mean, it's wonderful, because he's so kind and lovely and . . . Oh I don't know. This is the worst thing ever. At least where Ricky's concerned you're not in the same house as him, so you don't have to watch him with Lena Laurence the way I have to watch Alan with Mum in our house.'

'Well, you're the one who got them together,' Sasha reminded her snappily. 'You should be pleased they're happy.'

'I am. I mean . . . No, I am, but sometimes . . . You know, I really think he's interested in me too. Not just like I'm a daughter . . . Well, definitely in that way, but . . .'

'Why wouldn't he be interested in you? Everyone else is.'

'Oh, don't be like that. It's not true, and anyway, I only want him, but I can't have him because it's not *right*. He's my mother's partner, so he's supposed to be like a dad, and he is, most of the time, but . . .'

'He's not your dad. Not for real, and loads of people get involved with someone twenty or thirty years older than them. Look at Melinda's parents. Her dad's got to be at least thirty years older than her mum.'

Neve gave a shiver of nerves and closed her eyes. 'I wish you wouldn't say things like that,' she groaned, 'they make me go all funny.'

Sasha shrugged and got up from the bed. 'Listen, you know you've got the hots for him, and he's bound to have them for you too, so why don't you stop going on about it and do something for once in your life?'

Neve looked at her aghast. 'What do you mean?' she mumbled, not sure she wanted to hear the answer, while dying to.

'Well, when he drives you home later why don't you tell him how you feel? Or put your arms round him to say thank you for something and turn it into a snog.'

The mere thought of it turned Neve so weak inside that she couldn't even summon a reply. She was only able to stare at Sasha and wonder wildly, terrifyingly, wonderfully, if she could ever find enough courage to take her advice. If she did, what would happen then? But she wouldn't, she just knew it, because he might get angry, or disgusted, or worse tell her mum, and if he did that she'd never be able to face either of them again for the rest of her life.

Chapter Thirteen

The persistent ringing of the phone beside her bed finally brought Patsy up through many layers of sleep to a place she didn't immediately recognise, or, in fact, even want to be part of, her head was pounding so hard. The bed seemed to be swinging on some kind of pendulum, making her feel nauseous and giddy, then it steadied and she began to register fierce blades of sunlight spilling in through the cracks in the shutters to dissolve in a misty glow over her surroundings. She blinked a couple of times to try and clear her vision, then, as though a veil was being slowly peeled away from her senses, it started coming back to her. She was in Monte Carlo, the Hotel Hermitage, and the piercing shrill of the phone was what had hooked her out of blessed oblivion.

Wincing as she fumbled for the bedside receiver, she tried to remember how much she'd had to drink last night, but it wasn't a good idea because the mere thought of alcohol started her insides churning again. 'Hello,' she mumbled, hardly able to get her mouth open, it was so dry.

'Pats, it's me. Is it OK to talk?' Susannah whispered. 'We've been trying your mobile for ages . . .'

'What?' Patsy struggled to sit up, but thought better of it as everything started swooping and rolling again. 'What time is it?' she asked, wanting water now more than air.

'It must be about ten where you are. Are you still in bed? We've been dying to hear about your dinner last night, but if it's not convenient to talk . . .'

'No, it's fine,' which it clearly was not, but that wasn't Susannah's fault. She looked around the room, and slowly, like a horror scene coming into terrible focus, she began to register the other side of the bed. There was a dip in the pillow and the covers were turned back. 'Oh my God,' she muttered, feeling horribly faint.

'What?' Susannah prompted.

'Don't let this be true,' Patsy implored, the words sounding breathy and desperate on her parched lips. Then, realising she didn't have any clothes on, she let out a whimper of pure despair.

'What's going on?' Susannah cried.

'I don't know,' Patsy said weakly. 'I can't . . . Oh no,' she wailed. A purple jacket was slung over the back of a chair, looking as comfortable as if it had lived there all its life.

'For heaven's sake,' Susannah urged, 'what went on last night? The last we heard you were outside the palace, about to go in.'

'Hang on, I have to do something,' Patsy said, and dropping the phone on the bed she wrapped herself in a sheet and stumbled over to the bathroom to press an ear to the door. Nothing. She waited. Still nothing. Turning the handle she gave a tentative push, and the door creaked open.

Half-expecting a monstrous 'Boo!' or worse, a naked *Fronk*, or even worse, both, she peered in. The room was empty and didn't, thankfully, appear to have been used in recent times. Next she went to the main door, opened it briefly, spotted a 'Do not Disturb' sign hanging on the handle and closed it again.

After sliding the bolt she went back to the phone. 'Susannah, this is a disaster,' she croaked. 'I think I might have slept with *Fronk*.'

Susannah spluttered with laughter. 'What do you mean, you *think*?' she said. 'How can you not know?'

Not sure herself, Patsy said, 'I was drinking this stuff last night . . . What was it called . . . ? I can't remember . . . Oh God, I need water,' she rasped, and headed off to the minibar.

'What about Albert and Caroline?' Susannah wanted to know. 'Did you meet them?'

Finding a bottle of Evian, Patsy sucked down half of it in one go, then repeated, breathlessly, 'Albert and Caroline. Yes, that's right. They came out of the restaurant to meet us.' She gulped down more water. 'The taxi dropped us in front of the palace . . . *Fronk* paid the driver – that's when I sent you a text – then this couple came out of nowhere throwing their arms around him, and me, even though I'd never clapped eyes on them before. They turned out to be Albert and Caroline Neuman, old friends of *Fronk*, residents of Monaco, and surprise, surprise, not a serene highness between them.'

Susannah was laughing so hard that Patsy might have too, were that appalling jacket not still winking at her from the chair.

'Go on,' Susannah prompted.

Returning to the bed, Patsy said, 'There's a restaurant right opposite the palace, which is where it turned out they'd sprung from . . . They were a lovely couple . . .' She was racking her brains, trying to force out the details, and after a while a fractured slide show started to emerge. 'He's American, into electronics of some kind, I think he said, and hilariously funny, though God only knows what we were laughing at, I just remember doing a lot of it. She's French, and designs pet clothes for the rich and stupid. We ended up going back to their place – you should see it, it's straight out of Hollywood, all art deco and movie posters – and that's where we got stuck into whatever it was . . . Oh God,' she groaned as her stomach recoiled from the mere thought of the colourless liqueur that had seemed to have some kind of golden-egg quality about it: once her glass was empty it simply, magically, refilled itself. 'I don't know how we got back to the hotel,' she went on, 'it's all a blank, but *Fronk*'s jacket's here, and the other side of the bed's obviously been slept in, and . . .' Her eyes closed in abject misery. 'I don't have any clothes on.'

Susannah burst out laughing.

'Please don't,' Patsy complained. 'I know it might seem funny, but I have to face him now, *and* I have to work with him, and I can't believe I've got myself into this mess. I mean, I know nothing happened, but . . . What the hell was I drinking?'

'You tell me,' Susannah replied. 'Grappa? Marc?'

'Marc, that was it,' Patsy confirmed. 'Ugh, God,' she added, almost gagging.

Susannah gave a murmur of sympathy. 'Did you know that stuff can be over a hundred per cent proof?' she said.

'I do now,' Patsy replied, putting a hand to her head. 'What am I going to do?' she implored. 'I can hardly ask him if we did the deed. Knowing him, he'll say yes even if we didn't.'

'You must be able to tell. How do you feel, you know, down there?'

'I've no idea. My head's in such a state that the rest of me has given up trying to be noticed. Anyway, wait for this, I had a colonic rinse-out yesterday, so that might be confusing things.'

'This is getting more hysterical by the minute,' Susannah told her. 'I'm not sure you're safe to be let out alone.'

'I'm having serious doubts myself. Anyway, I'd better go. I need to shower and I'm supposed to be having another massage treatment at noon, I seem to recall. How come I remember that and nothing else? Ow. Mustn't get worked up, it hurts. Before I go, is everything OK with you?'

Still laughing, Susannah said, 'Fantastic. I won twenty quid at bingo last night, and my schedule's filling up so fast for the next few weeks that I have to go out later to buy a bigger diary.'

'And how are things with Alan?'

'Fine. We had a long chat after Neve had gone to bed last night, and he seems to be coming round to it all now. He's just popped out for the papers, actually. There's supposed to be quite a bit in them about the new series, apparently, and Neve's

278

sitting here, listening in as best she can to what we're saying.'

'Oh God, she doesn't know . . . Sorry, I have to go. Big white telephone. Urgent. Talk later.'

After dropping the phone she scooted to the bathroom and spent the next ten minutes on her knees in front of the loo wishing she was dead. Snatches of the return journey to the hotel were now starting to emerge through the fog, and unless her memory was playing her vile tricks she'd snogged Frank in the back of the taxi, and worse, *far, far, far* worse, she might have tried to seduce him in the lift. On the other hand she could be recalling a dream – *nightmare* – because everything after the scene that-please-God-didn't-happen-in-the-lift was still a blank.

When finally she managed to struggle to her feet she found that in spite of some lingering dizziness she was feeling marginally better. A vigorous splashing of cold water over her face improved things a little further, then going back into the room she began tracking down her mobile phone. She discovered it in one of her Manolo Blahniks, which prompted a nasty little memory flash of trying to order room service with a shoe, then turned the phone on to check her messages. Most were from Susannah, left that morning, a couple that had come in overnight were from friends, nothing was from Frank. She wasn't sure whether she was relieved or unnerved by that, but it hardly mattered when the bathroom was in urgent need of her presence again.

Eventually, after a very long hot, then cold, shower, a luxurious hairwash and a rather enlivening spell on the bidet, she downed another half-litre of water and climbed into a pair of tracksuit bottoms and a Dolce and Gabbana T-shirt. Though moving any further into this day remained a direction she did *not* want to take – given the choice, she'd be back-pedalling so fast she'd crash into yesterday and maybe even have the good fortune to land up somewhere in pre-noon Friday – reverse was sadly not an option, so she put on her sunglasses, assumed her bravest face and went off to confront her shame.

She found Frank having breakfast on the terrace, looking annoyingly perky and at one with the world as he soaked up the sun, read his paper and sipped his coffee.

'Ah, at last,' he smiled cheerily as she arrived at his table. 'I tried to wake you, but you could not hear me, or maybe you did not want to. How are you feeling this morning?'

Aware of how close they were to other guests who no doubt spoke both languages, she sank down in a chair and mumbled that she'd like a coffee too, please.

Summoning a waiter he ordered a double espresso and a refill for himself, then turned back to her with a mischievous twinkle in his eyes. 'Would you care for something to eat?' he offered kindly.

She almost felt her face turn green.

'I think that must be a no,' he decided.

'Just tell me,' she said, keeping her voice low. 'Did we . . . ? Last night, when we got back . . . Did you . . . ?'

His head was bent forward in order to hear her, but when she stopped he turned to regard her in confusion.

'You know what I'm trying to say,' she hissed angrily.

'I do?' he asked.

'Don't make me spell it out.'

He blinked. 'I am sorry, I think you must or I will not understand.'

Wanting to thump him, she cast a quick look round and said through her teeth, 'Did we have sex last night?'

He sat back in shock, then very slowly a smile started to creep across his face. 'You do not remember?' he said, clearly relishing this moment with every molecule of his sadly warped sense of humour.

'If I did I wouldn't be asking, would I?'

'No, I suppose you would not,' he agreed. 'Well, I could consider your poor memory an insult to my masculine pride, but I think I understand what is the case here. You are pretending not to remember because you are embarrassed, or maybe a little shy, about this very important milestone in our relationship.'

Patsy felt her fingers curl with intent. 'I'm neither embarrassed nor shy,' she lied, 'I just want an answer. Did we, or did we not make a terrible mistake?'

'For me there was no mistake,' he assured her.

'Oh God,' she murmured, starting to feel faint again. 'Frank, I was extremely drunk . . .'

'Yes, this is true.'

'Whatever I might have said, or done, I wasn't

in my right mind so you mustn't read anything into it.'

'I see. So you did not mean to happen what did?'

'*No*, absolutely not.'

'Then what did you mean to happen?'

She opened her mouth but instead of words only air came out. 'My brain isn't up to this, this morning,' she told him, 'you have to give me a straight answer. Did we, or did we not sleep together last night?'

Picking up her hand he held it tenderly between his own. 'It is not a problem,' he said wickedly, 'I am very discreet. Now I am afraid I must go. My next massage is at eleven forty-five and already I am late,' and after planting a friendly kiss on her knuckles he downed the rest of his coffee, tucked the paper under his arm and marched jauntily off towards the spa. The only thing he didn't do was kick up his heels in a chipper little quickstep, but he was clearly so pleased with himself he might just as well have done.

'I'm going over to Melinda's to do some home-work,' Neve announced, carrying her school bag into the kitchen. 'Janey's coming too, so her mum's picking me up on the way past.'

'No Sasha?' Susannah asked, sliding the Sunday papers on to a chair to make some room on the table.

'Don't you ever listen to anything I say?' Neve sighed. 'I told you earlier, she's gone to her gran's in Brighton today.'

'I'm sorry, yes, you did mention it. So how long are you going to be? We're eating about six, so I'd like you back by then. Alan can always collect you when he goes for Lola.'

'Cool. Oh, I expect that's them to say they're outside,' she cried as the phone started to ring, and grabbing her bag she took off down the hall.

'Don't I get a kiss?' Susannah called after her.

Spinning on her heel, Neve came to plant a peck on her cheek, and before she could zoom off again Susannah grabbed her in a giant bear hug. 'OK, off you go,' she said, turning to the phone. 'I'll let them know you're on your way out.'

Needing no more encouragement Neve ran back down the hall, and was already going through the door as Susannah said 'Hello,' into the receiver.

'Susannah? It's Michael Grafton.'

Feeling a leap in her heart, partly because she'd expected to hear Janey, but mainly because his voice had such a sonorous resonance, she cast a quick glance out to the garden to where Alan was putting in some new plants. With the door closed he wouldn't be able to hear, so feeling free to inject an equal warmth into her own tone she said, 'Hi, how are you?'

'I'm fine. I hope it's OK to call on a Sunday, but I believe your schedule's already pretty crowded for the coming week, and I wanted to find out if you'd be free to have lunch with me on Tuesday or Thursday?'

Experiencing another fluttering inside, along with a heady surge of elation, she said, 'That would be lovely. I think it'll have to be Tuesday because I'm pencilled in to go shopping with Lizzy from costume on Thursday.'

'Then Tuesday it is. I'll be at my London office, which is in Soho, but if it's not convenient to come into town I'll be happy to . . .'

'Soho's great. I'm meeting the publicists in Covent Garden at three thirty, so that should work out well.'

'Actually, it's very good timing, because I was hoping to have a chat with you before you got together with them. So shall we say one o'clock at Vasco and Piero's? I'll text you my mobile number in case something crops up in the meantime, but provided it doesn't, I'll see you then. Oh, and by the way, congratulations. We're all thrilled to have you on board.'

'Thank you,' she said softly. 'I'm thrilled too.' She wanted to ask if he was responsible for the change in her casting, but decided it might make her sound flirtatious, or perhaps eager to develop some kind of exclusivity with him, so she simply repeated the date and time they were meeting and said goodbye.

As she put the phone down Alan came through the door, stomping his feet on the mat and carrying a newspaper package of earthy bulbs he'd just taken from one of the beds. 'Brr, it's chilly out there,' he said. 'Seems someone forgot to tell the weather it's May tomorrow. Who was that on the phone?'

Susannah turned back to the sink. 'Just Michael Grafton,' she answered, making it sound as offhand as possible.

Alan looked up from the bulbs he was about to

plonk down on the floor. 'On a Sunday afternoon?' he said. 'Doesn't he have a personal life?'

'I've no idea, but I don't suppose making a phone call precludes one.'

'So what did he want?'

'To invite me to lunch on Tuesday.'

There was a lengthy pause before he said, 'I see. So would this be just you and him, or is anyone else going to be there?'

Since she didn't actually know the answer to that, even though she'd assumed it would be just the two of them, she prevaricated by saying, 'He wasn't very specific about who else he's invited, but I think it's a kind of welcome to the main cast. Anyway, I thought it was nice of him to ring and congratulate me, which was the other reason for his call.'

Alan nodded slowly, then catching the plaintive expression in her eyes he sighed heavily and said, 'I'm sorry. I promise to be more supportive and the next thing I know I'm down at the first hurdle. It's great that he called, and that he's invited you to lunch.'

Knowing he didn't really mean it, but appreciating the effort, she smiled affectionately and went to put her arms around him. 'I think he might be giving me, or us, some pointers on what to discuss with the publicists,' she told him, 'or that's how it sounded. Anyway, I'll find out on Tuesday. Right now, I'm much more interested in taking advantage of having the house to ourselves for a while. Neve's gone to Melinda's and won't be back until you pick her up at the same time as Lola.'

His eyes narrowed with interest as they gazed

down into her own. 'Really?' he murmured. 'So exactly how were you thinking we might spend this free time we suddenly have?'

With a coquettish smile she said, 'Why don't you tell me what you'd like to do?'

'Mmm. You really want to know?' he said, touching his forehead to hers.

She nodded. 'I really want to know.'

'Well, the first thing I'd like to do,' he said gruffly, 'is make love to you right here, over the table.'

As a bolt of desire flicked through her, she pressed herself to him and found him already hard. 'Then I think you'd better go and lock the front door just in case Neve pops back for something,' she whispered.

'Consider it done,' and after kissing her lingeringly on the mouth he went to turn down the latch.

By the time he returned she'd removed her shirt and camisole top and was reaching behind her to unclasp her bra. He stood in the doorway watching, moaning softly as her beautiful breasts were slowly set free.

'You're amazing,' he said huskily.

She watched him coming towards her, feeling her hair falling loosely around her shoulders and the erotic sensation of air on her skin. As he stooped to suck her nipples into his mouth she gave a gasp of pleasure and slid her hands into his hair, loving the feel of his tongue and fingers, and wanting to be naked now, with his body enveloping hers.

Neither of them had any thought for time as they finished undressing and began to make love tenderly, erotically, and even violently over the table. From there they moved to a chair where she sat across his lap; then they were against a wall with her legs around his waist, and eventually they were on the sitting-room floor panting and writhing as they began climbing towards an explosive climax. When they finally soared through the barriers of sensation she was sitting astride him, clutching his hands to her breasts and riding him with all her might.

'That was incredible,' he told her a while later, holding her close, his breath only now beginning to steady. They were still on the floor, naked and exhilarated and utterly exhausted.

She smiled and stroked his face as she gazed into his gentle brown eyes. She was thinking of all the lonely Sunday afternoons she'd spent worrying and stressing and feeling so afraid nothing would ever change that she didn't even dare to tell herself it would. And now here she was, in the arms of Alan Cunningham, her first big love, who'd rescued her from a well of sadness and difficulties too numerous to recall, and who made her feel so happy and cherished that she longed to do the same for him and more.

'I wish we could spend whole weekends like this,' he murmured, 'never bothering with clothes, making love whenever we feel like it.'

'We'll make them happen,' she promised, 'because it's what I'd love too.' Not that she wanted to shut Neve out, but if she was going to be away most weeks from now on, the time she spent with Alan was going to be more precious than ever.

Eventually they made their way back to the kitchen and had barely finished dressing when the front door burst open and Neve rushed in shouting, 'Hi! It's only me! Have to go to the loo.'

As she charged up the stairs Susannah turned to Alan, her eyes wide with disbelief. 'I thought you put the latch down,' she whispered.

'So did I,' he whispered back.

She looked along the hall again, and feeling the dizziness of such a narrow escape coming over her she started to laugh.

'Don't,' he said, laughing too. 'That was way too close for comfort.'

'You're telling me.' Pressing her hands to her cheeks, she took a couple of deep breaths. 'OK, it didn't happen,' she told herself firmly. 'She didn't catch us, so no need to be embarrassed, or to go on standing here like a couple of kids whose parents have just walked in on them.'

Putting an arm around her he went on laughing. 'I think we've been here before,' he reminded her drily.

'Oh my God,' she groaned as the memories came flooding back. 'Haven't we just? You must remember the time we bunked off school and went over to your place, and it turned out that all the time we were doing it your dad was asleep upstairs?'

He laughed as he cringed. 'How could I ever forget? He'd come home with the flu, and we only found out when Mum rang to check up on him and I answered the phone.'

'I wish you could have seen the look on your face,' she gasped, finding it as hilarious now as she had back then. 'You went completely white when you realised he was upstairs. I think you might even have whimpered before you managed to get any words out.'

With a roll of his eyes, he said, 'You know, I often wondered if he heard us and never said anything. He must have, unless he was in a coma.'

'Oh and then there was the time with Lola and Fred,' Susannah cried. 'Do you remember? They came back from bingo early and we were *in their bed*? How terrible was that, getting into their bed, but we didn't think anything of it then.'

'It might not have been so bad if our clothes hadn't been in your room,' he added. 'Creeping along the hall in the buff, with the living-room door open and them sitting there watching TV, is emblazoned on my memory for all time.'

'Mine too,' she replied breathlessly. Then, hearing Neve coming back down the stairs, she attempted a rapid sober-up.

'What's so funny?' Neve demanded, as she came into the kitchen. 'I could hear you all the way upstairs.'

'Nothing,' Susannah answered. 'Just a few old memories.'

Neve eyed her suspiciously. 'Well, as long as it wasn't about me,' she said, and going to tug open the fridge door she snatched out a packet of crab sticks and a seafood dip.

'Why would it be about you?' Susannah said, glancing at Alan before turning her attention to preparing their meal. 'You're not even funny.'

'Oh, and I suppose that was. Ha, ha, very good. Please excuse me while I get hysterical.'

Raising her eyebrows Susannah decided to let it drop, and said, in a chatty sort of way, 'So how come you're back early?'

'If you must know, we finished our homework so Janey's mum came to get us. Anything wrong with that?'

Not bothering to bite her tongue again, Susannah said, 'No, but something seems to be with you.'

Neve's cheeks flushed angrily. 'There's nothing wrong with me,' she said tartly. 'I just happen to find all this joking about and giggling a bit childish, frankly.'

'Oh, do you now? Well, there's a coincidence, because I'm finding your attitude a bit childish too, *frankly.*'

Neve glared at her in fury, but after her eyes flicked to Alan she only wrapped up the crab sticks again and stuffed them back in the fridge.

'Has someone upset you?' Susannah ventured, feeling certain it was her, though unable to think how she'd managed it.

'What's it to you?'

'I'm just trying . . .'

'I'm cool, OK, so drop it.' With a tight, stony face she grabbed an apple from the bowl and bit into it. 'So when are you off to Derbyshire?' she asked, as Susannah went back to scrubbing the potatoes.

'The last week of May. Why?'

Neve banged down the apple. 'For God's sake, I'm just trying to make conversation . . .'

'OK,' Susannah cut in, 'maybe we should start this again. I'm leaving . . .'

'Oh forget it. I'm not staying around here to be got at. I'll be upstairs in my room if anyone wants me. Let me know when dinner's ready.'

'Actually,' Susannah said, as she started to flounce off, 'you might think about helping to prepare it. We're not slaves . . .' She looked down as Alan put a hand on her arm.

'Let her go,' he said softly. 'There's no point getting into an argument about nothing.'

Not feeling at all inclined to take his advice, Susannah watched Neve stalk off down the hall, annoyed and baffled and still on the brink of calling her back.

'For what it's worth,' Alan said quietly as Neve stomped up the stairs, 'I think it's me she's unhappy with, she's just taking it out on you.'

Susannah looked at him in surprise.

'It was something that happened last night in the car,' he said with a sigh. 'When we got back here she gave me a hug to say thanks for picking her up, and then she kissed me in a way that was borderline inappropriate.'

Susannah's mouth fell open. 'Oh my God, she's taking this crush too far,' she said harshly. 'I'm sorry. I'll talk to her . . .'

'No, don't do that. It'll only embarrass her further if she knows I've told you, and she's clearly already having a hard enough time. She'll get over it. Any day now she'll fall head over heels for someone her own age, and along with all her father issues I'll be forgotten. Now, shall I put the chicken in?'

Susannah nodded distractedly. 'Tell me,' she said after a while, still appalled by the image of it, 'how did you handle it when she did that? What did you say?'

He shrugged dismissively. 'I just made light of it, as though it had been a mistake,' he answered, 'and for all I know it might have been. So the best thing now is to let it drop, because blowing it out of proportion won't help at all.'

'No,' Susannah mumbled, 'I don't suppose it will.'

With merriment in his eyes he said, 'Will you please take that frown off your face, beautiful woman, while I go and get Lola?'

After he'd gone Susannah went on debating whether to go and talk to Neve, feeling she ought, but unable to work out how to broach the matter without putting Neve on the defensive. Embarrassment would inevitably make her prickly, and when put together with teenage hormones and the angst of unrequited love the scene was very likely to flare up into something they'd both rather avoid. However, to think of Neve bewildered and imagining herself in love, without trying to do something to help her, was going right against her maternal instincts.

'Hello?' she said, drying her hands as she answered the phone.

'I swear there's a conspiracy going on somewhere to throw me together with this idiot at every possible opportunity,' Patsy declared angrily.

Susannah burst out laughing. 'Where are you?' she said. 'I thought you'd be on your way back to Paris by now.'

'So did I, but the flight's been delayed so I have to go on suffering this twit for many more hours than is humanly possible without one of us ending up injured.'

'I take it he still hasn't told you what happened last night?'

'No. He just gives me a knowing little wink every now and again and says it has made him very, very 'appy. Bastard! It didn't happen though. I know it didn't.'

'Then you've nothing to worry about.'

'Exactly. He just wants me to think it did, because it amuses him to watch me suffer. And if he bangs on about discretion one more time I'll knock his flaming teeth out. In fact, I might anyway, because they're getting on my nerves. OK, now that's off my chest, how are things your end?'

Still laughing, Susannah said, 'Believe me, nowhere near as entertaining as at yours, but you'll probably be interested to hear that Michael Grafton rang earlier.'

'I certainly am. What did he say?'

'He's invited me to lunch on Tuesday. I'm not entirely sure whether it's just the two of us, but I kind of got the impression it is.'

'How cosy. Did he say anything else?'

'Only that they were all thrilled to have me on board.'

'And privileged,' Patsy added, 'but they might not fully realise that yet. Have you told Alan about the lunch?'

'Yes. He didn't take it too well at first, but then he remembered his promise to be supportive and we've just had a lovely afternoon together, so I think he's finally beginning to realise that he has no need to be jealous. Whereas Neve, on the other hand, is a different story. I can't go into it now, because she's in the house, but basically she might have come on to Alan last night.'

'Oh God,' Patsy groaned in dismay. 'I was afraid of something like this. What happened?'

'She tried to kiss him, apparently. He seems to have got out of it pretty well, but she's obviously been left feeling hurt and angry and I don't know whether to try discussing it with her, or to do as Alan says and leave it. What do you think?'

'Mm, I'm not sure. It's a tricky one. I guess my initial instinct is to agree with Alan, but left unchecked there's no knowing how far she might go. Still, she's got her head pretty well screwed on, so I can't really see her doing anything too stupid.'

'No, me neither, which is why I'm daring to hope that it was just a rash moment that might have the happy outcome of sobering her up enough not to want to try anything like it again.'

'I'm sure it will,' Patsy said. 'Now I have to go, I'm afraid, our flight's finally boarding. I wonder if I can bribe someone to give *Fronk* an al fresco row all to himself?'

Chapter Fourteen

Susannah was finding it so energising being in the heart of the West End that she was unable to keep the smile from her face as she strode through the warm, cluttered streets of Soho. She could have been walking on air. Everything, from the noise of the traffic to the decrepit stateliness of the buildings, to the sheer vibrancy of the people rushing about, was like an electric charge shooting straight into her veins. She was someone at last, not just a blonde making a few heads turn with her long legs and captivating smile, but an actress soon to be on their screens and in their papers virtually every day of the week. More than that, she was someone with somewhere to go and not just anyone to meet, because Michael Grafton would be known to virtually everyone who worked in the numerous production and facility houses all around her. His name was one of the most highly respected in the business for the many successful dramas his company had produced. Knowing that he had chosen her, was actually *trusting her*, to take on his next major project was so exhilarating that the emotion of it all was as dazzling as the bright sunlight in her eyes.

'Mr Grafton's already at the table,' she was told as she entered the busy restaurant on Poland Street. The deliciously pungent smells of sautéing garlic and sizzling herbs was as prevalent in the air as the persistent burble of voices, mainly male, and the path she was shown through the tables was as crowded with briefcases, handbags and laptops as the ochre-coloured walls were with hazy paintings and soft lighting.

Seeing her coming, Michael Grafton put aside his menu and rose to his feet. 'Hi,' he said, leaning forward to kiss her cheek. 'I think you've just made me the envy of every man in the room.'

Feeling herself sparkle, she said, 'I'm sure you manage that without my help.' Then, realising he might not have understood she was referring to his success, she was about to explain when his smile reassured her and caused her to laugh.

After she was settled at the table and the maître d' had vanished, Michael regarded her in a way that made his dark eyes seem even more intense than she remembered. The rest of his features were large and slightly crooked, and seemed to emanate an easy confidence that made her feel relaxed and safe. This was an odd thing to think, she acknowledged, but it was due to him that she was about to enjoy the kind of financial security she'd hardly even dared dream about these past few years. His thick, greying hair conformed to no real style or length, nor did his casual attire, making him entirely his own person, both in character and look, and why not? Being as successful as he was, he had nothing to prove and no reason to waste time caring about trends or images, or what anyone else might think.

'Why don't we start with a glass of champagne to toast your success?' he suggested. 'Unless you'd rather keep a clear head for your meeting later.'

'I doubt one glass will do much harm,' she replied, 'and if I can't toast this amazing turn in my fortunes, never mind my life, with you, then I shouldn't be toasting it with anyone.'

Lifting a hand to signal the waiter, he ordered two glasses of the best they could offer, and turning back to her said, 'So how surprised were you to find yourself cast in the role of Marianne Rhodes?'

Her eyes widened. 'On a scale of one to ten, I think that would be a twenty,' she told him wryly. 'I didn't even know Marianne's name at that point, so I had no idea I was being considered for any other part than the one I was up for.' Her eyes narrowed playfully. 'Did you?' she ventured.

Seeming almost pleased by the challenge, he said, 'Not at first, but when I saw you again at the audition it occurred to me that we should at least bear it in mind.'

Recalling the way he'd whispered to Marlene at the start of the interview, she said, 'Am I allowed to ask if the others agreed, or did you have some persuading to do?'

'Some,' he admitted, 'but not much after the screen tests came in. The decision was unanimous then. Actually, for a beautiful woman you photograph extremely well, which isn't always the case, as I'm sure you know.'

She did, but slightly embarrassed by the compliment, she dropped her eyes to his hands, bunched on the table. Then, realising their elegant masculinity was also having an effect on her, she looked at him again, saying, 'I shall be doing my utmost to make sure you don't regret your decision. I'm starting riding lessons on Friday, by the way.'

'Good. I don't think you'll have too much trouble coming up to the standard we need for on-camera, because there are plenty of ways to make you appear an expert in the saddle. And I'm pretty sure you're going to be pleased with the horse we've cast to play alongside you. He's an eight-year-old Arabian stallion whose lineage, I'm told, can be traced back to the Bedouins. I'll go so far as to say that when you see him you might feel you're in the presence of equine royalty. He's magnificent.'

As such a vital part of the amazing new world she was entering into, Susannah was as excited about meeting the horse as she was about meeting anyone else. 'What's his name?' she asked. 'I know in the series he's Silver, but in life?'

He grimaced. 'I'm afraid you'll have to ask someone else, I don't have that information. However, to quote one of the directors, together you're going to make a visual feast with your blonde hair and the horse's silvery colouring. Thank you,' he said, as a waiter set down their champagne. Then, raising his glass, 'I guess we should drink to you, Marianne, Silver and *Larkspur*.'

She smiled into his eyes. 'Thank you,' she said softly. 'To everyone involved in the Larkspur Centre of Equitation.'

As their glasses touched his eyes remained on hers, and feeling a slight dissembling sensation inside her she looked down as she sipped.

'Do you ride?' she asked, putting her glass back on the table.

He nodded. 'I have several horses at my home in Derbyshire.'

She looked surprised. 'Does that mean you live near where we'll be shooting?'

'About ten miles away, but I'm generally only there at weekends. During the week I'm here, in London, or in Europe or the States.'

She wanted to ask what his house was like, if it was where he'd lived with Rita Gingell and what kind of relationship he had with her now, but it would be wholly inappropriate to start digging into his private life, so she merely said, 'You evidently travel a lot.'

'More for business than pleasure, unfortunately. How about you?'

She almost laughed. 'Hardly ever,' she said. 'I have a daughter, Neve, at school and . . . Do you have children?'

He nodded as he sipped. 'Three. Two sons and a daughter. Thomas, Elinor and Christian. Thomas is on a gap year at the moment. The last I heard, which was yesterday, he was still in Thailand. The other two are at boarding school during the week and either come to me at the weekend, or to their mother.'

'Rita?'

'That's right. She lives in Cumbria now with her new partner and his children. Occasionally they all come down to Derbyshire so we can get together as a family – or families – for the weekend, but it doesn't happen often.'

'That sounds as though your break-up was amicable.'

'Not at the time it was happening, but we'd reached the end of the road as a couple, so there was no point stringing it out. How about you? You're married, I believe.'

'Yes, but we're not together any more.' She took another sip of champagne, and was on the point of telling him about Alan when the menus arrived, and by the time they'd decided what to eat the subject had returned to the programme.

'Ordinarily,' he said, picking up his glass again, 'Marlene would be taking you to lunch now, but as she's one of the topics I want to discuss with you, she was happy for me to meet with you instead.' He took a sip and continued. 'She, and the two series producers, will be hosting a lunch for the others next week, by the way, which you'll also be invited to. Today . . . Well, I wanted to start by talking to you about rumours you may already have heard . . .' He stopped expectantly.

She shook her head.

'If you haven't, then I'm sure they'll come your way soon enough. There are some murmurings on the industry grapevine that I coerced Marlene into casting you against her better judgement. I want to stress here and now that this isn't true. Marlene was completely supportive of your casting, and frankly had she not been it wouldn't have happened, because there would be no point in me sanctioning a series where the executive producer was unhappy with the choice of a leading character.'

'No, of course not,' Susannah mumbled, appalled to think that a few malicious minds were turning her casting into something so embarrassing for him and humiliating for her.

'Don't look so worried,' he smiled, 'these things always happen and the rumours will die down soon enough. I just wanted to be clear where you stand with Marlene. However dour, sharp, critical or downright fierce she might seem – and believe me she could win awards for it – please don't make the mistake of taking it personally. You have her full support, and you'll soon discover that she's a first-rate producer who doesn't see it as her job to win a personality contest, only to get the programme to the top of the ratings, which is something she has an excellent track record of doing. She'll give the series one hundred per cent of herself, and will expect no less from you.'

Feeling herself relaxing a little, Susannah said, 'Does she usually use you for a character reference?'

His laugh made her laugh too.

'I admit I'd heard how exacting she can be,' she said, 'and I was a little nervous – now I think I'm terrified.'

Still laughing, he said, 'I don't think you'll have too much trouble standing up to her. And do so. She has a lot of time for plucky spirits, and remember, as one of the leads, you will have your own power, just don't use it in a way to make yourself unpopular, though I somehow don't imagine you will.'

Sitting back in her chair, almost as though to

escape the pull of his charm, she said, 'So how involved will you actually be with the programme yourself?'

'On a day-to-day basis, not very,' he replied. 'I'll probably visit the set once or twice a month, depending on other commitments. I'll be viewing each episode before it goes out though, and occasionally I might give a few notes, but only ever through Marlene, never directly.'

'So we won't know if they've come from you?'

'Unless she wants you to.'

Glancing up as their food arrived, Susannah watched the Caprese salad she'd ordered being set down in front of her, and in spite of how delicious it looked she knew already that she was too excited to manage more than a few mouthfuls.

'The next subject I want to bring us on to,' he said, after the waiter had finished grinding black pepper over their meals, 'is publicity. You're probably starting to get an idea by now of how much is going to come your way over the next few weeks as we get ready for the launch. Obviously it won't stop at transmission, because once the series is under way the public's interest in you will almost certainly grow. So my advice to you is make a friend of the press. Be available, up to a point that's reasonable, be charming and accommodating, again where reasonable, but whatever you do, don't lie to them. If you do you'll be found out and the last thing you'll want is them turning against you.' He took a mouthful of food, then filled their glasses with water.

'I know what I'm saying is basic common sense,' he went on, 'and the publicists will go over it again this afternoon, I'm just keen to stress how important it is for you to start dealing with any skeletons you might have in your cupboard now. Whatever they are, presuming you have some and most of us do, once you're in the public eye you can be certain that sooner or later the skeletons will be too. So you could do yourself an enormous favour by outing them yourself right at the beginning, then you should have nothing to fear from some ambitious young hack eager to make a name for him or herself somewhere further down the line.' His eyes started to twinkle. 'This is the point at which I invite you to tell me your deepest, darkest secrets, but it's OK, you don't have to answer. This is simply to get you to think about what I'm saying, so you can assess the situation for yourself before you start spilling the beans. How awful would it be for you, or your family, if the whole world knew . . . It's up to you to fill in the blank.'

After only a brief hesitation Susannah heard herself saying, 'If the whole world knew that Neve's father has just been released from prison?'

Though his head tilted to one side he appeared neither shocked nor worried, only mildly intrigued.

'I wouldn't mind for myself,' she went on, 'but I don't think it would be very pleasant for Neve if the papers were to make an issue of it.'

'What was the offence?'

'Drugs. A young boy almost lost his life thanks to some cheap substance Duncan supplied.'

'I see. Where is he now? Your husband, not the boy.'

'In Glasgow, making a new life for himself. He's a director, mainly theatre. We have as little contact as possible.'

'Well, I'm sorry to say, this is exactly the sort of thing that you should get out right at the start. Tell the story your way, before he jumps on the bandwagon and uses your fame for his own ends.'

'Which he probably will,' she muttered. She looked down at her plate for a moment, her heartbeat starting to slow as she thought of her other secret, the one she'd only ever confided in Patsy, but once her face was out there, someone would be sure to recognise her . . .

'Until recently,' she said, 'I was working at a gentlemen's club in Kensington.' Immediately her cheeks started to burn, certain the connotation must already be speaking for itself. 'My job was behind the scenes, in the offices, but occasionally I helped out in reception, greeting clients, taking their coats, showing them to their tables.'

Though his eyes were on his plate she could tell he was listening intently.

'The kind of things . . .' She stopped and started again. 'My financial situation had become . . . Neve needed . . .' She took a sip of water and tried again. 'One evening I waited on a party in a private dining room. I'm not sure if you know what that means . . .' She paused, praying she wouldn't have to spell it out.

'I think so,' he said, 'but it can depend on the kind of place we're talking about.'

'This one is a little more . . . upmarket than some, I think, but I can't speak for what everyone gets up to in the private rooms. I only know what happened the night I served half a dozen or so men with their food and drinks without, well, topless – and actually not very much else either.'

He nodded soberly, and she suddenly felt so ashamed that she wished she'd never mentioned it.

'I didn't even sit on a lap, unless I was pulled on to one,' she went on hastily. 'If anyone ever says differently, they'll be lying.'

When his eyes came up they were regarding her in a way she couldn't quite fathom. 'Then you'd have our entire legal team to back you,' he assured her. 'And now I'm going to say something you probably won't like very much, but here goes anyway: this is exactly the kind of thing, given the right spin, that the publicists can really go to town with. If you're willing to talk about why you did it, which by the sound of it had a lot to do with providing for your daughter, there won't be many TV viewers or tabloid readers who won't be glued to their screens or rushing out to buy a paper. It's sexy, you're glamorous and it's a mother's sacrifice for her child.' He was regarding her earnestly. 'I'm sorry to be so blunt, but I'm sure you know that's how it's going to read. Men will love you because you look the way you do, and they'll all wish they'd been in that room – and women will empathise with the terrible dilemma that drove you to it. Husband in prison, wife fighting to make ends meet for a daughter who is as subject to social and peer pressure as any of theirs.'

Susannah swallowed hard and lifted her glass. 'Apart from my best friend you're the only person

I've ever told about this,' she said, 'and you're right, I can see why it would make a good story, but . . .' There were so many thoughts chasing around in her head that she hardly knew which direction to go in first. 'There are other actresses working at the club,' she said finally, 'who I know won't be able to keep my session in the private room to themselves, so yes, it would be best if I beat them to it. I'm worried about Neve though, and my aunt Lola who's more like a mother to me.'

'Then obviously you must tell them before you green-light the publicists.'

She nodded and gazed down at her glass. 'Actually,' she went on, looking at him again, 'I'm probably even more concerned about my partner, Alan. I just can't see him liking the idea of me going on chat shows or appearing in papers over something like that.'

Michael took a sip of water. 'The decision has to be yours,' he reminded her. 'If you want to keep it hidden and hope that no one comes forward . . .'

'That would be crazy. Even if one of the girls didn't try to sell their story – and I know they will – there are always the men I served. One of them could easily recognise me, though I suppose it's a bit naive to think anyone was looking at my face.'

His eyes lit with humour as he dabbed his mouth with a napkin. 'Probably,' he agreed in a way that made her smile too.

'As I said,' he went on, 'you get to call the shots, so take some time to think it over. Talk to your daughter and your aunt, *and* your partner, and then decide whether or not to confide in the publicists. As far as I'm concerned it will go no further than this table.'

'Thank you,' she said.

An hour later, when they stepped out into the street, blinking at the sudden glare of the sun and still smiling at the manager's cheery goodbye, Susannah felt so alive that she could have flung her arms round Michael and kissed him.

'OK, I guess you're off to see the publicists now,' he said, checking his watch, 'which means we're going in opposite directions, because I have a meeting in Cavendish Square. Thank you for coming today. I've enjoyed getting to know you a little better.'

She gave him a winning smile. 'I've enjoyed it too,' she told him. 'Very much. In fact I could be in danger of gushing now, so to spare your blushes, perhaps we should make the parting swift.' She held out a hand to shake.

'Consider me gone,' he told her, and leaned forward to kiss her cheek. 'You've got an extremely busy few weeks ahead,' he warned, 'but you have my mobile number if you need it. Otherwise, I'll see you at the pre-shoot meeting on Sunday 21st.'

'I'll look forward to it,' she said warmly. 'Oh, and thank you for lunch.'

'My pleasure.'

As they turned their separate ways she was so thrilled and excited that she'd have called Alan right away to tell him how well it had gone, had she not been afraid he'd say something to burst her bubble. So once again she called Pats instead.

'I have to remember,' she said when she got

through, 'that all this is happening to me, not to *us* as a couple, which has to be difficult for anyone, no matter how supportive and happy they might be for their partner.'

'True,' Patsy agreed, 'but don't let it stop you enjoying the moment. When's he back from Zurich?'

'Friday. I think, when I speak to him later, I should just skim over the lunch and talk about the meeting I'm on my way to now, with the publicists.'

'Could be wise, because I have to tell you the way you just talked about Michael Grafton to me probably won't play terribly well with Alan.'

'Oh God,' Susannah groaned, 'did I sound besotted, because I think I am. Not in a romantic way, but in a . . . you know, starry-eyed, grateful sort of way.'

'So you don't fancy him?'

'No! I mean, he's attractive, I'll give him that, and incredibly charismatic . . .'

'Not to mention rich, powerful . . .'

'Stop! Yes, he's all of that, of course he is, but none of it makes a difference to my relationship with Alan. Pats, I swear, I'm not making the mistake of letting him go again. My head was turned once before by someone I thought was the god of showbiz and look how badly I got burned then. So no, as far as Michael Grafton's concerned, I'll admit, *but only to you*, that I've probably got a bit of a crush, but I can tell you right now that it's no more going anywhere than the one Neve has on Alan.'

* * *

'Oh my God! That is so wild,' Neve laughed, her eyes as round as the giant silver hoops in her ears. 'You seriously did that?' She looked from Susannah to Lola, her grin widening all the time. 'Did you know?' she asked Lola.

'Not until today,' Lola answered, appearing somewhat less impressed, but as she'd said herself when Susannah had told her about the little fiasco at the club, it took a lot more than a flit about a private room in fancy knicks to shock someone her age.

Neve turned back to her mother. 'You actually took off your top and served men drinks,' she repeated, seeming far more jazzed by the idea than shocked, or embarrassed, or even ashamed. 'You are amazing, do you know that? You never cease to surprise me.'

'Nor you me,' Susannah assured her drily. She wouldn't tell her it had been to pay for her trip to Barcelona; it was too great a burden for her young conscience to bear, and besides Pats had funded it in the end. 'It's likely to come out in the papers,' she warned, 'so how are you going to feel about it then?'

Neve gave it some thought, then shrugged. 'Who cares?' she said. 'It's so out there . . .' She started to laugh again. 'My mother is going to be this major sex symbol,' she cried in excited disbelief. 'It's *so wild*.'

'OK, so we can take it you don't have too much of a problem with that,' Susannah said, glancing at Lola, who was clearly becoming quite entertained by Neve's reaction, 'but how do you feel about your father's jail sentence being made public? I wish it wasn't an issue, obviously, but I don't want you . . .'

'Oh, don't mind me,' Neve interrupted hastily. 'I honestly couldn't care less about him. I mean, it's not as if all my friends don't know he was in the clink, so why would I bother about complete strangers finding out? No, as far as I'm concerned it's his problem, not ours. And actually, it makes sense to be getting all the embarrassing stuff out in the open ourselves, because we definitely don't want him doing it.'

Susannah regarded her with wonder and no little pride. This was the Neve she loved so much she couldn't even begin to express it. Not that she didn't love the other Neve who was whirling around on a rollercoaster of emotions, but this one was so much easier to adore, and always seemed so wonderfully in tune with her mother.

'I mean it, Mum,' Neve told her earnestly, 'you shouldn't let anything stand in your way now. You really deserve your success, and whatever it's going to mean for the rest of us, we'll handle it, won't we Lola?'

'Of course we will,' Lola clucked, smoothing out her lap. 'When have we ever not handled anything, us three?'

Adoring her too, Susannah said, 'I have to admit I'm a bit worried about how Alan's going to take it when I tell him, so it means a great deal to hear you two being so supportive.'

'He will be as well,' Neve assured her confidently. 'He's really cool with everything, so there's no way any of this will blow his mind. After all, it's not as if he was the one who went to prison, is it? And as for you jigging your top bits about for everyone to see, where's the big deal? I've seen them often enough and do I look excited?'

Not quite sure how to respond to that, Susannah looked to Lola for help, but Lola only chuckled.

'Seriously,' Neve said, 'he'll be dead cool about it. You'll see.'

Smiling at how an infatuation could so easily make someone an authority on the object of their passion, Susannah dragged her into an embrace, saying, 'What really matters is that you are.'

'Yeah, yeah. I'm cool, you know me. Anyway, I've got to go now. Sasha's dad's picking me up at the bus stop in a minute on his way back from Hastings. I'm staying there tonight, in case you'd forgotten.'

Susannah nodded. 'By the way, I had a text earlier from Sandrine, you remember, from Patsy's office? She wants to move into our old house at the beginning of June.'

Neve looked pleased, then suddenly worried. 'Oh God, what about Dad?' she said darkly. 'As soon as he finds out what's going on, you know, about all the money you're going to be earning, and the rent that's coming in, he's bound to try and get some of it.'

'Leave him to me,' Susannah told her firmly. 'Now, if you've got everything ready I'll walk you to the high street. I need to pick up a few things before I catch the bus home.'

'You'll have a chauffeur soon,' Neve told her, and promptly disappeared into her bedroom, leaving Susannah to try calling Alan in Zurich again, but he was obviously still in conference so

311

she left a quick message saying, 'Still nothing urgent. Just wondering how it's going over there. Lots happening here, but really missing you.'

'What's he over there for?' Lola asked as Susannah rang off.

'Some kind of seminar, apparently. All a bit beyond me, but he sounded quite upbeat about it when he was invited to step in last minute.' She pulled an anxious face. 'Let's hope the good mood prevails when he gets back on Friday and hears about the kind of publicity I might have in store.'

Alan stood looking at Susannah in wide-eyed amazement, until starting to laugh he pulled her into his arms. 'I'm sorry you've been so worried about telling me,' he said, holding her tightly. 'I'm such a fool to plant so many doubts in you. All that really matters to me is that you're happy, and if you don't mind talking about Duncan in public, then I can't think of a single reason why I should.'

Lifting her face, she gazed into his eyes, and though she wanted only to go on hugging and kissing him for caring so much, she still hadn't told him everything yet, and couldn't help feeling that his reaction to her next confession might be rather different to the last.

'It's clearly going to be pretty manic for you over these next few weeks,' he said, holding her face in his hands, 'what with having a documentary crew following your preparations, all the photo shoots you've been telling me about in your emails, the interviews and coaching. Not forgetting the riding lessons. How did it go today? Wasn't it the first one?'

She nodded and grimaced. 'So treat me gently,' she warned, 'because I'm a little tender in the nether regions.'

Laughing, he ran his hands soothingly over her buttocks. 'I brought you something back from Switzerland,' he told her. 'Would you like it now?'

Her eyes lit up. 'Mm, why not?' she answered, loving the idea of a surprise, and him even more for thinking of bringing one.

Going to fetch his bag from the hall, he tore the BA flight label from the handles and delved inside.

Realising right away what was inside the glossy wrapping, she made herself keep smiling. 'Pralines,' she said, thinking of the strict diet she'd put herself on ready for the cameras. She'd have to eat a few, but then she'd slip the rest to Neve and Lola.

'I've brought smaller boxes for Neve and Lola,' he told her, as they chose one each from hers. 'Where is Neve, by the way?'

'Gone to a concert with a couple of friends. She's been at Sasha's most of the week, actually, but she'll be home in the morning. Which reminds me, I meant to send her a text asking if she'd like to join the gym with me. I thought we could go together when I'm here at weekends. You too, if you feel up for it.'

'Absolutely, count me in. I'll be wanting to spend every possible minute I can with you while you're here. Any sign of a schedule yet?'

'No, but I had a long chat with Marlene on the phone yesterday – I don't know if she intends to sound like an old dragon, or it just comes natur- ally. Anyway, apparently immediate family will be welcome to visit the set any time, and to spend the night in the various residences that are being prepared for us all – cast and crew.'

He was looking interested, but slightly worried. 'Would that extend to me, even though we're not married?' he asked.

'Of course. You're my partner, so don't even think you'd be excluded. It includes Neve and Lola too, of course, but space is at a premium, so if you all came together they'd have to stay at a nearby hotel.'

'And what's your living accommodation going to be?'

'An old lodge, apparently, but I've no idea what it's like, or how close it is to the Centre yet – except everything's in the same valley, I'm told.'

'Well, it's all sounding like a mighty big adventure to me, and the important thing is that you enjoy it. Now, I'm going to unpack and shower after the journey, and if it's just us this evening, how would you like to go out for dinner?'

'I'd love to. Somewhere close by so we don't have to drive?'

'You choose and make a reservation.'

He'd got as far as the kitchen door when Susannah said, 'Actually, there's something else I need to tell you about the publicity. It's quite . . . Well, delicate, and I'd like to get it over with . . .'

His expression turned to one of amused curiosity. 'Do I need to sit down?' he teased.

'Maybe.' She took a deep breath, and in as few words as possible told him about her topless stint at the club. 'Nothing happened,' she hastily assured him. 'I mean, a couple of them tried to

314

grab me, and they kept asking me to take off everything, but obviously I didn't.' She took another breath. 'I know I'm probably making too much of it, but it was a pretty big deal for me. I hated it, and I've felt really terrible about it since, but I can see the sense in making it public myself, rather than leave it to someone else to turn it into something it wasn't.'

Alan's expression was tightening; a pale line was forming round his mouth.

'Look, I know . . .'

'It's not that I have a problem with you doing it,' he interrupted harshly, 'well I do, but I understand your reasons, obviously. It's the fact that you're going to allow it to be exploited for the programme's interests. It's tacky, Susannah . . .'

'Which is why the programme's publicists need to put their spin on it first. Surely you can see how . . .'

'And I'd like to know how come they get to hear about it before I do? Why is . . .'

'They didn't. They don't know anything yet. I've only discussed it with . . .' Too late she realised she'd walked herself into a trap of her own making. 'I don't have to tell them if I don't want to,' she finished lamely.

He was staring at her hard. 'Who did you discuss it with?' he demanded. 'Who thinks airing your indiscretions for the world to salivate over is a good idea?'

'You're getting this out of perspective,' she said angrily. 'It's *you* who's turning it into something salacious, trying to make me feel ashamed . . .'

'That is not my intention, but it sure as hell isn't

something to be proud of. And frankly, I don't want to be the man whose girlfriend is the one who struts about in nightclubs . . .'

'It happened *once*,' she shouted. 'And this isn't about *you*. It's about me, and it's not as though my entire publicity is going to revolve around it. As soon as it's out there it'll be a topic for a few days, then it'll be gone.'

'Says who? And what are you going to do when offers start coming in for you to pose topless for calendars and men's magazines and tabloid news-papers, because I hope you realise that's bound to happen?'

'If it does I'll turn them down. Listen, this really doesn't have to be as big an issue as you're making it . . .'

'You still haven't told me who's been advising you,' he cut in, 'but actually you don't have to, because I can guess. It's Michael Grafton, isn't it? You discussed it with him when the two of you had lunch on Tuesday.'

'Yes,' she answered, seeing no point in deny-ing it.

His face was reddening with temper. 'How cosy,' he said bitingly, 'and how very erotic – for you both. I can just see you, sitting there confiding in him, batting those big beautiful eyes as you taunt him with images of you naked . . .'

'It didn't happen like that,' she cried, 'and how dare you even suggest it did? He's not the kind of man who'd go after cheap thrills like that, and it really doesn't do you many favours to . . .'

'Don't try turning this around on me. The fact is, you confided something deeply personal about yourself to a man you hardly know, before you'd even discussed it with me. How do you think that makes me feel?'

'Obviously not good, but I had no idea the subject was going to come up until it did, but do you know what, I'm not going to go on standing here trying to defend myself. You're being totally unreasonable, and as far as I can tell you're determined to stay that way. So if you'll excuse me I have some calls to make, and I believe you were about to take a shower.'

'No, no, wait,' he cried, as she started to walk away. 'I'm sorry, you're right. I am being unreasonable. It's just . . .' He took a breath and wiped a hand over his face. 'I understand that you need to do publicity for your job . . . I'm simply . . . I just don't think this is the way to do it.' His eyes went to hers, but it was evident she wasn't going to back down. 'OK, it's not my world,' he conceded, 'so I'm probably not supposed to have an opinion . . .'

'Of course you are,' she insisted, going to put her arms around him, 'and I want to hear it – apart from anything else you might make a point no one else has thought of. In this instance though, I have to take the advice I've been given, because I know it's right, but at the same time I accept that I need to be more sensitive to how it's affecting the people I love. That's really behind what Michael was trying to say, because any kind of publicity, no matter how salacious, perhaps the more salacious the better, will work for the programme. What he wanted me to understand was how important it is to get things right behind

317

the scenes, for me and my family. And for that I need your help.'

He nodded slowly as he gazed into her eyes. 'Jealousy is a destructive beast,' he murmured, 'so I have to learn to keep it on a tighter rein.'

'You don't have anything to be jealous of,' she assured him. 'It's just a job. All the publicity, gossip, innuendo, it's an illusion. This, you and me, is what matters, because it's real.'

Smiling, he said, 'Thank you for that, because I needed to hear it.'

Going up on tiptoe she kissed him gently on the mouth.

'Can I ask one favour?' he said.

'Of course.'

'Please don't bring me into your publicity. It's not my thing, so I probably wouldn't be much of an asset anyway.'

Immediately putting on hold her plan to tell him about the interview she'd recorded with GMTV that day, she kissed him again, saying, 'It's a deal.' It wasn't due to be aired until the end of the following week, so there was still plenty of time to prepare the ground, and she hadn't actually said that much about him anyway. For now, however, it was probably safer to change the subject and ask about his stay in Zurich.

'Well, they were impressed enough to invite me to take part in another seminar in the States next week,' he told her, going to the fridge to take out some wine, 'but I've already used up too much of my patients' goodwill, changing their appointments last minute the way I did at the beginning of the week. I can't do it to them again, so I had

318

to turn it down. However,' he went on, filling two glasses with a Chilean Sauvignon Blanc, 'I have agreed to go back for five days in July. I know there's little chance you'll be able to come with me, but I'm going to ask anyway. Can you?'

Realising that this was very likely a taste of things to come, when she'd have to turn him down for all kinds of events, she felt awful as she shook her head. 'The cameras will already be rolling by then, so I doubt very much I'd be able to get away.'

'But if you can, you will?'

'Of course. Even if it's only for a night.'

He smiled and passed her a glass. 'Knowing you'd do that is enough,' he said softly, and after brushing a hand over her face he took his drink upstairs, leaving her to wonder, with no little trepidation, just how great the pressure was going to become on their relationship over the months ahead. Perhaps if their worlds were more similar it would be easier for him to accept the occasional overspill of limelight, but they could hardly be more different. And even if that weren't presenting a problem, there was still the issue of Michael Grafton, which didn't appear to be going away.

Chapter Fifteen

'Did you go to Switzerland to get away from me?' Neve asked quietly.

Taking his eyes from the road Alan glanced at her sitting in the passenger seat of his car, her lovely young face looking pale and strained, her beautiful hair twisted into a plait for school. Reaching for her hand he gave it a gentle squeeze. 'No,' he answered softly.

'Then why did you go?'

'You know why. I was asked to speak at a seminar.'

She pursed the corner of her mouth and tilted her head to one side. 'So why have you been avoiding me all weekend?' she challenged.

Her hand was still in his, so he linked their fingers as he said, 'Unless my memory is playing me tricks, I don't think you came home until last night, and then you went straight to your room. So maybe I should be asking if you're avoiding me.'

Her head went down. 'You know I wouldn't do that,' she said. 'It's just that . . .' She let the sentence hang hoping he'd prompt her to finish, but he didn't.

'The chocolates were nice,' she said. 'Thank you. They're Mum's favourites.'

'I know.'

Feeling an unsteadying rush of blood to her head she said, 'She shouldn't have thrown them away. I'd have eaten them for her.'

When he made no comment she wished she hadn't told him what her mother had done – it wasn't only disloyal, it was spiteful, and now he'd think she was a bitch.

She looked down at the loose tangle of their fingers, and felt a tightness in her heart that almost hurt. 'She's got another riding lesson this morning,' she said.

'And her acting coach this afternoon, and an interview with heaven only knows who this evening,' he added. 'She's very busy right now.'

Neve nodded. He wasn't trying to take his hand away, even though he was driving, and feeling it holding hers, thinking of what she'd really like to say, and do, was making her miserable and breathless and dizzy. 'When she goes up to Derbyshire,' she said. She waited for his prompt, but it didn't come, so she took her hand away and turned to look out of the window, not wanting him to see the tears that were suddenly burning her eyes.

He still hadn't mentioned the kiss last week and she couldn't find the courage to do so herself. Sometimes she thought she'd imagined it, but she knew she hadn't. She'd put her mouth on his and he hadn't pulled away. So it wasn't a real kiss, exactly, but it had lasted for at least three seconds which was a long time really. And then he'd said that it was probably best if neither of them mentioned it to anyone.

'It's not that it was wrong,' he'd whispered, 'but it could be misconstrued, so let's make it our secret, OK?'

She wished she'd never told Sasha now, but Sash had sworn she wouldn't repeat it, and she didn't usually break any secrets.

Neither of them spoke again until he was pulling up outside the school for her to get out of the car. She wouldn't be able to kiss him with everyone around, so she didn't try. Then she felt crushed when he didn't either. A small peck on the cheek would have been all right, wouldn't it? There was nothing wrong in that.

'Neve,' he said, as she started to get out.

She turned round to look at him, knowing her eyes were probably red, but she couldn't help it.

'It'll be all right,' he told her softly. 'We'll work it out, I promise.'

'Honestly, I'm up to my eyes with costume fittings, hair consultations, riding lessons, and don't get me started on the publicity,' Susannah was saying down the phone to Patsy. 'The writer's bible turned up yesterday containing everything from character backgrounds, to show-horse training, to major competitions, to story development. I need to get through it before the big pre-shoot meeting on the 21st, but you should see the size of it. Double an encyclopedia and you might be there. Alan finds the whole thing highly amusing, and slightly mad, it has to be said, and he's probably not wrong.'

'He's probably sizing you all up with a view to

expanding his client list,' Pats responded drolly. 'Have there been any shocking revelations in the papers yet, about Susannah's soirée of sin?'

'Very funny. No, but the press release only went out this morning. Apparently the publicists have already been inundated with interview requests – amazing how sex sells, isn't it? – and I'm due to re-record my GMTV piece later today so they can include it. Which is lucky, because it'll give me a chance to ask them to take out any mention of Alan from the previous piece.'

'So where are you now?'

'In the back of a cab about to be late for lunch with Marlene Wyndham, thanks to the documentary crew that's following me around. They've gone off for their own lunch now, because Marlene doesn't want them there for ours. You know, it's weird having a camera watching your every move. It starts to feel like a person after a while. I keep talking to it, like it's a friend.'

'Which they must love. Anyway, going back to Michael Grafton, when are you likely to see him again?'

Feeling a pleasurable swell of anticipation, Susannah said, 'Actually, not until the pre-shoot meeting which is still a couple of weeks away. Oh, that reminds me, Alan's suggested taking us all out for a kind of good luck/send-off dinner, just before I go. Any chance you can come? Friday the 19th or Saturday the 20th?'

'Hang on, I'm just checking my diary, and that's looking very possible. I'll write it in immediately, and make sure my secretary has a note of it too, so she doesn't commit me to anything else.'

'Great. Now, let's get down to serious matters. How are things with *Fronk*?'

Patsy gave a protracted sigh. 'Would you believe, absolute bliss?' she replied. 'This is because he's been in our New York office virtually ever since we got back from Monte Carlo, because Christopher Mackey, the resident head honcho, has broken his leg, so *Fronk*'s taken over the helm.'

'Oh,' Susannah said, disappointed by the lack of development. 'When's he due back?'

'This weekend, and though it pains me to say it, it actually can't happen soon enough, because I'm in the middle of retail hell right now, and I think he might have a far better chance of getting the concept of customer service across to our uniquely French sales teams than I ever will. In fact, it was his idea to promote this "revolutionary business practice" to the top of the agenda as a way to turn our flagging retail sales around. He thinks, and I agree, that a more personal service will do wonders to help put our company into the public consciousness, here in France, where we still don't have as high a profile as we'd like. And being polite and helpful to the customer should give us a cutting edge over our competitors, who tend to operate along the lines of "The customer is an annoying part of the transaction that must be put in its place at all times, or preferably ignored altogether, or given the wrong, or a faulty, product so you can have a good row when they try to bring it back." Being American, Bryce Beauty Inc. takes the view that "The customer should be made to feel welcome, appreciated, right even if they're wrong, and if they bring something back they receive a smile, an apology and are asked what can be done to rectify the problem." You can always vent with a good slagging-off when they've gone.'

Laughing, Susannah said, 'I can't imagine the French assistants are really that bad.'

'Believe me, anyone who shops in these overblown, overpriced excuses for department stores, of any nationality, including French, will know exactly what I mean. So it's going to be quite a contest getting a team of Miss Congenialities installed amongst all those snooty little *vendeuses*, but if anyone can do it *Fronk* can.'

'What a hero! So, if he's been away all this time I guess he still hasn't told you what happened that night.'

'What night?'

'The one in Monte . . . Oh, I get it. Total memory loss now. OK. So, would you like to bring him to my send-off?'

'Are you crazy? No thank you. I only socialise with him when forced at work-related events. Now, I have to go in a few minutes, so tell me quickly, how are Lola and Neve?'

'Lola's great, apart from a bit of a dizzy spell yesterday. Luckily Alan was there helping with some form she had to fill in, so he took her to the doctor. Blood pressure, again, so they've upped her medication. And Neve I've hardly seen anything of. We manage to text one another every few hours, and pass on the stairs once in a while, so based on that I think she's OK.'

'Any more incidents with Alan?'

'Not that he's mentioned, so I'm daring to hope

it's starting to die a death. He's getting our phones changed, by the way, so I'll have my own number at the house. He'll keep the old one, because some of his patients have it, then, if they ring, they can go straight through to the machine in his study without having to speak to me.'

'OK, well don't forget to let me have the new number, I don't want to find myself lumped in with the saddos and psychos who ring up to chew the fat with him. Having said that, looking around this place, that's probably exactly where I am. Send him my love, Lola and Neve too. Let's try and speak again at the weekend.'

As she rang off Susannah barely had time to draw breath before another call came in, and seeing one of the publicist's names appear she clicked on right away.

'Hi, Harvey,' she said chirpily.

'Hi, yourself,' he responded. 'You're needed at the Ladbroke studios to do an interview and photo shoot for the *Mail*.'

'When?' she asked, taking out her diary.

'As near to now as you can make it. It's just come up and Marlene wants you to make it a priority. You're already booked in at the same place for the series photo shoot at three thirty, so it works perfectly. George Bremell's going to be joining you for that, and the stylist is on her way now so she can oversee what's happening with the *Mail* as well. Oh, and Lizzy's organised some outfits for you, they're on their way by taxi, and . . .'

'Hang on, hang on,' Susannah interrupted, 'I thought I was re-recording the GMTV interview at five.'

'Oh sorry, did I forget to tell you? That's been changed. You're doing it live tomorrow morning now, so what went before will be scrapped, or used in some other way, I guess. This evening, you're down to record . . . Let me see, is it Graham Norton, or Jonathan Ross?'

'Oh my God,' Susannah gulped.

'Actually, they're both tomorrow evening. It's *Soap TV* tonight. The stylist will be there for that too, and yours truly. Where are you now?'

Susannah checked out of the window. 'Heading down the Mall towards Trafalgar Square, so I'll have to redirect the driver. What about lunch, or don't I get to eat?'

'I'll make sure there's something waiting when you arrive at the studios. OK, abandoning you now. Phones are going crazy. Call if you need anything,' and he was gone.

With her head still spinning Susannah called out the new destination to the driver, then gave herself a moment to take stock of the changes Harvey had just given her. The best part of them, without a doubt, was the rescheduling of the GMTV interview. True, she was going to have a sleepless night thinking about appearing live, but at least it was giving her the opportunity to drop any mention of Alan. And while she was at it, she'd better try not to get into any kind of discussion about Michael Grafton, because Alan probably wouldn't like that too much either.

Pats was walking back to her office from the boardroom after a particularly trying meeting with the department heads. It was close to the end of the day now, and she'd give anything to kick back and open a bottle, maybe watch a movie, or go out to a restaurant with friends. The trouble was, she still hadn't had time to try and make any yet, apart from at the office, and that was proving about as successful as a knees-up in a nunnery. Not that she didn't have plenty of business functions to attend, but they were always so formal and serious and full of the kind of people who seemed to draw down their shutters and put out the cat by ten, just when things should really get going. What she felt in sore need of was the kind of raucous girls' night she used to enjoy in Sydney, where people really knew how to let their hair down, even if the boss did happen to be around.

With a sigh, she dropped an armful of ledgers and files on her desk and sank down in her sumptuous leather chair. She wasn't sure who she was trying to kid that she fancied a night on the tiles; the truth was she could hardly keep her eyes open past ten thirty these days, she was working so hard. And she'd be here again tonight until gone nine by the look of it, answering emails, reading and writing reports and dealing with all the other urgent issues she hadn't yet got round to today.

Clicking on to her inbox she began scanning her emails, knowing subconsciously that she was hoping to find one from Frank. It bothered her to realise how much she was missing him, though she knew the instant he walked back through the door he'd say or do something to annoy the hell out of her. Still, there was no getting away from the fact that the place had more life in it when he was around. The hours ticked by with a jaunty sort of trip and meetings ended on an up note, rather than the sober agreement to review and reconvene next week that she'd left ten minutes ago.

Though Claudia had warned her that the Europe assignment would be tough, she really hadn't been prepared for so much resentment towards her just because she was a woman – and a foreigner and unmarried and younger than most of the senior executives to boot. It made everything so much more complicated and time-consuming and exhausting than it needed to be, which was why, for the main part, she was missing Frank. When he was around he seemed to bridge the gap between her and the others in a way that made it barely noticeable. Without him it had become so glaringly obvious that she resolved there and then to do something about bridging it herself.

Hearing the chime of a new message dropping into her mailbox, she clicked on again and felt a little smile perk the corners of her mouth when she saw it was from him.

Just to let you know that Madame la Comtesse will be taking the same flight as me to Paris on Saturday. I have arranged for us to meet with her on Tuesday morning at 10.30. If this is not suitable for you please to let me know and I will change the rendezvous.

Looking forward to seeing you.

Your Frank

With a start she wondered if there was an s missing at the end of 'your', and decided there must be, because he certainly wasn't her Frank, nor did she wish him to be. In fact, as far as she was concerned he could be anybody's, and probably was the way he fizzed about the place like a sexed-up firework.

Quickly checking her diary she made a note for her secretary to move the meeting she had scheduled for Tuesday morning, then sent an email back to Frank letting him know that the date and time worked for her, but she'd like to meet with him first on Monday to discuss the presentation.

After pressing send she returned to the rest of her emails, and once they were dealt with she called up the PowerPoint she'd begun creating for the comtesse – who was flying back to Paris with Frank. Funny, she was thinking, as she began entering some new images, how until this evening she'd assumed that Madame la Comtesse du Petits-Louvens was old and slightly frail and far too rich for her own good. Certainly that was how she looked on the official website, but the carefully coiffed wrinkly smiling back at her from the top right-hand corner was the company's founder. There was nothing to say she was still running the show. In fact, for all Pats knew she could have croaked decades ago, and some gorgeous little Fifi from the new generation of this obviously wealthy and titled family had taken over the company's affairs. If that were the case then it might not be as great a pleasure doing business with her after all.

Alan's face was taut with anger as he watched Susannah coming in through the front door. She was clearly so engrossed in the conversation she was having on her mobile phone that she hadn't even noticed he was there. Certainly she wouldn't have been expecting him, since it was almost nine o'clock in the morning, and his car was parked further down the street thanks to someone blocking their carport last night, but he'd waited to confront her following her live interview on GMTV.

After kicking off her boots and hanging her coat, she padded towards the kitchen and came to a sudden stop when she saw him. 'Hi,' she said, starting to colour, 'I thought you'd have left by now.'

'I imagine you did,' he replied shortly.

'Harvey, I have to go,' she said into the phone. 'I'll call you later.' And after ringing off, 'Is Neve still here?'

'She's upstairs getting ready for school. So why did you do it?' he challenged. 'I told you I didn't want to be drawn into your publicity . . .'

'I swear, I wouldn't have mentioned you if she hadn't asked, but . . .'

'All you had to do was say that you wanted to keep your private life private . . .'

'I would have, but when I recorded a piece with them the other day I talked about you then, how we were each other's first love, and how we got back together through Friends Reunited. So when she brought it up this morning I had to go with it, or I'd have made her, or myself, or both of us look fools.'

'But it's all right for me to look one, the pathetic jerk of a lonely heart who surfs the Net looking for his old girlfriend . . .'

'Oh, for heaven's sake! Everyone's signing up

to those sites these days, and you must have heard me say it was Neve who instigated it . . .'

'For *you*, yes, but not for me – and it still doesn't get us away from the fact that I made my feelings perfectly clear about being used in your publicity. I do not want to be a part of it. I'll do my best to be supportive in every other way, but I *do not want* the spotlight on me, or my home, or my career.'

'Well, that really does spell it out. Thank you. Please be assured that from now on you will remain the shadowy, reclusive figure in the background who takes himself so seriously that he can't, even for a minute, or for someone he's supposed to love, allow his name or face to be revealed. Christ, anyone would think you worked for MI5 the way you're carrying on. You're a psychologist, Alan. Plenty of people in your profession have become celebrities themselves . . .'

'That's their choice. Mine is not to be dragged into a promotional circus that has absolutely nothing to do with me. If you want a clown or performing seal, you need to look elsewhere, because those particular talents are no more in my repertoire than sycophancy and star-fucking.'

Susannah's eyes blazed. 'Then we really do have a problem on our hands,' she said furiously, 'because a star is what I'm about to become, and if you can't bring yourself to sleep with me . . .'

'That's not what I meant, and you know it. I'm simply saying that I don't want to be seen as one of the halfwits basking in the glory of knowing you, the way half the nation does with celebrities.'

'And in your opinion partners or husbands come across that way?'

'Some, yes.'

'You know, I might be finding it a lot easier to apologise if you were at least trying to be reasonable.' She glanced round as Neve came down the stairs, then turned back as Alan said, 'Being reasonable to you means seeing everything your way, while not bothering to see it mine.'

'No. I accept that you have a right to your privacy, and from now on I will respect that right, and at the same time maybe you could try to have a little more respect for me and what I do. I know you think it's trivial and a waste of time, but whether you detest celebrity and soap operas or not, they still have a place in our society and right now I am about to become a part of it. If you find you can't live with that, then maybe we need to review our relationship.'

His face turned white. 'Well maybe we do,' he agreed, and snatching up his keys he stormed down the hall. 'Come on,' he said to Neve, 'or you're going to be late.'

As he tore open the front door Neve looked worriedly at her mother.

'Go on,' Susannah said, 'I'll be all right.'

'I'll talk to him,' Neve promised, coming to give her a hug. 'And by the way, you were brilliant in the interview. I was dead proud of you.'

After she'd gone Susannah took several steadying breaths in an effort to try and calm herself down. She really didn't have time to stand here thinking about this now, but at some point she and Alan had to have a very serious discussion about how they were handling things between them, or those bitter parting words were going to turn into a reality neither of them wanted.

Alan and Neve had been edging through the traffic for some time in silence, half-listening to the radio, but both still caught up in the scene at home.

'Do you think I'm being unreasonable?' Alan finally blurted.

Neve stopped pressing in a text to Sasha, but carried on staring at it as she said, 'Personally, I can't see anything wrong with letting Mum talk about how you got back together, but if you don't want to be famous by association, then that's up to you.' Her head stayed down as she added, 'I think you hurt her feelings though.'

Sighing, he said, 'I'm sure I did.'

Still not looking at him, she said, 'Are you going to say sorry?'

'Do you think I should?'

She shrugged. 'I don't know. I mean, I can see it from your point of view too, so maybe you both have to apologise.' She really didn't want to be having this conversation. She wanted to talk about other things like what he'd meant the other day when he'd promised they'd work things out, but she didn't know how to change the subject without seeming desperate, or obvious, or maybe annoying him for not talking about what was on his mind.

In the end she said, 'Is it because . . . Are you angry with Mum because you don't want your stepchildren to see you having a good time? You know, like your life has moved on and you're not really bothering about them any more?'

Reaching out for her hand he squeezed it warmly. 'You're a very perceptive young lady,' he told her, 'because yes, in part, that is behind my reluctance to enter into the limelight. I need to consider their feelings, even though I'm not really a part of their lives any more.'

'Do you ever hear from them?' she asked, already jealous of the daughters whether he was still in touch with them or not. 'You know, by text or email or anything?'

'No,' he sighed, 'which is a pity, because I'd like to, very much, but it helps a lot to have you.'

Neve's throat dried as she tried to swallow.

As they stopped at a red light he put his fingers under her chin and turned her face towards him. 'You've come to mean a great deal to me,' he told her softly, 'so please don't think I'm going to give up on my relationship with your mother, because if I did I'd lose you too. And I don't think either of us wants that, do we?'

Neve's eyes were burning with emotion as she looked at him. 'No,' she whispered shakily. 'No, we don't.'

Chapter Sixteen

I am very sorry but I have small crisis which mean I cannot make the meeting this morning. Perhaps we can speak later on the phone to discuss strategy for tomorrow. Your Frank.

This time Patsy really did conclude an s was missing, mainly because she was angry and disappointed, so certainly didn't want to lay any claim to him. She was a little concerned too by what kind of crisis might have arisen. If it came in the shape of a young comtesse whose ancestors had irritatingly escaped the guillotine, then she hoped they both turned rigid in the act and when surgically parted *Fronk*'s offending member remained plugged in. On the other hand, it could be something serious, so maybe she should call to see if there was anything she could do. She had his home number, naturally, but she didn't want to appear interfering, or inquisitive, or *God forbid* jealous, and besides, if he'd wanted to talk to her, he could have picked up the phone instead of sending an email.

In the end she hit the reply button and typed a message back.

I'll be in the labs until six, shall we speak after, say

around six thirty? Meanwhile if I can offer assistance,
please let me know.

Before sending it she read it through several
times, worried that it might sound too formal, or
intrusive, or even sarcastic, but after reminding
herself that the French liked formal, she opted for
that slant and clicked it on its way.

The rest of her day was taken up with meetings, mostly within the building, until she left at
four to make her rendezvous at the labs. They had
a new fragrance in the works, so she was going
in person to see the 'nose' whose olfactory skill
was in control of perfumery development. As
ever, it turned into a contentious encounter, since
Marcel Vigneau was as notoriously prickly in his
attitude as he was gifted in his nasal concha and
made little secret of his contempt for lesser
mortals, particularly of the female variety, and
very definitely for her. Still, she somehow
managed to leave his peacock feathers in a less
ruffled state than she usually did, and by the time
she returned to the office she'd turned her attention to the scheduled phone call with Frank.

However, to her dismay, when she opened her
emails it was to find one from him apologising
for being unable to keep to their arrangement,
but he was attaching the notes he'd made in
preparation for the morning.

Not sure whether she was more angry or worried
by this uncharacteristic lapse in his company
loyalty, she opened the first of three files and began
to read his suggestions for how to proceed. To her
relief, though not surprise, he had some very good
ideas which suggested he really had been giving

337

the matter his attention. Whether he was being tipped off by the pert little comtesse herself she wouldn't allow herself to contemplate. What mattered was that though the ideas were easy to expand on, they were not necessarily straightforward to present. So, just in case he was holed up in a genuine crisis, she decided to devote her evening to putting together a detailed document incorporating his brilliance, and her own flair for concise and comprehensive delivery that even the stupidest of bimbos could understand. Not that the comtesse was that, she felt sure, but just in case.

By the time ten o'clock came round she was so tired and hungry that she was becoming word blind. Accepting that to push herself any further tonight would inevitably prove self-defeating, she attached what she'd come up with so far to an email and sent it to Frank in his love nest, or centre of crisis. She would come in at six in the morning to finalise and add more polish, in the hope that by nine, when her secretary was due to arrive, it would be ready for her to assemble in a user-friendly PowerPoint file.

As she started to pack up her desk, careful to store confidential material in a locked cabinet, and placing pens, Post-its, paperclips and a pile of brochure proofs in a top drawer, she kept glancing at the screen to see if Frank had emailed back yet. Not that he'd have had time to read anything by now, especially if he was in a restaurant, or even in flagrante, but he might confirm having received her email, and perhaps reassure her that he'd be at the meeting tomorrow.

After drawing out her departure for over twenty

minutes, she finally shut down her computer, turned off her desk lamp and started through the concourse to the lift. All the partitioned offices were in semi-darkness, a *Mary Celeste* sort of look about them with so much seeming to have been abandoned halfway through. Apart from a cleaner, and the security guard at reception, she saw no one else on her way out, and didn't pass many in the streets either as she made the short walk home.

Once inside Claudia's apartment, which was very typically Parisian with its lofty ceilings, elegant furniture and shuttered windows, she kicked off her shoes and went to pour herself a drink. Though she'd brought Frank's phone number with her, she had no real intention of using it, but she did keep checking her BlackBerry to see if an email had popped its way through.

By the time she'd prepared and eaten a sandwich, replayed a programme on Sky that featured an interview with Susannah, sent a text to congratulate her on being fabulous again, then wandered through to the bedroom to start getting undressed, she'd finally managed to persuade herself that she wasn't going to hear from him tonight. He was probably whirling it up at the Moulin Rouge, or maybe he'd fallen into a post-coital slump, or perhaps he was still dealing with a very real crisis, and she felt awful for hoping he was.

Lying down on the bed, she turned out the light and lay staring hard at the darkness. She'd known Frank for two months now, but apart from being in the throes of a divorce, she had no idea what his personal circumstances actually were. She didn't even know where he lived, though she could easily find that out from human resources. Not that she'd bother, because actually she wasn't all that interested, it was just another missing piece in the puzzle that was *Fronk*. And now she came to think of it, there seemed to be a lot more blanks in that particular jigsaw than there was any kind of discernible picture.

The following morning there was still no sign of Frank. Though Patsy tried his home, and involved both their assistants in trying to track him down, by the time ten thirty came round there was still no word.

'Has he ever disappeared like this before?' she asked Virginie, his PA, who, for once, was looking genuinely perplexed, rather than face-smackingly superior.

'Mais non,' she replied. 'Only when he has to . . .'

Patsy's eyes narrowed as the girl stopped. 'Has to what?' she prompted.

'It is nothing. I . . . No, I do not know where he is, and it is not like him to vanish without telling me where he is going to be.'

Since her own assistant was announcing the comtesse's arrival, Patsy had no time to pursue this, but had every intention of doing so as soon as the meeting was over.

Slightly cheered by the fact that the comtesse was downstairs so therefore not shacked up somewhere with Frank, she grabbed everything she needed and hurried towards the lift. She'd intended all along to greet the comtesse and her team in person, and Frank's absence hadn't changed that. As she went she could sense the buzz following in her wake. Madame le Directeur is looking for Frank who has gone missing. She is angry, she will screw up the presentation, she will soon be history. It is OK Frank to come back now.

As the lift doors opened for her to step into the lobby, Patsy performed a quick mental shakedown and glanced at the receptionist. The woman nodded towards a small but extremely elegant older lady in a fur stole and navy two-piece, whose photograph Pats had seen in the top right-hand corner of the Louvens website. Clearly the illustrious founder was still breathing. Hiding her relief, she assumed her most welcoming smile and went towards her.

'Madame la Comtesse,' she said warmly, hoping it was the right form of address and wanting to kick herself for not having checked. 'Thank you for coming, it's a pleasure to meet you.'

The old lady's hyacinth eyes were like a bird's, quick and watchful, and reasonably friendly. 'My dear,' she said, taking Patsy's hand between both of hers as she rose to her feet, 'it is a pleasure for me too. I have liked very much the products you have send for our approval. My board of directors also. It is my hope now that we shall do some business together.'

Patsy glanced towards the door. 'Are we waiting for anyone else?' she ventured, having expected a marketing manager at the very least, but more likely an entire team of advisers.

'No, Frank call this morning and ask me to come alone, so it is just me.'

Patsy blinked in astonishment. 'You've spoken to him this morning?' she blurted.

The comtesse nodded, and Patsy couldn't be entirely certain, but she might have smiled. Then the worst imaginable suspicion struck her a terrible blow – had Frank spent the night with this bony old crone? Was that how he was drumming up business?

Quickly pushing the absurd suspicion aside, she said, 'Did he happen to mention whether or not he was going to join us?'

The comtesse's thinly pencilled eyebrows rose. 'He is not here yet?' she said. 'Well, I suppose I am not very surprised, but I think we can continue without him, no?'

'No. Uh, yes, of course.' Why wasn't the old lady surprised? How come she seemed to know more about what was going on than Patsy did? 'Second floor,' she told a security guard, who was waiting to call the lift, and a few minutes later she was walking the comtesse into a small but fully equipped conference room, its windows already blacked out ready for the on-screen presentation.

'Can I take your stole?' she offered, not really wanting to touch a dead animal, but this was hardly the time to get activist. 'Nancy will serve us some coffee, or tea if you prefer,' she said, pointing the comtesse in the direction of a catering assistant who'd made an excellent job of laying out refreshments for twenty people.

After requesting a coffee the comtesse sat down at the table and treated Patsy to a charming smile.

'I'm sure Frank will be along any minute,' Pats told her awkwardly. 'So perhaps we should wait?'

The comtesse nodded agreeably, and they

proceeded to spend the next ten minutes making small talk about Paris and New York, and Claudia, who, it turned out, the comtesse knew well.

'She is coming to Europe at the beginning of next month, I believe,' the comtesse said, placing her tiny coffee cup back into its saucer.

Patsy nodded, and wondered if the comtesse knew that Claudia was simply passing through en route to Switzerland for yet another facelift. Even if she did, it was hardly the kind of detail one mentioned without being certain. 'Are you planning to see her while she's here?' she asked chattily.

The comtesse twinkled. 'You are living at her apartment, no? So I have invite her to stay at my home with me.'

Wondering about the rarefied world of these rich old biddies, and shuddering again at the thought of the role Frank might be playing in their boudoirs, Patsy glanced at the time and said, 'Perhaps we should make a start?'

'Yes, why not? I am happy for you to speak me in English, but if you can do in French, it will maybe be a little better for my hearing.'

'Of course,' Patsy assured her, and really wanted to wring Frank's neck now, because they'd agreed he would take over if the comtesse preferred to hear French. She'd had no time to prepare, so her translation would have to come off the cuff, which meant that if the dear old soul went away fully appraised of the amazing package they'd put together for her, a minor miracle would have occurred.

In the event, a slightly bigger one turned up

just as she was about to begin, when the door opened and Frank himself breezed in, all five o'clock shadow, psychedelic shirt and a takeaway carton of frothy cappuccino.

'I am so sorry to be late,' he cried earnestly. 'Everything takes so long to achieve these days, and the traffic was terrible . . . Céline, how are you, *chérie? Tu es ravissante, comme normale.'*

Patsy could only stare as he kissed the comtesse on both cheeks and kept hold of her hands. Clearly they knew one another well, given his use of 'tu' and their air of intimacy seemed to increase as he continued to murmur to her in French.

'*Et tu,'* he said, smiling affectionately as he turned to Pats, '*tu es enchanteresse.* I hope I have not caused you to interrupt. Please, continue.'

'Actually,' Patsy said, almost failing to keep her tone sweet, 'Madame la Comtesse would prefer to hear it in French, so perhaps you would like to take over.' Let him get out of that, she thought feistily.

'*Mais bien sûr,'* he responded, and binning his coffee he went to take up position at the computer, where, to Patsy's amazement, and no little frustration, he launched into an extremely relaxed but no less professional presentation of their proposals for the comtesse's salons and spas. It was as though he'd been up half the night compiling and rehearsing it, which couldn't have been possible, when she'd only emailed her final draft to him an hour ago.

By the end of the morning she was fighting more sinister misgivings than a sane mind could cope with, but fortunately she managed to appear perfectly calm as the comtesse made her farewells and Frank took her downstairs to the waiting taxi.

Patsy was waiting when he came back to the conference room, her green eyes flashing with outrage. 'What the hell is going on?' she demanded. 'Where have you been for the past twenty-four hours, and why didn't you tell me how well you knew the comtesse?'

'Patreesha,' he cried, throwing out his hands in surrender, 'please do not be angry. I am in a bad situation with my wife and so . . .'

Patsy's eyes boggled. 'Are you seriously telling me that you went AWOL because of some wrangle with your wife?' she cried furiously.

He frowned. 'Excuse me, what is AWOL?'

'It means you disappeared off the face of the planet as far as I was concerned, and I want to know why.'

'I just explain I have a bad situation with my wife . . .'

'That's not good enough. There are phones and computers. You could have let me know where you were, and at least put my mind at rest that you would be here for the meeting. Or was this some deliberate ploy to ride in at the last minute to rescue the comtesse from my inferior French and make me look . . .'

'Stop, please, Patreesha,' he said, assuming his most mournful expression. 'There was no ploy, only a small crisis that I must deal with. It is over now, and I think we do very well for the comtesse, no?'

'Yes, and I'd like to know how you were able to turn it on like that, when you'd hardly had the final draft an hour, and most of it was put together by me.'

'But we have had many discussions about the presentation,' he reminded her, 'and when I send you my suggestions I can make very good guesses how you will incorporate them. So when I see what you send by email this morning, it is then not difficult for me to, how you say, turn it on.'

Only just buying it, she said, 'That still doesn't explain why you asked the comtesse to leave her team at home.'

Still not appearing in the least bit fazed, he said, 'To put it very bluntly, I was concerned, if I did not get here in time, that it would be a little intimidating for you to present alone in front of so many French people. Especially if you have to do it in French, which I suspected she would prefer.'

'But what are you to her, that she would do as you ask just like that?'

He gave her a smile.

Her lip started to curl. 'Please don't tell me . . . Frank, you can't. It's . . .'

'You need the boo-kett?' he offered.

'If what I'm thinking is true, then yes, I do.'

He started to laugh. 'I am 'appy to tell you that you are wrong. I know Céline very well, it is a fact, but not in this way you are meaning, because then it would be incest and that would not be good.'

Patsy blinked.

'Céline is the sister of my father,' he explained.

Resisting the urge to slap him, she said, in as contemptuous a tone as she could muster, 'The Comtesse du Petits-Louvens is your aunt.'

He nodded.

'And you didn't tell me this before because . . . ?'

He merely shrugged in his typically Gallic way.

'I want some answers, Frank,' she said fiercely, 'and if I don't start getting them, *now*, I will be speaking to Claudia when she comes about making some changes around here, and yes that means what you think it does. And don't try telling yourself she won't back me, because I know she will.'

Frank's expression was a little tragic as he said, 'Please, promise me, for your own sake, that you will not put it to the test.'

Patsy's jaw dropped in shock.

'Claudia is an old friend of my family,' he told her, almost apologetically.

Patsy could only stare at him, so confounded by this emerging net of connections that she began to feel unnervingly entangled, even betrayed. 'I should feel surprised by that,' she said coldly, 'but for some reason I don't.'

'I believe that Claudia tell you this herself,' he confessed. 'Her husband, before he die, was the partner of Céline's brother in their company of law. Now, it is the son of Céline and my cousin, Bertrand, who are the senior partners of the firm.'

'I see,' she said tightly. 'And you, Frank? Why aren't you at the top of this company, where we all know you should be?' Then with an acid sarcasm, 'Especially considering your connections.'

He threw out his hands helplessly. 'I don't know what to tell you,' he said, sounding genuinely sorry. 'I am just Frank, and you are running this company with very good efficiency, I think everyone agree about that, and I am extremely 'appy to work for you.'

Despairing of ever getting anywhere, she began gathering up her files and laptop. 'You weren't straight with me about your relationship with the comtesse,' she reminded him, 'or about how close you are to Claudia. Those two facts alone prove that I can't trust you, and if I can't trust *you* then life around here could start to get very difficult indeed. Unless I leave, which I think is what this is really all about.'

He could hardly have looked more stunned. 'This would be the very last thing I am after,' he assured her. 'You must surely know that I have *une vraie tendresse* for you that I have never tried to hide.'

'No, you've used it to try and make a fool of me, and I'm sorry to say you've succeeded. But no more, Frank . . .'

'Patreesha,' he interrupted, sounding surprisingly harsh for him, 'you will listen to me, please. I have great admiration and respect for you, I also have other feelings for you that I think you would rather not hear of now. But that does not stop them existing, nor does it mean that I will allow you to go on thinking bad things of me. You have my complete loyalty and support, and though I will admit there are certain things I find it very difficult to discuss, they do not at all alter who I am.'

'I don't see how . . .'

'I know you have had your heart broken,' he said over her, 'and because of this you are suspicious and mistrustful of others, but you have no need to be that way with me because I have had my heart broken too. It is not a good thing, but it does not make me afraid of you, or of the life that do this to me. Instead it make me value it more. The mask you have seen, he is another part of me that sometimes I need to get me through the day. He is my guardian, my entertainer to distract the world when the other parts of me want to break down. Now I will leave you with this, because I need to go home and shave,' and making her a courteous little bow he walked out of the room.

'Alan, your lawyer's on the line,' Janet announced through the intercom. 'Shall I put him on?'

'Sure,' Alan replied, and turning away from his computer where he was researching case studies of paternal abandonment, he pressed the connection and picked up the phone. 'Ken,' he said with a forced brightness. 'How are you?'

'I'm fine. Bit overworked, but nothing new there. I've some bad news, I'm afraid.'

Alan's face drained of colour. 'Please tell me Helen's not going ahead with her threats,' he said shakily.

'Not exactly, but it seems she saw Susannah's interview on GMTV – more to the point, so did her brother.'

Alan's eyes closed in despair. This was exactly what he'd been afraid of, and why he'd reacted so angrily after Susannah had gone back on her word. They'd made up again now, but clearly the damage had already been done. 'Have you spoken to either of them?' he asked.

'The brother, about ten minutes ago, and it wasn't pleasant. We could have him arrested for attempted blackmail, but I don't think you really want to go that route, any more than anyone else.'

'Absolutely not,' Alan confirmed.

After a pause Ken said, 'You're in a very vulnerable position, now they know you're involved with Susannah.'

Turning back to the screen, Alan looked at the report and closed his eyes against the anguish building inside him. Far, far more vulnerable than his lawyer realised, but he didn't need to tell him that yet.

'So what do I say to the brother when he rings back?' Ken prompted.

Taking a breath, Alan closed down the screen and said, 'Ask him if he really wants to do this to his sister's children, and if he's prepared to, tell him I am too.'

'He'll know you're bluffing.'

'But I might not be.'

'I hope you are.'

'It's got to end some time, Ken, and I'm not having Susannah's life torn apart over something that has nothing to do with her.'

'I understand what you're saying, but you have to think of her daughter too. This isn't . . .'

'I do, all the time,' Alan interrupted. 'Now, if you'll forgive me, I have a patient waiting,' and after promising to call back later in the day, he rang off and speed-dialled Susannah's mobile.

'Hi, darling,' she said, coming cheerily on to the line. 'To what do I owe this pleasure in the middle of the day?'

350

With a tender smile he said, 'I was thinking about you and wanted to hear you. What are you doing?'

'Right now I'm at a hair salon being videotaped having highlights, and talking to you.'

'Remember your promise, no names,' he said softly, even though it was already too late. But there was no point aggravating the situation by putting it out there again and again.

'Don't worry, I haven't forgotten. What are you doing?'

'Actually, I was wondering if you'd like to go up to Derbyshire this weekend to take a look at the set, if it's allowed. We could stay in a hotel nearby and start familiarising you with the surroundings, as you're going to be there such a lot.'

'Oh darling, that is such a wonderful idea, and I'd love to . . . Can you stop recording a moment, please,' she said to someone in the background. Then, coming back on the line, 'I have a double riding lesson on Saturday morning, and costume fittings in the afternoon. Then on Sunday, the main cast is getting together with the writers and producers at the Savoy to talk about interpretation and character development.'

'I see,' he said, suppressing a flash of irritation. 'Well, it was just a thought.'

'And a really lovely one. It means so much to me that you're taking an interest.'

'I'm trying,' he confirmed, 'but already losing you for an entire weekend isn't making it easy.'

'I know and I'm sorry. Things will settle into a proper routine once the shooting starts, then we'll be able to make plans and stick to them.'

Stifling a sigh, he said, 'Let's hope so. Anyway, I'll let you get on with your video. Will I see you this evening?'

'Unless things change between now and then I should be home around seven.'

After ringing off he sat quietly in his chair, thinking, planning, trying to come to decisions that could cost him so much more than he was willing, or even able, to pay. In the end, pushing everything else aside, he picked up the phone again and called Neve.

She didn't answer so he left a message. 'Hi, it's me,' he said, 'I was wondering what you were doing at the weekend. Mum's going to be quite busy apparently, so I was thinking, if you're free, I could take some photographs of you to put in a frame for her to keep in Derbyshire. We can make it a surprise if you like, and I wouldn't mind one or two shots for myself to put up here at the office. Call when you can,' and ringing off he went back to his study of the short- and long-term effects of paternal abandonment.

'Oh my God,' Neve murmured, her cheeks turning crimson as she listened to Alan's message.

'What?' Sasha prompted, sliding into a chair in the dining hall with a tray full of food.

'He wants to take photos of me,' Neve told her, feeling a buzzy sort of sensation coming all over her.

Sasha was searching the table for ketchup. After shouting for someone to pass it when they'd finished, she said, 'What kind of photos?'

'I don't know.' She didn't want to admit they were for her mother or it might not sound as good. And anyway, it might just be an excuse.

As Sasha fell into conversation with some others at the table, Neve sat staring at her food, not seeing it, only feeling the unsteadying force of a heat growing inside her as she imagined herself striking all sorts of poses. She was showing her legs and her midriff and her cleavage, and pouting into the lens like a model. She began wondering what she'd do if he asked her to take off her top, but as she started to imagine herself doing it the burn between her legs became so intense she had to make herself stop.

'Aren't you going to eat that?' Sasha asked, her fork ready to plunge into Neve's spag bol.

Neve shook her head. 'No, you can have it if you like,' she said.

It wasn't until much later in the day that she rang Alan back to say she'd love to do some photos. 'When's a good time for you?' she said shyly into his voicemail. 'I can be free whenever you like.'

Ten minutes later she received a text saying *How about Saturday afternoon?*

Feeling almost sick with anticipation, she pressed in *Cool*, then clutched the phone hard as if to stop the text leaving it, even though it had already gone.

All that night she lay awake in her room planning and imagining and becoming so aroused by her thoughts that she felt dizzy and almost queasy with excitement – and shame. It wasn't as though she'd never touched herself intimately before, because she had, plenty of times, but tonight was the first time she'd allowed herself to do it while thinking of Alan.

When she stopped she wanted to tear at her skin, or rip out her hair as though to get rid of her disgrace, but by morning the burning sensations were back, hotter and more piercing than ever. She could barely look at him as they sat across from one another at breakfast, and wondered how much of what her mother was saying was reaching him, because almost nothing was getting through to her.

Finally she heard Alan say, 'Well, now you're free for the afternoon I can tell you what Neve and I were planning to do, so perhaps you can join in.'

Shock and misery drained the colour from Neve's face as she looked at him, then at her mother. 'I thought you had costume fittings this afternoon?' she said dully.

'It was cancelled just before you came down,' Susannah told her. Then to Alan, 'Whatever it is, I'd love to join in. Is it possible that Lola can too?'

'Absolutely,' he answered with a laugh. 'In fact I should have invited her anyway. I was going to take shots of Neve to frame for you to keep in Derbyshire, but now you can be in them too, as can Lola . . .'

'And you too!' Susannah cried, wrapping her arms around him in delight. 'Oh God, I love you so much for thinking of it. You're amazing and wonderful and I know I'm embarrassing Neve . . . Don't go, darling,' she begged, trying to grab Neve's arm. 'I'm sorry, I just got a bit carried away.'

Neve shrugged her off. 'I've got homework to do,' she said shortly.

'What about your breakfast? You haven't eaten anything yet.'

'I don't want any. Actually, I'm not sure I can make the photos either, because Sasha's asked me to go shopping.'

After she'd gone Susannah turned to Alan in dismay. 'I think I've just stolen her thunder,' she said quietly.

He nodded a wry agreement. 'If she's not down in fifteen minutes I'll go up and have a chat with her,' he said.

When Neve failed to show, true to his word he went upstairs to knock on her door. 'It's me,' he called when there was no answer. 'Can I come in?'

There was the muffled sound of her moving, followed by a tragic, 'OK.'

He found her sitting on the edge of the bed, brushing her hair, and trying to keep her face averted, but it was evident right away that she'd been crying. He didn't mention it, only went to turn a chair away from her dressing table to sit facing her.

'I'm sorry if you're feeling a bit let down about this afternoon,' he said, attempting to catch her eye.

'It's cool. I don't mind,' she answered with a shrug.

'I think it would have been quite special if it had been just us,' he told her softly. 'But there'll be other times.'

She swallowed hard as her cheeks flamed.

'We can take photos, or go for a walk, or simply

hang out together, here at home,' he suggested. 'Would you like that?'

Her chin went up, but she still wouldn't look at him as she said, 'If that's what you want.'

'It is, very much,' he whispered, and reaching for her hand he held it between his.

They sat that way for several minutes until finally she brought her eyes to his.

'Can I have a smile?' he asked tentatively.

In spite of trying to stop them her lips started to curve.

'That's better,' he told her. 'And now, how about a kiss?'

Her face flushed beet red as her heart did a violent flip. Did he mean like before? Or . . . She looked at his lips and felt her head starting to swim.

'Perhaps you'd like me to kiss you?' he offered gently.

Her eyes stayed down as she gave a breathy sort of sob and tried to nod.

He leaned forward and she stayed where she was. His lips felt warm and spongy on her own, and wet on the inside as he parted them slightly.

'There,' he said, a moment later, 'does that feel better?'

She swallowed hard.

He got to his feet and slipped a hand under her hair. 'You can have one of those any time you like,' he told her softly, 'but it has to be our secret, OK?'

She looked up at him, and as he smiled she felt as though her heart might explode with fear and elation. 'OK,' she whispered.

After he'd gone she went on sitting where she was, still feeling the pressure of his mouth on hers, and the fierce pounding of the beat in her chest that seemed to be getting louder and harder until she couldn't hear or feel anything else. What had happened was seriously wicked, and she didn't know whether she wanted to scream or cry or lie down on the bed and curl up and die.

Chapter Seventeen

It hardly seemed possible that the day of departure for Derbyshire was coming around so fast. After a month of almost constant press and publicity, and the kind of build-up worthy of a Canaveral launch, Susannah had finally arrived at the point where she was almost as familiar to the public as she was to herself. Already she was finding it virtually impossible to go anywhere without being recognised, and hardly a day passed that she wasn't featured in at least one newspaper, magazine or TV chat show.

'It's amazing,' she told Patsy as they strolled arm in arm on Clapham Common the day before she was leaving, 'half the time I'm pinching myself to make sure it's real, and the other half I'm convinced it's all about to come crashing down around me.'

Patsy's smile was wry. 'I don't think that's going to happen,' she said confidently.

Susannah suppressed a shiver. 'In retrospect I'd like to have gone in quietly, just in case of implosion,' she said, 'but it's too late now. The cameras start rolling on Monday, and two weeks after that the public will get to see for themselves what all the fuss has been about. I'm absolutely dreading it, because after this sort of hype expectations are going to be soaring beyond any possibility of satisfaction.'

'How are the scripts looking?' Pats asked, amused by a jogger who almost hit a post as he recognised Susannah.

'My answer to that changes by the minute,' she confessed, 'which is nerves, of course. I'm in all of the first six episodes, and I've got some great storylines. I haven't told Alan yet that one of them involves seducing two of the judges at a county show in order to make sure Silver qualifies for Horse of the Year.'

'At the same time, or individually?'

'Don't be shocked, but at the same time. I even toss a coin to decide who goes first.'

'My God! What kind of woman is she?'

'Sly, conniving, deadly ambitious and sex-mad. And that's her shy side.'

Laughing, Patsy said, 'So not exactly casting to type?'

'No, she's definitely nothing like me, which is why she's going to be so fantastic to play. I can really get my teeth into how scheming and bitchy she is, but she has a few redeeming qualities, well, one anyway, she absolutely adores her horse – which reminds me, I've only been approached by *Playboy* to do a centrefold, on horseback, as Lady Godiva.'

'Which you had to know was coming. Are they offering a small fortune?'

'Actually, quite a large one, but I've turned it down. It's not the kind of thing I want to get into.'

'Does Alan know?'

'Yes, and needless to say he thoroughly approved of my failure to be tempted by untold riches. However, he was pretty keen to take some risqué shots himself, which we had quite a bit of fun with before he erased them. Now, enough about me. We've hardly spoken this last couple of weeks, so I want to hear what's been happening with you. Have you found out any more about Frank's aristocratic connections, or who broke his heart?'

'I'm presuming that was his wife,' Patsy answered, 'but there's no one to ask . . . Correction, no one I'm *prepared* to ask about him, apart from Claudia, and since it's not something I want to get into on the phone I'm waiting until she flies in at the end of next week. At which point, maybe she'll be able to explain how Frank knows my heart has been broken.'

'Well, obviously she must have told him,' Susannah replied, 'how else could he know? And I think it's good that he does. It gives him a better understanding of *you* as a person, instead of you as his boss. Anyway, all that aside, have you seen much of him?'

'Less than usual, because we've both been all over the place, me in Rome and Prague, then Madrid, while he's been visiting the regional sales people in France about customer service, and how we can beat off the competition with ours. I have an incentive plan, but I need a good feasibility study and the go-ahead from Claudia before I can put it into motion. But we don't want to talk about all that, tell me more about the series and the other members of the cast. What are they like?'

Susannah waggled a hand, *comme ci comme ça*. 'Mostly great,' she said, 'George especially, but the jury's still out on a couple of them, like Polly Grace who got the part of Penelope. We detest one another on screen, and I fear it's not going to stop with the cameras, because apparently I stole Marianne from one of her closest friends, who everyone *just knew* the part had been written for.'

'Is that so? Sounds to me more like sour grapes that you got a better part. Have you seen Michael Grafton at all since you had lunch?'

'Only once, at a drinks party last week, but the place was packed and as I was supposed to be one of the star attractions I had to spread myself around, which meant we barely said more than hello. I'll probably see him tomorrow at the pre-shoot meeting.'

'Is Alan taking you up to Derbyshire?'

'No. It's cast, crew and production personnel only this weekend. We have to get settled into our accommodation and familiarise ourselves with the sets. He's going to try and take some time off during the week, though, to come and spend the night, which'll be great if he can, because as luck would have it I'm supposed to be sharing a cottage – or they call it a lodge – with, guess who, Polly Grace.'

Patsy chuckled. 'That should be fun,' she commented. 'Can't you get it changed?'

'Probably, but if I do it'll only set her back up more, and she's not actually in very many scenes, so it's not as though she's going to be around all the time, or for very long.'

'Well, that's a relief. Now, what about Neve? How's her crush going? God, even thinking of all the hormones flying about in your house is bringing me out in spots.'

With a laugh, Susannah said, 'On the whole she seems to be handling it fairly well, I think, but she still has moments when she gets quite down or querulous and short-tempered with me. Alan's incredibly good with her. Her attachment to him, and sudden mood swings, aren't only about her age, he tells me, they're about the way she perceives her father to have abandoned her . . . Speaking of whom, wouldn't you just know it, he popped out of the woodwork again a couple of days ago, wanting to know if I'd agree to sell the house now I'm doing so well.'

'So you informed him it's let and that he could go bury himself again?'

'Kind of. I said I'd share the rent with him after he's repaid what he owes me from the last three years' mortgage. He wasn't thrilled, as you can imagine, but once I'd reminded him it was the only way he was going to get half the value of the house when it is eventually sold he let it drop.'

'Did he ask about Neve?'

'Actually, yes. He wanted her mobile number, but I couldn't give it to him until I'd checked with her first, and she was absolutely adamant that I must not, under any circumstances, let him have it.'

'Mm. What did Alan have to say about that?'

'That it was sad, but not especially surprising. He thinks it'll change in time, but it's probably best not to try pushing her, at least until she's become more used to me being away a lot.'

'I guess that makes sense. So, all in all, every-thing seems to be falling into place at last.'

Susannah smiled as a wave of happiness coasted through her. 'Don't let's tempt fate,' she cautioned, 'but yes, it's feeling pretty good right now. I just wish you weren't seeming so down.'

'Me?' Patsy cried in surprise. 'I'm fine. What makes you say that?'

'You just don't seem your usual lively self.'

'Probably because I've been working all hours, and I have to admit, I don't always find it easy being in an office where I have to try so hard to get along with people. My natural charm has always worked its magic before, but if I've ever come across a cultural clash it's now. It didn't happen in Australia at all, but in France, which is so close it's like stepping out of your front door on to the path by comparison . . .' She sighed. 'We just don't seem to think the same way, never mind behave, but the differences are so subtle that half the time you can hardly even put them into words.'

'Does that mean you're starting to become jaded with Paris?'

'Not with Paris, just with some of my colleagues, and now Frank's not around much lending his support my valiant efforts to integrate are like trying to carve my initials in sand – no sooner have I finished than they're swept away by the next tide of bigotry, or resentment, or whatever the hell else they've got on their agenda.'

'Well, you're the boss, is it possible you could base yourself in another European city, such as here, in London?'

Pats shook her head. 'Claudia wouldn't want that. She's keen to conquer France in a way she hasn't managed up till now, and I'm not ready to give up yet, anyway. However,' she went on, forcing a smile, 'it feels really good to be here, because look where we are. Do you remember how we used to consider it a huge adventure to come down here to Clapham Common for the day when we were kids? It seemed such a long way away from our estate, didn't it?'

'Miles. And when the circus was here we'd think we were going on a major expedition. We couldn't sleep for days beforehand and you were actually sick with excitement once, I remember.'

Patsy laughed. 'Does it still hold that much appeal for children?' she wondered. 'For us, it was an amazing magic kingdom. Stand aside Lion, Witch and Wardrobe, or Harry Potter, or Lord of the Rings. We had Clapham Circus.' She smiled ironically. 'And now here you are, about to enter a magic kingdom for real.'

Susannah squeezed her arm. 'But not before Alan's taken us all out for dinner tonight,' she responded. 'I'm so glad you were able to make it. As Lola said earlier, with you here it feels as though the family's complete.'

'That's so sweet of her,' Patsy replied, meaning it. 'But tomorrow we all go our different ways again.' As well as Susannah's new journey she was thinking of her own Eurostar to Paris, and Frank, and whether he was due to be in the office on Monday.

'The good thing is,' Susannah said, 'no matter where we are or what we're doing, we'll still always have the invisible threads that tie us.'

'Without which,' Patsy added, 'there wouldn't be a lot of point to anything really, would there?'

Laughing at her gloomy tone, Susannah said, 'I suppose not. Now, if I were you, Pats, I'd start facing up to the fact that you're falling for that man, because as long as you're in denial, you're going to be in this depression.'

'This isn't a depression,' Patsy informed her hotly, 'this is an all-out black despair, because I swear I can't stand him really, I just can't seem to stop thinking about him.'

'He's definitely got through to you,' Susannah chuckled, clearly enjoying Patsy's struggle, 'so when you do finally get it together, make sure you're on the phone to me the minute it's over, because I'll be wanting every detail. And no pretending next time that you can't remember what happened.'

'I swear there was no pretence the last time,' Pats said earnestly. 'Those hours are still a complete blank to me, and remain the source of high amusement for him. Or I suppose they do, it's hard to know for certain when I rarely see him these days, and it's annoying the hell out of me that I seem to mind about that.'

With a sigh, Susannah tightened her hold on Patsy's arm as she said, 'Love's never easy, is it?'

'Definitely not where I'm concerned,' Pats retorted, 'but I'm not in love with Frank so it doesn't apply. And I'm not sure you can say that about you and Alan. Unless we're talking about Michael, of course.'

Susannah cast her a glance of surprise. 'I was absolutely meaning Frank,' she assured her. 'And whatever you say, as soon as it's possible, I'm coming over there to Paris to meet him.'

'Fine, but I'm starting to wonder if I might be needed in Derbyshire first to help put out the flames of a hotter than hot affair.'

Susannah's eyebrows rose. 'You mean with Michael?' she said. Then with a mischievous twinkle, 'Well, actually, put like that, what can I say but bring it on,' and laughing delightedly they turned tail to begin a much brisker walk back to the house, where Neve, Alan and Lola were setting up aperitifs before the taxi arrived to take them for dinner.

'Here's to Susannah,' Alan toasted when they were all settled at their table in the restaurant later.

'Susannah,' everyone echoed.

'Long may she shine and far may she reign,' Patsy added.

'Pats, that's really good,' Neve told her, almost choking with her determination to get in fast.

'I'm known for it,' Patsy commented wryly.

'Amongst other things,' Susannah muttered and they all laughed.

Susannah was looking sensational in a black and silver dress that clung lovingly to her figure, while her glistening blonde hair fell like shimmering bands of silk around her shoulders and back. Already a waiter and another customer had come to ask for her autograph, which was an interruption Alan had seemed to consider an intrusion, while Lola had been tickled pink, and Neve had almost burst with pride to be at the same table as someone famous, even if it was her mum.

'OK, shall we all choose what we're going to eat?' Alan suggested. 'Then we can really get stuck into the fizzy stuff.'

No sooner had the ordering been done than Patsy's mobile bleeped with a text, causing everyone to groan. 'No work tonight,' Neve protested. 'You have to turn it off.'

'It might be *Fronk*,' Susannah told her.

'In that case,' Neve said, 'can we all read it?'

'It won't be him,' Patsy said, opening up the message. 'He's in Toulon.'

'Oh, like the end of the world where phones don't work,' Neve declared knowingly. 'So come on, what's he saying?'

'It's not from him,' Patsy insisted, her cheeks starting to colour.

'Liar!' Susannah laughed. 'I can tell by your face that it is.'

'OK, but you're not reading it. Any of you.'

'That's not fair!' Neve cried. 'I'd show you if it was from one of my boyfriends.'

'One of?' Lola chipped in. 'How many do you have?'

Neve blushed. 'Enough,' she answered, throwing a girlish glance at Alan.

'That means too many,' he said with mock sternness.

'Well, anyway, I would show you,' Neve insisted. 'So come on, Pats. Hand it over.'

'Absolutely no way,' Patsy retorted, and turning the phone off she opened her bag, dropped it inside and zipped the bag up again. 'So, where were we?' she enquired with an eye-fluttering smile.

'I think it was good,' Susannah whispered to Neve.

'I do too,' Neve replied. 'She's trying to pretend she's not interested, but you can tell by the way . . .'

'Will you stop,' Patsy cut in. 'Alan, do you have no control over the women in your life?'

'Now how dumb a question is that?' he responded, throwing out his hands. 'Look at them. How can I be expected to have anything as grand as control? But in their royal munificence they do allow me to think I have a little every now and again.'

'When it suits us,' Neve confirmed, and immediately blushed at her own temerity. 'So come on, Mum,' she said quickly, 'talk us through what's going to happen tomorrow. I know you've got a taxi picking you up at ten in the morning – have you finished packing, by the way? I hope you haven't nicked anything of mine, because if you have . . .'

'Don't worry, your precious Topshop collection is safe.'

'It better be. Anyway, the taxi takes you to Hyde Park, where you transfer to a bus . . .'

'Luxury coach,' Susannah corrected.

'. . . that will chauffeur you and God knows who else to the Derbyshire dales.'

'About forty other cast and crew,' Susannah supplied. 'We'll then be taken to our various lodgings, which I'm assured are home from home, and everything's in the same valley so we'll never be too far from the set.'

'You mean they've bought an actual valley?' Patsy enquired, ready to be wildly impressed.

'Leased, I think, from a local farmer or landowner. It's got everything from an enormous manor house to stables, barns, cottages, manèges, gallops, paddocks and obviously the Peak District right on the doorstep. Everyone else has already managed to get up there to have a look around, but tomorrow will be my first time, because I've been too tied up here with publicity and all the rest of it. Polly, who's obviously *not* going to be my best friend, has already informed me that she's moved her things into the lodge, and she hopes I don't mind, but she's taken the bedroom that has the en suite, because she has to get up a lot in the night.'

'Probably gets lonely,' Patsy decided, 'or has to check her incontinence pad.'

Alan gave a splutter of laughter.

'If she's a cow to you, Mum,' Neve jumped in, 'make sure you don't let her get away with it. You're the star, remember? You could probably have her fired.'

'Oh, the power's going to my head already,' Susannah joked.

'I'm serious,' Neve said. 'I bet you could. I mean, Michael Grafton himself chose you for the lead so that's got to mean something.'

'He was only a part of the decision-making process,' Susannah informed her, throwing a pained look Alan's way. 'The final say was with Marlene Wyndham.'

'My reckoning is,' Alan pronounced, 'that you're going to have a much easier time of it with the men than the ladies, so if you go out of your way to make friends with your own sex, you should be a winner all round.'

'And this isn't control?' Patsy cried with a laugh.

'Friendly advice,' he corrected.

'Mum's so brilliant with people, she'll be fine,' Neve weighed in. 'She gets it from Lola.'

'Who else?' Lola wanted to know. 'Actually, I could have been a TV star myself once, but they hadn't invented anything risky enough for me when my bits were in the right places.'

'Don't go there!' Neve cried. 'Alan hates thinking about Mum doing love scenes, don't you?' she challenged.

'Unless they're with me,' he responded.

Was there really, Pats was thinking as she went along with the banter, an undercurrent of tension around the table, or was it her imagination? Since she was slightly wound up by the text she'd received, her perspective was skewed, so she couldn't be certain, but she seemed to be sensing something, she felt sure of it. However, as the evening wore on, and they drank more champagne, she decided to give up trying to read a subtext that probably didn't even exist. Everyone seemed happy enough, and hopefully she did too, but by the time she sank into the new king-size bed in the guest room she couldn't help feeling relieved to be able to drop the facade.

Michelle and I in Marseilles Mon till Wed, then Bordeaux till Friday. This means will be unable to make marketing meeting on Thurs. Email with detailed itinerary to follow. F.

He was going to Marseilles with Michelle Maurice, the company's Director of Beauty, and a more aptly titled individual Pats had rarely come across. She was a sumptuously brunette version of a young Deneuve, with a figure that could make grown men fall to their knees and weep. It was only recently that she, Pats, had started to notice how friendly Frank and Michelle had become, or perhaps they'd always been close and she hadn't been interested enough in their personal lives to care. Now she felt sure they were having an affair, in spite of Michelle being married to a lawyer Pats had actually heard of, he was so successful. Not that Pats had pulled Michelle's personnel file to find that out, exactly, because she'd asked for the Director of Fragrance's details too, in order to review both their bonus schemes.

The dossiers were back at human resources now, and it was on Patsy's agenda to discuss her proposed increases with Frank at their next meeting. She was interested to see how he responded to discussing his mistress's financial rewards – if she was his mistress, and Pats was becoming increasingly certain that she was. To say it didn't bother her would be ludicrous self-deception, because she was hardly able to get it out of her mind. She kept imagining the two of them together, seeing their bodies entwined, erotic, steamy and sensuous beyond bearing. She was doing it now, and wanting to scream at the detestable images her mind was conjuring up.

In the end she got out of bed and went down-stairs to make herself a hot drink. To her surprise there was a light on in the sitting room, and pushing the door open she found Susannah curled up in the corner of a sofa with a script open on her lap.

'Hi,' Susannah whispered. 'Can't sleep?'

Patsy shook her head and came to sit down.

'Me neither,' Susannah said, 'so I thought I'd go over my lines.' After a beat she said, 'Is it the text? Did he say something . . .'

'It's fine,' Patsy interrupted. 'He was just letting me know that he's going to be in Marseilles and Bordeaux next week.'

'Is that a problem?'

'No, not at all.' Reaching for the script she began flicking through it, but then handed it back. 'Everything's changing, isn't it?' she said quietly. 'We're on the threshold of something new, you especially.'

'You too. Your job's still only a couple of months old.'

Patsy turned to her and put a hand on Susannah's cheek as she smiled. 'Your life's already moving forward in ways you hardly dared imagine,' she said. 'You have Alan now, this house, your newfound fame, but it's going to be what happens up there in Derbyshire that will bring about the biggest changes of all.'

'I know,' Susannah responded, 'it's why I can't sleep, because thinking about what they might be scares me half to death, but nothing in the world would make me back out now.'

'It's going to be a wonderful journey,' Pats said with certainty, 'just make sure you remember to enjoy it, and don't forget who your friends are.'

'That's something,' Susannah told her with feeling, 'that I know I will never forget.'

Chapter Eighteen

Just as Susannah had been told, the Larkspur Centre of Equitation was set entirely in its own valley, a rich, dramatic sweep of natural land buried deep in the Derbyshire dales. As far as the eye could see the fields, forests, peaks and streams had been taken over by Michael Grafton's production company, as had the small village that straggled over one of the slopes. Several more individual cottages were scattered through the vale, along with a collection of variously converted barns, sheds, stables and mews and other outbuildings, all tucked randomly into the swathe of land. Sitting resplendently at the valley's heart was the seventeenth-century mansion which was to be home to *Larkspur*'s fictitious family by day, and to senior members of production and crew by night. Though Susannah had already seen pictures of it, and read about it in the publicity handouts, the soaring turrets and ivy-clad walls were so thrilling in reality that it made her heart swell with pride to see it.

As the bus began its descent into the valley she was eagerly drinking in the magical landscape, and feeling so much emotion that she couldn't even murmur her admiration as many of the others were. If there were anywhere in the entire country more beautiful than these sweeping hills and fells, she had never been there. Even on a day like today, when the sun wasn't much in evidence and the startling and soothing colours of early summer were veiled by the drabbing fall of rain, its charm was so encompassing that she could feel herself being drawn into it as though she really was Marianne, and this was where she'd always belonged.

At the end of a narrow winding lane the bus paused for a barrier to swing upwards, and just beyond it Susannah caught her first glimpse of the lodge she was to share with Polly Grace. It appeared every bit as quaint and inviting as the photographs she'd seen, nestling amongst the trees with its wisteria-covered walls and newly thatched roof. Surrounding it was a small garden with a freshly laid patio area and a privet hedge to mark out its borders.

Since the itinerary called for everyone to be taken straight to the big house on arrival, the bus continued along the beech-lined drive, passing carefully tended manèges and a small fleet of horseboxes, before turning around an enormous stone barn that was announced as the production offices and a prop store. Beyond that was another, smaller barn with a vast parking area behind it, much of which was taken up by cranes, lorries, forklift trucks and various other construction vehicles.

Then they were crunching over the gravel of the stableyard, which was littered with benches, brooms, buckets and hoses. A handful of grooms and handlers were going about their business either on foot or horseback: one trotted off towards the exercise fields, while two others rode in from the gallops. Each of the horses Susannah could see was a chestnut, so no sign yet of Silver, whom she was as nervously excited about meeting as she was about starting the shoot.

When the bus finally came to a halt outside the house Harvey and Jayna, the publicists, were waiting to take everyone through to the kitchens where the caterers had refreshments waiting. The large stone-walled room with its bank of ovens, rack upon rack of utensils and dark oak cupboards was, like most of the rest of the house, doubling as a set. On the days it was being used for filming, meals would be served in the recreation barn on the far side of the stable blocks.

As everyone milled around, sipping tea and biting into triangular sandwiches, Susannah wandered outside with George Bremell, who was also seeing the Centre for the first time.

'It's beyond amazing, isn't it?' she murmured, as they strolled towards a manège where a groom was putting a proud-looking stallion through its paces.

'I've never seen anything like it,' he replied, his wrinkly face appearing genuinely overawed. 'Quite humbling, in its way,' he added. Then, as they reached the fence and leaned against it, 'How are you feeling about tomorrow?'

Susannah inhaled the wonderfully invigorating scent of horseflesh and fresh country air. 'I think I'm ready to get started now,' she finally answered. 'How about you?'

'About the same. If there's time later, I'm happy to run lines.'

Touched, and honoured, considering how established he was, she said, 'I'd love to. Thank you. Where are you staying, by the way?'

'Here, at the house, I believe. And you're at the lodge with Mzz Grace?'

Susannah smiled as she flicked him a look.

His only response was an eloquent raise of his eyebrows, but it was enough to confirm him as a friend, perhaps even an ally, should she need one.

'Hey, you two!' Harvey shouted through his cupped hands. 'We're about to tour the house. Are you coming?'

Taking the arm George offered, Susannah fell into step beside him, and didn't miss the sarcastically knowing look she received, courtesy of *Mzz* Grace, as they caught up with the group inside the main hall. The walls were crowded with a macabre display of stuffed animal heads, along with various trophies, old-fashioned tapestries, and an impressive collection of family portraits adorning the stairs. It wasn't until they'd been shown around the main drawing room, morning parlour, library and an extremely grand study, and were on their way up the stairs that Susannah recognised one of the portraits as her own. It was a strange and slightly unsettling experience, seeing herself as a member of another family, and the subject of a painting she didn't even know had been done. Clearly the artist had worked from a photograph, but it was still as though she had some kind of doppelgänger who was watching her from the other side of a mirror.

The master bedroom suite, belonging to her and George – or more accurately Marianne and Jerome – was almost as high as it was wide, with an intricate network of studio lights cluttering up the ceiling, a deep bay window overlooking the stableyard, and a vast four-poster bed, its monstrous headboard crammed with carvings of gargoyles and griffins. It was the only room upstairs that was to act exclusively as a set – the others were private living quarters for the producers, directors, designers and a very pleasant suite at the back for George.

The last port of call was the stables, but only for Susannah, since the others had either seen them before, or were keen to start settling into their quarters before the evening's welcome meeting in the production barn.

As she crossed the stableyard with Jayna, the publicist, Susannah was already falling in tune with the sound of hooves clattering on the cobbles, and the occasional breathy rumble of a horse snorting or munching on feed. She could smell the potent scent of hay and manure, and inhaled it like a perfume. Though she might still be a long way off the riding standard required for her character, it didn't mean she hadn't developed a love of horses, because she certainly had. Of all the new experiences that had come her way over the past few weeks, acquiring the confidence to mount a beast whose back was higher than her own head, and then to let go of her ego so she could become one with the animal, had proved by far and away the most thrilling. If she'd had more time there was no doubt in her mind she'd have spent it having more lessons, not only to help with her character, but because she truly loved being in the saddle.

'Josie's here somewhere,' Jayna informed her, as they walked into the enormous complex of purpose-built stables. 'She's Silver's groom, and I know she's really looking forward to meeting you.'

As they passed, the stable hands, all of whom were to act as support cast in their own real-life roles, stopped work to come and shake Susannah's hand and welcome her. They were so kind and pleased to see her that she was starting to feel like a visiting monarch, until they reached a much larger stable at the rear of the building, and then, just as Michael Grafton had predicted, she knew she was in the presence of true royalty.

'Oh my God,' she murmured, putting a hand to her mouth as the most magnificent horse she could ever have imagined was led out of its stable. 'He's beautiful,' she said, swallowing hard.

'He's been very impatient to meet you,' Josie, the groom, informed her. 'We've had such a fuss on, haven't we, you old tyrant,' she said, giving a tug to Silver's lead rope.

Susannah spluttered with laughter as Silver gave a haughty toss of his head, then treated Josie to a retaliatory nudge.

'You be on your best behaviour now,' Josie warned, 'and remember, you're the beast half of this partnership. OK? I know you think you're the beauty, but she's that. Got it?'

As though he'd understood, Silver let go a derisory snort, then with a swish of his luxuriant tail and an elegant pawing of the straw he took a step closer to Susannah, stopping just short as though to challenge her to do the same. Delighted, Susannah moved in to stroke him, putting her head back to gaze up into his watchful dark eyes. Silver allowed the caresses, and even nudged her for more when she stopped, but then he required a reward for such graciousness, which Josie passed to Susannah to deliver.

As Silver's soft rubbery muzzle took the Blue Chip treats from her palm, Susannah laid a cheek against his neck, inhaling the wonderful warm scent of him and revelling in the incredible silkiness of his coat. The power that emanated from him was as thrilling as an elixir. She longed to ride him now, and as though sensing it, Josie said, 'Your saddle and bridle are ready and waiting in the tack room. I can get them if you like.'

Susannah looked at Jayna, whose lips flattened as she shook her head sadly.

'I'm sorry, there's isn't time,' Jayna grimaced. 'Unless you want to go to the lodge after the meeting, instead of before.'

Though torn, in the end Susannah decided she really ought to freshen up before the big get-together, so after giving Silver a hug, which earned her an affectionate-seeming brush with his nose in return, she followed Jayna out to where a unit bus was just returning from dropping off some of the others.

To her surprise, and relief, Polly Grace alighted, saying, 'Oh there you are. The lodge is all yours now. I hope I haven't used all the hot water,' and with a stiff splay of her fingers to affect a wave, she started off towards the main house.

Susannah glanced at Jayna, smiled, then taking the key Jayna was holding out to her, she hopped on to the bus.

Minutes later she was letting herself into the lodge, which turned out to be just as quaint inside as out. The small hallway was generously equipped with coat pegs and boot racks, and the dog-leg staircase was secured by a white spindled banister. Her bags were already there, having been delivered while she was being shown round the house, but she decided to check out the downstairs before going up to her room to change.

The sitting room was bigger than she'd expected with low, beamed ceilings, an inglenook fireplace with a built-in wood burner, plush navy carpeting and a capacious burgundy leather three-piece suite grouped around a mahogany coffee table. The kitchen, by contrast, was small, but there was enough room for a breakfast table in front of the window, and plenty of storage in the melamine-fronted units. She soon discovered which cupboards Polly had claimed for herself, since her name was pinned to several of the inside shelves. She'd also claimed her space in the fridge, freezer and walk-in larder. Amused, Susannah wondered which side of the dishwasher she might prefer, but didn't bother opening it to find out. Instead she stopped at a noticeboard to scan a list of the Centre's phone numbers which had been thoughtfully provided, along with all kinds of useful information about the local area, including times of buses and trains.

Apparently Polly had already divided up the

welcome grocery pack to the point that she'd opened a box of tea bags, counted them out and left Susannah's share in a heap on one of the unmarked shelves. Feeling tempted to cut the fruit in half, rather than taking a whole apple, orange and banana, Susannah returned to the hall and carried her bag up to the landing. She found Polly's name Sellotaped to the first and second doors, her own to a third and no one's to a fourth.

Intrigued to know why Polly had two rooms when she'd already informed Susannah she was taking the en suite, Susannah decided to investigate. The answer soon became apparent – the en suite only had a shower, whereas the main bathroom had both a shower and a bath. So apparently Polly had abandoned the en suite bedroom in favour of a fully equipped bathroom. The fourth door turned out to be a linen cupboard where once again Polly had left her markers, having claimed, Susannah learned from a quick glance at the inventory, three extra pillows, a blanket and two pairs of sheets. On Susannah's unlabelled shelves there was a single sheet, a pillowcase, and a blue chenille throw. Starting to find this quite amusing now, Susannah popped into the main bathroom to count up the loo rolls, then crossed over to her own en suite to discover less than half the number. Polly had also hoarded the lion's share of complimentary soaps and shampoos, as well as *all* the cleaning products.

Hearing her mobile ringing, Susannah ran back to her bedroom, which was rather cosy, she thought, with its deep springy mattress and mauve and lavender draperies, and grabbed it up.

'Hi,' Alan said. 'Can you talk? How's it going?'

'Your timing is perfect,' she told him, wandering to the window. 'This place is . . . Actually, I don't know how to describe it. The countryside around is stunning . . . I'm at the lodge now, which is very quaint and cosy, but I'm starting to wonder if I might wake up tomorrow to find myself sawn in half.'

'What?'

'Don't ask,' she laughed, deciding she didn't want to waste time on Polly. 'I've met Silver, which for my part was an out-and-out *coup de foudre*. He redefines magnificent, which I guess is only to be expected considering how many prizes he's won. I can hardly wait till tomorrow when I get to ride him.'

'You know, it feels strange to think of you in a place I've never seen,' he said. 'I'm not sure I like it.'

'It'll help once you've been here, so let's hope you manage to make it up for a night some time this week.' As she spoke she was unzipping her bag to lift out the framed shots he'd taken of her and Neve. 'I'm so glad Neve decided in the end to join us the day you took the photographs,' she said. 'She looks so lovely in them.'

'So do you,' he reminded her.

'We all do,' she smiled, coming across one of the three of them together. After placing it next to her bed, she carried the others to the tallboy, saying, 'It's really helping me to feel at home having them here, but I still think I'm going to find it odd sleeping alone tonight.'

'You and me both. I'm already missing you like

crazy. Remind me when you're back, just in case I can't make it up in the week?'

'On Friday evening, provided everything goes to plan with the schedule. I'm due to wrap at five, so I should make the six o'clock train.'

'Which'll get you into London around eight, I guess. Home by nine at the latest. I'm sure you won't feel like going out, so I'll cook something special. Neve might give me a hand, if I'm lucky.'

'Or maybe we should gently ask her to stay at Lola's?' It wasn't actually what she wanted, but feeling sure he would, she ought at least to suggest it.

'Actually, I don't think we should exclude her for your first weekend back,' he said.

Smiling with relief, she said, 'How is she? Have you taken her over to Lola's yet?'

'Just about to. She's upstairs in her room if you want to give her a call.'

'I'll have to do it later, because I should be going now or I'll miss the start of the meeting. Send her my love. Lola too,' and after assuring him again that she missed him and loved him she rang off and went to turn on the shower.

Discovering that Polly had, indeed, used up all the hot water, she soaped herself hastily in the lukewarm flow and managed to get out again before it turned ice-cold. Then, selecting a pair of tailored white jeans to wear with a strappy white T-shirt, she pulled a brush through her hair, snapped it into a low-rise ponytail, and throwing a shimmery grey pashmina over one shoulder she dug her feet into a pair of silver ballet pumps, ready to walk back up to the house.

However, she'd just reached the lodge gate when the security barrier rose and a sleek black Mercedes came through into the drive and pulled up alongside her. As one of the darkened windows went down she started to smile.

'Can I give you a lift?' Michael Grafton offered.

'Such great timing,' she told him, and tugged open the passenger door.

He waited for her to fasten her seat belt, then drove on, listening with amused interest as she gave him her first impressions of the Centre.

It wasn't until they came to a stop in front of the production barn that it occurred to her how their joint arrival was going to appear to those inside. Feeling her cheeks starting to burn, she turned to look at him.

'Well, I could always kiss you now and really get them going,' he said drolly, 'but I should probably take the wiser route and carry on as though everything's as straightforward and above board as it actually is.'

'Mum's going to call you later, after the big meeting,' Alan was saying as he dropped Neve's bags into the boot of his car.

Neve nodded vaguely while unravelling the wires of her iPod earplugs.

'Are you OK?' he asked, coming to put an arm around her as she stopped next to the passenger door.

Her head went to one side as she stood stiffly in his embrace. She wasn't really sure what she wanted to say, or do, she only knew that she wanted to go to Lola's, but at the same time she really, really didn't.

'It's only until the weekend,' he said softly, 'and I'll be by to pick you up from school on Wednesday, just as we planned.'

'Are you going up to Derbyshire?' she asked.

'I don't think I'll have the time.'

'Mum'll be disappointed.'

'I know, but I'll do my best to make it up to her. In the meantime, you're my main concern. Now tell me what's the matter, because I know something is.'

She shrugged and shook her head.

'You want to stay here, is that it?'

She turned away, gazing down the street towards the common.

'You know I'd be more than happy for you to stay,' he told her, 'but if you did, people would take it the wrong way, even though there wouldn't be anything wrong in it at all.'

She took a breath as though to say something, but whatever words were trying to come out melted back into the confusion inside her.

'Come on,' he said, giving her a squeeze, 'Lola's cooking for us, remember, so we don't want to be late.'

She turned her face up to his and gazed solemnly into his eyes. 'I really love Mum,' she said shakily.

'I know you do,' he replied, pressing a kiss to her forehead. 'We both do, and I hope we love each other too.' He looked at her expectantly.

'Yes,' she whispered, and feeling she was about to blush she quickly opened the door and got into the car before he could think she was waiting for him to kiss her, which she was, but there again, maybe she wasn't. And anyway he couldn't when they were standing in the middle of the street.

The production barn was even more crowded than Susannah had expected as she and Michael walked in, with people spread out all over the place, slumped in chairs, leaning against desks, perched on filing cabinets and even sitting on the floor. Leaving Michael at the door talking to one of the directors, she crept through the throng to a long wooden bench, close to the front but tucked away to one side, where George Bremell had saved her a space.

'Quite an entrance,' he whispered from the corner of his mouth as she sat down beside him.

'Pure coincidence,' she whispered back.

'Tell that to your room-mate.'

Following the direction of his eyes she saw Polly Grace staring at her pointedly, her attractive face soured by an expression of outright disdain.

Susannah treated her to a winning smile, but Polly's only response was to mutter something to the actress next to her, who gave Susannah a quick look before muttering something back.

Next to her George chuckled, which made Susannah laugh too, in spite of the jarring inside her, then someone began banging a desk for quiet. As the streaming burble of voices receded slowly into silence, all eyes turned towards the space at the front that had been cleared for the most senior members of the team. Michael Grafton took a seat slightly apart from the series producers, directors, script editors and Marlene Wyndham. He was still able to be seen, but suggested by his position that he wasn't going to be a part of the everyday scene.

Showing impressive agility, and no evident embarrassment, the diminutive Marlene stepped up on to a box that had been strategically placed for her in front of a microphone. After checking it was working with a tap of her fingers, she said, 'OK. I'm going to start by welcoming you all, and thanking those who aren't involved in tomorrow's shoot for coming anyway, so we can all be together for this momentous occasion.' Pausing as one of the production managers encouraged everyone to give themselves a round of applause, she waited for it die down, then said, 'I'm not going to make this long, but I thought it would be a good idea to precis what we're about and how we're going to work. I apologise in advance to those who've heard what I'm about to say before, but better that you hear it twice than not at all.'

She looked up, her owlish eyes travelling around the room as though in search of dissent. Apparently finding none, she continued.

'You will have met our two producers by now, Alex and Gillian. Gillian will be in charge of the red unit, and Alex the blue. At any one time two episodes will be shooting, while eight more will be in various stages of pre- or post-production. The logistics of this need only concern those in charge of scheduling; as far as the rest of us are concerned, we have only to do as we are told by the scheduling managers. If we do that, everything should tick over like clockwork. Should you find yourself needing to change your days off at any time, you can always make your request and it will be considered. But I want to emphasise this point very strongly indeed, whilst I appreciate that you all have lives outside *Larkspur*, when you are here this place and the programme will be your life, and if we don't all pull together we'll end up in trouble. So please, before you request any change to the schedule, think first how vital it really is, and how your needs are going to impact on everyone else. Sick children – I'm talking measles, flu, stomach upsets etc. – visits to the doctor and dentist, family birthdays, even invitations to appear on chat shows or at some kind of celebrity function, will not rate as important enough to make a change to the schedule. *Larkspur* and your commitment to it has to have an ongoing priority for you, or I'm afraid you will find yourselves being dropped from the team.'

She looked around the room again, spreading her warning with a meaningful gaze, then continued. 'As far as all your living arrangements go, if anyone would like to change their current situation the person to talk to is Nadia Wilson who's around somewhere . . . Yes, there she is, give us a wave . . . Nadia is our housekeeping manager, which means she's responsible for everything to do with your accommodation. She has a small army of domestic engineers, as she likes to call them, who will take care of your laundry – bedding, towels etc., not personal items – and the cleaning of your rooms, but they are not cooks, drivers or personal shoppers. If you want to enter into a private arrangement with any of them for additional duties, that's for you to work out – and to pay for.

'On the subject of money, there is a cash office here in the production barn, but it is for programme use only. If you need any personal money there are banks in Matlock with twenty-four-hour cash dispensers.'

Looking down at her notes, she slid the top page to the bottom, quickly scanned the next sheet and looked up again. 'Regarding access to the sets: this is a secure site, and no one who is not a part of the *Larkspur* unit will be allowed anywhere inside the perimeter without having first obtained the necessary permits. These can be acquired through the press office, so if any of you have friends or non-immediate family who'd like to visit, please don't bring them without going through the official channels or they'll be escorted back out of the valley. Yes, you can laugh,' she said as a titter went round, 'but it'll be highly embarrassing for both you and your guests should it happen, so be warned.'

She looked down again, flicked on, and then said, 'This next point of business concerns the actors, probably Susannah most of all. Fan mail will be dealt with by Cordelia, who's also our telephonist, where are you, Cordelia?' A plump, pretty girl stood up at the back and waved. 'She already has a good stock of signed photographs,' Marlene went on, 'and we can keep them coming as the series unfolds. Susannah has a photo shoot scheduled with Silver for Wednesday afternoon, I believe?' Receiving a nod from Jayna, she continued. 'Anyone wishing to deal with their own mail is welcome to, but I cannot stress this strongly enough, if anything appears even remotely off colour, or contains any kind of threat, veiled or otherwise, you are to give it straight to Nadia, or one of the producers, or to me. Most communications of this kind turn out to be harmless, but where personal security is concerned we can't be too careful.'

She consulted her notes again, scanned to the end and then said, 'OK, to finish up I want to make three quick points concerning democracy, diplomacy and dedication. First: as far as I'm aware everyone present is a member of the appropriate union governing our industry – if that's not the case, then you shouldn't be here. Second: we're going to be living in very close quarters with one another, so a thought or two before any angry explosion would serve everyone very well indeed. Third: I personally will not tolerate any less than one hundred per cent dedication to this series. We have invested in you, so in return I expect you to invest in us. There are always going to be things you disagree with, or that upset you, or that might seem unjust in some way. If that proves the case, my door is open, so are Alex's and Gillian's. Be assured, should any of you decide to go to the press with a gripe before coming to us, you will find your contract under negative renegotiation when the time comes. We must all work together, and I believe we can, so please don't let petty grievances lead you to make a mistake that we'll all end up regretting.'

After a final check of her notes she turned towards Michael Grafton, who said something Susannah couldn't quite catch, then returning to the mike she said, 'Michael's just reminded me that we've changed location for the press screening of the first two episodes. It's now going to happen in the viewing theatre here, at the Centre. We've moved it from the London venue, because so many of you will be working that day it seemed to make sense for the press to come to you, rather than the other way round.'

As everyone nodded agreement and approval she stepped down off her box, then the room fell silent again as Michael came to take over the mike.

'Since Marlene's covered just about all bases,' he said, 'it's only left for me to say that what we're hoping to achieve is a series that we can all be extremely proud of. Everything that can be done behind the scenes has been done, it's now up to you to turn *Larkspur* into a twice-weekly, highly rated, sometimes shocking, but regularly all-round entertaining drama series.' He smiled, and Susannah felt her hero-worship go up several more levels. 'Welcome, congratulations, and thank you for being here,' he said. 'Now, I believe drinks are being served in the recreation barn. Yes, I'm told they are . . .'

'On the house,' one of the production managers announced over the mike, 'but only for tonight. After that you're buying, and there will be no tabs.'

Half an hour later, finding herself in the thick of the throng, a virtually untouched glass of champagne in one hand and a barely nibbled vol-au-vent in the other, Susannah could hardly have felt more humbled or ecstatic. Everyone she spoke to from the crew and production teams was being so friendly and welcoming that she might have known them all her life, and already she could sense a spirit of camaraderie starting to weave its way around them all. It didn't matter that Polly was being bitchy and petty, she'd get over it eventually, and besides, to imagine she'd be liked by everyone would be self-delusional, or just plain arrogant.

Seeing Michael Grafton watching her from the group of people surrounding him, she smiled and raised her glass. He raised his too, but as she went to take a sip something inside her drew back. She really didn't have the stomach for it tonight, or anything else come to that. The pressure was on for tomorrow, and right now she was feeling it intensely.

'Are you OK?' Michael asked when he finally made his way over to her. 'You're looking a little pale.'

'Nerves,' she confessed with a laugh. 'Just thank God I'm not in the first shots of the day tomorrow, because I'm not sure how well I'm going to sleep tonight.'

Smiling, he said, 'I guess your stunt double will be galloping Silver into the valley for the series opening?'

She nodded. 'I'll be taking over for the mid and close shots.'

Appearing to envisage it, he said, 'I think together you and that horse are going to make quite an impact.'

Deciding not to tell him about the Lady Godiva offer, she said, 'Will you be there for the first action call in the morning?'

Swallowing some champagne, he said, 'I'm afraid not. I have to be in London for a meeting, but the rushes are being sent down the line to me at the end of the day.'

She nodded and tried again to sip her drink. Though she managed a small mouthful, her insides almost immediately rebelled.

'It'll pass,' he told her, seeming to understand what was happening. 'You'll be fine.'

'I hope you're right,' she said, forcing a smile.

'I know I am.' Then, after a moment's thought, 'I'll be back again on Friday. Perhaps I can take you for dinner, if you're not rushing off, and you can tell me how your first week has gone.'

Though she'd have loved nothing more than to accept, she knew how crushed Alan would be if she didn't keep her promise to take the six o'clock train. Worse was how he'd feel if she told him why she was going to be late. 'Were it any other day I'd love to,' she assured him earnestly, 'but after being away all week my family will be waiting to see me. On the other hand,' she went on carefully, 'if something happens and we have to shoot on Saturday, I'll still be here on Friday so . . .'

'Let's speak later in the week,' he said, and giving her hand a gentle squeeze he moved back into the crowd, leaving her to wonder how on earth she was going to get through the rest of the evening without anyone else guessing quite how terrified she actually was.

Chapter Nineteen

The following morning at eight o'clock sharp Susannah stepped out of the lodge to find the unit bus waiting at the gate, already warmed up and ready to transport her to the Centre. Since the crew and stunt riders had all risen much earlier to make a six o'clock start, and she and George Bremell were the only main cast required for the first scene of the day, there was no one else on board the bus apart from the driver.

As far as she knew Polly was still sleeping. Certainly there had been no sign of her while Susannah was preparing to leave, a circumstance for which Susannah could only feel grateful. With such a fist of nerves inside her it was all she could do to breathe, never mind try to make small talk with someone who detested her. No doubt Polly would show up before too much longer though, since everyone was planning to be up at the gallops for the camera's first roll of the day. By then Susannah would be in full costume and make-up, ready to take over from the stunt double who, even now, would be rehearsing the opening shot of the very first episode.

Gazing out at the valley as the bus trundled

through the trees and the driver regaled her with a weather report, Susannah began wondering if they'd actually be able to turn over with so much mist hanging over the fields.

'Oh, Jane, the director, was that excited when I drove her up top an hour ago,' the driver told her in his gruff Yorkshire accent. 'Says it's just the sort of atmosphere she wants, seeing Marianne emerging through the fog on that horse. She was a bit worried in case the rain comes on though, which it's forecast to, but not till around midday according to local radio. Right you are then, lass, this is your stop,' he said, pulling up in the stable-yard. 'There's our Carrie waiting to take you in.'

'Hi, good morning,' a rosy-cheeked, curly-haired girl cried cheerily as she yanked open the door for Susannah to climb down. 'I'm Carrie, the third assistant for blue unit today. I'll take you straight through to your dressing room so you can get yourself settled in, then I'll come back to collect you for make-up. Jane asked me to say good morning from her, and if there's anything you need, or want to ask, we can get her on one of the walkie-talkies, or on her mobile.'

Warming to the very young and bouncy girl, Susannah stepped out into the damp morning air and followed her in through a double swing door that was part of a newly constructed block behind the main house. This was the first time she'd been to the dressing rooms, and she was quite taken aback to find that hers was so plush and cosy, with a large corner sofa angled around a square glass table, a smart Berber carpet, a plasma screen covering most of one wall and a hanging rail up against another, crammed with various costumes and tack.

'Becky's already taken your riding gear to press it,' Carrie told her. 'She'll be along in a minute to help you dress. I just need to let her know you've arrived. Coffee's there, in the flasks, and tea. If you want a full breakfast you can get it up at the gallops where the caterers have set up.'

At the mention of breakfast Susannah's stomach started to churn. 'Actually, where's the nearest loo?' she asked faintly.

'Oh, there's one right through here,' Carrie informed her, pushing open a door that was partially hidden by the clothes rail. 'Shower, wash-basin and WC. OK, I'll leave you to it for now, and come back in about twenty minutes.'

After she'd gone Susannah felt her nausea subside, and turned to survey her reflection in a large spotlit mirror. Seeing how haunted and anxious she looked filled her with a sinking dismay, but she could do this, she reminded herself firmly. Everyone was depending on her, and she'd rather die than let them down – at the same time she couldn't help wondering what on earth she was doing here. This was too much for her. She'd never played a part this big before, never mind had to carry so much responsibility for a programme's success. She wondered why the enormity of it all was only coming home to her now. Why hadn't she realised sooner just how huge an undertaking this was going to be? She could have prepared for it then, psyched herself up for the challenge and been ready to school herself through these terrible nerves.

Starting as her mobile rang, she dug it out of her bag, and seeing it was Neve she immediately clicked on.

'Hey Mum! How's it going? Have you done anything yet?'

'No, I'm still in my dressing room,' she gasped. 'I'm going to pieces and I don't know how to put myself back together.'

'OK, deep breaths and think of England,' Neve commanded.

Expelling a sigh in a gust of laughter, Susannah said, 'You're just what I need to help me feel grounded again. Thank you, darling.'

'No problem, all free with the slavery of being a daughter. Seriously though Mum, you'll be fine once you're out there doing it. I'm really rooting for you. We all are. Here, Lola wants to talk to you.'

Loving them for thinking to call now, Susannah started undressing as Lola came on the line saying, 'Now, I don't want any of your nonsense, my girl. You can stop those nerves this instant and remember you're a very talented actress who they wouldn't have cast if they didn't think you was up to the job.'

With a smile, Susannah said, 'Thank you for that. It was just a funny five minutes. I think I'm almost past it now. It would probably help if I could eat, but the very thought of it turns my stomach inside out.'

'You'll be all right once everything's under way. It's always the build-up that's worse. Anyway, you'd better not let us keep you. We just wanted to send you our love and wish you good luck –

am I allowed to say that? I'm not keen on break a leg, knowing you're going to be riding a horse.'

Laughing, Susannah assured her it was fine, and after promising to call as soon as she wrapped, she began pulling on the cream-coloured undies and socks that had been laid out for her. A few minutes later Becky, her dresser, arrived with one of the exquisitely tailored riding jackets that was part of Marianne's high-quality wardrobe, along with beige jodhpurs, white shirt, riding hat, whip, boots and a silk polka-dot cravat.

No sooner were the garter straps fastened on her boots than Carrie returned to take her through to make-up. A smock was put over her costume for protection while her hair was coiled into a bun and covered with a black sequin-studded net, and a lavish coating of foundation was applied to her face, followed by thick layers of mascara, heavy lines of kohl and a cheekbone-defining blusher. Finally her lips were transformed into a sumptuous scarlet slash.

'We'll touch that up again before you go on camera,' Ricky, her make-up artist, informed her.

'You look a treat,' George Bremell commented as he sauntered over from the washbasin where his own make-up artist had just given him a shave. 'Let's hope the weather stays dry now so we get this in the can today. It would be a great pity if rain stopped play before we'd even gone in to bat.'

Susannah was about to reply when Carrie came bustling in with a squawking walkie-talkie. 'OK, jeep's outside ready to take you up to the gallops,' she announced briskly.

'Oh my God,' Susannah gulped, pressing a hand to her mouth. 'Do you think I could have a moment?' she said plaintively to Carrie.

'There's one right through here,' George informed her helpfully.

Dashing in the direction he was pointing, she tugged open the door, locked it behind her and managed to get to the basin just in time. Or what felt like just in time. The fact was she had nothing to bring up, and she wasn't even retching, it was just a sensation at the pit of her stomach that was making her feel queasy. She was simply beside herself with fear.

However, by the time they reached the sprawling mass of vehicles spread out across the top of a far hillside, and Jane had sent word that she'd be over asap to talk them through what was happening, Susannah was becoming aware of an unexpected, but very welcome sense of calm starting to trickle into her veins. It was as though another part of her was emerging from the trembling mess she'd been all morning, a part that was confident, assured, and most of all outwardly poised, even if the inside continued to teeter on the edge of collapse.

Since a glistening mist was still suspended over the treetops with fine droplets of rain dampening the air, Ricky insisted she stay undercover while they watched the stunt double gallop in from the woods for the first shot.

'Everyone seems to be on the catering bus,' George informed her, and holding out an arm for her to take he led her across the grass to join the other cast members who'd come to witness the first episode getting under way. Though they had a ringside view of the action from the bus and offered Susannah a seat next to the window, there was very little to see for the moment, beyond a line of camera tracks running parallel with the gallops and a small clutch of people standing so far distant they were almost obscured by the mist.

Then finally it was announced over the walkie-talkies that they were going for a take. An excited buzz immediately spread around the base unit, followed by a breathless anticipation as the set-up progress was transmitted over the airwaves.

'Are you OK, Bridget?' someone shouted. 'Are you in position?'

'I'm there,' a voice replied. 'Ready when you are.'

Since Bridget was her stunt double, Susannah felt almost as tense as if she were on Silver's back herself. Bridget was out there somewhere, masked by fog and forest, preparing to urge Silver into a thrillingly daredevil gallop before bursting into shot and taking the viewers by storm. How she'd love to be able to do it herself, but neither insurance, nor inexperience would allow.

'Right, you lot,' they heard Jane saying, 'as soon as you see her coming, start the track back. Keep them in wide shot the whole time, Tom, bringing them along the gallops until you reach the end, then let them go past. If you can manage to get close on the horse's hooves churning up mud at that point, you'll be my everlasting hero.'

'Now there's an incentive,' came a jocular reply.

'OK, everyone?' another voice shouted. 'We're ready to go.'

Seconds later, 'Camera rolling.'

'Episode one, scene one, shot one, take one.'

Susannah's heart fluttered with a wonderful sensation of pride, mixed with nerves and elation. Being any part of this would be a dream come true; playing such a significant role was quite simply beyond anything she'd ever even dared imagine.

'OK. And . . . *Action!*'

For several moments nothing seemed to happen, then the camera began tracking back, going faster and faster across the hilltop until finally Silver came thundering out of the mist, a vision of pure magnificence and power as he charged along the gallops, his rider perfectly poised over her saddle bottom up and weight on her knees, and dressed in the exact same costume Susannah was wearing now. The spectacle was stupendous: Silver was spellbinding as he sailed along with all the grace of a racehorse and the majesty of the great Arab stallion he was. Everyone watching was silent with awe, feeling, to a man, as though their heartbeats had become one with the colossal pounding of hooves.

Eventually the camera stopped tracking, and swung in a whip pan as Silver galloped by. Then Bridget began slowing him up. When finally he came to a halt great clouds of steam surrounded his body, and his head tossed up and down as he jogged with the urge for more action.

'Now I really know I'm in love,' Susannah commented, making everyone smile – apart from Polly, who muttered something to the person next to her, and didn't even deign to look in Susannah's direction.

Then, with no warning at all, the heavens opened, prompting a collective cry of protest.

'They'll never be able to carry on in this,' Polly stated knowledgeably, unable to disguise her pleasure at the prospect of Susannah's own debut being postponed.

'They won't even be able to get a second take for safety,' someone else remarked.

'We might as well all go back to the Centre,' Polly added. 'We're wasting our time here now.'

Feeling desperate at the very idea of having her big moment delayed, Susannah looked hopefully at George, but he only grimaced apologetically, as though wishing he could disagree with the consensus, but he couldn't.

'OK, Bridget, bring Silver in,' they heard the first assistant shouting into his walkie-talkie. 'Can someone tell me where Susannah is?'

'Catering bus,' Carrie replied.

'Tell her not to move, Jane's on her way over. Is George there too?'

'Affirmative.'

Seconds later Carrie jumped on to the bus.

'It's OK, we heard,' George told her.

Giving him the thumbs up, Carrie leapt back down again and disappeared off across the grass towards Silver's horsebox.

'Bloody rain,' Jane grumbled, tugging off her hood as she came to join them, 'but I want to wait for a while to see if it eases off. Meantime, will someone please get me a coffee and some kind of bun? I'm ravenous. They don't feed the directors, you know.'

'Keep 'em lean, treat 'em mean,' the first

assistant added as he came on board too. Then, following an expressive nod from Jane, 'Right, everyone, could you clear this bus please and go over to the next one? Sorry to make you go out in the rain, but none of you's on camera this morning, so I'm afraid that's the way it is.'

To Susannah and George, Jane said, 'Marlene's on her way up with Alex and Gillian. They might want us to do your shots in the rain. Will either of you have a problem with that?'

Glancing at George, Susannah shook her head.

'Is it going to be possible to see us in this sort of downpour?' George wanted to know.

'No, but if it goes over a bit, it should be OK, and the producers sure as heck won't want to start the week behind schedule. So my darlings, better brace yourselves for a soaking.'

In the event the rain did ease off, and by the time the camera was moved into position it had virtually stopped. Susannah was standing with Josie and Silver by now, her riding hat on and the whip grasped tightly in one hand.

'Ready to go up?' Josie asked, with a twinkle in her eyes.

Susannah turned to Silver and lovingly stroked his nose. 'How about you?' she murmured. 'Are you ready for this?'

Silver gave her a nudge, and pressed his muzzle towards Susannah's pocket.

'Shameless creature,' Josie snorted. 'As you can see, he's not above bribery,' and handing Susannah a treat she waited for Silver to crunch it up, while two props guys put the mounting block in place.

Seconds later Susannah was on Silver's back,

gazing down at the valley and feeling, for a moment, as though only she and the horse were on the hilltop. She could hear the crew, but she was only really aware of the way Silver was prancing restlessly beneath her, and how much she was already starting to feel like Marianne. Susannah was melting away, making room for a stronger, darker force to press its way through all the various dimensions of her self. She didn't feel like Susannah any longer, she was the woman who owned all she could see, and who ruled over it with a will of iron and heart of malice.

She looked down at George and saw his eyebrows twitch in recognition of what was happening. Then someone was calling for first positions, while Jane spoke to the cameraman and Marlene watched from the wings with coldly assessing eyes.

Susannah turned Silver round and urged him back towards the forest, aware of everyone watching her, but not really caring. She was sensing the horse, just as Silver was sensing her. They'd rehearsed this three times by now, so were already getting to know one another in a way that had no sound or vision, only instinct and trust. When she reached her mark she eased Silver round again, feeling how willingly the horse obeyed, but never for a minute losing the sense of his power.

As they waited Silver pawed the ground, showing his impatience, but not until the first assistant's arm went down and Susannah squeezed gently with her heels did he start to move forward. Within seconds he'd sprung into a canter, heading back towards the unit at the pace they'd rehearsed. Susannah could feel the air on her cheeks and the pounding motion of the horse. The reins were soft in her hands, all the control centred in her thighs and knees. Dimly she registered the crew watching and shooting and waiting for her to come to the appointed stop. When she did she raised her chin high and turned to gaze down her nose at the valley below, aware of the camera beneath her capturing the image of haughty grandeur.

After a count of three she heard Jane whisper, 'And turn.'

Obediently Susannah lowered her head and turned to George who was camera right, an unholy contempt blazing from her eyes.

'And *cut!*' the first assistant shouted.

'Jesus, Mary Mother of God,' George muttered crossing himself. 'I'll be lucky to make it to episode four at this rate.'

As everyone laughed, Susannah leaned down to smooth Silver's neck while Josie fed him another Blue Chip treat and Jane came up to congratulate them both.

'You look sensational on that beast,' she told Susannah. 'It's my prediction the two of you will become an iconic image of these times.'

'No pressure then,' Susannah laughed, and as Marlene beckoned her over she slid down from the saddle and passed Josie the reins.

'You're to be commended for how quickly you've acquired your riding skills,' Marlene declared as Susannah joined her. 'That was most impressive, because to my inexperienced eye you looked as though you've been doing it all your life.'

'Marianne has,' Susannah reminded her.

Marlene gave a rare smile. 'Indeed,' she acknowledged. 'Now, I won't take up any more of your time. There's still a lot to get through today, but I'd appreciate it if, as soon as you wrap, you'd come and find me in my office. Something's come up that we need to discuss.'

By the time the day's shoot was over Susannah had worked herself up to a pitch of high anxiety about Marlene's summons to her office. Not even the director's praise, still ringing in her ears as she crossed the stableyard, nor the euphoria of reaching a wrap with every scene in the can, was doing much to ease her concern. She felt like an impostor whose real identity was about to be uncovered, or the butt of a joke that was now over, so time to go home – which was how everyone felt, George assured her, when success was staring them in the face, 'or hanging in the balance, since the programme hasn't actually gone out yet,' he added.

When she reached Marlene's office and finally learned what it was all about she could only blink in confusion at the printed email she'd been handed, needing a moment to absorb the very last thing she'd imagined.

Take care of your daughter. I wouldn't want the same happening to her as happened to mine.

Her eyes went back to Marlene. 'Who's it from?' she asked. 'When did it arrive?'

'Some time over the weekend,' Marlene told

her. 'As for who sent it, you can see that the address is merely a random sequence of letters and numbers.'

Susannah's heart was tightening as she looked at the message again.

'My guess is,' Marlene went on calmly, 'that it's a caution from someone in your own profession whose child suffered as a result of their fame. Since you've mentioned Neve a few times in interviews, it's obviously triggered something for someone. I'm afraid it happens from time to time. Children get carried away with a sense of their own importance just because Mum or Dad is on the screen, and the next thing you know they're doing drugs or getting into situations they wouldn't otherwise find themselves in. Or it could simply be a cry for attention from one of the unhappy souls out there who concoct messages such as this one in the hope of getting themselves noticed. We've sent a copy to the local police as a matter of course, and I can only say that I'm sorry this sort of thing is upon us so soon. I take it you haven't had any other messages like it, sent to your personal email?'

Susannah shook her head.

'That's good, because it shows the sender is only able to make contact through the programme. Obviously, if you do find anything similar you'll let me know.'

'Of course,' Susannah assured her. Then after thanking her, she folded the message and slipped it into the pocket of her jeans as she walked back through the production concourse. Before doing anything else this evening she was going to ring Alan, partly to thank him for the beautiful flowers she'd found in her dressing room after the wrap, but mainly to get his expert take on the mind that had sent the email.

'Mm,' he said ponderously after she'd finished reading it to him, 'I guess I'm inclined to agree with Marlene's assessment, that it's someone from your own profession whose child has gone off the rails.'

'So you don't think it's anything to worry about?'

'It's not sounding that way to me. Read it again.'

After she'd repeated it, she said, 'Please don't mention it to Neve. I don't think she needs to know. Or Lola.'

'Of course not. There would be no point to that at all. I suppose there's no way of knowing whether it was sent by a man or a woman?'

'No. Why? Does it make a difference?'

'Probably not. Gender rarely plays a defining role in this sort of compulsion.'

'What sort is that?'

'The sort that makes someone want to be noticed, but only obliquely, or they'd come out into the open with their warnings. Or it could be someone who gets a thrill from knowing they've unnerved someone in the public eye. It provides them with a sense of power. There are all kinds of explanations, but without knowing who it is, or anything about them, it's impossible to say for certain which cap might fit.'

'Do you think whoever it is might pose any kind of threat?'

'I doubt it very much. People who send anonymous letters are a bit like frustrated puppeteers, never seen, but trying to pull the strings anyway. If they get a response it reminds them they're alive.'

'How sad.'

'Very, but in this instance not worth losing any sleep over. The police clearly aren't if they haven't come to talk to you, and as there's nothing malicious or even particularly personal in the messages, you might as well ignore them too and tell me how it went today. I know, you were spectacular.'

Laughing, she said, 'Modesty prevails, but everyone seemed really happy with my performance and I have to say I loved every single minute I was out there, in spite of the rain. Best of all, though, was riding Silver. He's something else, honestly. If I could, I'd take him out again right now this minute, but there are strict rules forbidding recreational rides, for our own safety and the horses'. Why are there always rules against things we enjoy? Anyway, what about your day? How was that?'

'Nothing like as exciting as yours,' he responded drily, 'but it had its moments when a very generous patient invited me to join her book club in Wimbledon, and another sent me a video of himself that he's posted on YouTube.'

Laughing, Susannah said, 'I'm sure there's a whole slew of great characters passing through your doors, if only you could discuss them. Have you seen Neve this evening?'

'No, Sasha's housekeeper was picking them up today. It's my turn on Wednesday. So I'm having a bachelor dinner in front of the TV, then I might do some work on the computer before I go to bed. How about you?'

Hoping he wasn't going to mind about this, she said, 'A few of us are talking about going to a pub. Nothing special. I'd much rather be with you.'

'I'm glad to hear that, it might help my Lean Cuisine go down a bit better. Are you still due to come back on Friday evening?'

'It's looking that way,' she replied, 'but there's still no knowing how the week might develop. If it carries on raining and we fall behind, I might not make the early train.'

'Then let's hope the weather's on our side. Oh, by the way, you're not the only one who had flowers today. I had some too, from Pats, thanking us for the weekend.'

'Really? How thoughtful, especially when she's so busy. I'll send her a text to say thank you and try to call tomorrow. She's obviously not quite herself at the moment. I'd better ring off now, because I still have to speak to Neve and Lola before I go out. And the marvellous thing is, I'm famished at last. I was beginning to think I'd never be able to eat again.'

'Then *bon appétit, chérie*, and come home soon.'

After putting the phone down at his end, Alan sat staring into space as too many thoughts whirled around in his head. In the end he turned to his computer and composed an email to his lawyer, telling him about the message Susannah had received and asking for his comments.

Half an hour later his mobile started to ring. Seeing it was Ken he clicked on.

'There's probably no connection,' he was told, 'but I'll make some enquiries. If it does turn out to be from your wife, or her brother, what do you want me to do?'

'I'm not sure,' Alan replied. 'Let's get an answer to the question first, then we'll speak again.'

Chapter Twenty

'Frank! What are you doing here?' Patsy demanded, sounding much more brusque than she intended as he came sauntering into her office. 'It's only Wednesday. I thought you weren't back until Friday?'

'Aha,' he said, looking extremely pleased, 'does this mean that you 'ave been missing me?'

'*Nooo,*' she replied, drawing out the word. 'It means I thought you weren't back until Friday.'

Pulling out a chair to sit down, he said, 'I agree, that was my intention, but then I find I am missing you so Michelle has carried on alone.'

Patsy sat back in her own chair and folded her arms. 'OK. So now, let's have the real story,' she said. 'Why are you back early?'

'I have to say, you are a very difficult woman to compliment,' he told her. 'Most women would be very 'appy to know they are missed . . .'

'Frank, come to the point.'

With a more tempered Gallic shrug than normal, he said, 'I am here, because I receive your email about the advertising budgets and I think maybe, it make more sense for me to be at the meeting tomorrow than to be galvanising around Bordeaux.'

Suppressing a laugh she said, 'I think you might mean gallivanting. Or there again . . . Anyway, I'm glad you've taken that decision, because it would be extremely helpful to have you there. There's also –' was she really adding this? – 'an invitation to the opera tonight, courtesy of *Elle* magazine as a thank-you for our patronage. Since it's a major event in the social calendar I thought you might like to go.'

He seemed surprised and pleased. 'With you?' he ventured.

'No. Alone.'

He scowled. 'Now I am not so interested. Why are you not also going?'

'I don't like opera.'

'I will go if you will go,' he said, folding his arms.

'Frank, don't be childish, it doesn't suit you.'

He laughed and she lowered her eyes because she liked the look and sound of it too much. 'Please come,' he said. 'I will teach you how to love opera.'

'Maybe I don't want to learn how . . .' She stopped, realising she was being childish now. 'OK,' she said, cringing at how fast she caved in. 'There are drinks first, in one of the salons, so I'll meet you there at seven.'

Standing up, he pushed the chair forward, saying, 'I will pick you up at six thirty. Please do not keep me waiting, unless, of course, you would like some 'elp with your zip.'

'In your dreams,' she muttered, and before he could see her smile she turned back to her computer, willing, but only reluctantly, to admit how much lighter she felt inside knowing he was around again. Then, seeing the staff appraisals she'd been working on when he'd turned up, she raised an eyebrow. Luckily for them, they were likely to have a much easier time of it now their champion had made an unscheduled return. Then her smiled dropped as for one uncomfortable moment she wondered if it was a coincidence, him walking in when she was right in the middle of trashing them all. Not that she'd actually intended posting any bad reports, it was just a way of getting things off her chest before she got round to the kind of assessment that none of them deserved, but with any luck might help her win a few friends and influence some people.

Realising she was in danger of seeing a conspiracy in her own mirror if she carried on like this, she pushed the suspicion away, and continued to type.

Wouldn't it be odd, she was thinking, if she turned out actually to like opera?

'Shut *up* already,' Neve giggled. 'I am so not going to do that.'

'Why?' Sasha demanded. 'It would be dead easy, and I bet anything it would work.'

Neve shook her head and stared down at the open homework books spread out between them on the desk in Sasha's room.

'It would,' Sasha insisted. 'Look, he said just now, when he dropped us off, that he's picking us up again next Wednesday, right?'

Neve didn't answer.

'Right,' Sasha said for her. 'So all you've got to do between now and then is ask if we can stay the night at your place, then at the last minute I can be "sick" and you can go on your own. Easy. No-brainer. It'll work.'

Feeling a thousand knots tightening and twisting inside her, Neve said, 'I don't know. I mean, what if he says, "OK, then I'll have to take you back to Sasha's, or Lola's?"'

Sasha shrugged. 'So he brings you back. But he won't. You'll see. He'll definitely let you stay at home for the night. I'll put money on it.'

Inhaling shakily, Neve said, 'I don't know. I mean . . .'

'Oh come on, it's you who keeps on about it all the time,' Sasha reminded her. 'I'm just telling you how to make it happen.'

'I really want to,' Neve said, 'but . . .'

Sasha threw out her hands. 'You're just scared, which is normal, but it'll be OK once you're there.'

Neve's eyes stayed down. 'No, it won't.'

'Why?'

'I don't know. It just won't.'

'You know what your trouble is,' Sasha declared. 'You're all talk.'

'I so am not!' Neve cried defensively.

'Yes you are. You got like this over Brendon Draycott, saying you were going to go all the way, then backing off at the last minute.'

'Because I didn't fancy him any more.'

'So you've stopped fancying Alan?'

Neve's eyes went down again. 'No. It's just . . .'

'What?'

'Nothing.'

'Oh, well, suit yourself. I've told you how to do it, if you decide not to bother, then it's up to you.

415

Just don't blame me when people start calling you a tease, because actually, that's what they're starting to say.'

Neve's face turned pale. 'No it isn't,' she protested.

'Yes it is. Ask anyone. I keep telling them it's not true, but the way you're carrying on I'm beginning to think it is.'

Patsy couldn't believe she'd just said what she had. It was as though the words had grown wings and flown straight out of her mouth, unassisted by her, unprogrammed by her brain, and were now creating all kinds of havoc. Worse, *Fronk* was clearly finding it highly amusing.

She should never have agreed to go to the opera, chanting, screaming, undulating debacle it had turned out to be. It might have helped if she understood more than three words of German instead of having to depend on the *sur titres* – and a fat lot of good they'd been, because she still had no idea what the plot was about. However, she had to admit the costumes were impressive, and the parties before and after had been fun . . . Anyway, it was bad enough that she'd let him coerce her into sitting through all that shameless overacting and scary music, but to have allowed him to talk her into an after-theatre supper in this alarmingly intimate little bistro tucked around the back of the Champs Elysées, all soft music and low lights, had been the biggest mistake of all. She'd only agreed because she was hungry, and well, why not admit it, he was reasonably good company – or he had been until she'd just blurted the most idiotic question of her entire grown-up career right into his face.

It had to be the drink, she told herself. The thought wouldn't even have entered her head if she hadn't downed all that champagne before the show. And now, here she was, halfway through a second glass already, and the *amuse-bouches* hadn't even turned up yet, never mind the entrée. Or maybe it was still the first glass, and just felt like the fourth. Whatever. If he didn't stop grinning at her like a Hallowe'en pumpkin with idiosyncratically perfect teeth, she was going to . . . Well, she'd do something, she just hadn't worked out what, yet.

'It's OK, you don't have to answer that question,' she told him, sounding amazingly relaxed. 'It's absolutely none of my business . . .'

'You would like to know if I am having an affair with Michelle Maurice,' he said, repeating it in a way that made her wince and want to throw the rest of her drink in his face, or maybe her own.

She'd only asked because she now felt sure he wasn't, which made this entire scene more farcical than any she'd just suffered from an opera box, and even more ludicrous than the lorgnette he'd brought with him and perched on the end of his beaky nose. Except it had made her laugh when he'd produced it, as he'd clearly known it would, which was quite possibly why he'd done it.

'OK, the truth,' he declared.

'I don't want it,' she told him hastily. 'I'm honestly not interested. I'm not sure what made me . . .'

'I am very madly in love with Michelle,' he told

her earnestly. 'I have been since the day I first see her, but alas, she is 'appily married and I have not yet been able to persuade her to have an affair with me. So you see, your . . . How you say? Intuition? Is very good. I thought maybe no one notice, but you, Patreesha, know me so well. I think, perhaps, you know me better than I know myself.'

Far more flummoxed than she could deal with in an instant, Patsy picked up her glass and drank. He could be winding her up, of course, and she was almost willing to believe he was. On the other hand, everyone knew the French were into extra-marital affairs big-time, with so many blind eyes being turned it was no wonder all the traffic kept ramming into itself.

'So the answer to your question,' he said mournfully, 'is that I live in 'ope. I think, maybe when we are in Marseilles, that she will succumb to my irresistabilityness – is that a word?'

'No, but I get the picture.'

'*Mais, hélas,*' he went on, with a fountain of hands, 'her husband arrive just as we are getting into bed.'

Patsy's eyes widened.

'So you can say maybe that my charm work its magic, but then the wrong genie pop out of the bottle.'

In spite of it all Patsy sniggered. 'You are a terrible storyteller,' she informed him, inexpressibly relieved to realise he was teasing her.

'Actually,' he said, 'it is not entirely a story, because I am, of course, very attracted to Michelle and I would like, more than anything, to make

418

love with her as often as is possible. She is desiring of this too, but, unfortunately, my life is very complicated right now, so it is better that I do not make it any more that way.'

As the laughter dried on Patsy's lips, she looked down at her glass and wished she could leave now.

'I am sorry, I feel this is not the answer you were hoping to hear,' he said softly.

'No, no. It's exactly what I thought,' she assured him. 'Well, more or less. Anyway, I'd like to talk about our customer-service plan, and now seems a very good time.'

He nodded soberly. 'I believe it does,' he agreed. 'Please tell me how you are going to revolutionise *La France*. I am very interested to hear.'

'It's my intention,' she said, passing over his irony, 'to send our senior salespeople to a seminar in California, which, as I'm sure you're aware, is the customer-service capital of the world.'

'*Mais, bien sûr,*' he agreed, appearing impressed. 'I find this an excellent idea, but a very costly one, no?'

'Of course, but I think it'll be worth it. I'd prefer you not to mention it to anyone for the time being, I'm still costing it, and I need to discuss it with Claudia before I put anything into . . . practice.' She trailed off as his mobile started to ring.

Checking to see who it was, he gave her an apologetic look as he said, 'I'm sorry, I must take it. Please excuse me,' and getting up from the table he put the phone to his ear as he walked away saying, '*Oui? J'écoute.*'

Unsure whether she was more annoyed or

intrigued to know who he had to speak to at eleven o'clock at night, she gestured to the waiter to refill their glasses.

It was ten minutes or more before he returned, by which time Pats was so mad she was on the point of storming out and leaving him to find an empty space when he finally deigned to come back. Had the food not arrived when it did she might have done so, but she was hungry and actually, she wanted to hear his explanation, because to her mind nothing warranted this sort of rudeness.

'Patreesha,' he said, coming back to the table, 'I am very sorry, but I have to go 'ome. I know it is inexcusable to leave you like this, but I will make sure to pay the bill first.'

Patsy stared at him in mute astonishment. He was seriously going to abandon her, in the middle of a dinner? No, surely not. She couldn't have heard right.

'The tarte tatin is excellent here,' he told her. 'I can recommend it very highly,' and after downing what was left in his glass, he turned around and left.

The week had sped by so fast that it was hard to believe Friday was upon them already. Fortunately the weather had undergone a dramatic improvement since Monday, so both red and blue units were set to finish on schedule, meaning that the first two episodes of *Larkspur* would be in the can and ready to edit by the end of the day. Everyone was delighted with the relatively smooth start to the series, and the few rushes Susannah had managed to see had left her both relieved and thrilled to discover that she hadn't completely disgraced herself.

Having been so busy she'd all but forgotten about the anonymous email by now; however, at Alan's insistence, she'd checked yesterday with Cordelia, the mail manager, to find out if anything else had arrived, and apparently it hadn't. Since Susannah had an idea who might be trying to make mischief, she wasn't altogether surprised. However, if she was right and no more turned up, it would be best to leave her suspicions unaired. If they did, then she'd try to deal with it herself rather than create a fuss.

It was eight thirty in the morning now and she was still at the lodge, enjoying a more leisurely start to the day than she'd had so far, thanks to a nine fifteen make-up call. She'd already showered and washed her hair, and was towelling it dry as she wandered down to the kitchen. To her surprise she found Polly sitting at the table, dunking a biscuit in a cup of coffee and reading her script.

'Good morning,' Susannah said pleasantly, in spite of the sudden tension inside her. 'I thought you had a seven o'clock start.'

'It was changed last night,' Polly replied without looking up.

Susannah carried on rubbing her hair as she went to unhook a mug from an overhead beam. This was the first time they'd actually been at the lodge together, apart from when sleeping or passing one another on the way in or out, and she couldn't help wishing they'd adhered to the tacit agreement at least to try and avoid one another.

On set was a different story, since they had several scenes together so had no choice about facing one another, but as there was no love lost between their characters those occasions often provided a gratifying outlet for her frustration, thanks to Marianne's unerring ability to deliver a gloriously stinging last word. Usually Penelope was left open-mouthed with shock, or swollen with rage, or perhaps muttering some kind of ludicrous vow to get even. Yesterday, however, Marianne's cruelty had reduced her to tears, an outcome that had clearly incensed Polly beyond reason. Though she hadn't embarrassed herself by venting her fury then, it had been plain to see. Though it seemed absurd now, Susannah began wondering if that was why Polly was still here this morning, to try and settle a score that wasn't even real.

Reaching for the jug of freshly brewed coffee, she was about to help herself when Polly said, 'Actually, that's mine.'

Susannah managed to stop before spilling a drop, and putting the jug down again she went to fill the kettle. There was no point getting into something so petty, and anyway, she'd prefer to have tea.

Several minutes ticked by as Polly continued studying the script and Susannah brushed her hair while gazing out at the beautiful sun-drenched valley. She thought about opening the window to absorb the fresh, grassy air, but decided against it in case it provided Polly with another reason to object.

Once the kettle had boiled she dropped a tea bag in her mug, covered it with hot water, then pulled open her cupboard to take down her share of the welcome pack chocolate chips.

'Would you like one?' she offered.

Polly merely turned over a page and carried on reading.

'I'll take that as a no thank you,' Susannah said with a smile, and helping herself to one she put the packet away again.

After a while, still keeping her head down, Polly said, 'Tell me, how does it feel to know you were cast for your looks rather than your talent?'

Susannah became very still. She couldn't even begin to think how to answer that without sounding defensive, or aggressive, or, God forbid, pathetic.

'I was just wondering, that was all,' Polly said affably.

Still Susannah said nothing. Even if she were able to come up with a suitable rejoinder, which it seemed she couldn't, the last thing she wanted was to end up in the kind of slanging match that Polly, being such a practised bitch, would no doubt win hands down. In the end she decided to take her tea upstairs out of the way.

'What's the matter, cat got your tongue?' Polly said as she passed. 'Or no, I'm forgetting, you need a writer to give you the lines.'

Susannah reeled. She could hardly believe Polly was being so insulting, and never having dealt with anything like it before, she remained flummoxed for a reply. In the end, managing to muster what mettle she could, she said, very calmly, 'Polly, I'm sorry if you feel cheated on your friend's behalf that I got the part of Marianne, but please can we try to move past it? We have to work together, and share this house . . .'

'Oh, as for that,' Polly broke in, 'I'm sure you already know they're moving me to one of the cottages with Wendy Shilton.'

Susannah frowned. 'No, I didn't know,' she said, 'but frankly I think it's a pity, because being here together might have given us the opportunity to get to know one another a bit better.'

Polly's cynicism cast her lips in an unpleasant curl. 'Why don't we cut the crap,' she sneered. 'We both know you want me out of here so you can have this place to yourself for when Michael Grafton drops in.'

Susannah almost gasped, but somehow managing to stay calm she said, 'You can tell yourself whatever you like, Polly, but spreading rumours about me and Michael Grafton isn't clever. To begin with . . .'

'I'm finished here,' Polly said, standing up.

'Well, that's a shame, because I'm not,' Susannah told her. 'As far as I'm aware I've done nothing to make you . . .'

'Let me pass,' Polly said, white-faced.

'Why? What are you running away from?'

'I have a make-up call,' Polly replied tightly.

'Really? You didn't seem in such a hurry a moment ago, so maybe . . .'

'You are in my way. Please move.'

'What are you afraid of, Polly?'

Polly's eyes widened incredulously.

'Look,' Susannah said, 'I really don't want to fall out with you. We're going to be working together . . .'

'More's the pity, but at least I wasn't cast on my back . . .'

'Stop!' Susannah broke in angrily. 'Why are you doing this? I have no grudge against you, we hardly even know one another . . .'

'Oh puhlease! This Miss Innocent act might fool everyone else, but . . .'

'Polly! What the hell have I done to upset you? Is it something from when we worked together before?'

'Oh give me a break. You always have everyone falling at your feet. You never even know what's going on around you, you're so up yourself.'

'That's not an answer,' Susannah cried, as Polly pushed by and started up the stairs. 'If I've done something, at least give me the chance to apologise.'

'This conversation is *over*,' Polly shouted, and slammed into her room.

Susannah, barely able to contain her anger, was waiting at the bottom of the stairs when she came down again.

'If you don't want to tell me what your problem is, Polly,' she said, 'then perhaps you'd like to tell me if you're responsible for an anonymous email I received at the beginning of the week.'

The look that came over Polly's face told her instantly that her suspicion was wrong.

'Do you know what, I really don't have time for all this crap,' Polly hissed, 'but before I go I'll tell you this much . . .'

'No, don't tell me anything,' Susannah cut in over her. 'Even though you barely know me, you've decided to spread malicious rumours about me, and behave in a hostile way whenever you can. Whatever reason you have for doing that is your business, but I hope for your sake that you get over it, because carrying that much resentment inside will end up causing you far more damage than it ever will me. It's already starting to show on your face, so unless you want to end up *looking* like a bitter middle-aged woman, I'd do something about it now,' and grabbing her towel she stormed up the stairs, leaving Polly gaping much like Penelope at the end of a showdown with Marianne.

As she closed the door to her room, Susannah was shaking, as much with anger as regret at having lost her temper. The last word might have felt satisfying in the short term, but it wasn't going to help improve things, and in truth she'd far rather try to make friends with Polly than let the sun set on an angry exchange. Having already done that once in her life, with her brother, she never wanted to suffer for her temper again, even though Polly might have deserved it.

'She just really wound me up,' she told Pats a while later as she walked towards the Centre, 'but I'm going to try to put it right if I can.'

'That makes you a lot bigger than most of us,' Patsy commented drily. 'If it were me, I'd probably have clocked her one. Damn nerve of the woman, suggesting you were cast for your looks, not your talent.'

'Apparently she's moving out of the lodge,' Susannah said, 'which is fine by me, even though it might be better if she stayed. At least then she'd see for herself that Michael Grafton isn't dropping in whenever he feels like it.'

'Who cares what she thinks?' Patsy cried. 'Get rid of her, is what I say. You know what, you're too nice, that's your trouble.'

Susannah laughed. 'I'll try to do something about it,' she promised. 'Anyway, you didn't ring to hear all this, so tell me how things are at your end. Oh, by the way, I received a huge box of your Cachet range to review yesterday. Did you send it?'

Sounding surprised, Patsy said, 'Not me, but it proves someone in our UK office is on the ball. I think you'd better pass on it, though. They obviously don't know we're friends, and if it comes out that we are, and you rave about it, we'd both end up losing our cred.'

'OK, will do. So what's new with *Fronk*? Have you found out where he took off to on Wednesday night yet?'

'No, I haven't. In fact, I've barely seen him since. He breezed in yesterday for a budget meeting, then disappeared again straight after, and whether or not he puts in an appearance today still remains to be seen.'

'How extraordinary,' Susannah commented, waving out to a couple of grooms who were leading their charges from the stables over to the horse-walker. 'When does Claudia arrive, so you can start getting some kind of lowdown?'

'It should have been today, but she's put it off till Sunday week, so I won't actually see her until she comes in for a meeting on the Monday. At which point I may, or may not, gain some insight into the peculiar species called *Fronk*, depending on how forthcoming she decides to be, or how much she actually knows.'

'Remember to send her my love when you see her, won't you? And to your parents too when you call to tell them that the series is probably going to be sold to Australia.'

'Are you kidding? That's fantastic news. They'll be over the moon. It might even help my mother to forgive me for disgracing her. Now, back to you. What are you doing for the weekend?'

'I'm not sure what Alan's arranged, but whatever it is I hope it includes Neve. I've really missed her this week. Now, I'm afraid I have to go. I've just walked into my dressing room and I'm already running late. Call and let me know the instant you have any news about *Fronk*.'

It was only a matter of seconds after she'd rung off that Becky turned up with her first costume of the day, and ten minutes later she was sitting in the make-up chair going over her lines. That morning's scenes were dialogue-heavy, and she could see from the corner of her eye that George was intent on his own. By the time they walked through to the study to take up positions for their first scene of the day, word had reached her that George had fallen off the wagon the night before, which would account for how anxious he seemed. Taking hold of his hand she gave it a squeeze of encouragement, and received a rather pathetic look of gratitude in return.

The morning soon turned into something of a trial, thanks to the problems George was having with his memory. Jane, the director, was doing her best to be patient with him, but the first assistant was constantly watching the time. No one wanted to fall behind today, when they'd done so well all week and were now looking forward to going home for the weekend.

In the event, they did manage to finish George's scenes by lunchtime, but only just, and George was so relieved that he pressed Susannah and Jane to accompany him to the bar for a drink. In an attempt to discourage him Jane gently suggested they eat instead, which he happily agreed to, and after promising to join them in ten minutes Susannah returned to her dressing room to check her mobile phone for messages. Finding a handful of texts from Neve suggesting all kinds of outings and events for the weekend, she felt a warming swell of pleasure. They were going to have so much to talk about after being apart all week, and the Sunday papers were likely to prove a real trip for them both. According to the publicists the programme had front- or centre-page spreads in at least three of the tabloids, which were bound to feature shots of Susannah, which Neve could add to the scrapbook she'd started.

It wasn't until she'd finished texting Neve back that she realised there was a voicemail waiting, and after going through to messages she was pleasantly surprised to hear Michael Grafton saying, 'I know from Marlene that you've had a successful first week, so you'll be taking off as soon as you've wrapped. Have a great weekend, try to relax and you have a rain check for dinner.'

After disconnecting she sat down on an arm of the sofa, still holding the phone as she wondered whether or not she ought to ring him back. He hadn't asked her to, so she guessed there was no need.

Jumping as the phone suddenly rang, she saw it was Alan and clicked on right away. 'Hi darling,' she said. 'On a lunch break?'

'I am. I guess you are too. How was your morning?'

'Oh, fine . . . Well, actually, not as great as it should have been. Poor George had some trouble remembering his lines.'

'Booze?'

'You guessed. I had a bit of a showdown with Polly, this morning,' she went on. 'I'd like to try to repair that before we all take off this evening.'

'I see,' he said darkly. 'Does that mean you won't make the six o'clock?'

'That's not what I said . . .'

'And what do I tell Neve? That she has to stay at Lola's or Sasha's again, or can she come home?'

'Of course she can come home. I just said, I'll be back.'

'Good, because we've missed you.'

'I've missed you too.' Then with a sigh, 'Please don't let's fall out now. I've been looking forward to the weekend . . .'

After a pause he said, 'Me too, and here I am threatening to spoil it, because I can't wait to see you. How perverse is that? I'm sorry. If you need to make up with Polly . . .'

'No, I don't. It can wait till next week. I'll be home on the six o'clock.'

Chapter Twenty-One

'Frank? Is that you?' Patsy said, stopping on the way into her office as she spotted someone on their hands and knees in his. Yes, it was him all right, with a score of documents spread out over the floor in front of him. 'It's Sunday morning,' she informed him as if he might not have known. 'Don't you have anything better to do than crawl around here?'

Looking a little ragged around the edges, in spite of his usual debonair grin, he clambered to his feet saying, 'I am here since seven o'clock, because I have many things to catch up on. And you are here because . . . ?'

Flashing him a look through the partition glass, she went to stand in his doorway. 'Actually, I've popped in to pick up my laptop,' she told him, 'but I'm glad to have this opportunity to speak to you at last.'

From his expression it was clear he already knew what it was going to be about, and he wasn't exactly welcoming it.

'So,' she said, folding her arms, 'I'm dying to hear your excuse.'

'*Oui*,' he said.

'Well, are you in the habit of abandoning people halfway through dinner? Or is it just me?'

'Ah,' he said solemnly, 'I am afraid it is just you.'

Since she'd walked right into that one she narrowed her eyes in a menacing sort of way and said, quite firmly, 'You owe me an explanation.'

He nodded agreement. 'This is very possible,' he conceded.

She leaned against the door frame and waited.

Drawing in his breath, he scratched his stubbly jaw as he thought. 'This is very difficult,' he confessed.

'I can't imagine what could be so difficult, or bad, or outrageous that I won't be able to understand, or perhaps even excuse it,' she insisted.

'I think you probably can excuse it, no, I am sure you can, but I cannot excuse myself to discuss it at this time. I am very sorry, Patreesha. I do not wish to make you angry, or to ask you to make allowances for me because of my position . . .'

'Frank, the allowances are already happening, because I sure as heck wouldn't be letting anyone else get away with showing up late to meetings, or absenting themselves for a day or more without some kind of explanation. So now, I'd like a straight answer please.'

He looked down at the files spread out around his feet. 'Do you know this woman?' he asked, pointing her to the stunningly beautiful face of an actress who'd endorsed the Cachet range a few years ago.

'Not personally, no,' she answered, wondering how this little tangent might be connected to the main issue, if it was at all. 'Do you?'

'*Mais bien sûr,*' he replied.

Of course he would, the campaign had been run from Paris, and to her dismay she felt a dull sort of spinning in her head that surely couldn't be the first stirrings of jealousy.

'She would like very much to be the face for Cachet again,' he said, 'but it is not possible.'

He was right about that, because apart from the actress being too old by now, with something of a blighted reputation, it was never a good idea to go back. However, she felt sure there was more to it than age, scandal or timing. 'Why are you going through these files?' she enquired.

'Because she ask me to. She is desiring of some of the photographs and I am interested to see if there is a strategy we did not use back then that might work for a new campaign.'

'I see.' Why was she so tense? And what did it matter that he knew the woman personally and was apparently still in touch with her? 'I still don't seem to be getting a whole lot of straight answers, Frank.'

His eyes came to hers. 'No,' he said softly.

Again she waited. 'Is that it?' she prompted.

He nodded. 'Oh, except I receive the email you send to all directors about the teenage cosmetics. I agree it is a very good idea to embark upon a nationwide search for an ordinary girl who has the beauty to become the face. So you can count on my support.'

With no little irony she said, 'Without which I probably wouldn't get it through, but we'll leave that for another time. Now, as you're obviously intent on resisting me at every turn, perhaps you'll consider making an exception for lunch. I was about to go and get some, so will you join me?'

His expression turned to regret. 'I am very sorry, because I would love nothing more than to eat with you, but I am afraid I have to go home as soon as I finish here.'

Shaking her head in an effort to cover the smart of rejection, she said, 'Frank, you've either got a mistress, a gay lover, or some kind of habit I probably don't want to know anything about. Whatever. I'm not going to press you any more over your reasons for disappearing on at least three occasions this past couple of weeks, I'm simply going to leave it to your conscience and sense of integrity to decide when to tell me the truth,' and having collected her laptop from her office, she left without another word.

'Oh blast,' Neve said, getting into the car and fastening her seat belt.

Glancing at her as he started the ignition, Alan said, 'What is it?'

'Nothing. Just something I forgot to ask Mum, that's all.'

'Well you can always get her on the mobile. The train probably hasn't even pulled out of the station yet.'

'I know.' Then after a beat, 'Hey, that was really cool, wasn't it, the way those people came up and asked for her autograph? And the programme hasn't even gone out yet. Imagine what it's going to be like when it does.'

With a dryness that belied his aversion to having strangers crash into his personal space, he said, 'I can hardly wait.'

Neve gave a distracted sort of laugh, then after checking her mobile for texts and voicemails and finding none, she sat in awkward silence as they began heading away from St Pancras back through London to Lola's. She couldn't work out what to bring up first – on the one hand it made sense to go on with what she'd already started, about having to ask her mother something, but on the other she wasn't sure if she really wanted to ask him instead. Well, she did, but at the same time, she didn't. In the end, she said, 'Are you still mad about how much time Mum spent learning her lines over the weekend?'

His eyebrows rose as he pulled out to overtake a bus. 'No,' he replied steadily, 'but I could have wished she'd spent more time with us.'

'Is that what you rowed about last night?' she dared to ask. 'I'm sorry, I couldn't help overhearing.'

'I'm sure you couldn't.'

'So was it?' she prompted when he didn't go on.

'If you overheard, then you already know,' he pointed out.

Embarrassed, and even a little rattled, she said, 'Yeah, well, I don't think getting on her case is going to help, you know. I mean, she has to learn the lines, and probably the weekends are going to be the only time she has spare.'

After a beat, he said, 'You're a good champion and a loyal daughter, and what's more you're right, because complaining about it and picking fights doesn't help anyone. So,' he went on, reaching for her hand, 'in peril of falling out with you, I promise never to do it again.'

She gave a little hiccup of laughter, and

promptly looked out of the window, aware of their joined hands and feeling her insides seeming to lurch and stretch around a barrage of emotions. 'Actually,' she suddenly blurted, 'I suppose I could ask you what I was going to ask Mum.'

He simply continued to drive, allowing her to come to the point in her own time.

'In fact, really, you're the one it most concerns,' she said, 'so definitely it makes sense to ask you.'

Still he waited.

She took a breath that shook and shuddered in the middle. 'I was thinking,' she said, tensing so tightly now that without realising it she was crushing his fingers, 'what if . . . I mean, maybe one night me and Sash could . . . Well, we could come and stay at our house. I meant to ask Mum if it would be all right, but then I forgot.'

'I see,' he said in a tone that didn't at all betray the fact that he'd read every word of the subtext. 'Well, I don't think there should be a problem with that. I'll have to run it past her, of course.'

Neve shrugged, not too sure how she felt about that. 'I expect she'll say no,' she decided, 'but that's cool. I was just wondering, that was all.'

'Leave it with me,' he told her, 'I'm sure it'll be fine if Sasha's coming too.'

Saying no more, Neve turned to stare out of the window again. After a while he threw her another look, but all she could see in the dazzling orange glow of dusk was the ghostly image of her own reflection as it floated over the passing buildings – and all she could feel was the firmness of his hand still holding hers.

* * *

'Ah, Susannah, you got my message,' Marlene said, turning away from the monitor she was watching as Susannah tapped on her door. 'Come in, sit down.'

Still in her riding gear from the day's shoot, Susannah closed the door and tucked her crop under one arm as she went to sit in the guest chair in front of Marlene's desk.

'Did you have a good weekend?' Marlene asked, going to open her drinks cabinet. 'Gin and tonic? Vodka? Wine?'

'A white wine would be lovely,' Susannah replied, not because she wanted one, but because it seemed more polite to accept than refuse.

After opening a bottle of Pinot Grigio and half-filling two glasses, Marlene passed one over and returned to her chair. 'So everything's OK at home?' she said, saluting Susannah with her own drink.

Puzzled, Susannah said, 'It's fine, thank you.' Surely Marlene didn't know that she and Alan had rowed, and anyway, they'd made up again before she'd left.

'Good, excellent,' Marlene stated, seeming genuinely pleased. Then, dispensing with any more niceties, 'I'm afraid another email has come through.'

Feeling her smile fade, Susannah said, 'What does it say?'

Handing over a printout, Marlene said, 'We'll be passing it to the police again.'

I'm not trying to scare you, I just want to be sure you take care of your daughter. Please don't let her end up like mine.

Susannah's eyes were showing unease as they went back to Marlene. 'I suppose the police haven't had any luck tracing the other yet?' she asked.

'I'm sure they'd have let me know if they had,' Marlene replied. 'The problem is, they're unlikely to give this any kind of priority when there's no specific threat, or even the hint of one, in fact. Which is why,' she went on, looking carefully at Susannah, 'I've taken the decision to alert Michael Grafton to the situation so that he can help to assess it. He now has a copy of both messages, and, like me, he doesn't see any reason for alarm, but we do need to ask if your daughter's mentioned receiving any unusual emails herself. Or has she been approached by anyone showing undue interest or concern about her welfare?'

Susannah shook her head. 'If she had, I'm sure she'd have told me.'

'Does she know about the message you received?'

'No. My partner, Alan, and I were both quite certain it was just a cry for attention, so there didn't seem anything to be gained from telling Neve.'

'I'm sure that's the right decision,' Marlene said with a smile. 'However, just to be on the safe side, Michael's instructed the company lawyers to hire a private firm to try to trace the sender. Hopefully we'll have some insight into who's behind it before too much longer.'

Feeling more than a little thrown by the lengths they were going to, as well as bewildered by how concerned she should, or shouldn't, be herself,

Susannah said, 'I take it Cordelia's sent a message back asking who the person is, and if . . .'

'Yes, yes,' Marlene interrupted. 'All that's been done, but nothing's come of it. Now, I suggest you put it out of your mind, and let the professionals do their job. I just wanted to find out if your daughter had received any similar messages, and to let you know what Michael proposed.'

Realising she was dismissed, Susannah got to her feet. 'Thank you,' she said uncertainly. 'I guess I should thank Michael too.'

Marlene only smiled.

It wasn't until she reached the door that it occurred to Susannah to say, 'I'm sorry. This isn't a good start, is it? Only just into our second week and already . . .'

'It's not your fault,' Marlene interrupted. 'This sort of thing happens a lot more than most people realise, and I'm sure it's nothing to worry about.'

As soon as Susannah returned to her dressing room she called Alan. After reading him the email and repeating what Marlene had told her, she said, 'So what do you think? Should we be worried? If they're getting a private investigator involved . . .'

'That seems to be taking it a little far,' he said, 'but I guess they'd be failing in their duty if they ignored it completely.'

Sinking down on the arm of the sofa, Susannah said, 'So you don't feel overly concerned? And Neve seems perfectly OK to you?'

'No – and yes. We were both with her at the weekend, so we could see for ourselves that she's absolutely fine, and I've no doubt that's the way she's going to stay.'

'I just wish I knew what this person meant by saying that she – or he – doesn't want her to end up like their daughter. If they'd just say what that was . . .'

'Darling, ask yourself, if you had a real warning to give someone, wouldn't you come right out and tell them what you were afraid of and why?'

Realising how much sense that made, Susannah felt some of her tension starting to ebb. 'Yes, I suppose I would,' she agreed.

'So there you are. What we're dealing with here is someone who gets off on the idea of causing someone else to be worried. It's a mild form of what we in the trade call socio-sado-gratification. These people are almost always harmless in themselves, and after the first few attempts of trying to draw other people into their sphere of confusion they tend to let go.'

Feeling even more relief at having it explained so simply, and reassuringly, Susannah said, 'Thank God I have you to tug me down from the ceiling. Not that I was quite there yet, but I was definitely heading that way, so it really helps to hear you sounding so unfazed by it.'

'Well, I am, and I'm sure I can be of even more help if you're able to tell me which firm they're using to try and trace the emails.'

Losing her next words to a sudden yawn, she said, 'Apparently it's going through the company lawyers, so I guess they're the only ones who know.'

'OK, just see if you can find out, and I'll get my lawyer to have a word with them. We only want to be kept in the loop.'

With a sigh of tiredness she peeled the net from her chignon, and yawned again as she shook her hair loose. 'How would I manage without you?' she said, 'especially when I feel so exhausted tonight that I barely know what I'm thinking, never mind what I need to do.'

'A hard day in the saddle,' he teased.

She smiled. 'It was, quite.' She hadn't told him yet about the seduction scene she was due to shoot next week, but there was still plenty of time, and she certainly didn't want to end up in a row tonight. So, changing the subject again, she said, 'Have you seen Neve today?'

'No, but actually, I did want to talk to you about her. She's asked if she and Sasha can come and spend a night here, and I thought it would give Lola and Sasha's parents a bit of a break if they did.'

Susannah frowned. 'I guess that should be OK,' she said, 'as long as you don't mind.'

'Not a bit,' he assured her. 'Ken, my lawyer, and his wife are coming on Wednesday, so we can turn it into a bit of a party – provided the girls can take being with the oldies.'

Susannah laughed, and stifled yet another yawn. 'If you're sure you really want two giggly, or stroppy, or overconfident teenagers stomping about the place while you're entertaining, then I wish you luck. I guess we still shouldn't mention anything about the emails though?'

'I don't think so. There's really not any point.'

'No. And at least when she's with you I know she's as safe as when she's at school, or with Lola, or at Sasha's.'

'Safer,' he corrected. 'Now, I'm afraid I have to ring off. I've a late consultation and unless I'm mistaken, I think he's just arrived.'

After putting the phone down, Susannah flicked a button on the remote control to bring up off-air transmission, rather than the Centre's output, which would be blank by now, anyway. Then, stripping off her costume, she hung it ready for her dresser to collect, and once she was wearing her own jeans and a thin, flowery shirt she started over to the bar to join the others for a pre-dinner drink.

However, she was barely halfway there when she realised that she really didn't feel up to it tonight. For some reason she was shattered, and not at all in need of any more wine after the few sips she'd managed with Marlene. So, rerouting, she began heading down the drive to the lodge, falling into step with one of the sound guys until he peeled off to take a walk through a leafy copse to his own place of residence.

It was about an hour and a half later that the sound of a phone ringing dragged her out of such a deep sleep that it took her several moments to remember where she was, and then to realise it was the lodge phone that had woken her, not her mobile. 'Hello,' she mumbled into it. 'Susannah Cates speaking.'

'It sounds as though I've woken you,' Michael Grafton said, in a voice that sounded mildly amused.

Immediately she shook her head, trying to clear it. 'I admit I did drop off,' she told him. 'What time is it?'

'A quarter to eight. I was calling because I've just spoken to Marlene. So you're OK about us hiring a private firm to trace the emails?'

'Of course,' she replied. 'I thought, from what she said, that you'd already done it, but if you haven't, yes, please go ahead. Thank you.' Then, after a pause, 'I'm sorry if it's a bother . . .'

'It isn't.'

She swallowed as she tried to think what else to say. 'Are you back in London now?' she asked.

'I drove down this morning. Did you have a good weekend?'

With a roll of her eyes, she said, 'It had its moments. How about you?'

'My kids were with me, so pretty hectic. You'll have to meet them one of these days. They wanted to know all about you, especially Ellie, who's the same age as Neve, I believe.'

'If you mean fourteen going on forty, you're right.'

With a smile in his voice he said, 'Sounds exactly like Ellie.' Then, 'I guess I should let you go back to sleep, I'm sorry to have . . .'

'Before you go,' she jumped in, 'could we . . . I was wondering . . . I mean, if you're up here again on Friday . . .'

'I'm afraid I'm not,' he broke in gently, 'but I am planning to be around next week for the press preview. So, if you were about to cash in your rain check . . .'

Smiling, she said, 'I was.'

'Good. Then let's make it next Tuesday, as it'll probably be too late on Monday after the screening.'

'I'll look forward to it,' she told him, and still smiling she rang off, certain that by next week she'd have found her appetite again, and definitely slept off this debilitating bout of tiredness.

However, two days later she still wasn't able to stomach very much food, and felt so weary that it was all she could do to drag herself through the day. By the end of it word had reached Marlene that she wasn't herself, and when she left the set it was to find the unit nurse waiting to whisk her off to a local doctor.

'He thinks it's a kind of come-down after the build-up to everything,' she told Alan when she got back to the lodge. 'He's given me a tonic to take and told me to make sure I eat something, even if I don't feel like it.'

'Actually, I noticed at the weekend that you seemed to be off your food,' he commented, 'but I put it down to your obsession with shedding pounds for the camera. Are you sure it's not that?'

'Positive. I'm just not hungry, but hopefully once I've taken this tonic I'll start eating again. Are you cooking tonight? It is tonight Ken and his wife are coming, isn't it?'

'That's right. They're not here yet, but the girls are. I'm just about to give them some tea, then I'll get round to thinking about dinner.'

'OK, I'll have to leave you with that, I'm afraid, because I'm not too good even talking about food at the moment,' and after promising to call in the morning she turned off her mobile, unplugged the landline next to her bed and snuggled down to sleep the night through.

*　　*　　*

As Alan clicked off at his end he was watching Neve coming along the hall into the kitchen. He'd told Susannah that Sasha was there too, but Sasha had had to go somewhere with her parents at the last minute, so Neve had come home alone. He knew it had been her intention all along, but he was willing to play the game. He'd even added his own embellishment to the story, telling Susannah that Ken and his wife were coming for dinner, and to stay the night, but no one else was coming tonight. It was only him and Neve and the crush that had brought them together, a little sooner than he'd expected, but that was fine.

In spite of the many years he'd been in his job, the way history repeated itself still never failed to amaze him. He'd been in this very place once before, with his elder stepdaughter, Julia. She'd fallen for him, too, and there had been no holding her back. She was a vibrant, passionate girl, who knew her own mind, and who'd refused to allow the difference in their ages, or the fact that he was married to her mother, to stand in her way. Like many adolescent girls she was competing with her mother on several levels, preparing herself to fly the nest. She'd never seemed to understand, or accept, that their relationship would be frowned upon by society, and could even land him in prison should they get caught. They needed to be subtle in their exchanges, he used to tell her, always appear to be father and daughter and utterly devoted to her mother. That way, there would be no reason for suspicion to alight on them, like a moth eating away at the fabric of what was pure in reality, but a crime in the eyes of the world.

He should have known that a girl of her age, and temperament, wouldn't be able to resist boasting about her conquest. Whether she'd ever told her friends he still had no idea, but in one randomly cruel moment she'd used it to taunt her younger sister, Kim, and Kim, feeling horrified and betrayed by the stepfather she loved, had gone straight to their mother and repeated it all.

He had denied it, of course, and had kept on denying it throughout the unravelling of his marriage and the break-up of his and Julia's relationship. Distraught, Julia had begged him to tell her mother the truth, to make her understand that they were in love and planning to make a life together, but as far as he was concerned there was only one truth – she had fallen for him in a typically teenage way, and was describing her fantasies as though they were reality. It was what adolescents did. Everyone knew that, and because Helen hadn't wanted to put her daughter through the trauma of going to the police, or the ignominy and finger-pointing that would follow, particularly when her word was challenged, they'd agreed he would leave and have no more to do with them.

Unfortunately, Helen's brother, Julia's uncle, had not been a part of that agreement, but he had no real power, apart from physical. It would always be Alan's word against Julia's, and Alan knew that if it ever went to the wire, Helen would protect her daughter before she'd allow her brother to put her through any kind of public humiliation or pain.

So he'd left, come back to London, and then one day a message had turned up on Friends Reunited . . .

Neve was feeling weird and uneasy and so nervous that she thought she might be sick. Her head wasn't right, or her skin, or anything about her. Everything seemed wrong, especially sitting here at the table, without her mother, knowing that she and Alan were going to spend a night under the same roof. She didn't know what to do, or to say to him. The truth was, she didn't really want to be here. At least she didn't think she did. It was all mixed up in her head, and she wished Sasha had said she'd come over when she rang just now, but Sasha had said, 'No way am I playing gooseberry,' and Neve couldn't really blame her, because she wouldn't want to either if she was in Sasha's shoes.

'What would you like to eat?' Alan asked, as he poured himself some wine. 'I can make pasta, or salad, or we have all the *Nigella Express* recipes on Sky Plus.'

'Um, pasta would be good,' she answered, tucking her hair behind one ear. 'Actually, I should probably make a start on my homework. I've got loads tonight. Is it OK if I go and do that?' She hesitated. 'Or do you want me to stay and help?'

'Whichever you'd like,' he told her kindly, and taking out a pan he began filling it with water.

Torn, and horribly self-conscious, she said, 'I'll go and do some homework, OK?' Maybe she could call Sasha again and tell her . . . Tell her what? She didn't know, she just wanted to talk to her, but if she tried to back out Sasha would end up accusing her of being all talk and a tease again. She wasn't, because she'd let Jason Davidson feel her up at Melinda's party, and had even put her hand on his thing . . . She felt really spacey inside when she thought of doing that to Alan, like she was being sucked into some kind of secret place that left her hand separate from her, so it wouldn't really be her doing it. Anyway, she didn't have to, because Alan didn't even know what she was thinking, so there was no need to do anything.

As she reached the kitchen door Alan said, 'If you're going to have a bath you can use the jacuzzi if you like. I'm just going to get this under way, then make a few calls. I'll give you a shout when dinner's imminent. Shall we have some candles?'

His expression was so playful that it made Neve smile. 'Yes, cool,' she said. 'Mum bought some more on Saturday. They're in the dresser drawer, over there.'

Leaving him to it, she ran upstairs to her room and closed the door. She didn't actually have very much homework, and Sasha had already promised to let her copy, so instead of getting out her books she put on some music, then went to sit on her bed. So many thoughts were chasing around in her head that she hardly recognised one before another fell in and blocked it out. She could hear voices saying, *You're here now, this is your opportunity, so take it.* Or: *Everyone says you're a tease.* Or, *Why don't you leave now and go home?*

But she *was* home. Lola would send a taxi if she asked her to. She wouldn't ask though, because there was no need. He was only downstairs making pasta, and she was up here being really juvenile and all talk, when what she really wanted to do was kiss him again. At least she thought she did . . . No, she definitely did. Now she was getting used to the fact that it was just the two of them in the house it was starting to feel OK. A bit random, but kind of OK. She trusted him. He'd never do anything to hurt her, so why not go downstairs and use the jacuzzi? She'd done it often enough when her mother was around, so it would just be stupid to start behaving differently now. She didn't have to let him see her, or anything, the way she had before, when she'd had a bath in the middle of the night and he'd come downstairs and found her. Or she could, if she felt like it. If she didn't, she only had to lock the door.

Taking off her clothes, she wrapped up tightly in her dressing gown, picked up a towel and crept downstairs. She could hear his music playing loudly in the kitchen, Country and Western, which made her and Mum want to puke it was so bad. They never let on how they felt. It wouldn't be fair, because he never complained when they put on their favourite sounds. He even danced with them, and learned some of the words to sing along. He was lovely really. The best. Actually, she didn't really fancy him, she just liked him a lot. Well, she did fancy him, but not as much as she thought. And that was all right, because he didn't know she'd ever fancied him anyway, and the kiss he'd let her give him that time was just him being nice. He was always nice, so she shouldn't keep twisting things round, and reading things into situations that just weren't there.

When she got to the bathroom she found that he'd already turned on the taps, so the water was gushing into the bath and the room was becoming all steamy and hot. Closing the door behind her, she put her towel down then went back to turn the lock. It made her feel better to do that, because now she was down here she was starting to feel a bit weird again, and wished she'd stayed in her room. Still, she might as well have a jacuzzi now, or it would be wasting hot water and Mum always said they shouldn't do that.

When the bath was full and fluffy mountains of bubbles were coasting over the surface she peeled off her robe and slipped into the water. It was lovely and deep and smelled of the Fiore perfume Pats had given them. She'd turn on the jets in a minute, then the bubbles would really go wild, billowing up like giant snowy alps all around her, smothering her in their airy scent. She wouldn't think about Alan, because it kept making her feel strange and uneasy, and anyway he was listening to one of his operas now so maybe he'd forgotten she was here. She hoped so.

A few minutes ticked by, then sitting forward to turn the controls she realised the opera had finished. She waited for something else to go on, but it didn't. For some reason it felt spooky having no music, but it would be OK once it started again. She hardly dared to breathe as she waited and strained to hear something. Maybe he'd just turned the volume down, or he might be on the phone in his study.

Then the door handle started to turn and she almost leapt from her skin. *He was trying to get in.*

Her eyes bulged in their sockets, her heart began to throb in great big painful beats. *No! Mum!* She didn't want him to come in. He had to go away. Please God, make him go away.

Quickly she drew herself back, hunching to the far end of the bath as though to hide behind the bubbles. Her eyes were fixed on the handle, wide with horror. It was turning again and her chest was burning with fear. It's only Alan, she tried telling herself. He wouldn't hurt her. But she'd let him think this was what she wanted and now, if she said no, he might get mad and make her. He wasn't like that though. He was kind and understanding, and if she just explained that she'd got a bit muddled about things and said she was sorry . . .

The handle turned again and she almost screamed. Somehow she stayed silent and rigid, as though pretending not to be there, but he had to know she was or the door wouldn't be locked. Maybe he only wanted to look at her, the way he had before, but she didn't want him to do it again. She just wanted her mother to come home now. Or Lola to ring, or Pats. Anyone to make him go away. Tears were rolling down her cheeks and she was shaking so hard that the water was moving around her. This was all her fault. She should have stayed at Sasha's, or at Lola's, but she'd come here, alone, even though she hadn't really wanted to. So she only had herself to blame if something horrible happened, and it was going to, she just knew it, and it was *all her fault.*

Outside, in the bedroom, Alan let go of the handle and turned away from the door. She was afraid and he understood that, so he'd give her some time to calm down. She'd have to come out sooner or later, and it would be better if he wasn't there waiting when she did. It would only frighten her more.

Going back to the kitchen he put on more music, the final act of *Tosca*, letting her know that the coast was clear for her to come out. Returning to the kitchen doorway, he stood staring along the hall into the mirror at the end that reflected the landing above.

For a long time nothing happened. There was only the music, passionate and rousing, climbing to the ceilings, covering the floor, pressing the walls. Every other sound was sucked into it. He hummed for a while, but only the vibration reached his ears. His eyes were trained on the mirror, watching, occasionally blinking, until finally she came on to the landing. After the first few tentative steps, she made a dash up the second flight of stairs to her room.

He went on standing where he was, until the last doleful chords faded into silence, then after locking the front door he started up the stairs.

Chapter Twenty-Two

'Claudia.' Pats was smiling warmly as her boss came sauntering, unannounced, along the corridor towards her office, a picture of unrelenting glamour, with her tight cap of sleek dark hair, pale pink Chanel suit and matching pumps. 'Why didn't you tell me you were coming early? I haven't had time to put out the red carpet yet.'

'Yes, I noticed it was missing,' Claudia retorted drily. Then, treating her star executive to a frankly assessing once-over, she said, 'You're looking gorgeous, honey. Well done,' and throwing aside her designer purse and glasses she held out her arms for an embrace.

'A pretty compliment,' Patsy smiled as she hugged her, 'but I've a way to go before I catch up with you.' And she wasn't being entirely untruthful, because though Claudia might be seventy-one and a little creased around the edges now, the lustrous topaz eyes that had made her one of the great beauties of her day were still every bit as arresting as her inimitable air of wealth and perfectly capped smile.

'Your emails have me crackling with excitement,' Claudia informed her, in a Southern drawl that seemed to belie any such effort. 'I'm going to call a meeting in New York sometime in the next couple of months that I want you to be at. By then you should be able to give us a fair assessment of how well your promotional ideas are working here in France. I like the search for a teenage face very much. Have you got TV backing for it yet?'

'Frank's meeting with one of the channel heads even as we speak,' Patsy replied, glancing at the time. 'Now, I want to know why you don't look jet-lagged. Really, Claudia, you are disgustingly fresh for a woman who's just crossed the Atlantic.'

Twinkling her appreciation, Claudia sank down in a chair and caused a little static as she crossed her expensively pantyhosed legs. 'I came early,' she said, 'so we can have a little chat, *entre nous*, before the meeting starts. Frank will be back for it, I hope?'

'I fully expect him to be, unless he stages another of his vanishing acts.'

Claudia's eyebrows rose in a question.

'I was hoping you might fill in those particular blanks,' Patsy told her, 'but I'm sure you'd like a coffee first.'

'Oh, I'm sure I would,' Claudia agreed, flipping out a black lacy fan to cool herself down.

After buzzing through for her secretary to do the honours, Pats returned to her own chair saying, 'Are you still scheduled to leave on Thursday?'

'I'm afraid so,' Claudia sighed, 'and I so love Paris, but I expect you'll be glad to be rid of me by the time it comes round. You don't want the old lady in your hair, interfering and messing things up, when you're doing such a great job of putting this office on the map here in France. I have to hand it to you, Pats, you've taken next to no time to make your mark, and I know it won't have been easy in this deplorably chauvinistic environment. You haven't even sent any emails screaming for rescue, which I was fully expecting. So, can I take it you're happy and willing to stay?'

Patsy was surprised. 'Do I have another option?' she ventured, curiously.

'Not one that's on the table at present, but I wouldn't want to lose you so if you did want out, I'm sure we could find you something in the US.'

Patsy was shaking her head. 'It's a challenge here at times,' she admitted, 'but I don't give up easily and I'm still hopeful that I can win at least some of my male colleagues round, if not all. Frank, I have to say, is an exception. He seems to have no problem either with my gender or my nationality.'

'No, I didn't imagine he would. When he turned the job down he gave me his word that he'd support you in every way he could.'

Patsy's eyes narrowed slightly. 'I'm curious to know *why* he turned it down,' she said evenly. 'He was the obvious contender when Marcel jumped ship to join L'Oréal, so why am I in this chair instead of him?'

Claudia gave a little shrug. 'The way he told me was he didn't want to do all the travelling,' she answered. 'Being the senior executive for France is more localised than taking on the top job for all of Europe.' She twinkled mischievously. *'Entre nous,'* she went on quietly, 'I couldn't have been happier, because it's long been an ambition of mine to get a woman to the top in this testosterone-charged environment, and I knew if anyone could do it, you could.'

Smiling briefly at the compliment, Patsy said, 'Did he ever give you a reason for not wanting to travel?'

'Oh, I knew why without him telling me,' Claudia replied breezily. 'Just like I guessed, when I offered him the job, that he'd turn it down, because unlike most of the rest of us Frank has his priorities in the right place, as well as possessing that rarest of commodities, a well-ordered male ego.'

Pats glanced up as her secretary brought in the coffee, somehow keeping the irritation from her face at such an untimely interruption. She waited, impatiently, as the haughty young thing, all sweetness and light with Claudia, Pats noticed, poured, sprinkled, stirred and served, before finally leaving them alone.

'Back to Frank and his priorities,' Patsy said, making sure the thread wasn't lost before Claudia wandered on to another subject.

Claudia sipped her coffee, then replaced the cup in its saucer. 'I take it from your interest, and tone, that you don't know what they are,' she said blandly.

'Correct, I do not, but in the light of recent events I'd certainly like to.'

It was Claudia's turn to look intrigued. 'Recent events?' she repeated. 'Is there something you want to tell me, Pats? I have no rules concerning office relationships, you know that . . .'

'You're misunderstanding me,' Patsy interrupted, wishing her cheeks hadn't decided to burn out another story. 'There's no personal relationship between us, but . . .'

'You would like there to be,' Claudia cut in knowingly, 'however, you're not willing to commit yourself until a few questions have been answered.'

Trying not to bristle at the assumption, Patsy said, 'You're right in thinking I'd like some answers, so what is the big secret? Where does he go when he disappears? And why would he back off the top job when he must have been working towards it for years?'

Putting her cup on the desk, Claudia steepled her fingers as she said, 'Did you know that Frank was – still is, in fact – married to Juliette de la Frenais?'

Patsy blinked as her heart turned over. 'You mean the same Juliette de la Frenais who was the face for Cachet until five or six years ago?' she said, her mind flipping back to last Sunday morning when she'd come across Frank with the Cachet files spread out around him. It hadn't even entered her head that there might be a serious personal connection between him and one of the most beautiful women on the planet, let alone that she could be his wife. And why would it, when she could hardly imagine a less obvious match, Juliette being so gorgeous and him being so, well, bald, and portly and . . . Actually, she had to admit, the more she was getting to know him, the more attractive he was becoming, even physically, but still . . .

'They have a son, Jean-Luc,' Claudia told her.

'He'll be four years old by now, I imagine. An adorable little boy who Frank is devoted to. I guess his mother probably is too, but Juliette has problems, which you might have heard about. She got in with the wrong set while she was globetrotting for Cachet and before anyone realised how bad it was she'd already become hooked on the white stuff. She went through a very promiscuous phase that kept landing her in the gossip columns for reasons that were unsavoury, to say the least. There was one scandal after another, after another, and so many men . . . It broke dear Frank's heart, but there was nothing he could do, she was out of control, and in the end Marcel was left with no choice but to drop her. She took it very hard, and blamed Frank for the decision. In her book, he should have fought Marcel, but as devoted as he was, Frank was never stupid. He knew the image she was portraying was all wrong for the product, so he refused even to try to step in, and ever since she has been threatening to divorce him.'

With a sigh, she took another sip of coffee, then went on, 'Speaking personally, I wish she would let him go, because no one should have to put up with the kind of crap she throws his way. As far as I know they are living separately now, but she uses the boy to keep Frank on as tight a leash as she can manage. If you say he is disappearing at odd times and with no explanation, it will be because she is back on the drugs, and if she decides she has to go to a party, then he must come and get his son, no matter what time of the day or night. I think he sleeps at her apartment sometimes, usually when she's depressed, to make sure she doesn't do anything to harm herself or the boy.' She sighed again and shook her head. 'So, my dear, that, in a nutshell, is what's happening in Frank's world. His priority is his son, and he turned this job down because he was afraid of the clash of responsibilities.'

Still absorbing it all, Patsy said, 'But if Juliette's a danger to her son, why doesn't he take full custody?'

'As far as I know he tried and the courts did not rule in his favour, which isn't to say he can't try again, of course, but his aunt tells me he is afraid of what she will do if he wins. She's attempted to overdose a couple of times, and had to be pumped out.'

'But she has to take responsibility for herself,' Patsy protested, 'and the child's welfare should come first. He's obviously going to be better off with his father, especially if she's getting high on drugs, or taking off to parties at a moment's notice. What if Frank can't get there for some reason? Anything could happen to the child.'

'Juliette has live-in help, which minimises the risk,' Claudia assured her. 'I think that's why the courts were more sympathetic to her. If it were just her and Jean-Luc, Frank, I'm sure, would have the boy with him by now.'

Patsy turned to look at the empty desk in the next office. 'He hides it all very well,' she said. 'You'd never know from how good-humoured he is around the office that he must be sick with worry inside.'

'Céline tells me that being here, throwing himself into his work and the relationships he has

459

with his colleagues is a very welcome release. He can be Frank the executive; Frank the manager; Frank the fast thinker, even Frank the clown, because I know he has that tendency at times. It's only when he leaves here that he has to be Frank the father.'

'You missed out Frank the flirt,' Patsy muttered, 'but I think we need to change the subject because he's just come up in the lift. Before he gets here, should I let on that you've told me any of this? Or should I let him think his secret is safe?'

'It's up to you,' Claudia replied, getting up to greet him, and opening her arms she treated him to one of her most affectionate smiles as he came to embrace her. 'Frank, my dear, I swear you get more devilishly sexy every time I see you,' she teased.

'And you, Claudia, should be the face for our products, because you get younger by the day. Just looking at you is enough to seduce a song from my soul.'

Laughing and groaning, Patsy continued to watch him, aware of a stirring inside that she recognised as her defences melting in the face of who he really was. Frank the father. She decided it suited him, and made him even more appealing than he already, bizarrely, was, in spite of the difficulties he'd bring into a relationship. Realising what she was thinking she brought herself up short, and turned to check her mobile as it conveniently bleeped.

Call as soon as you can. Very urgent. S x

* * *

460

Susannah was in her private shower room at the lodge, staring at a short white wand that was confirming her worst fears. She hadn't wanted to think it, hadn't allowed herself to entertain even the slightest suspicion until this past weekend, because she simply couldn't accept that life would deliver such a blow as to make her pregnant now. In the end, though, she'd had to face the possibility. The tiredness, loss of appetite and queasiness weren't going away, and though she'd started taking the Pill after she and Alan had got back together, there were the few occasions at the start, when they hadn't used contraception – and there was no knowing either, how long it had taken to kick in when she had begun taking it.

As she sat there, fighting back tears of frustration and despair, she could only thank God that she wasn't required on set again today. She'd have to be there for this evening's press launch, however, and somehow she'd have to make herself face Michael Grafton. The mere thought of it caused a sob to catch in her throat. He'd remember only too well how her pregnancy with Neve had lost her the first series he'd cast her in, and she'd almost rather die than have to break the same news to him again. What the hell was he going to think of her? He might even wonder if she'd delayed telling him in order to make sure she got the part first.

Hearing her mobile ringing she ran into the bedroom, and seeing it was Pats she clicked on in a panic. 'Thank God,' she gasped. 'Oh Pats, you're not going to believe this. I'm bloody well pregnant.'

There was a moment's stunned silence before

Patsy said, 'Well, this has to be the worst timing in history. I thought you were on the Pill.'

'I am, now, but the first month . . . I must be about eight weeks gone.'

'Not too late for a termination? Is that what you're thinking?'

'Yes. No! I don't know. Oh Pats, I can't be pregnant now.'

'I wouldn't argue with that, but if you are . . . Have you told Alan yet?'

'Good God, no. I only found out myself just before I sent you the text.'

'How do you think he'll take it?'

With a sinking dismay Susannah said, 'He'll be over the moon. He even said at the weekend that he hopes my job doesn't rule out the possibility of us trying at some stage.'

'And you didn't mention anything then about the fact that you might already be?'

'No, I couldn't. I know this is awful . . . Oh Pats, you're going to think I'm dreadful, but I don't actually want him to know.'

'Maybe it's best he doesn't until you've sorted out what you want to do. What about Neve? How do you think she'll respond to the idea of a brother or sister so much younger than she is?'

Susannah shook her head, at a loss. 'There was a time I'd have said she'd be delighted,' she replied, 'but she's all over the place at the moment. She was really edgy with me on Saturday, sulky and uncommunicative, then she took herself off to Melinda's and didn't come back again. I hardly saw her, and I haven't had a text from her yet today either. Oh Pats, what am I going to do about this? If I tell Alan I'll have to keep it, but if I don't tell him it'll be cheating him of his own child, and I don't think I could live with myself if I did that.'

'The best thing is not to make any decisions right now,' Patsy told her firmly. 'You need some time to get over the shock, then you might be able to think more clearly. Are you still feeling crap?'

'Yes, but it comes and goes. If it carries on, though, someone's going to put two and two together, and I don't even want to think about how Marlene Wyndham's going to take it. Plus, I've arranged to have dinner with Michael Grafton tomorrow night. How am I going to get through that knowing I'm about to screw up the entire series when it's hardly even had a chance to get on air? I know this is going to sound crazy, but I feel like I've betrayed him, and actually, I have, because this is the second time he's given me a big break, and now I've gone and blown it again.'

'Not necessarily,' Patsy said comfortingly. 'A termination is the most likely answer, but don't let's be hasty. You're obviously really worked up right now, which is hardly surprising, but you have to try and relax a little. Try some meditation if you can, and drink some herbal tea – what was in that tonic the doctor gave you last week, any idea?'

'No, but I don't suppose I should take any more. And what about riding? I'm scheduled to be with Silver virtually all day on Wednesday. Oh God, Pats, this is a nightmare. Please tell me I'm going to wake up any minute.'

'I wish I could, but we'll find a way through this, I promise. Meantime, put your feet up and don't do anything rash like telling Alan, or booking into a clinic, OK? No decisions have to be made today, or tomorrow, so we still have time to be sure it's the right one when you do come to take it.'

Feeling slightly calmer after speaking to Pats, Susannah put the phone down and lay back against the pillows. In spite of the turmoil inside her it wasn't long before her eyelids started to droop, then remembering that she still hadn't heard from Neve today, she forced herself up again and pressed in a text.

Getting worried. Where are you? Please call to let me know you're OK.

Neve was staring down at the text, not really focusing on the words. The phone was lying loosely in her hand, like an object that was already forgotten. She was in one of the toilet cubicles at school, the door locked and the lid of the seat pulled down for her to sit on. The closeness of the walls was making her feel safe from the people and noises outside. Dimly she was registering the sound of girls playing and shouting, occasionally getting louder when someone came in, then fading again as they left. She didn't listen to their conversations, she was only aware of words in the air passing over her like birds in the sky.

Absently she pressed in two letters, *OK*, and sent them. Then she went on staring at the phone, thinking of the message and imagining it was her, flying away over the rooftops and countryside and not stopping until she was miles and miles away and with her mother. Safe in her arms, tucked up in her bed.

She wasn't going to think about what had happened last week, because it was her own fault and now nothing could change it. Not thinking, or crying, or even cuddling up to Lola, who'd always made everything better.

He'd told her it was what she wanted, and he'd kept on telling her, even though she'd said it wasn't, and she'd begged him to stop. He'd wiped away her tears and told her not to be afraid, but she couldn't help it. She'd wanted to scream, but there was no one to hear her, and later she'd wanted to run to her mother, but her mother wasn't there. She'd lain alone on her bed, like she was sitting alone now, knowing that if she ever told anyone it would spoil everything for her mum. She wouldn't be able to stay in Derbyshire any more, and maybe the newspapers would find out why, and then the whole world would know and that would be worse than anything, because it was all her fault.

'You know this is what you want,' he'd whispered, 'so don't be afraid. I'm not going to hurt you.'

She was so ashamed that she couldn't even speak to Sasha any more. She only wanted to be with Lola. They watched TV together, Neve with her head in Lola's lap as Lola stroked her hair and her back, as though stroking the badness away. It was still there when she got up, though, and she knew in her heart that it would never go away.

'You wanted me to see you, didn't you?' he'd said. 'That night in the bathroom.'

She'd denied it, but it was the truth, because she had. It had seemed like a game then, thrilling and terrifying, with no consequences to pay. Now she knew better.

'You're as beautiful as your mother,' he'd told her, and she'd closed her eyes like a child who thought it made them invisible.

It was what she was doing now, closing her eyes to make herself invisible, but she was still here. She could feel herself from the inside out. Everything was dull and heavy, her heart, her mind, her limbs, her shame. She'd made it happen.

'It was your idea to come and spend the night,' he'd reminded her, 'so you see, it is what you want. You're just feeling apprehensive now, but it'll be all right.'

It wasn't, and it never would be again. Her mother was in love with him, and would probably marry him, so they'd always have to live with him. And her mother would be working on the series, a long way from home, and she would be in London, where he was, unable to get away from him. He'd said he was going to pick her up from school tomorrow night, but she didn't want him to. She'd rather walk all the way to Lola's, or take the bus, but if she did that he'd said he would tell her mother what had happened and it would break her mother's heart to know that her own daughter had betrayed her so badly.

Moving through the party, smiling, laughing, pretending to sip champagne and to be as euphoric as everyone else wasn't proving quite as difficult as Susannah had feared. She'd felt certain that her inner turmoil would show, and even spoil the evening, but the screening had received such a warm reception from the press that her personal issues had receded into the background for a while. Now, she was enjoying being steered from one showbiz reporter to another, all eager for sound bites, or an actual live interview down the line to their various programmes.

'Susannah Cates is set to become an overnight sensation,' she'd heard one of them announce to his studio in London, having to shout to make himself heard above the noise of the party. 'I can highly recommend that everyone tunes in tomorrow at eight thirty, because you won't be sorry.'

Compliments were flying as fast as champagne corks were popping. Everyone was in high spirits, and provided she kept her thoughts away from the dreaded truth she was carrying around with her, the elation was very easy to slip into.

She'd seen Michael Grafton several times, but only across the room. He'd spotted her once and raised his glass, but a few minutes ago, when she'd noticed him coming towards her, she'd linked George Bremell's arm and kept him by her side as Michael congratulated them both. Then Marlene had come to whisk Susannah away. Everyone wanted to meet her, and she was delighted to meet them. This was everything she'd ever dreamt of and more than she'd dared hope, because the press was on her side – at least for now. She knew that could change at any time, but for tonight, and tomorrow, she would allow herself to bask in their enthusiasm and to enjoy their attention.

'I heard you were unwell last week,' a voice said behind her.

Turning round she smiled into Michael Grafton's eyes with more warmth than she'd intended. It caught him off guard and he raised his eyebrows inquisitively, which made her laugh and blush.

'I'm fine now,' she assured him. 'Just a passing bug, or virus.'

'Good. So we're still on for dinner tomorrow evening?'

'Of course. I'm looking forward to it.'

He eyed her curiously, as though sensing there might be more behind the smile, but then someone was calling for his attention and he moved away.

'It was heaven and hell in equal measures,' she told Pats when she finally collapsed into bed later and rang her. 'But at least I got through it without throwing up, or fainting, or disgracing myself by breaking down and sobbing my heart out, which is what I feel like doing right now.'

'Did you see Michael Grafton?'

'Yes, but we didn't speak for long. There were so many people there and everyone wanted to talk to the actors.'

'I can imagine. Anyway, it was a success and now you're all feeling very positive about tomorrow's transmission?'

'I think so. I mean, there are bound to be one or two bad crits, it would be naive not to expect it, but the early feedback was everything we could have hoped for. I'm sure Marlene's ecstatic, but she'd never let it show. I only wish I could say the same for how furious she's going to be when she finds out about me.'

'Does that mean you've come to a decision?'

'Not really. I just keep weighing every scenario in my mind, and each one seems to be worse than the last. The only person who's going be thrilled about this is Alan.'

'Whom you still haven't told?'

'Actually I've hardly spoken to him today, so I should probably call before I go to sleep. The trouble is, I don't know if I can face it.'

'Send him a text and say you're still at the party, so don't wait up. He might not like it much, but at least it'll let you off the hook for tonight.'

Susannah nodded vaguely.

'Then tomorrow,' Patsy continued, 'I think you should consider telling Michael Grafton what's happened.'

Susannah groaned as her insides rebelled against the very idea.

'I've been giving it some thought,' Patsy went on, 'and I reckon, from what you've told me about him, that even though he won't be thrilled, obviously, he might appreciate your honesty, and if anyone can advise you about what it could mean for your future with the series, it has to be him. Or Marlene, of course, but I'm sure you'd rather it was him.'

'Yes, I would,' Susannah said weakly. 'In fact, I'd more or less come to the same conclusion, and now I've heard you say it . . . I just wish to God it wasn't happening, because it feels such a betrayal of Alan, telling someone else before I've even told him.'

'He doesn't have to know that, so don't lose sleep over it now.'

'I'll try not to. Thanks for listening, and being there. I don't know how I'd get through any of it without you. Now before I go, tell me, how did it go with Claudia today? Have you had a chance to ask her about Frank yet?'

'Yes, but I'll put it in an email tomorrow. You're tired now, and so am I.'

'Is it good or bad?'

'Coming at it from my perspective I'd say good, I suppose. From his . . . I'm not sure what he'd say. I guess I'll find out in the morning when I tell him what I know, and very possibly what I think.'

Frank was watching Patsy with cautious eyes. His smile was slightly crooked, and his eyebrows were forming a pointed roof over the bridge of his beaked nose. They were in the small conference room, behind Patsy's office, where the other company directors were due to join them soon for the weekly update. This perhaps wasn't the best time to have told him what she now knew about his private life, but she'd wanted it out in the open before he could perform another of his vanishing acts.

'I just wish you'd told me,' she said, leaning against a windowsill and folding her arms. 'In fact, I don't understand why you didn't. It's hardly anything to be embarrassed about.'

He appeared to give this some thought, then said, 'It is my personal life, and I think that has no place in the office.'

'But you're giving it one when you disappear without a word,' she pointed out.

He looked away.

'Frank, having a son, and doing what you have to to keep him safe, is your duty, and caring about him as much as you do is something to be proud of. You surely can't think I'd have viewed it any other way.'

'You have no children. Maybe you do not understand . . .'

'That is a particularly offensive assumption,' she told him angrily. 'I don't need children to have compassion, and clearly you have a problem in your personal life that deserves it.'

'But I do not want your pity.'

'That was not the word I used. And for what it's worth, as well as my compassion, you have my admiration and respect, but not for the way you've dealt with it here. Here, with me, you only had to be honest.'

'Then you have my sincere apology for not confiding to you the reality of my situation. Now, is that, per'aps, an end to this conversation?'

Her heart jolted. It was so unlike him to be sharp that she was momentarily thrown. 'OK,' she said, feeling as though he was taking the upper hand. 'But it's not an end to the matter,' she added, struggling to get it back again.

He looked at her steadily. 'No,' he said, 'I think it is not, but please do not think that you can become involved in the situation, because you cannot,' and turning away he quickly assumed one of his more charming smiles as the door opened and Michelle Maurice came sailing in, followed by two rather harried-looking directors.

It wasn't until the middle of the afternoon that Patsy found time to send Susannah the promised email, adding an account of that morning's unsettling encounter. *I don't understand why he's being so defensive,* she finished. *There again, I'm not sure I understand anything about him at all.* After sending it, she sat thinking about it for a while, wondering what her next step should be from here, or if she should leave it to him.

In the end, still with nothing resolved in her mind, she was about to close down her email and carry on with some work when she remembered what Susannah was facing this evening. Immediately she began typing another message wishing her good luck, and promising to watch the programme when it aired at nine thirty, French time.

If you get a chance, call me before you go out and we'll have a chat. Otherwise let's speak when you get home. Don't worry about how late it is, I'll be wanting to hear how you got on. Love Px

Chapter Twenty-Three

More than anything Susannah wished it was Patsy's number she was dialling right now, because she could desperately do with the moral support before facing Michael, but there simply wasn't the time. He'd rung earlier, suggesting they watch the programme in the screening room at his house, which meant he'd be picking her up from the lodge at seven forty-five. It was now seven thirty.

She was already dressed for the evening, and feeling as nervous as hell, as well as extremely thankful that Polly was nowhere around. She was still waiting for Polly's big move out, but it hadn't happened yet, and she guessed it probably wouldn't now, since the tiresome woman's contract was due to finish in a couple of weeks. Presumably she was somewhere up at the Centre this evening, and with any luck she'd stay there for transmission, or at least for the next fifteen minutes. Even so, having the lodge to herself wasn't making it any easier to ring Alan, but she had to, not only because he'd worry, or find it odd if she didn't, but because she wanted to ask him about Neve.

'Hi,' he said cheerily when he answered, 'I was hoping it would be you. We're all looking forward to the big event this end. Eight thirty prompt, we'll be glued to the screen.'

With a smile Susannah said, 'Where are you watching it?'

'Actually, I'm home alone. I was going to watch it with Lola and Neve, but Lola's invited a few of the neighbours in to make a bit of a party of it, so I thought I'd give them some extra room and settle down here with a glass of wine and a TV dinner.'

'I'm sorry we're not watching it together,' she told him, feeling relieved that he had no idea about who would be watching the programme with her. That it was Michael Grafton would be bad enough, in a private screening room at Michael's house would be totally unacceptable. In some ways she wasn't even sure about it herself, since it didn't seem right not to be at the Centre for the first transmission. However, blue unit would still be shooting at that time, so not everyone would be there anyway. And if anyone should ask why she wasn't . . . Well, she'd deal with that when, if, the question arose.

'Have you seen Neve today?' she asked, wanting to get on to the real reason for her call. 'She sounded quite down when we spoke earlier, and she hasn't answered my text asking where she's watching the programme. I know she's at Lola's now, but I just wondered how she's seemed to you after she vanished off to Melinda's for the weekend.'

'I haven't seen her since,' he told her, 'but I'm

picking her up from school tomorrow, so maybe I'll be able to find out more then.'

Susannah looked up as someone jogged past the lodge. Relieved to see an actress she sometimes jogged with herself, and not Polly, she waved as she said, 'OK, it's probably just the time of the month, or she's had some kind of upset at school that she doesn't want to worry me with, but she doesn't usually hold back, or go for so long without being in touch, so I'm feeling a bit concerned.'

'I'm sure there's no need to be. Kids that age aren't always as forthcoming as we'd like them to be when it comes to letting parents know where they are, or what they're up to. But like I said, I'll have a chat with her tomorrow to see if I can find out if anything's on her mind.'

As she tried to thank him there was such a painful twisting of guilt in her heart for not being there for Neve, that her words were lost. 'You're so good with her,' she said, finally, 'actually with us all.'

'You're my girls,' he reminded her softly. 'You've made me happier in these few short months than I ever dared hope to be again.'

Swallowing the lump in her throat, she pressed a hand to her head as she said, 'I'm glad, because you've done the same for us. I'm just sorry we're having to be apart so much.'

'Me too. Where are you now?'

'In my dressing room,' she lied. 'The others are waiting for me to join them in the bar, before the transmission, but I want to speak to Lola before I go over there, so I'll have to ring off now.'

'OK. Just remember, I love you and I'll be sitting here at home rooting for you as the programme goes out. Will I speak to you after?'

Her eyes closed. Why hadn't she thought about that? 'Probably not immediately,' she answered. 'I think Marlene's going to give some kind of a speech and then no doubt there'll be the usual party and post-mortem. I'll call as soon as I can though,' and after assuring him she loved him too, she rang off, still hearing the words echoing emptily through her mind.

A few minutes later she was talking to Lola, but there was so much noise in the background as the neighbours gathered that it was difficult to make out what she was saying. Clearly it wasn't the time to ask her about Neve, so she had quick, lively little chats with a chosen few, apparently making their nights now they'd spoken to the star herself, then promising to call Lola later she hung up and tried Neve's mobile.

After the seventh ring she found herself being diverted to voicemail, so she left an upbeat message saying she was dying to hear what Neve thought of the programme, so please call as soon as it was over to let her know.

By the time she clicked off it was seven forty-five, and picking up her bag and a shawl she went outside to wait in the warm evening air, knowing if she stayed indoors she'd start pacing and agitating and working herself up into the kind of state that wasn't going to serve her well at all.

Alan's eyes were unfocused as he held two ready meals in his hands, one fish, one chicken. He wasn't hungry yet; he wasn't even thinking about what choice he might make. He was simply starting to act out what he'd told Susannah he would do, as though in some way programmed to follow his own words. In his mind he was picturing Neve's face, ravaged by tears and saliva, ashen with dread, stricken with confusion. She was sobbing and begging, her hair tumbling in straggly knots around her shoulders, her body a writhing mass of skinny limbs and tender young flesh. He could hear himself soothing her, whispering gently in her ear, telling her not to be afraid. 'This is what you want,' he'd murmured. 'You've been thinking about it for a long time, imagining how it would be. It's no different to what's in your head, because really it only exists in your head.'

She didn't believe him yet, but she would.

'If you change your thoughts,' he'd told her softly, 'you'll come to realise that everything's perfectly all right. Something is only wrong if you think it is. So you see, the power lies with you, not me, or your father, or even your mother. It's all up here in your mind, working its magic like an angel whose only desire is to make your wishes come true. And this is what you've wished for, isn't it?'

By the time Michael arrived to collect Susannah, five minutes late, she was standing in the country lane that skirted the Centre.

'I'm sorry,' he said, pushing the door open, 'I got caught up. Are you OK?'

'I'm fine,' she answered, inhaling the scent of leather, and him, as she slid into the passenger seat. 'I was just afraid that Polly might put in an untimely appearance, so I thought it best to wait out here.'

'Very wise,' he commented with a smile, and once her belt was fastened he accelerated to drive on.

'Now here's my next apology,' he said, as his phone started to ring. 'I have to take this call, and I'm afraid it probably won't be short.'

With a smile she gestured for him to continue, turning to look out at the passing scenery as he spoke to someone called Robert who, from what she could make out, was either in New York or LA.

Sorry that she couldn't use the time to call Pats, she continued watching the countryside go by, a green and golden blur, speckled with wild flowers and skittering birds. She was wondering if she'd be so worried about Neve, or feeling so guilty about Alan, if she weren't pregnant, when changing hormones often shifted things out of perspective. She could only hope it was that, because she could hardly bear to think of Neve being unhappy and feeling, for some reason, that she couldn't confide in her mother. On the other hand, Lola was there, so if anything was wrong Neve would be sure to tell her. Or Alan. In fact, now she came to think of it, there was a chance this crush of hers was starting to take its toll. Unrequited love was difficult at the best of times – at Neve's age it could seem like the end of the world.

Confident she'd hit on the cause of Neve's withdrawal, or at least a contributing factor, she made a mental note to mention it to Alan the next time they spoke, then refocused her attention on Michael as he finished his call.

'There, that's that sorted,' he said, removing his earpiece, 'and just in time, because we're here,' and pressing a button on the underside of the rearview mirror, he eased the car to a stop.

Susannah watched as two enormous black iron gates, set in a ten-foot-high wall, began to glide slowly apart, and the vista that opened up beyond caused her heart to stir and swell. Though she'd imagined his home to be impressive, it had never occurred to her that it would be anything like as grand or enchanting as this. As he accelerated to enter the grounds she gazed out at the immaculate lawns either side of the drive, one of which formed part of an intricate knot garden, while the other was divided by stone walkways leading to pergolas, fountains, or pyramid-shaped yews. The colours of the flowers were as vivid as if they'd just been painted in oils, and the sparkle of sunlight on the water seemed to turn it to jewels. At the far end of the drive a magnificent Elizabethan manor with pale limestone walls, long rows of leaded mullion windows and perfectly symmetrical wings sat at the heart of it all.

'I hardly know what to say,' she murmured, as they came to a stop on the gravelled forecourt, next to a curious piece of modern art. 'It's so beautiful it almost doesn't seem real, especially in this light.'

With a smile, he got out of the car, and as he came round to open her door a stout, elderly lady appeared in the front porch.

'I may have forgotten to mention,' he said, as Susannah stepped out, 'that some of the staff will be joining us for the viewing. This is Sheila, my housekeeper,' he went on, as the woman came towards them, all beaming smiles and old-fashioned curls.

'Welcome,' she said, squeezing Susannah's hands in a doughy grasp. 'We're considering ourselves very honoured to have you with us tonight. So come on in, the others are all waiting.'

With a humorous glance at Michael, who gestured for her to go ahead, Susannah followed the bustling old lady into a large flagstone hallway that was home to several elaborately carved settles, solid oak beams in its ceiling, and an eclectic collection of paintings that adorned the walls and continued up over a wide wooden staircase. Sheila was already beetling along a sunlit hallway, passing several closed doors until she reached the end and turned a corner.

'She's here,' Susannah heard her announce, and following her around the corner she found herself in an enormous atrium full of succulent plants and sumptuous cane furniture, with a breathtaking view down over the rear gardens to an orchard and a tennis court and a sprawling arrangement of outbuildings that nestled at the foot of the surrounding hills.

Smiling at the faces turned towards her, she shook their hands as Sheila introduced them: Bob, the gamekeeper; Millie, the cleaner; Greville, the chief gardener; Paulette, Millie's daughter who helped out when Mr Grafton hosted special functions; and Binkie, the children's old nanny, who still had to put them in their places now and again, and that went for her older charges too, who apparently included Michael and his brother, James.

'I live in one of the cottages next to the stables now,' she told Susannah, her rheumy green eyes and loose, crinkled cheeks seeming to pool and ripple as she spoke. 'You can't see it from here, but it's not far to walk, and the children are forever over there plaguing the life out of me about something or another. Never get a minute to myself when they're around, so I don't.'

Warming to the fondness in her tone, Susannah began asking more about the children, while Michael passed her a glass of champagne and after making sure everyone else had one, he proposed a toast to her and the programme.

As they all drank she forced down a sip herself, not enjoying the reminder of her condition and finding it particularly irksome that it should be champagne that made her feel the worst. After a little more small talk with the staff, Michael announced that they should all go next door now, and taking their glasses with them everyone shuffled off through a set of double doors that Greville had thrown open into what turned out to be a small and very sumptuously furnished media room. There were at least half a dozen deep, plum-coloured sofas and even more matching armchairs all turned towards a large white screen that wouldn't have looked entirely lost in an arthouse cinema. There were any number of TV monitors, speakers and pieces of hi-tech paraphernalia stacked against the back wall, and more refreshments laid out on a table just behind the door.

At the flick of a switch the screen came to life, showing the closing credits of the programme that was airing immediately before *Larkspur*.

'Oh, we're just in time,' Sheila declared, slumping down in one of the chairs. 'I'm sorted, come on the rest of you, you don't want to miss the start.'

Michael directed Susannah to one of the sofas, and after closing the door and dimming the lights he sat down next to her, stretching out his long legs and resting an arm along the back, and managing to look as at home in this small theatre as any man might in front of his own TV.

Feeling somewhat disoriented, yet enjoying the experience, she put her drink down on the glass table beside her and stretched out her legs too. As the commercials played she found herself thinking of Alan again, and Neve, and how unbalanced everything was feeling at home. Then realising Michael was watching her, she turned to him and smiled in an eager, nervous sort of way, as though she were thinking of the programme and nothing else. The opening titles of *Larkspur* were starting to roll, and as they both turned to the screen the tremendous opening shot of Silver galloping out of the forest and thundering across the hillside caused a murmur to thread around the room. Then her own face was filling the frame, haughty beyond measure as she gazed out at Marianne's magnificent estate. The shot changed and there was the valley in all its Avalonian glory, seeming almost like an apparition in a swathe of silvery mist.

As the episode played out she found her mind wandering again, back to Alan and Neve, Lola,

Pats, then returning here to Michael. She was becoming increasingly aware of him sitting next to her and wondered if he was paying as much attention to the programme as he seemed to be. He'd seen it often enough by now, so surely he was no more absorbed by it than she was, but of course they must pretend to be. Everyone around them appeared engrossed, sometimes tutting or even sighing at appropriate moments.

It seemed an eternity, and yet no time at all, before the end credits were rolling. Michael's staff applauded heartily and he joined in. Smiling, Susannah stood up and took a bow, feeling suddenly light-hearted and in the mood for a party. A milestone had been reached. The first episode had finally been played into millions of homes around the nation – in fact the world, thanks to Sky. People would be making up their own minds now whether to watch again, and everyone in the room was in no doubt about what they would decide.

'Are you ready for dinner?' Michael asked quietly.

Susannah smiled, and nodded, even though she had no appetite at all.

'We can either eat here,' he told her, 'or I've reserved a table at a restaurant a few miles away.'

Feeling a light going out inside her as she realised it might be better to make her dreaded confession here, rather than in a public place, she said, 'If it's not too much trouble, why don't we stay here?'

'No trouble,' Sheila assured her. 'I can have something dished up in no time at all.'

'Actually, why don't you take the rest of the evening off,' Michael suggested kindly. 'I can always throw a salad together, and I'm sure you've some cold chicken or smoked salmon tucked away somewhere.'

'I'll put it all out before I leave,' she informed him, 'and I made a peach crumble earlier so I'll put that out too. Lovely to meet you, Susannah. I think you're splendid in the programme. You did a wonderful job with that nasty little minx Marianne. I'm going to love hating her, so I am.'

'I think we all are,' Binkie added, coming to clasp Susannah's hands. 'I hope you're not really that devious or bad-tempered,' she teased, 'but somehow I don't think so.' Then, turning to Michael, 'It was good of you to let us watch the first programme here, dear. Thank you. If you have time in the morning, I'd like to have a chat about next weekend, when the children are here.'

'I'll pop over before I leave,' he smiled.

Ten minutes later everyone had gone and Michael was leading the way back along the hall through to the other end of the house, where an enormous kitchen and breakfast room, with a mezzanine library, occupied virtually the whole of the wing.

'You have a beautiful home,' Susannah told him, as he drew back a vast sliding glass door that opened out on to a vine-covered terrace. 'How long have you lived here?'

'Maybe not as long as you might think,' he replied. 'Just over six years, and most of the renovation was done by the previous owners. I've added a few things, though, such as the media room and the tennis courts. Everything else is more or less the way it was when I bought it.'

'For such a large house it has a wonderfully intimate sort of feel,' she said, stepping on to the terrace. She was immediately entranced to see a reflecting water garden, and walked over to look at herself and the sky in one of the ponds. There were koi, swimming around like slivers of ivory and gold, and frogs were performing a lazy sort of sunset chorus. She could hear Michael moving around in the kitchen and lifted her head to gaze out at the deepening reds and purples on the horizon. She thought of the others back at the Centre, celebrating and relaxing after the long haul to the start, and Marlene reminding them that they still had a long way to go. She wished she was there, if only because it would be so much easier than being here.

'Would you like some wine?' he called out from inside.

Going back to the door she said, 'Just a little, thank you.' She wanted to be sociable, even though her stomach was already rejecting the thought of it.

Bringing her a glass he tapped it with his own, and as he took a sip he kept his eyes on hers. She looked back and felt her heartbeat slowing, then quickening, as too many emotions gathered inside her. Her lips parted but no words came out. She almost couldn't bear this.

'Unless I'm gravely mistaken,' he said gently, 'there's something bothering you, so would you like to tell me what it is?'

She gave a mirthless little laugh. 'Am I that

transparent?' she said. 'As an actress, I should be doing better.'

'I'm not sure anyone else will have noticed,' he told her, and the intimation that he was watching her so closely made her turn her head away.

'What is it?' he prompted kindly.

She looked down at her glass, then turned to walk back on to the terrace. 'Before I tell you,' she said, 'I want you to know that I had absolutely no idea until two days ago. I wish to God I still didn't know, or better still that it hadn't happened, but it has and I just don't know what to do about it. My conscience is so torn . . .'

'Susannah,' he said softly.

She stopped and turned round to look at him. 'I'm pregnant,' she said, and to her dismay her eyes filled with tears. Quickly she blinked them back and swallowed a mouthful of wine. It tasted foul and she almost retched, but somehow managed not to.

He was very still. His eyes were telling her nothing, but his silence was terrible enough. In the end he turned back into the kitchen and poured more wine into his glass. 'I'm not going to pretend,' he said as she came to stand in the doorway. 'The timing of this could hardly be worse . . . How far along are you?'

'I'm not entirely sure. About eight weeks, I think. It's not too late for a termination, the trouble is . . .' She broke off, not really knowing what she wanted to say. 'You can't make me feel any worse than I already do,' she told him. 'I swear, it's the last thing I wanted, or expected. I haven't even told my partner yet, that's how undecided I am about what to do, but obviously

I'll have to. It wouldn't be fair, or right, to do something he wasn't aware of.'

'Of course not,' he said.

She couldn't look at him, she could hardly bear to be near him, she felt so raw and despairing.

In the end, putting his glass down, he came to stand in front of her and placed his hands on her shoulders. 'You have a very difficult decision to make,' he said, 'but maybe it will help if I tell you that if you do keep the baby we'll find a way to shoot round it, or even to script it in.'

Biting her lip to try and force back the tears, she let her head drop forward. 'Thank you,' she said brokenly.

'I think I should take you back to the lodge now,' he said, 'and in the morning I'll make Marlene aware of the situation.'

Susannah's head came up, her eyes wide with alarm.

'She won't be happy, of course,' he said, 'but she's pragmatic, and right now you need her on your side.'

'Neve, love, are you awake?' Lola whispered, pushing Neve's bedroom door ajar. 'Gosh, it's hot in here. What are you doing with all the windows closed in this heat?' When there was no reply, 'Mum's on the phone wanting to know what you thought of the programme.'

There was still no movement in the bed.

'She's asleep,' Lola said down the line to Susannah. 'Do you want me to wake her?'

'No,' Susannah answered. 'Get her to call me in the morning.'

'Tell her she was great,' Neve croaked from under the sheet.

'Why don't you talk to her?' Lola said, going closer to the bed.

'I can't. I'm too tired. I'll ring her tomorrow.'

'What's she saying?' Susannah asked.

'Hang on.' After closing Neve's door Lola took the phone back into the sitting room. 'I thought she'd already called you,' she said. 'She told me she'd done it straight after the programme.'

'She did. I got a message saying she'd seen it and I was great, but she sounded so . . . flat. I'm starting to get really worried about her, Lola. How does she seem to you?'

'Well, I have to admit, she hasn't been her usual self lately,' Lola replied steadily, 'but she's had that much homework. She's always in her room studying, and downsurfing stuff from the Internet. I think they overload them these days. You keep hearing about it on the news, and it's not right that she should be feeling the pressure already, when her GCSEs don't start till next year.'

'I know,' Susannah sighed. Then, 'Do you think that's all that's bothering her? I've never known her to be withdrawn like this before.'

'It's probably a bit of a phase she's going through,' Lola said comfortingly, 'and with you not being here all the time I expect it seems worse than it is.'

'I was afraid you might say something like that. Do you think I made a mistake taking this job? If she . . .'

'No, of course I don't. We all just need a bit of time to adjust, that's all. She misses you, but she's thrilled to bits with all that's happening to you.'

After a pause Susannah said, 'So you don't think there's anything seriously wrong?'

'No, not at all, so don't you go worrying yourself up there. You've got a lot on your plate now, my girl, and you've waited a long time to get where you are, and you deserve it. Everyone thought you were marvellous tonight, and I was that proud of you I had to keep putting a hand over my mouth to stop myself saying so. Now, it's getting late, and I expect you've got an early start tomorrow, so off you go to bed, and Neve'll call you in the morning.'

After she'd rung off Lola put the phone back on its stand and sank down in her favourite armchair. The truth was, she'd been worrying about Neve quite a bit lately for all the same reasons as Susannah, but there was no point admitting it to her when she was all that way away, and when the next thing anyone knew Neve would be bouncing back like nothing had ever been wrong. It went like that with teenagers. Lola still remembered it from when Susannah was the same age. One day up, the next day down, and in between it all, spots, hormones and more attitude than you could sail down the Thames in a barge at high tide. No, Neve would be all right. She had too many people looking out for her not to be, but all the same, Lola might have a quiet word with Alan the next time he was round, because he wasn't only really good with Neve, he was also a bit of an expert in these things.

Chapter Twenty-Four

It was Friday evening, and Susannah was on the train back to London. With all her heart she wished she was looking forward to getting there, but she was completely dreading it. Since Michael Grafton had dropped her back at the lodge on Tuesday evening she'd spoken to him only once, when he'd called to let her know that he'd spoken to Marlene who was now waiting for Susannah to inform her which course she was proposing to take. She'd like to know, she'd told Susannah on Wednesday evening, as soon as possible after the coming weekend.

Ever since, Susannah had been on such a roller coaster of emotions that she could only thank Marianne and Silver for her parallel existence. Without it she might have rushed into a decision they'd all end up regretting.

As the train hurtled towards King's Cross, she felt so weighted with trepidation for what came next that she couldn't even open her eyes when the steward asked if she'd like a drink.

'You can't spend your life with Alan if you don't love him,' Pats had objected on one of the many occasions they'd discussed this impossible dilemma over the past few days. 'It wouldn't be fair to either of you.'

'I'm not saying I don't love him,' Susannah protested. 'I'm just, I don't know, confused and . . . He's a good man, Pats, and he really loves me and Neve and Lola. I know he'll always be there for us, and this is his child. He has a right to be its father, not just sometimes, when I happen to be in London, but always.'

Those words were ringing in Susannah's ears as she hailed a cab outside the station and began the journey back to Clapham. Alan was already at home, preparing a candlelit supper, and Neve was at Lola's. So tonight was the obvious time to tell him . . . But to tell him what? She knew in her heart that she could never cheat him of his own child, so she guessed the decision was made.

Perversely, after the near exhaustion she'd suffered these past couple of weeks, Susannah didn't feel at all tired by the time she and Alan had finished eating. She could always fake it, of course, but that would be a cowardly thing to do, and besides, he deserved better than that. She was about to make him the happiest man in the world, so she should at least try to join in his elation.

He was loading the dishwasher now, stacking the plates neatly, large ones at the back, smaller ones to the front, while humming along to one of his Country and Western tunes. She wished she could hit the off button, not only because she detested the music, but his humming was grating on her nerves.

Carrying a stack of dishes to the counter, she

looked down at the soft whorls of hair on his scalp, and seeing the pale pink flesh beneath she realised it was starting to grow thin. It made him seem vulnerable somehow, less invincible than she'd always considered him to be. He was only human, she reminded herself, and as capable of being hurt, or broken, as anyone else. Considering the power she had over him now, she felt her heart fold around a wave of pity and tenderness – and a guilt that was fierce enough to undo her. She thought of how different things would be now if she'd known three months ago what life had in store. But she hadn't, so there was no point tormenting herself with futile what-ifs.

In her mind she'd rehearsed several ways to tell him about the baby, but none had included her blurting it out the way she suddenly did. 'I'm pregnant,' she said, while running hot water over a dessert bowl.

She'd taken herself so much by surprise that she didn't immediately realise he hadn't heard. When she did, she wondered if this was life giving her the opportunity to go back. If it was, should she, could she, take it?

'Pass the long plate,' he said, glancing up from the dishwasher, 'I think it'll probably fit at the back there.'

Susannah handed it over, then returned to the table to clear the remaining dishes. He'd prepared a delicious meal, she was sure, but she'd hardly tasted the few mouthfuls she'd managed. If only he'd become angry about it, or even appeared hurt. Instead, he'd been understanding. She was tired, and had probably overindulged on all the wrong things during the week, so she needed to let her system relax. Why had that irritated her, she wondered. He was only being kind and trying to make excuses for her to prevent her feeling bad, so why, suddenly, was his concern leaving her cold?

'Shall we watch some TV?' he suggested, wiping his hands on a tea towel as he stood up. 'I wouldn't mind seeing your programme again.'

Her smile was thin as she forced herself to meet his eyes. 'Actually, I have something to tell you,' she said, reaching for his hand.

He looked intrigued. 'What's that?' he asked, kissing her briefly.

Reminding herself again of what a wonderful father he would make, and how much he deserved this, she said, 'We're going to have a baby.' The instant the words were out she was sure she'd made a mistake. She shouldn't have told him yet. She needed more time, but she couldn't have it now. The truth had slipped from her to him and was already blooming inside him, just as his baby was growing in her.

His changing expressions started to melt the hardened edges of her heart. She watched as his initial uncertainty – had he heard right? – yielded to hope that he had, and then to inexpressible joy. He tried to speak, but emotion choked him as tears swamped his eyes.

Putting her arms around him, she held him close. She didn't seem to be feeling anything now, except, perhaps, a certain sense of gladness for him, the way she might if she were watching a stranger react to good news.

'How long have you known?' he finally managed to ask.

'Since Monday, but I didn't want to tell you on the phone.'

'I'm glad you didn't,' he said, holding her face in his hands and gazing fiercely into her eyes. 'This is how it should be, the two of us together, so I can look at you and tell you how much I love you and how happy you've made me.'

Her insides stayed neutral as he kissed her. She was thinking of a scene she'd played earlier in the week, when she'd done exactly this with George Bremell. She was acting again.

'I want to celebrate,' he declared, 'but I guess alcohol's out of . . .' He broke off as his eyes widened with understanding. 'That's why you're not drinking wine,' he said, and looking down at her abdomen he ran a hand over it, whispering, 'Thank you for taking care of our baby.'

She wasn't sure why she was crying, but he took it to be for joy and hugged her again. 'There are other ways of celebrating,' he said huskily, 'and I'd like to be as close as I can to you tonight.'

She allowed him to take her hand and lead her up the stairs, knowing already that she was going to plead tiredness, but not yet able to find the words. When they reached the bedroom she watched him undress and found herself registering, still in a detached sort of way, how physically attractive he was. She could do this, she told herself, and she should, because the closeness might help bring her back to her senses.

'I forgot to ask,' he said, turning round with a big smile, 'how pregnant are you?'

'About two months, I think.'

He laughed delightedly. 'He or she is going to make quite a gift for the next New Year.'

How strange that she hadn't worked out the dates herself. Realising what that told her, she quickly tried imagining the next seven months with her belly swelling and her breasts filling with milk. A part of her was fighting against it, trying desperately to pull away from the other part that was moving on to the first precious moments of holding a new life. If she stayed with that image a moment longer she knew she'd start crying again. Could she really be considering killing her own child? But it wasn't an issue now. The decision was made. She'd told Alan, which meant she was having the baby.

'Have you seen a doctor yet?' he asked. He was stripped down to his boxers by now and came to sit next to her on the bed.

'No, but I will,' she answered.

'I'd like to come too when you go.'

She smiled. 'Of course.'

He put an arm around her and she rested her head on his shoulder. 'Are you going to get undressed?' he whispered.

She nodded, but didn't move.

'It's OK if you're not feeling up to it,' he told her. 'We can just lie together and I'll hold you.'

Swallowing hard, she turned to look at him and touched her fingers to his face.

'We should decide when you're going to tell them at the Centre that you're leaving,' he said softly. 'They'll need to know soon, I guess.'

She became very still, so thrown by the

assumption that not a single word offered itself up for a response. How could she not have seen this coming? It was so obvious, and yet she was completely unprepared.

'Lucky you're not too far into the series,' he continued, 'they can probably write you out again without too much trouble.'

He knew nothing. Had no understanding at all of how anything worked in her world. 'I won't be leaving,' she told him huskily.

He smiled and smoothed back her hair. 'But you'll have to,' he said. 'I can see it's probably going to cause a few problems, with you only just joining and the first programme already out, but apart from anything else, you can't possibly ride a horse now you're pregnant.'

'I won't – I mean, they're going to shoot around it, or maybe write it into the script.'

His hand fell away as he looked at her in disbelief. 'You mean you've already discussed it with them?' he said.

Her eyes went down. 'I had to. I – I wasn't sure what to do . . . I . . .'

'What do you mean, you weren't sure what to do?' He got up from the bed and walked across the room. Then, spinning back, 'Were you considering . . . ?'

'No!' she said.

'Yes you were. You talked to them before you talked to me because you were going to put your job first.'

'That's not true,' she lied. 'I told them so that when I told you I'd be able to explain how we can make it work.'

'You're lying.'

'No. Alan, listen. I don't want to give up the part now. I can't. I've wanted this for so long. It means everything . . .'

'More than your own child?'

'Of course not. If that were the case I could have gone ahead with an abortion and never said anything to you.'

Clearly still stunned by the way things had suddenly turned, he dropped his head in his hands as he tried to take it in.

'Alan, you're going to be a father,' she said desperately. '*We* are going to be parents. That's what matters now, and I won't be doing anything to put the baby at risk. I wouldn't, *couldn't* do that to you, or to it.'

Coming back to the bed, he sank down next to her and took her hands in his. 'I guess I over-reacted,' he said. 'I can see why you needed to find out . . . I just think it would be better for us, and for the baby, if they wrote you out.'

'Please don't say that,' she implored. 'They want me to stay, and it's what I want too, so they're going to make it happen.'

'But it'll mean a very public pregnancy,' he objected, 'and you know how I feel about being dragged into the limelight.'

'You don't have to be. If I'm asked about you in interviews I'll just say that we're very happy. That's all anyone needs to know.'

Looking down at their hands, he held them very tightly, too tightly, as he said, 'I am happy, I guess I just need to get used to the fact that it's not going to happen the way I imagined it.'

'Barefoot and pregnant and chained to the kitchen sink?' she tried to tease.

He smiled. 'Something like that, I suppose, but OK, that's hardly you.' He suddenly kissed her hard on the mouth, then gazed deeply into her eyes. 'We're going to have a baby,' he said, as though it was still taking its time to sink in. Then he started to laugh. 'We're having a baby,' he cried, 'and I am the happiest, luckiest man on the planet.'

Putting on a smile she watched him, and might almost have felt caught up in his joy were it not hitting so many wrong chords. It seemed too intense, oddly harsh, and his eyes were so bright they were almost feral.

'I want to shout it out so the whole world can hear,' he was laughing.

'What happened to privacy?' she said, going along with it.

He threw out his hands delightedly. 'I have to tell someone,' he said, 'but it can wait till tomorrow, and then I guess the first person we should break it to is Neve. I wonder how she'll take it.'

'Yes, I wonder,' Susannah murmured. 'With any luck, it'll be just what she needs to help cheer her up a bit.'

Neve's face turned completely white. Her normally lively blue eyes turned dull, almost lifeless as they moved from her mother, to Alan, then back again.

'Isn't that great news?' Alan said encouragingly.

As he made to put a hand on her shoulder she sprang to her feet, knocking over her chair, and before anyone could stop her she'd run down the hall and was tearing out of the front door.

Susannah raced after her. 'Neve!' she cried. 'Come back! What's wrong?'

By the time she reached the gate Neve was already at the end of the street, disappearing around the corner towards the mayhem of Saturday shoppers on Battersea Rise.

'She'll be OK,' Alan said, coming up behind her. 'It was just a bit of a shock. She's used to being the only child, remember?'

'But she's always wanted a brother or sister,' Susannah said helplessly. 'What's the matter with her? I just don't understand why she's being like this.'

'Come back inside,' he said gently. 'There's something I want to tell you. I was saving it till after dinner last night, but then other things came up that took precedence.' He smiled at his own irony.

When they returned to the kitchen she watched him pick up the chair Neve had knocked over, barely registering his actions, only thinking about Neve and where she might go. 'I can't even ring her,' she said, seeing Neve's mobile on the table.

'She'll be fine,' Alan assured her. 'She'll go to one of her friends. Several live down that way.' After settling her into a chair he sat opposite her and said, 'I had a bit of a chat with her this week, like I said I would, and things are pretty much as I suspected.'

Susannah's heart turned over. 'What do you mean?' she said faintly.

His eyes deepened with feeling as he looked at

her. 'You remember the night she came to stay here with Sasha?' he said. 'When Ken and his wife were here too?'

Susannah nodded.

'Well, it didn't turn out quite the way I expected. Ken had to cancel last minute, and Sasha had to go somewhere with her parents. I had my suspicions at the time that there might be something afoot, Sasha's sudden commitment seemed a little too convenient, but I didn't say anything. In retrospect I should have, of course, but I didn't realise until it was happening what Neve was intending to do.'

Susannah felt a terrible stillness come over her. 'What did she do?' she asked, not at all sure she wanted to hear this.

'It's best I don't go into detail,' he replied. 'You can probably work it out for yourself. The point is, I had to be quite firm with her, and make her understand that while I was extremely flattered that she had a crush on me, her behaviour was inappropriate and she mustn't try anything like it again.'

'Oh my God,' Susannah muttered, pressing her hands to her face. 'This is awful. I have to speak to her . . .'

'No, it's best you don't for the time being. I promised not to tell you anything, so it won't help matters if she knows I've betrayed her confidence. Unfortunately she's taken the rejection as hard as I expected, mainly because of the abandonment issues she has with her father, but we're starting to work on them. We had a chat the other night, after school. I brought her here because it's less formal than the office, less daunting for her. She went back to Lola's after, and I was reasonably confident, by the time I dropped her off, that she'd found our chat helpful. The trouble is, passion in a teenager can be a bit of a wildfire. Just when you think you have it under control it's suddenly raging away again, and sometimes even hotter than before.'

Susannah's heart felt as though it was breaking in two. To think of Neve suffering so much was as bad as if she were suffering the pain herself. Worse, even, because there was nothing she could do to make it better.

'You have to remember,' Alan went on, 'that she has a lot to be dealing with right now. You're not a part of her everyday life any more, which isn't easy for her when she's been used to you always being around. I'm doing everything I can to fill the gap, as is Lola, of course, but she's taking some time to adjust to not having her mother there all the time. It's another reason why she's turned her affections to me the way she has. I'm becoming her mainstay, her rock, the one she can depend on, and I'm afraid promiscuity, as a means of holding on to someone, is quite common in teenage girls who have experienced paternal abandonment.' He smiled affectionately and reached for her hand. 'Don't look so worried,' he said softly. 'She's going to be fine. We have it under control and while she's too embarrassed and confused to discuss it with you, or Lola, at the moment, fortunately she is able to discuss it with me.'

As she looked into his gentle dark eyes,

Susannah felt an ocean of gratitude swelling through her. 'Thank you for taking such good care of her,' she said shakily. 'I hadn't realised, when I left, that it might have this kind of effect on her, but I suppose it's like both parents have abandoned her, isn't it?'

He nodded. 'I'm afraid so,' he confirmed. 'But it won't last. She knows you're there for her really, and before too much longer she'll be so busy enjoying your fame it'll be as though none of this has happened. Unless, of course, you do decide to drop out of the series. Then she'd feel totally secure and a lot of this inner angst of hers will evaporate overnight.'

Susannah couldn't have looked, or felt, more torn.

He smiled. 'Don't think about it now,' he said kindly. 'You just leave her to me, while you stay focused on taking care of yourself and our baby.'

Chapter Twenty-Five

Patsy's eyes widened in disbelief as she looked up from her desk to see Frank coming down through the concourse towards her, leaving ripples of laughter and applause in his wake. Since their encounter the other day, which hadn't ended on the friendliest of notes, he'd been keeping a low profile, in so far as his natural flamboyance was capable of such a feat, but that clearly wasn't his intention today.

'*What* are you wearing?' she demanded as he reached her door. His jeans were so white they were dazzling, and so tight they were positively indecent, while his metallic blue shirt was unbuttoned to his navel, exposing the hirsute splendour of his manly chest. All that was missing was the medallion. But no, there it was, lurking behind a little curly thatch, winking away like a bawdy come-on.

Affecting his best Adonis pose, he said, 'Now you know the secrets of my personal life I have lost my mystery, and a man without mystery is a man without appeal. So now, I do my best to show you what is waiting backstage, without opening the curtains.'

Patsy's jaw dropped, but she couldn't stop a bubble of laughter. 'They look fairly open to me,' she commented. 'You look ridiculous.'

'I do not want you to think that I do not know this,' he responded, 'but I tell myself that maybe it will make you hungry for me, and if you are hungry, I can take you for dinner.'

Groaning and still laughing, she shook her head in despair.

'So, have I once again made myself irresistible to you?' he challenged, turning around and giving a little wiggle of his tightly upholstered derrière.

'You were never that,' she informed him, even though it wasn't strictly true.

Waving a dismissive hand, he said, 'I know you are playing hard to get with me, so I am not deterred. Dinner, this evening. I will pick you up at Claudia's apartment, and I will not hear no for an answer.'

As he attempted a macho strut into his own office Patsy had to stifle another laugh, and yet another as he eased himself down in his chair with an agonised grimace. Then, giving her a friendly little wave, he picked up the phone and a moment later hers started to ring.

'Hello, it is Frank,' he told her. 'I forget to ask if you have an enjoyable dinner last night with Claudia and Céline?'

'Very enjoyable, thank you,' she replied, watching him through the glass partition. 'And you, did you have a good evening too?'

'*Impeccable*,' he answered. 'I spend it with my son, just me and him. He is very entertaining.'

'Then he's like his father.'

'I often think so, but happily for him, he have the look of his mother. Did Claudia tell you last night that she meet him during the afternoon?'

'Yes. She said he's adorable.'

'He think the same about her, but he use different words, like old and smelly, because she wears much perfume.'

Patsy smiled, and wanted to say how pleased she was that he no longer seemed angry with her, or anxious to keep her out of his personal life. She wished she could have told him that she'd like to meet his son too. In fact, there was quite a lot she'd have liked to say to him, but she merely excused herself and took another call.

'Patsy, it's Claudia. How are you this morning?'

'Very well, thank you. And you?'

'Excellent. I'm leaving shortly to get my plane, but I wanted to find out if you've spoken to Anita in London yet today.'

'No,' Patsy answered, looking at the time. 'It's still only nine o'clock over there. She doesn't usually get in until ten.'

'I guessed something must have come up, because she was going to call first thing. It turns out she has to go into hospital the week after next for a little procedure that's going to leave her out of action for about three weeks. Because of various deadlines and launches she has scheduled for that time, someone needs to be running the show over there. I've suggested you, or Frank. I'll let you make the choice. No need to come back to me on it, I'll be happy either way.'

And uncontactable in a Swiss clinic, Patsy mentally added.

After ringing off she went to stand in Frank's doorway. 'There's something we need to discuss,' she told him, 'so dinner tonight might be a good time, but don't you dare wear those terrible jeans.'

He grinned wickedly, but sensing what was coming she made good her escape before he could trot out another of his dreadful puns or innuendoes.

She'd been back at her desk for only a few minutes before her mobile rang, and seeing it was Susannah she clicked on. 'At last,' she said, 'how did it go at the weekend?'

Sounding tired and stressed, Susannah said, 'Sorry, it wasn't a good time to call before . . . Anyway, Alan's over the moon, just as I expected.'

'So this means you're going through with it?'

'I guess so. Neve didn't take it very well at all. She ran out on us, and I haven't seen her since.'

Patsy frowned. 'So where is she?'

'Right now at school, but she spent most of the weekend with Lola, apart from when I was there when she went off to Melinda's.'

'And where are you now?'

'In a field next to the Centre. We're going for a take any minute, so I can't stay. I just wanted to let you know how it went with Alan.'

'Have you told Marlene yet?'

'No. Actually, my main concern right now is Neve. There was an incident with Alan. He didn't go into any detail, but apparently it was inappropriate and he had to tell her so, which is why she's having such a difficult time. It's all about rejection, he says, her father going to prison, me suddenly taking off to Derbyshire every week, and now him resisting her advances.'

'Oh poor love,' Patsy murmured. 'I wish I knew . . .'

'I'm sorry,' Susannah broke in, 'they're shouting for me. I'll try and call this evening.'

'Make it tomorrow morning,' Pats told her. 'I'm having dinner with Frank this evening.' After ringing off she quickly changed the screen on her mobile and composed a text to Neve. *If you feel like having a chat, you know you can call any time, day or night. Love you, FGM.* Neve would know the initials meant fairy godmother.

'I'm really glad you're staying at mine tonight,' Sasha was saying as she and Neve strolled out of school at the end of the day. 'My mum's so been on my case asking what I've done to upset you, because you didn't come back all last week. Don't you just love her, that everything has to be my fault?'

Neve's smile was thin. She was reading Patsy's text, then closing her mobile down she put it back in her bag.

'So anyway, how did it go at the weekend, with your mum?' Sasha wanted to know. 'I bet she's dead chuffed about the programme. Even my mother likes it and that's saying something, because she never likes anything, especially telly.'

Neve staggered slightly as a crowd of girls pushed past, barely managing an apology, until they realised who it was.

'Hey, Neve. What are you doing later?' one of them asked. 'We're all meeting up at the Bluebird on King's Road, if you and Sash want to come.'

'Thanks, but we can't tonight,' Neve replied, knowing that her sudden increase in popularity was due to her mother's newfound fame. Not that she hadn't had lots of friends before, but apparently she was something really special now.

'Where's Ping?' Sasha murmured, as they emerged through the gates into the cluster of vehicles waiting to transport the girls home. 'Oh, by the way, when we go to Barcelona in the summer it turns out my aunt and uncle are going to be there at the same time, so they're going to see if they can take us for dinner. That'll be cool, won't it?'

'Yes,' Neve agreed.

Since there was no sign of Ping yet they leaned back against the wall and dropped their heavy bags as they waited. 'You know what,' Sasha said, 'even I was starting to think I might have done something to upset you. You've been . . . Well, it's like you've been avoiding me.'

'It's not that,' Neve assured her. 'It's just Lola hasn't been all that good, so I've needed to go back there every night.'

'But even at school . . . I'm not getting on your case, or anything, but you're like, distant, and you haven't even told me what happened that night with Alan yet. How did it go? Did it work out the way . . . you know?'

Neve turned her head away to look down the street.

'Well?' Sasha prompted.

'I can't talk about it,' Neve mumbled.

'But I'm your best . . .'

'Just leave it,' Neve seethed.

Sasha immediately backed off, and feeling awkward started to hunt around for Ping again. 'Ah, here she is,' she said, spotting the black Toyota Corolla pulling into the kerb a little way down the street. 'Are you ready?'

When she turned round it was to find Neve standing rigidly against the wall, a really strange look on her face. Following the direction of her eyes, she saw Alan getting out of his car across the road. 'Did you know he was coming to pick you up today?' she asked, unable to fathom what was happening.

'No. Come on, quick, let's go with Ping.'

As they reached the Toyota Sasha threw her bag into the back seat and hastily scrambled in after it. Before Neve could follow Alan was taking her arm.

'Hey,' he said, laughing, 'not so fast. Mum's really worried about you . . .'

'Let me go,' Neve growled, trying to wrench her arm free.

'Come on,' he said gently, 'we don't want to cause a scene, but we do need to have a chat.' Then to Ping and Sasha, 'I'll drop her off later. You go on now and don't worry about dinner, I'll make sure she has something to eat,' and taking Neve's bag from her he turned her around and steered her gently, but very firmly, across the street to his car.

Hearing a knock on her dressing-room door Susannah came out of the shower room, wrapped in a towelling robe. 'Who is it?' she called out.

Marlene put her head round. 'OK to come in?' she asked.

Susannah nodded, and knowing exactly why she was there she waited only until the door was closed and Marlene was leaning against the vanity shelf before saying, 'I told Alan at the weekend. He was thrilled.'

Marlene nodded. Her expression was severe, but not entirely without feeling. 'Then I guess I have my answer?' she said.

Susannah took a shuddering breath. 'I don't know how to apologise for this,' she said shakily. 'I promise, it was the last thing I wanted, or expected . . .' She broke off as her voice was swallowed by a gulf of emotion.

Coming forward, Marlene clasped her by the shoulders. 'It's lucky we have a good team of writers,' she said, 'they'll manage to work it in, and your stunt double can take over the riding scenes. Let's just hope you don't start showing too soon.'

Swallowing, Susannah attempted a smile. 'Will you tell Michael about my decision?' she asked hoarsely. 'Or do you think I should?'

Marlene's eyes showed a depth of understanding that brought Susannah to the verge of revealing all her confused emotions. Luckily she managed to hold back, since it would only end up embarrassing them both. 'I'll do it, if that's what you want,' Marlene said.

Not sure that it was, Susannah looked away.

After giving her shoulders a comforting squeeze, Marlene turned away and let herself out again.

For a long time after she'd gone Susannah stood with her head in her hands, until, picking up her mobile, she rang Neve's number, willing her to answer. Once again she was diverted to voicemail. 'Hi darling,' she said, trying to sound bright. 'I was wondering if you'd like to do some shopping for your Barcelona trip at the weekend? It's only about six weeks away, so we should probably start getting some things together. Let me know. I'd love to talk to you anyway. Oh, and I was wondering if you'd like to spend your summer holidays up here, with me? Polly's moving out of the lodge at the end of next week, so we'll have it to ourselves. We might even be able to find you a job of some sort while you're here, as a runner, or as one of the grooms. And you could learn to ride. Wouldn't that be lovely, if we could ride together?' Her words ran out as she remembered that she'd be able to do precious little of that from now on. 'Please call me, darling,' she said, hoping she wasn't sounding as emotional as she was feeling. 'I love you.'

As she rang off she was trying hard to hold back the tears. If Neve's young heart was broken over Alan, then she guessed it followed that his partner was the last person she'd want to talk to, but she was finding this rift between them almost impossible to cope with. It simply wasn't right for them to be this way when they'd always been so close. She wished she could think of a way to reach her, but all Neve's barriers were up at the moment, so in spite of being her mother and the one person who'd do anything for her, right now all Susannah felt she could do was follow Alan's advice and give Neve time to come through this. Just thank goodness he was there to offer his professional support and understanding, or her darling, precious girl would be all alone with her despair.

Looking at her mobile again, she tried to think of what she might say were she to call Michael. Nothing was feeling right, and she was so close to the edge that it wouldn't be wise to try, anyway. She considered ringing Alan then, but almost immediately dismissed it. To her shame she wasn't finding his happiness easy to deal with at all.

In the end she sent Michael a text saying *Marlene will be calling to let you know that the baby's going to be scripted into the programme. I'm sorry I'm not calling myself, I just don't think I can. S.*

A few minutes later she received a message back. *I understand.*

As she gazed down at the two words tears welled large in her eyes and rolled on to her cheeks. She felt a sudden urge to call him to say she'd changed her mind, she couldn't go through with the pregnancy, but even if she was serious, Michael wasn't the person she should be telling. She needed to talk to Alan, but since she knew she couldn't bring herself to hurt him so badly, she took the only other option open to her, and put it from her mind.

'My God, how much cologne are you wearing?' Patsy gasped, waving a hand in front of her face as Frank wafted into the apartment, dressed, rather soberly for him, in loose-fitting chinos and an electric blue polo shirt.

'It is to add to my irresistibleness,' he informed her cheerfully. 'And for you, here is a corsage, which is very old-fashioned and charming, and I am sure if I keep being this romantic that you will be begging me to . . .'

'*Stop*,' she cut in before he could go any further, and taking the flowers she popped them into a vase she found under the sink, and ushered him straight back out of the door.

'May I say you are looking exceptionally beautiful this evening?' he ventured, as they strolled along the Rue St Dominique towards the restaurant he'd chosen.

'You may,' she replied, feeling at her best in a deep-amber-coloured dress that sparkled and rustled and revealed all of her slender shoulders down to her semi-exposed cleavage. Had she been dining with anyone else she might have worn the matching sandals, but as she was already at least an inch taller than Frank, she'd rejected them in favour of some gold ballet pumps.

Since the restaurant was little more than a block from her apartment, they were soon being shown to their table on an elegant roof terrace where a young jazz trio was playing in one corner, and the tables were set with starched white linen and fresh red roses. 'At least if you run out on me tonight I'll have some idea why,' she remarked, as he held out a chair for her to sit down.

'I am confident it will not happen,' he told her, sitting down too and making a point of turning off his mobile. 'Jean-Luc is with my mother. *Deux coupes*,' he said to the waiter. Then to Pats, 'You are happy to have champagne to begin? It is a perfect June evening and we are in Paris, so . . . '

'Champagne's fine,' she informed him. 'Thank you.'

He smiled and a small frisson of response sparkled through her. Ignoring it, she looked around admiringly. 'This is a lovely place,' she commented. 'I don't think I've been here before.'

'It is one of my favourites,' he told her. 'They have excellent *confit de canard*.' Then promptly dismissing it, 'You say earlier, at the office, that we have something to discuss?'

It was a moment before she remembered it was why they were there. 'Yes, of course,' she replied, sitting up a little straighter. 'Anita's going to be out of action for a while, so one of us needs to go and run the London office for three weeks from the twentieth of this month. Unless you particularly want to do it, I thought perhaps I should, then you'll be on hand if your wife, or son, should need you at short notice.'

He nodded thoughtfully, then sat back as their champagne was delivered. 'That was a very quick discussion,' he remarked, as though impressed. 'And a very considerate decision. Thank you.'

'Not at all,' she murmured, and touched her glass to his.

After he'd taken a sip he put the glass down and regarded her steadily. 'So I am to lose you for three weeks,' he stated ruminatively.

'I'm sure you'll survive,' she responded smoothly.

Sitting forward and affecting a low, intimate tone, he said, 'I would like to know if you are very serious about me, because I don't mind telling you that I am very fast becoming that way about you.'

Feeling her cheeks starting to burn, she said, 'I doubt you can be serious about anything, Frank. Apart from your son.'

'And *l'amour*,' he added darkly. 'As a Frenchman I take affairs of the heart most seriously indeed.'

Her eyebrows rose. 'Really? You mean like you did in Monte Carlo?' she challenged.

At that a light of mischief sparked in his eyes.

'Frank, don't start playing games again,' she warned. 'I know nothing happened, because you're far too honourable to take advantage of a woman in the condition I was in.'

He was grinning. 'You are right,' he told her, 'I am too much of a gentleman for that, but I have to confess that I decide to have some fun anyway. So, I lie down on the bed to make it look as though I sleep there, and I leave my jacket behind to confuse you. I think maybe you will know right away that I am tricking you, but you didn't and then the fun becomes very much more enjoyable.'

Her eyes narrowed. 'For you, maybe.'

He was still grinning. 'Possibly. The fun for you will come when we do make love.'

Feeling a catch in her breath, she said, 'It's not going to happen.'

'I think that maybe it is,' he corrected, 'but it is good to linger in the candlelight, letting burn the anticipation, because it make us both very much in the mood, *non*?'

'*Non*,' she agreed and drank more champagne.

He continued to gaze at her in a rapt, but slightly teasing sort of way.

'You're impossible,' she told him.

'No, I am very possible, but I must warn you, I will remember your name in the morning, and I will bring you coffee in bed, and I will send you flowers, so maybe this is something that will turn you off?'

Shaking her head in mock despair, she said, 'Tell me how you can be so certain I'm going to give in.'

At that one eyebrow arched itself assertively. 'It is because I am fantastic lover,' he replied with unabashed pride, 'so now you know that, I think you will be very happy to surrender.'

Laughing, and fearing she'd never find a way to cool him down, she said, 'I don't think I've ever known anyone quite like you.'

'This is good?' he said.

She nodded. 'Yes, it's good.' Then, glancing past him, 'I think the waiter's trying to attract your attention.'

'Neve, love, what are you doing here?' Lola exclaimed, coming out into the hall as Neve let herself in the front door. 'You gave me a bit of a fright. I thought you were staying at Sasha's tonight.'

'I was, but I changed my mind,' Neve said, keeping her head down as she took off her jacket and hung it next to Lola's everyday coat behind the door.

'You should have rung,' Lola told her. 'How did you get here?'

'I walked.'

Lola tutted and shook her head. 'You'd better not tell your mother,' she said. 'She won't approve of you being out at this time of night on your own. It's gone ten o'clock.'

'I know. Actually, I'm really tired, so I think I'll go straight to bed if that's OK.'

'Have you had anything to eat?'

'I don't want anything.'

Lola watched her walk to her bedroom door, head still down. 'Have you been crying?' she asked. 'Did you and Sasha have a row, or something? Is that why you're here? And where's your bag?'

'I left it there, OK?' Neve snapped. 'Stop keeping on. I've got a headache and I don't need anyone getting on my case right now.'

As she slammed her bedroom door Lola stood looking at it, blinking with as much dismay as concern. Then, feeling a wave of dizziness coming over her, she went back into the sitting room to sit down for a while.

A few minutes later, Neve came out of her room to apologise. 'I didn't mean to bite your head off,' she said. 'I'm really sorry, it's just I'm feeling a bit stressed at the moment.'

When Lola didn't respond she stole a glance at her, then suddenly the colour drained from her face. 'Lola!' she gasped, dropping to her knees and grabbing Lola's hands. 'Are you all right?'

'Yes, yes, I'm fine,' Lola managed to croak. 'Just a bit of a turn. Nothing to worry about.'

'Are you sure? Shall I get you something? Maybe I should call the doctor.'

'A glass of water would be nice,' Lola rasped, 'and my blood-pressure pills. I must have forgotten to take them today.'

Dashing into the kitchen Neve grabbed the pills, poured some water into a glass, and ran back again. 'Here,' she said, tipping the bottle into her hand and feeding two into Lola's mouth.

Lola sucked them in, then drank some water to wash them down. 'That's better,' she said breathily. 'I'll be right as rain in a minute.'

'I'm going to call Mum,' Neve said, standing up.

'No, no, you don't want to go worrying her now. I'll just sit here a minute, then you can give me a hand getting into bed.'

Neve gazed into her beloved old face, and wanted to cry because she loved her so much and she'd been so horrible to her just now that maybe this was all her fault too, like everything else that was happening.

'Oh my, those aren't tears, are they?' Lola chided. 'Come here, you daft old thing.'

Sinking into Lola's ready embrace, Neve swallowed hard on the lump in her throat and snuggled up warmly against her.

'Would you like to come and sleep in with me tonight?' Lola offered.

'Yes, please,' Neve answered.

Helping Lola to her feet, Neve walked her into the bedroom and started to unbutton her blouse. 'You don't have to go fussing now,' Lola told her, pushing her hands away. 'I can manage. You go and get yourself sorted out, then you can come and read me a story. We'll have some *Harry Potter*, shall we? And there's a nice bar of chocolate in the fridge, we could have a bite of that each, mm?'

After changing into her nightie Neve came back into the room to find Lola lying against the pillows, already starting to doze. 'It's probably a bit late for a story,' she said, realising Lola needed to sleep.

'You're a good girl,' Lola murmured as Neve climbed in beside her.

For a while Neve lay staring into the darkness, listening to Lola's deepening breaths and wishing the night would swallow her up so that she wouldn't have to worry about anything any more.

'What is it, my love?' Lola whispered, reaching for her hand. 'I know there's something, so why don't you get it off your chest?'

Thinking of the turn her great-aunt had just had, Neve said, 'There's nothing, honestly.' After a lengthy silence, not really knowing if Lola was still awake, she said, 'I was thinking, do you happen to have Dad's number?'

There was a beat before Lola said, 'No, I don't, but Mum will, we can . . .'

'No, it's OK,' Neve interrupted. 'Don't worry. She'll only want to know why I'm asking and it might upset her if she thinks I want to get in touch with him. Don't even tell her I mentioned it, all right? It's better that she doesn't know.'

Chapter Twenty-Six

'Polly, would you have any idea what's happened to all the cosmetics that were here, on the table?' Susannah asked as Polly came into the lodge kitchen.

Polly tossed a quick glance at the few face masks and samples Susannah was holding and said, 'I shared them out, the way we're supposed to.'

'I see,' Susannah said carefully. 'But there were at least a dozen boxes here last night, now there's only this. That doesn't seem a particularly equal sort of sharing.'

'Oh, for heaven's sake, if you want to make an issue of it . . .'

'Only in so far,' Susannah cut in sharply, 'as they were sent to me, personally, to review, and because of a conflict of interests I brought them here, for you, to ask if you'd like to try them out instead.'

Reddening to the roots of her hair, Polly said, 'I assumed one of the PR people had left them there.'

Susannah's eyebrows rose, and handing over the rest of the products she said, 'A thank-you would be nice, but in your own time,' and smiling sweetly she swept out of the lodge to start walking along the drive to the Centre.

Scoring points off Polly might be gratifying for five minutes, but it was soon forgotten as everything else came crowding back in on her. She'd had a brief conversation with Neve this morning, who was now saying she didn't want to go to Barcelona. Then Lola had broken the disturbing news that Neve wanted to be in touch with her father. It wasn't that Susannah objected, particularly, she just didn't understand why Neve had suddenly changed her mind now when she'd been so adamant about having nothing to do with him before.

'Actually, the answer's quite simple,' Alan said, when she rang to tell him. 'The way she's perceiving things is that she's lost me, so now she's going in search of her real father to try and fill the void.'

Feeling her heart contract with an overpowering need to fill every void Neve could ever possibly have, Susannah said, 'So should I give her Duncan's number?'

'I don't think so, not yet. In the long run it might be a good idea if she is in touch with him, but let's be sure she's prepared for it. She still has quite a lot of anger stored away towards him, so any kind of scene with him could cause her a lot of emotional damage while she's still quite fragile.'

'Oh God,' Susannah murmured, 'I wish there was something I could do.'

'You're doing exactly what you should in telling me, so I can try to sort it out.'

'But if it's you she's heartbroken over, surely it's making it worse for her to keep seeing you?'

'On the contrary, as long as she understands that I'm not rejecting her in a paternal way, she'll always have our relationship to hold on to. She just needs to get things into balance, and she will, you can be sure of that. Now, where are you at the moment?'

'Walking up to the Centre.'

'No riding shots today?'

Her eyes went longingly to the stables as she said, 'No.'

'Or love scenes?'

'No.' That was a lie, but by the time the episode went out he'd have no idea which day it had been shot. 'Where are you?' she asked, feeling she should return the interest.

'Almost at the office, so I should go. I've a busy day ahead, but I'll try to call between consultations.'

'You don't have to. I'll be fine, and I've got a fairly full day too. I'll call you later, after we've wrapped.'

'OK, and make sure *no riding shots*.'

Clicking off before she snapped at him, Susannah quickened her pace as though it might put some distance between her and her own irritation. Just thank God he hadn't mentioned the baby for once, at least not directly, because their conversations now were hardly ever about anything else. Not that she had much desire to discuss other things, apart from Neve of course, and since he was being so supportive and wonderfully patient with her, she, Susannah, should get a grip on her temper and focus more on being thankful he was there. *Except he's the damned cause of Neve's problems*, a voice inside her seethed. But it was hardly his fault Neve had fallen for him, and since she and Duncan, as Neve's parents, were far, far more responsible for the angst she was going through, she needed to ease up on Alan and remember that there weren't many men who'd be as generous with their time and expertise as he was being.

The trouble was, no matter how grateful, or even affectionate, she managed to feel towards him, she knew in her heart that she no longer loved him. She was even starting to wonder if she ever really had. Though it had felt completely right at the beginning, the answer to all her prayers, looking back she could see more clearly now just how vulnerable she'd been at the time, so needful of affection and desperate for something to change. She'd jumped in too quickly, had never even questioned her feelings, had simply assumed that the whirlwind romance was a heady prelude to a much deeper and more lasting kind of love. And now, to make matters even worse, though she'd given Marlene her decision about the baby, deep down inside she still didn't feel as though one had been taken. But it had, because even if she could bring herself to break Alan's heart, which she couldn't, she still had to face the fact that she didn't really have it in her to kill an innocent child for the sake of her career.

Taking out her mobile as it started to ring, she saw it was the director she was working with that day and quickly clicked on. After assuring him she was fine about the upcoming scenes, and would be in her dressing room in about five minutes to discuss them, she rang off again and gave Pats a try. Finding her mobile still switched off, she left a message letting her know she'd rung and telling her that the text Pats had sent last night had come out as gobbledegook, so she either needed to call back or send it again.

Have lost mind. Going to b^% w!&**@ Will call so@*st. Px*

By the time Susannah reached the Centre two other actors had fallen into step with her, and she was managing to impress herself with how light-hearted and enthusiastic she was sounding as they chatted about the day ahead. However, going next to naked in front of a crew, even on a closed set, was the very last thing she felt like doing today. Just thank goodness her pregnancy wasn't showing yet, and once again she was trusting to Marianne to carry her through.

In the event exactly that happened, because once she was in character it was as though her real self ceased to exist, or at least went into retreat some-where safe and discreet, along with her almost constant fatigue and girlish inhibitions. Marianne was a bold, confident woman who rejoiced in her sensuality and revelled in her power over men. For a woman like that, peeling off her clothes to make sure a show judge qualified her horse was no more daunting than throwing herself into the saddle and galloping off into the hills.

'Are you OK?' Lindon, the director, asked, when the time came for her to disrobe.

Susannah was in one of the stables, wearing only a dressing gown over a fancy pair of lace panties and long black riding boots. She was to be shot from behind first, waist up to see her bare back, then thigh down to show her legs and boots. After that the camera would move round to take a medium close-up of her head and shoulders to include the tops of her breasts as she smouldered seductively into the lens.

'I'm fine,' she said, and she was, because she was already becoming Marianne, and Marianne wasn't pregnant, or embarrassed, or even particularly concerned about who was watching her out there. Marianne had an exquisite body that she had no problem making work for her in every way possible. It was only when they began framing the head and shoulders, taking care to avoid her nipples, but coming low enough to make it clear that she wasn't wearing anything on top, that she started to feel self-conscious. She was standing amongst a handful of men, with only one other woman present, completely exposed from the waist up. She could hardly begin to imagine what Alan would say if he could see her now, though in truth it wasn't him she was thinking about. It was Michael, and whether he might see the rushes, and how he would feel if he saw her like this. For one horrible moment it made her feel cheap and worthless, and so distanced from the sophistication of his world that she came close to grabbing her robe and running back to her dressing room.

Realising she'd slipped back into her own persona, she quickly began psyching herself into Marianne again, holding her head high and arching her back in a way that raised her breasts and caused the cameraman to laugh and groan.

'I had it just right,' he complained, 'then you go and put your shoulders back so I can see everything.'

'Sorry,' she apologised. 'I promise not to move again.'

What was it going to be like, she wondered, when they came to shoot an actual sex scene and she had to roll and writhe about the bed, wearing nothing at all, with a man who was naked too? She could already feel herself shrinking from it, but reminded herself firmly that Marianne would be there to take control. Thank God for her alter ego, because if everything was left to Susannah her life on-screen, and off, might be in an even bigger mess than it already was.

Trying to understand the self was always a fascinating exercise, Alan was thinking, as he sat in the car waiting for Neve to come out of school. His own personality was more intriguing to him than any other, simply because it was his. There were so many facets and dimensions to the enigmatic prism that made up Alan Cunningham, any number of complexities, motivations, fears, desires, passions, aversions, all combining to create the behavioural patterns of one outwardly unremarkable man. What interested him greatly was how he, much like the rest of humanity, always thought he'd know exactly how he'd react to any given situation. The truth was, however, that until a particular challenge or deviation from the norm arose, no one could ever really know how they'd handle it – and very often the response turned out to be the complete antithesis to the one expected.

He was keeping a record of how both he and Neve were responding to their current state of affairs. The depth to which they could self-delude, or control the other, was especially intriguing, though unsurprisingly he was the more adept at control, while she remained confused, frustrated and occasionally afraid of her own instincts and desires.

She would find her way through though, he was sure of that, and no harm would be done in the long run. He simply needed to help her gain a greater understanding of herself and of what was happening, most particularly the role she was playing in bringing it about. Once she was able to accept responsibility for her actions and to distinguish reality from fantasy, she would come to realise just how powerful an individual she actually was. Until then she'd probably go on seeing herself as a victim, which was why he'd decided it would be best to focus her away from her relationship with Susannah for now, or misunderstandings would be bound to occur, and the last thing he wanted was any undue stress being inflicted on Susannah while she was carrying his child.

As soon as Neve came out of the school gates and saw Alan waiting she started to walk the other way, praying she'd be masked by the crowd. However, he spotted her, and was out of the car and coming across the road to take hold of her before she could get very far.

'We need to talk,' he said, smiling pleasantly.

'I know what that means,' she hissed, trying to wrench her arm away.

'People are staring,' he told her, 'so unless you want to cause a scene . . .'

'I don't care.'

'Yes you do. Now come along. I don't have time to take you home, so I'll drop you at Lola's. We'll talk on the way.'

Only because he wasn't taking her to *that house*, which she hated with all her soul and wished she never had to set foot in again, she allowed him to walk her over to the car that she also hated, but not nearly as much as she hated him.

'I hear you want to make contact with your father,' he said chattily as they drove away.

She turned to look out of the window. She should have known Lola would tell her mother, even though she'd promised not to. Did it matter? She didn't know, because she didn't know anything any more.

'Don't you think it's a little selfish to be upsetting your mother now you know she's pregnant?' he said, making it sound like a genuine question.

She kept her head averted, digging her nails into her palms and wanting to scream and scream until everything stopped and she ceased to exist.

'Your mother's sacrificed a lot for you,' he went on, 'you've always been at the very centre of her world, and that doesn't need to change, but I think it's best, at least for the next few weekends, that you stay at Lola's when she's here. I'll bring her to see you, of course, but she's tired when she comes back from Derbyshire, and now, with the baby, it wouldn't be good for her to have you bothering her.'

With tears stinging her eyes Neve continued to

stare out of the window. She hated him so much that she'd like to kill him, but he scared her, because maybe he'd like to kill her too. Sometimes she wished he would, at least then he wouldn't be able to do things to her any more, and she wouldn't have to be a worry to her mum or anyone else.

This was the third morning in a row that Patsy had woken up to find Frank lying next to her in the bed, snoring softly, with a sheet tangled loosely around him and an arm draped protectively over her. She was still slightly dazed by what was happening, and kept wondering if it might be a dream – in some ways she hoped it was. Just like on the previous mornings, however, she found herself moving closer to him, inhaling his musky scent, and responding warmly to the feel of his skin.

As she'd told Susannah when she'd finally confessed that the deed had been done, he really hadn't been joking, or exaggerating, when he'd claimed to be a fantastic lover. In all her thirty-six years she'd never known anything quite like it, hadn't even realised it was possible to climax so many times in one night, or to make each one feel as though the last was a poor rehearsal. He made love with his entire being, heart, body and soul. He was right there with her every moment of the way, making her his complete focus, taking her tenderly and passionately, holding himself back and watching her as she became lost in more sensations than she'd believed it was possible to feel. When he joined her in the final throes of ecstasy he somehow kept her there, making it go on and on, infusing more and more potency into her release than she could bear without crying out for him to stop, even as she urged him on. And when it was over and he was holding her while the pounding in their hearts receded and their breathing steadied, he invariably said something to make her tighten her arms around him, or to make her laugh, or very often both.

Looking at him now, she smiled at the lovely crookedness of his nose, and the blue-black shadow that darkened his jaw. His mouth was slightly open and as she touched a finger gently to his lips, she found herself thinking of how exquisitely he used them, and started to become aroused again. Sliding a leg over his she waited for him to feel it, and a moment later one of his crazy eyebrows arched before an eye opened cautiously, as though taking a secret peep at who might be there.

'Good morning,' she whispered.

He blinked a couple of times, then drew her in more tightly. His body was both hard and soft, and coated in thick dark hair that she'd always imagined she'd find repulsive, but she didn't, at all.

'We can't be late again today,' she told him huskily. 'People will start to talk.'

'This is sad, but true,' he murmured. 'You understand, I do not care for myself, it is the way my wife will react if she knows there is someone else in my life, that is my concern.'

'Do you think she wants you to go back to her?' she asked with a pang of alarm.

'This is what she says, but it is not possible for me to live with her again.'

'Not even if she went into rehab and managed to stay clean?'

He shook his head. 'I care for her very much, and always I will want to help her, she is the mother of my son, so this is necessary. But she have broken my heart in too many places, and since it start to go back together it has no room for her any more.'

Knowing that to lose his love would be difficult when he was such a loyal and decent man, with even more kindness and integrity in his soul than he had wit and charm in his heart, she pressed her mouth into his neck and kissed him hard. 'She's à foolish woman to have squandered what she had with you,' she told him. 'There aren't enough good men out there to be careless with one when you have him.'

There was a pause before he said, 'You know, Patreesha, I think you just give me a compliment.'

'I'm sorry, it just slipped out.'

He grinned, and sensing it she looked up.

'For many weeks I have wanted to be with you like this,' he told her. 'You think always I was joking, *non*?'

'I was never entirely sure,' she confessed.

'And now you are?'

'I think so.'

'Be sure,' he told her, 'because it is my pleasure to make you understand how special you are, and how 'appy you make me just to be in my world.'

Smiling as her heart melted, she said, 'That's such a lovely thing to say.'

He touched his mouth to hers, and as he kissed her she felt more flickers of desire coming to life inside her. 'I'm starting to feel very, very lazy about getting up,' she murmured.

'Then we shall stay here for the day,' he declared.

'Is that an executive decision?'

'It is one that has been taken out of my hands.'

Laughing as she caught his meaning, she wound herself more tightly around him and lay very still as he began stroking her, his fingers moving softly over her back and arms, then down over her buttocks to her thighs.

They both groaned in frustration as her mobile started to ring, and reaching out to the bedside table she fumbled around until she had it, but by then it had gone silent again.

It wasn't until an hour later, as they were walking to work, that she replayed the message that had been left, fully expecting it to be someone from the office, or possibly Susannah. However, what she heard slowed her pace to a halt, because someone was sobbing down the line, saying nothing, simply crying as though her heart would break. Pressing a key, she played the message again.

'What is it?' Frank asked, coming back to find out why she'd stopped.

'I'm not sure,' she replied, 'but I think this is my god-daughter, Neve.'

Taking the phone he listened for a moment, then scrolled to the call log. 'Yes, it is her,' he said, seeing Neve's name come up. 'She is sounding very upset, so you must call right away,' and pressing to reconnect he passed the phone back.

'Neve? It's Pats,' she said when Neve answered.

'Are you OK? I just got your message. What's wrong, sweetheart?'

'Nothing,' Neve answered, sounding quite different from her earlier call. 'It's all right now.'

'But what was it? You were crying so hard . . .'

'Honestly, it's OK. I'm at school and the teacher's about to come into class, so I have to go.'

'Will you call me later?' Pats urged.

'If I can, but don't worry, everything's cool. We're looking forward to when you come over. Mum said it'll be for three weeks.'

Patsy's eyes went to Frank as she said, 'I'm arriving the weekend after next. We'll go and have some dinner, just the two of us, shall we?'

'That would be cool. Sorry, I have to ring off now,' and the line went dead.

To Frank, Patsy said, 'You go on ahead. I have to speak to Susannah about this.'

After squeezing her hand he walked on down the street, leaving her to wander into a pavement cafe as she pressed in Susannah's mobile number. To her surprise, Susannah answered on the second ring. 'Great, you're there,' she said. 'I thought you might be on set.'

'I will be any minute,' Susannah told her. 'Is everything OK? How's the fantastic lover?'

'Bloody outstandingly fantastic, but that's not why I'm calling. Neve left me a message earlier. I couldn't make out what she was saying, she was sobbing so hard. I rang back, but she's at school and couldn't speak, so I wondered . . . Do you have any idea what it was about?'

With a sigh that sounded tired and a little

short-tempered, Susannah said, 'This morning, no. In general though, she's still upset about Alan, and she's making it impossible for anyone else to get close to her. I wish she'd talk to me, but I've barely been able to get a sensible word out of her since I told her about the baby. The fact that she's called you could be a good sign though, maybe she'll find it easier to open up with you.'

'I've told her we'll get together when I come over,' Pats said. 'Do you think it can wait that long?'

'Probably. With any luck it'll all have blown over by then, because I'm getting close to the end of my tether. I don't want to sound unsympathetic, and I'm not, but I can't imagine what she ever thought might come of this crush.'

'She probably didn't think,' Pats responded. 'Has she discussed any of it with Lola at all?'

'No, but she asked her for Duncan's number the other day. I haven't sent it to her yet, mainly because I'm not supposed to know, and since she's apparently trying to fill a void, I'm sure you'll agree that Duncan's hardly the person to do that.'

'Definitely not,' Pats replied, glancing up as a waiter started to hover. After ordering an espresso she said, 'Poor lamb. She's obviously having a really tough time of it lately. Someone needs to spoil her a bit, and if a godmother can't do that, I don't know who can. I'll take her shopping when I get there. Barcelona's coming up, isn't it?'

'Oh, as for that, she doesn't want to go any more. Of course, I haven't mentioned anything about the money, but it was right on the tip of my tongue, I can tell you. No doubt she'll change her mind between now and then, and meanwhile, a shopping trip with you will probably do her the power of good. OK, coming,' she said to someone else. 'I'm needed in make-up,' she told Pats. 'We'll talk later. Give my love to Fantastic Frank and tell him we're all looking forward to meeting him.'

After she'd rung off Patsy thanked the waiter for her coffee as he set it down, and sat staring across the boulevard to where a group of tourists was spilling out of a bus on to the pavement. She was having some difficulty putting her thoughts into any kind of order, mainly because the last few minutes had left her feeling more unsettled than perhaps was reasonable. In the end she had to concede that sitting here, drinking coffee, wasn't going to make things any clearer. She could only wait until she got to London and found out for herself exactly what was going on. It was just a pity, she thought, as she dropped a few coins on the table, that she wasn't going this weekend, rather than next, because Neve must be feeling pretty heartbroken and lonely right now to have called her, Pats, in such a terrible state.

'You go on,' Neve said to Sasha as they gathered up their books to leave the history class. 'Save me a place in the dining room.'

'Where are you going?' Sasha asked.

'Nowhere, I just need to call my mum.'

Shrugging, Sasha hoisted her bag over one shoulder, and began filing out into the corridor with the others.

When the room had cleared, and the teacher had gone too, Neve switched on her mobile phone.

Her face was ashen, her mind was a turmoil of unhappiness and dread. She didn't know if this was the right thing to do, but she was going to try anyway.

Taking a scrap of paper from her pencil case, she dialled the number written on it. After the second ring a bright cockney voice came down the line saying, 'Hello, Cates Exports, can I help you?'

'Yes, I um . . . Can I speak to Mr Cates, please?' Neve asked tentatively.

Sounding vaguely taken aback, the telephonist said, 'I'll see if he's available. Who's calling please?'

'It's . . . Um, I'm his niece. Neve.'

'Oh, hello love. We met once, a long time ago. I don't expect you remember me, but I remember you. Anyway, I'm sure your Uncle Hugh would love to talk to you. Hang on, I'll put you straight through.'

Waiting, Neve's face grew paler than ever as her hand clenched tightly round the phone.

Finally Hugh's voice came down the line, saying, 'Neve? Well, there's a turn-up for the books. How are you, chicken? What can I do for you?'

Neve took a breath. 'I was wondering,' she began. 'I . . . Um . . . Do you happen to have a number for my dad?'

Hugh chuckled. 'Of course I do,' he replied. 'I thought you already had it, but here it is. Have you got a pen?'

Neve quickly fumbled in her pencil case and as her uncle gave her the number, a digit at a time as though she were simple, she jotted it down on the same scrap of paper. 'Thank you,' she said when he'd finished.

'No problem. So how are you? Things are going well for Mum, I see. Bet you're enjoying all that fame she's getting.'

'Yes,' Neve said faintly, and after mumbling something about hoping he was well she ended the call.

With her heart in her mouth she dialled her father's number. Her head was swimming, her hands were shaking. *Please let him answer,* she begged silently. *Please don't let me have to leave a message.*

'Hello?' Duncan's voice shouted down the line.

Relieved, Neve started to speak, but there was so much noise at the other end that she knew already he was going to have trouble hearing her. 'Dad, it's me,' she shouted back, but her voice was mangled by tears.

'Who?' he said.

'Neve.'

'Who? You'll have to speak up.'

'It's Neve,' she sobbed. 'Your daughter.'

There was a moment of only background chaos before he said, 'Neve? Is that you?'

'Yes, it's me.'

'Well, I'll be . . . Hang on, sweetie. It's a madhouse here. Let me go outside.'

As she waited Neve dashed the tears from her cheeks. It was going to be all right, she was telling herself. He sounded pleased to hear her, so she could go there and everything would be fine.

'Neve, honey. Are you OK?' Duncan said,

coming back on the line. 'This is a big surprise. What's happening with you? Where are you?'

'I'm at school,' she replied, 'but I was thinking . . . Dad, can I come and see you?'

'Come and see me?' he echoed, sounding stunned. 'Well, of course, sweetie. I told your mother you could whenever you want. When are you thinking?'

'I checked the trains and there's one to Glasgow tonight that gets . . .'

'*Tonight?*' he broke in. 'Oh, Neve, honey. It would be lovely to see you, but I don't have anywhere for you to stay, and I'm right in the middle of a rehearsal at the moment. We're working round the clock. Why don't you come during your summer holidays? The play will have opened by then. You'll be able to see it, and we can spend some proper time together.'

Neve was fighting hard not to cry. 'I just thought . . . It was like . . .' There was no point, he was too busy. 'OK, I'll come in the summer,' she said.

'You do that, hen, but don't book anything before telling me, will you? I'll have to make sure everything's going all right with the play before I can take any time off. It might only be a few days, but that'll be better than nothing, won't it?'

Neve tried to say yes but the lump in her throat was too big.

'I'd better go now, sweetie,' he said. 'You take care, OK? It's lovely to hear you. Call again any time, and all being well I'll see you in the summer.'

* * *

Susannah's schedule was so full over the next few days that by the time the weekend came round it was all she could do to get herself on a train back to London. She was so exhausted she slept the entire way, then dozed off again during the taxi ride to Clapham.

Just as he'd promised, Alan had supper waiting, which he served in the patio garden since it was such a lovely balmy evening. The clematis and sweet peas were in full bloom and candles were flickering in their glass holders, almost seeming to dance to the gentle melodies that drifted from the speakers he'd set up on one of the fences. It was all very romantic, and thoughtful, but she was still so tired that by the time she'd finished eating she could only excuse herself and go off to bed.

By the time he joined her the sun had disappeared, leaving the moon to fill the shadows with its pale blue light. Hearing him tiptoe quietly into the bathroom she lay very still pretending to be sleeping, and when he came to snuggle up behind her she only murmured drowsily and continued to pretend.

The next morning he brought her breakfast in bed, then told her what he had planned for the day, most of which entailed shopping for baby paraphernalia, or visiting the interior designer he was thinking of commissioning to convert the guest bedroom into a nursery. Deciding the easiest course was simply to go along with what he wanted, she showered and dressed and got into the car ready to be taken to his various rendezvous.

Though she tried several times to call Neve throughout the day her phone was always turned off, and none of her messages were returned. She spoke to Lola who said she'd get Neve to ring, but by the evening there was still no word, and Susannah was so worn out by the day's activities that she simply sank into a sofa and let Alan wait on her again.

On Sunday they went to Lola's for lunch, only to discover that Neve had taken herself off to Melinda's for the day.

'I don't understand why you're avoiding me,' Susannah cried into Neve's voicemail when she and Alan returned home. 'If you're upset about the baby, or with me, we need to talk about it, because this isn't getting us anywhere and I'd really like to see you.'

An hour later Neve sent a text saying *Going to cinema with M and parents. Love Nx*

When Susannah rang there was no reply, and she almost threw her phone across the room in her distress and frustration.

'Calm down,' Alan advised gently. 'It won't do any good to get worked up over it. She's making a stand of some kind, and when she's finished I'm sure she'll let us know.'

'But I have to get the train first thing in the morning,' Susannah protested, 'and I haven't even clapped eyes on her since I came home. Did I tell you she rang Patsy earlier in the week sobbing her heart out? I have to talk to her, before this gets out of hand.'

'Do you know what she said to Patsy?' he asked, stroking her hair.

'She was crying too hard, Pats couldn't under-stand her, but if she's that unhappy I can't let her go on that way.'

'Leave it to me,' he said. 'You don't need the stress and forgive me for pointing out the obvious, but I'm better qualified to deal with her problems than you are.'

'I'm her mother,' Susannah snapped, jerking her head away. 'Whatever's bothering her, I need to know about it, even if it is about you.'

His smile was solemn. 'Think how difficult it is for her, being jealous of her own mother,' he pointed out. 'She loves you, very much, but you have the love of the person she thinks should be hers. She knows it's wrong, and that nothing can happen between us, but that doesn't stop her wanting it, or hurting because she can't have it. She's very confused about her feelings, but we're working it through, and though it might not seem so to you, we are making progress.'

Susannah was shaking her head, only half-listening to what he was saying. All she could think of was how desperate she was to get hold of Neve and do whatever it took to make her open up to her, the way she always used to.

'She's got a lot of issues right now,' he reminded her, 'not only with her father, and the void he's left in her life, but having to share you with a new baby, and me *and* the rest of the world. That's a big leap from having you all to herself.'

'If it's affecting her like this then maybe I should rethink everything,' Susannah said irritably.

'Well, let's explore that. How difficult would it be to get out of your contract?'

541

Her eyes darted to his, then away again. Since she hadn't actually been referring to the series, but to the baby and him, she could only feel thankful that he'd misunderstood. That was a scene she really didn't want to get into now. 'Next to impossible,' she answered shortly.

'Are you sure?'

'Of course I'm sure. Listen, I'm sorry I can't discuss this now. I have lines to learn, and ...'

'Don't run away from the issue,' he broke in gently. 'Things aren't working out very well with you being away, and you have to face it.'

It was on the tip of her tongue to tell him that the problem was him, but finally registering how worried he was, and how helpful he was trying to be, she bit the words back. 'I will,' she sighed, going to put her arms around him as much to avoid looking at him, as to show him affection, 'just as soon as this first stint on the programme is over.'

'And when will that be?'

'August. I have a week's break at the beginning of the month, so perhaps we can all go away somewhere, or both of us can sit down and chat to Neve. Oh God, it seems such an age away. What if she can't hold on that long?'

'Of course she can,' he said, drawing back to look at her. 'I'm due to have a chat with her again on Wednesday, and she generally looks forward to our little sessions, so I'll try to find out then if there's anything else she might be holding back. Maybe there's a situation at school that's upsetting her, or a boyfriend issue.' He gave a laugh. 'I'd be happy to hear that was on the agenda, at least then I'd know she was no longer carrying a torch for me.'

Turning away, Susannah pulled open the fridge and poured herself some wine. Coming up behind her, he removed the glass from her hand and replaced it with a juice.

Keeping her eyes down to disguise her annoyance, she thanked him and took a sip. It was a bitter irony that Neve should be suffering a broken heart over him, when she herself was feeling so stifled by his constant attention.

Michael Grafton spun his chair away from the window as Naomi, his PA, came in through his open office door carrying an armful of scripts and DVDs. There was a post-weekend sort of glow about her that lit up her smooth, angular features, reminding him of how recently she'd married, and making him feel pleased that she was so happy. She'd been with him for over fifteen years by now, so he knew better than most how close she'd come to giving up on ever meeting the love of her life.

Putting a hand over the mouthpiece of the phone, as she looked at him in a 'where do you want these?' sort of way, he said, 'What is all that?'

'It just came in from LA,' she told him. 'There's a note from Dan at CAA explaining it all. I think it's something you must have asked for.'

Remembering, he said, 'OK, put it on the table over there. Any word from Marty Filbert at Ocean yet?'

'Too early in the day, but as of Friday our bid was still the highest, so, with any luck, we should have the rights to the latest Jean Crowther by the close of play today.'

With a comical raise of his eyebrows he said, 'At which point the woman will be a three-time millionairess, and we'll have to start borrowing as fast as . . . Yep, I'm still here,' he said into the phone. 'It's OK, I don't mind waiting.' To Naomi he said, 'I'm trying to get hold of my son, who's somewhere in Laos, according to his latest email. He desperately needs two hundred quid he informs me, but neglected to say where to send it.'

'Do you want me to sort it?' she offered, turning back from the table that ran the entire length of one wall of his penthouse office.

'No, it's fine. It'll be good to hear him, if this person, whoever she is, manages to track him down.'

'I'll leave you to it then. Oh,' she said, turning back as she reached the door, 'I picked up an email from Marlene Wyndham asking if you'd had time to look at the *Larkspur* rushes over the weekend. She's keen to know if you have any comments for the director before he takes episode three into the edit suite this morning.'

Puzzled, Michael said, 'Is there a particular reason why she wants my comments?'

'I'll take it from that that you haven't set eyes on them. Apparently, episode three features the first nude scene of the series.'

A kind of mask dropped over Michael's features as he said, 'Tell Marlene I have every faith in her, and I'll be happy to watch the transmission copy when it's ready.'

'By which time you'll be in New York.'

He nodded. 'Exactly. They don't need me nurse-maiding them any longer, she's just being polite. Oh hell,' he groaned, as a single tone sounded down the line. 'I've been cut off.'

'Let me deal with it,' she said, coming back to press redial, 'you need to go or you'll be late for your meeting with Grant Mason.'

Getting to his feet he said, 'Remind me again what I'm seeing him about.'

'Top of the agenda is the Cheeseman affair,' she replied, referring to a libel suit his lawyer was bringing against a small publishing house for accusations of plagiarism. 'You also want to ask him if there's any news about the email trace his investigators are carrying out after those messages popped up for Susannah. Have there been any more, do you know?'

'I'm presuming not, or Marlene would have sent a copy through. OK, I'm out of here,' he declared, unhooking his jacket from the coat stand. 'I'll keep my mobile switched on, so ring the minute there's any news on the Crowther auction.'

Susannah was on the unit bus returning to the Centre after a long day's shoot at a specially convened horse show in the neighbouring valley. After listening to the first assistant announcing a few changes to the next morning's call times, she switched on her mobile and felt her tiredness evaporate as she saw that one of the messages was from Michael.

'I thought you'd like to know,' he began, 'that a small breakthrough has been made in the search for the person who sent you the anonymous emails. Still no identity yet, but apparently they're coming from an Internet cafe in Dewsbury, which is about midway between Huddersfield and Leeds. As soon as there's any more to report I'll be sure to let you know.'

As the message finished she hit 1 to replay it. With so much else going on she'd all but forgotten about the emails and now, in a perverse kind of way, she felt almost glad of them for the distraction they were providing. However, when the bus eventually pulled up in the stableyard she realised she'd slept the entire way, and twenty minutes later, after changing out of her costume, she discovered she really wasn't in the mood to join the others in the recreation barn this evening. It had been a long day thanks to a six a.m. make-up call, and tiring, thanks to how often she'd had to get on and off Silver, and hectic, with too many scenes being scheduled into too few hours. Added to which, it was already seven thirty, so by the time she'd prepared some kind of snack supper and learned her lines for the next day it would probably be after ten, and then she'd have to be up again at dawn.

As she strolled back through the evening sunshine she began wrangling with herself over whether or not she should call Michael. It seemed only polite to thank him for letting her know how the private investigators were getting on, but when she tried his number she was diverted to voicemail. 'Hi, it's Susannah,' she said. 'Thank you for your message. I appreciate you keeping me informed. Uh, well, I guess that's about it. I hope you're well and happy with what you've seen of the programmes so far.'

As she rang off she was already wishing she hadn't added the last bit, in case it sounded as though she was fishing for compliments. However, it was too late to take it back now, and she could hardly call again to assure him it hadn't been her intention, so trying to push it from her mind she connected to Alan's number.

'Hi, it's me,' she said when he answered. 'What are you up to?'

'Actually, I'm just sitting here having a nice little chat with Neve,' he told her.

Her heart immediately jolted, as much with guilt that she hadn't rung Neve today, as with the hope that things were as relaxed between them as Alan's tone was suggesting. 'How is she?' she asked, aware that he might not want to give a full answer with Neve right there, but needing to ask anyway.

'Fine. She's looking lovely, thanks to a bit of a tan she picked up at the weekend.'

'Can I speak to her?'

'Uh, maybe tomorrow.'

Understanding that he was probably at some crucial point in their discussion, she said, 'If you get the chance and feel it's appropriate, please tell her how much I love and miss her.'

'Of course.'

'Has she mentioned anything about the baby?'

'Not really, but I think it's OK. I'll call you later, before you go to sleep.'

Not until she'd rung off did she realise that she'd forgotten to ask where he and Neve were. 'Sitting here having a nice little chat,' was what he'd said, and she supposed she'd assumed they were at home, possibly in the garden given how warm it was, but now she realised that wasn't very likely. Still, wherever they were, in a park, outside a pub, or at Lola's, it was lightening her mood to know that Neve was communicating with someone, even though she'd have far preferred that someone to be her.

It was as she was about to climb into bed that she received a text from Michael saying *Very happy with programmes I've seen. Am in New York all of next week. If any developments while I'm away lawyers will contact Marlene. Goodnight. M.*

She sat looking at the message for a long, long time, hardly aware of what she was thinking, or even feeling. Then her thoughts moved on to Neve and Alan and her eyes slowly drifted closed.

Chapter Twenty-Seven

After spending eight days at the Bryce offices in Geneva, then Prague, Patsy made a brief return to Paris to clear her desk before decamping to London for the following three weeks. Since she and Frank hadn't seen one another for so long, he insisted on accompanying her on the journey, and spending the entire weekend helping her to settle into the serviced apartment she'd rented in Knightsbridge.

Having such a distraction as him around meant that it was Sunday lunchtime before Pats finally got to see Susannah.

'Frank's very demanding,' she'd informed her when they spoke on Saturday night to make arrangements. 'I won't go into any more detail than that, because I'm sure you can figure it out for yourself. Would you like us to pick up Lola on the way past?'

'It's OK, Alan will collect her when he goes over to Sasha's for Neve,' Susannah replied. 'Come around midday and we can have a glass of champagne in the garden before we eat.'

At noon on the dot Pats and Frank clambered out of a black cab, arms loaded up with champagne, foie gras and a generous assortment of cosmetics not yet on the market. Leaving Frank to pay, Pats went off up the path to ring the bell, loving the very air of London, though perhaps not as much as she was now coming to love Paris.

'Neve! Can you get it?' she heard Susannah shout from somewhere inside. 'It'll be them.'

Thinking of Neve, Pats felt a pang in her conscience for not having been in touch with her over the past couple of weeks, but her days had been so full that she'd barely had time to eat, never mind to make personal calls – apart from to Frank, of course, but even they had been mainly about business. The only time she'd spoken to Susannah was for about five minutes while she was waiting at Prague airport on Thursday, and to her further dismay she realised they'd barely even mentioned Neve then. However, if Neve had been uppermost in Susannah's mind, that was all they'd have talked about, so presumably the crisis of a fortnight ago, whatever it might have been, was over and past.

Indeed, when Neve pulled open the door, there were no indications, such as red eyes, that she was unhappy. She was looking as lovely as ever – not that Pats had really expected her to burst out in floods of tears, or to stage a tragic fling into her godmother's arms. She did look a little thinner though, Pats thought, and her complexion seemed a tad blotchy, but that could be anything from the time of the month to staying up late watching TV.

'How are you?' Patsy said, dropping her packages and hugging her hard.

'I'm fine,' Neve answered, giving an unusually lacklustre hug back.

Noting it, but not commenting, Pats cupped her face between her hands, saying, 'We've come bearing gifts and I think you're going to like them.'

Neve glanced down at the glossy bags with their red ribbon ties, something she'd normally have pounced on. Today she only said, 'Cool.' Then, peering past Pats, 'Is Frank here?'

'Oh yes, he's here,' Pats answered, and turning around her eyes softened as she watched him pocketing his wallet with one hand, whilst hoisting a magnum of champagne with the other as he came in through the gate. 'I know he's a bit weird to look at,' she muttered, 'but he has a heart of gold and he's an absolute demon in the sack.'

To her surprise Neve didn't giggle, as she'd expected her to, she only watched Frank, and seemed about to shake hands with him when he thrust the champagne at Pats and opened his arms ready to kiss Neve on both cheeks. To Patsy's amazement Neve shrank away, but then appeared to collect herself and allowed Frank to greet her in the normal French way.

'This is Neve, my god-daughter,' Patsy told him, eyeing Neve with growing concern.

'*Enchanté*,' Frank gushed with all his Gallic charm. 'I am hearing so much about you that it is already like I know you. My name is Frank, by the way. I tell you this, because Patreesha keep forgetting who I am.'

To Patsy's relief Neve laughed, then Susannah was coming down the hall, arms outstretched ready to hug them. 'Pats, you're positively blooming,' she told her, hugging her tightly. And turning to Frank, 'Welcome, Frank. We've heard so much about you that we're in love with you already, aren't we Neve? Please come in. Alan's outside trying to set light to the neighbourhood, and Lola's fanning herself down in a deckchair, too hot to get up.'

'We have bring some champagne with us,' Frank told her, as they followed her through to the kitchen. 'And foie gras from the Périgord region, which is the very best foie gras. I will apologise now in case Patreesha become out of hand. She is a little wicked when she has the luxury food and sparkling wine inside her.'

Laughing delightedly as Pats rolled her eyes, Susannah called to Alan who came in, wiping his hands on the apron he was wearing. 'Frank, welcome,' he said, holding out a hand to shake. 'It's good to meet you. I'm sorry I don't speak French.'

'It is no problem, I am 'appy to speak English,' Frank assured him.

'Thank goodness, because I need to know how good you are at lighting barbecues. I'm having the devil of a time trying to get ours going.'

'I will see if I can 'elp,' Frank said, starting to follow him out. 'I have much experience when I am younger, at the summer home of my family in Provence, but that is some years ago.'

As they disappeared into the garden, Pats turned to Susannah. 'So what do you think?' she whispered. 'Weird, isn't he?'

Susannah laughed. 'First impressions, I absolutely adore him,' she declared. 'Anyone who can make you glow the way you are is always going to be a winner with me. Now, come on, let's get this champagne open and some nibbles under way. Neve, where are you?'

Patsy glanced round but Neve had disappeared.

'I swear that girl's on an elastic that pings her straight back to her room the instant no one's looking,' Susannah grumbled.

'How is she?' Pats asked. 'I wasn't sure when I saw her. She looks a little, well, I guess peaky is the first word that comes to mind.'

Susannah grimaced. 'She's up and down, but I think she's finally starting to get over all this nonsense with Alan. He feels sure she is, and he's in a better position to know than the rest of us, as he's the only one she's talking to.'

Pats frowned. 'Do you think he's the right one to be doing that, as the object of her desires?' she asked.

'Ordinarily he wouldn't, he tells me, but her issues are more paternal than she realises, so he's trying to get her to work on that, and understand how it's tied in with her feelings for him.'

Patsy nodded understanding. 'Poor thing,' she murmured. 'She's so young to be all mixed up and broken-hearted, but looking back, I suppose I was about her age when Jamie Stone dumped me. I still remember how I truly believed I'd never get over it.'

'So do I,' Susannah commented drily.

Giving her a playful shove, Pats pulled open a cupboard and started to take down some glasses as Susannah tackled the champagne.

'How long's Frank staying in London?' Susannah asked, as she began easing out the cork.

'Till tomorrow morning. If he weren't needed in Paris he'd probably stay longer, but he's got a particularly busy week ahead, and he has his son next weekend, so unfortunately we won't be seeing one another again for at least a fortnight.'

Giving a sigh of satisfaction as the cork popped with such perfection that only a wisp of vapour escaped from the bottle, Susannah said, 'When are you going to meet his son?'

'I'm not sure. The wife's the problem – apparently as soon as she knows about me she's likely to start acting up, so we have to tread carefully. But don't let's depress ourselves with that now, tell me about you. You're not showing yet, I see. How do you feel?'

'Actually, not too bad considering how crazy my schedule's been this past couple of weeks. Certainly a vast improvement on when I first found out, anyway.'

'And Alan's still over the moon?'

Susannah made a growling sound under her breath as she slanted her a look. Then, after checking he was out of earshot, 'Between us, it's driving me nuts. He rings me up at least five times a day checking to make sure I'm not riding, or overdoing things, or wanting to recommend some baby website or other. I have to keep reminding myself this is his first child so of course he's excited and overattentive, not to mention an overnight expert on prenatal care and birthing methods. Beware, he can bore on for England if you get him on the subject, so *please* don't.'

With a spark of amusement, Pats said, 'You can count on me,' and adding a slab of foie gras and some toasties to the tray of glasses she carried it out to the patio, where Frank was charming the blushes out of Lola, while Alan was hovering over a merrily flaming barbecue trying to decide what to put where.

After passing round the drinks, Pats went to sit beside Lola in the shade of a small cherry tree that looked almost as weary in the heat as its refugee. 'So how are you enjoying having a famous niece?' she asked, tapping her glass to Lola's.

With a glowing smile Lola said, 'Can't hardly go anywhere without seeing her in the papers, or on the front of magazines these days. I miss her though, her being away all week, but don't let on I said that, or it'll only make her feel bad.'

'My lips are sealed,' Pats promised. 'And what do you think of the programme?'

'Oh, I love it, I do,' Lola clucked proudly. 'And I'm not just saying that because of Susannah. I think it's really good. You know it's up in the top four already, do you?'

Patsy nodded.

'And so it should be. I reckon it'll be number one before much longer, you see if I'm not right. Everyone's talking about it – on the telly, in the papers, all my mates down the bingo. I've become quite the celebrity, myself, lately. They'll miss me this week when I don't turn up, because they love getting all the inside gen.'

'Where are you going this week?' Pats asked, taking a sip of her drink and smiling at Frank, who was gamely taking on the role of sous-chef to Alan.

'Oh, nowhere,' Lola answered. 'I'll just be at home. A couple of places came up last minute for a coach trip to Eastbourne, so Nora and Stan took them. She usually wheels me round there of a Wednesday, but it won't hurt to miss a week.'

'I'll tell you what,' Patsy said, 'I'll have a look at my schedule, and if I can swing it, I'll come and take you myself. It's years since I had a game of bingo, and it'll be fun seeing all the old faces.'

Lola chuckled. 'I expect they'd love to see you too,' she told her, 'but don't go putting yourself out now. Like I said, it won't hurt to miss a week, save me a couple of quid, apart from anything else. Not that I'm ever short these days with all the money Susannah keeps giving me for taking care of Neve. I don't want it, but she won't have it back, so I'm putting it away for a rainy day. Now,' she said, after slurping down half her champagne in one go, 'I want to hear about Prague. It's somewhere I've always wanted to go, don't ask me why, I just have, so I'll fasten me seat belt and let you take me on a tour.'

Remembering again why she loved Lola so much, Pats delivered what she hoped was a reasonable description of the Czech capital, though having spent most of her time in hotels or meetings, it was a little scant on the kind of detail Lola was after. She'd heard about the luxury spas, and all the shopping around Wenceslas Square, but she also wanted to know if Pats had come across something called a strip crochet tour. 'They was talking about it on the telly,' she said, a wicked twinkle in her eyes, 'and it didn't sound to me as though it had very much to do with knitting.'

Laughing, Patsy said, 'I have to wonder what kind of programmes you're watching, and the answer's no, I didn't run into anything like that, but I rather suspect it's more for stag parties than female execs. Like another drink?'

'Oh, yes please,' Lola replied, smacking her lips as she passed over her empty glass. 'Lovely champagne.' Then, with a nod towards Frank, 'He's a bit of all right too. Lovely and . . . you know, *French*.'

Treating her to a resounding kiss on the forehead, Patsy went into the kitchen for a refill, saying to Susannah, 'Unless there's something you need me to do, I think I'll just pop upstairs to find out what's going on with Neve. Lola's glass is empty.'

Susannah glanced up from the dressing she was making. 'It rarely stays full for long,' she commented. 'She'll probably be asleep before we eat at this rate.'

On arriving at Neve's bedroom door Pats found it firmly closed, and when she knocked, to her surprise, there was no reply. There wasn't any music coming from inside either, or the sound of a TV, or of Neve chatting to one of her friends on the phone.

'Are you in there?' she called as she knocked again. 'It's me, Pats. Can I come in?'

There was still no response, but then she heard a kind of dragging noise and when it stopped the door swung open.

'Hi,' Patsy said, putting her head round and finding Neve sitting on the edge of the bed. 'How come you're up here all on your own?' *And how come the door was barricaded*, she wondered, noticing the small armchair that was out of its normal position.

Neve only shrugged and continued sitting on her hands while kicking her legs to and fro.

'It's really warm in here,' Patsy said, looking up at the skylights. 'Don't they open?'

'If you like,' Neve replied. 'The thing's over there.'

Going to fetch the pole, Patsy unlocked the handles and drew down the windows. 'There, that's better,' she said, 'we've got a bit of air so we can breathe.'

After replacing the pole she turned to look at Neve, not sure what to say now she was here. To weigh straight in about broken hearts and how they healed would be clumsy and trite, and very probably inappropriate, since it would tell Neve that her mother and Alan had been discussing her – and not only between themselves.

'Do you want to tell me what's on your mind?' she ventured as an opener. 'It seems to me like something is, and after the call you made a couple of weeks ago . . .'

Neve shook her head. 'It's nothing,' she said. 'It doesn't matter now.'

'It does if it upset you that much. What was it about?'

Neve glanced at the door, then put her head down again.

Going to sit next to her, Pats slipped an arm round her shoulders. 'Come on, you can tell me,' she said gently. 'What is it?'

'I'm just a bit fed up, that's all,' Neve mumbled.

'About anything in particular?'

'No. I just am.'

'Everything OK at school? When do you break up, by the way?'

'In three weeks.'

'So what plans do you have for the summer? Mum mentioned you'd changed your mind about going to Barcelona. Why's that?'

'I just have.'

'But it'll probably do you good to get away for a while, be in a different place with all your friends, no school or anything else to worry about.'

Neve shrugged. 'Maybe.' Then, 'If I don't go, I'll save up and pay you back the money. Mum says I might be able to get a job up at the Centre for the summer.'

Giving her a squeeze, Pats said, 'You don't have to pay me back. I'm just wondering why you've suddenly decided you don't want to go. I thought you were looking forward to it.'

Neve merely shrugged again.

'How would you like to come to Paris for a while?' Pats suggested. 'You can stay with me and I'll show you around. It could be fun. And if I get to meet Frank's little boy, you could be just the ally I need.'

Neve's head was still down as she said, 'That would be cool.' Then suddenly, to Patsy's surprise, she turned and buried her face in her chest.

'Oh my love,' Patsy murmured, holding her close and smoothing her hair as she started to cry. 'What is it? Come on, you know you can tell me.'

'It's so horrible, Pats,' Neve sobbed. 'I hate it and I hate him and I wish I was dead.'

Knowing who they were talking about, and

remembering only too well the various stages of rejection, Pats said, 'Ssh. It's OK, it'll be all right.'

'No it won't, because Mum's going to have a baby and then she'll marry him and we'll always have to be here.'

'Oh darling, I know it's hard right now,' Patsy said gently, 'but I promise you it'll get better.'

'You don't understand,' Neve cried. 'He tries to say it's all in my head, but I know it isn't. It's real and I hate it and I wish we'd never gone on to that website.'

Feeling for how cruelly it was backfiring on her, Patsy said, 'This is just a bad patch you're going through. It'll pass, I promise, and I'll always be there for you, at the end of the phone, or if you want to . . .'

'Hello, and what's going on in here?' Alan said jovially from the door.

Feeling Neve stiffen, Patsy held her more tightly and mouthed, 'She'll be fine.'

'Come on,' he said, 'we're about to start serving up and we've got guests, Neve, so you know better than to be hiding away up here.'

'It's OK, I'll bring her down,' Patsy told him.

Shaking his head, he indicated for Pats to go first. 'Let me deal with this,' he said quietly.

'No!' Neve snapped, springing to her feet. 'Come on, Pats. Let's do as he says,' and grabbing Patsy's arm she dragged her past Alan and down to the first landing, where she hooked Patsy's arm and continued, side by side, to the hall, not letting her go until they were in the kitchen on their way out to the patio. Once there, she seated herself next to Lola, and apart from when she was asked to help, that was where she stayed for the entire afternoon.

'It is very plain to see,' Frank commented as he and Patsy took a taxi back to her apartment later, 'that Neve is a very unhappy *jeune fille.*'

'Yes,' Patsy murmured, feeling even more disturbed about it than she could manage to put into words.

'It is per'aps a good thing that you are going to be here for a while,' Frank continued. 'I know they are like a family for you, and my perception, when we were in that house, is that the, how you say, *harmony* is all wrong.'

'Mm,' Patsy responded. 'Then your perception is very sensitive, *chéri,* because you're right, things are definitely not as they should be, and not only with Neve, because the vibe between Susannah and Alan is not what it should be either.'

'But most of all I think the problem is with Neve,' he insisted. 'However, I will say no more, because it is not my place to. I just think you need to make yourself available for her whenever she might need it, especially with her mother being a long way away.'

'Yes,' Patsy murmured, 'I think you're right, I probably should.'

It was Tuesday now, and Susannah was on the unit bus en route to Chatsworth House, where they were to shoot a scene in the famous Painted Hall. She was already in costume: an extremely revealing red cocktail dress, copious amounts of fake diamond jewellery, and black hold-up stockings. The four-inch stilettos to complete the outfit were still with her dresser, ready to slip on just before the camera rolled. Until then she was in flat sandals, with an umbrella at her side because the forecast was for occasional showers.

She wondered if it were possible to feel less like playing the kind of scene that lay ahead. Marianne and a local landowner were to sneak out of the party into an anteroom to engage in a fast and furious bout of unbridled lust. Today she was relying on Marianne heavily again, because the mere thought of allowing anyone to see her, Susannah, even partially undressed, much less touch her, was turning her stone cold. If the truth were told, all she really wanted was to be with Neve, because no matter how often Alan insisted he was making progress, it certainly wasn't looking that way to her. If anything Neve seemed more depressed than ever, and it wasn't helping at all to be reminded that broken hearts don't mend in a day, or that it was normal for someone with psychological issues to plunge right down into the darkness before properly coming up again.

She just wished Alan would give her some space to talk to Neve herself, but on the rare occasions she saw her these days he was always there, hovering over them, fussing and advising and criticising in a way that made her want to scream at him to go away. She never did, because it wouldn't help, and anyway, he'd just accuse her of being hormonal, or overworked, or, like many women in her position, frustrated by the way her career was affecting her family.

Though she kept reminding herself that he meant well, and was doing his utmost to make sure he was there for Neve, she could only feel thankful that the school holidays were almost upon them. At least then she and Neve should be able to spend some time together, provided, of course, Neve was still willing to come up to Derbyshire and learn to ride as they'd planned.

Looking up as the bus drove into Chatsworth's magnificent grounds, where modern sculptures and hugely elaborate fountains nestled amongst lavish garden beds and carefully tended lawns, she found her thoughts drifting to Michael and his own beautiful home. She guessed he must be back from New York by now, and was probably in London, rather than here, in Derbyshire. She'd heard no more about the emails, so perhaps the person sending them had found someone else to pester, and she was about to dismiss them from her mind when their content came into a sudden, unexpected focus. They were cautioning her to take care of her daughter, advice she hadn't taken too seriously at the time. Nothing was more important than Neve, so of course she was taking care of her. But her heart was starting to twist with the realisation of how worried she was about Neve now . . .

It had to be coincidence, because there was no way an outsider, a complete stranger, could know about the turmoil Neve was in, much less warn against it. And it wasn't as if the emails had mentioned her by name, so they could apply to anyone in the public eye with a daughter. Nevertheless, if there should be any more developments in tracing the sender, she would mention to Michael how difficult Neve seemed to be finding life right now. She should probably bring it up with Alan, too, to see if he thought there might be a connection.

Hearing those around her murmuring in amazement, she turned to look out of the window and saw that the bus was following the drive along the crest of a hill that offered a breathtaking view of the estate. As she gazed down on the sheer splendour of the house's Palladian frontage, and considered its centuries of history, she could almost feel its magic starting to lift her. But then her mobile bleeped with an incoming text, and seeing who it was she sank back into a swamp of despondency.

Just to say I'm thinking of you and our baby. With all my love the happiest man in the world. Xxxx

With a bizarre sense of unreality she closed the message down and stared out of the window again. She must remember that it wasn't the baby's fault she felt the way she did; it was an innocent little life, and in her better moments, she was finally starting to experience some maternal feelings towards it. In fact, were she able to put all her misgivings and torn loyalties aside, she could easily feel the urge to hold it in her arms and watch its tiny face as its eyes opened and its mouth searched for her breast. She would love and cherish it every bit as much as she did Neve, because it was hers, so how could she not?

Letting her thoughts drift on as the bus circled round to approach the side of the house, she began imagining how it would work with her schedule when the baby eventually came. She probably wouldn't have to take too much time off, and when she returned to the set she could hire a nurse, or a nanny, to take care of it while she was shooting. She wondered how he, or she, would be scripted in after the birth – would another baby be brought in to play the part, or should she allow her own to take it on? She was in little doubt of how Alan would feel about that, he'd hate it, and as its father he'd have every right to object. Her heart clenched with anxiety as she wondered how on earth they were going to be a united and happy family if she continued to stay with the series. The baby would have to be here with her, but it would be unfair to Alan to give him a child that he could only see at weekends. Unless he moved up to Derbyshire, and the thought of that left her feeling flat and empty inside.

By the time they arrived at the house and wandered through to the Painted Hall, most of the lights had already been rigged and the camera was rehearsing positions.

'About ten minutes,' the first assistant told her, when she asked how long it might be before she was needed.

After letting her dresser know where to find her should anyone shout for her sooner, she wandered off along the cloisters to a secluded niche at the far end, where she took out her phone to call Neve. Even though she'd be in class at this time, Susannah would rather leave a message than have no contact at all. As she waited for the greeting to end she was trying to think of something to say that wouldn't sound like a nag, or a mere repeat of the messages she'd left before.

'Hi, it's me,' she began after the tone. 'I'm in this amazing house called Chatsworth. I thought you might like to look it up on the Internet. It's one of the country's grandest stately homes. We can come here during the summer if you like. There's so much to see and do, not just old paintings and furniture and stuff. Oh, and I meant to say, if you want to invite Sasha to come and keep you company for a couple of weeks, why don't you? We should probably get Lola up here too. I have a week off at the beginning of August, so think about where you might like to go then. The world's our oyster now, remember?'

Running out of ways to try and make Neve happy, at least for the moment, she rang off, and was about to put her phone away again when it started to ring. Seeing it was Alan she stared down at his name, waiting for the call to go through to messages, until at the last minute her conscience made her click on.

'Hi, how's it going up there?' he asked.

'OK. We're about to start shooting so you were lucky to catch me. Is everything all right with you?'

'Of course. I've just ordered this amazing new baby video from the Internet. I thought I could drive up there on Wednesday and stay the night so we can watch it together.'

Unable to think of anything else to say, she mumbled, 'Lovely.'

'And we still haven't reached a decision about whether or not we want to know the sex. What's your latest thinking?'

'I guess it's helpful in some ways,' she began. 'But it takes away the element of surprise. If it's a boy I'd like to call him George. Does that work for you?'

It didn't, but all she said was, 'Let's talk about it later. I have to go now.'

'OK. Maybe we should let Neve help choose a name. It might make her feel more included.'

'Yes, it might,' she agreed, and turned to gaze into the inner courtyard as a violent downpour began pounding the flagstones.

'I'll put it to her when I collect her from school later,' he said.

At the sound of footsteps echoing along the stone walkway she looked round and saw the director approaching. 'I have to go,' she said to Alan. 'I'm wanted on set,' and ringing off she took a deep breath with a rapid instruction to Marianne, and made herself smile.

'OK,' the director said, rubbing his hands together, 'before we start on the party scene, I want to take you and Adam into the side room with a dresser to check how easily, or not, the dress comes off.'

Michael Grafton was walking into his office as Naomi announced a call from the company's chief lawyer.

'Put him through,' Michael told her, and going to hit a button on his speakerphone he shrugged off his jacket as he said, 'Grant, what can I do for you? If it's about the Cheeseman business, I'm afraid I haven't had time to go over everything yet.'

'No problem, still plenty of time,' the lawyer assured him. 'It's about these emails. I've got a name for you.'

Michael paused in hanging up his jacket. 'OK, shoot,' he said, going back to his desk.

'Carl Pace. Does it mean anything?'

Michael frowned. 'No. Should it?'

'I don't think so, I just wanted to check. The investigators are still on it, so I'll get back to you when there's more.'

'Thank you,' Michael said, and after jotting down the name, he asked Naomi to find out where Susannah was today.

When the reply came back a few minutes later he called Marlene on his private line.

'Have there been any more emails since the last one you told me about?' he asked, after explaining why he was calling.

'None that I'm aware of,' Marlene replied, 'and Cordelia would be sure to let me know. I confess I'm surprised it's a man. I'd assumed it was a woman.'

'Me too. We need to find out if the name means anything to Susannah, but I gather things are falling behind at Chatsworth.'

'A combination of technical problems and weather,' Marlene confirmed, 'and the forecast isn't good, which is going to give us a real headache for the night shoot if the rain doesn't let up.'

'Which is why I didn't contact her right away. They'll be under a lot of pressure over there, and I can't see any reason for urgency, unless you tell me differently.'

'None I can think of,' Marlene assured him, 'but while you're on there are a few budget issues I'd like to discuss if you have time.'

* * *

'Ken,' Alan said down the line to his lawyer, 'sorry it's taken me a while to get back to you, I was with a patient. Janet said it was urgent.'

'It could be,' Ken confirmed. 'I had a call from Carl about an hour ago. Apparently a private investigator's been trying to get hold of him.'

Alan's face drained so rapidly it was as though a main artery had burst. 'Why?' he asked.

'They haven't said what it's about, only that they want him to get in touch.'

By now Alan's throat was so dry that he could barely speak. 'So why did Carl contact you?' he asked hoarsely.

'At the moment he seems to think we've hired the investigator, trying to dig some dirt that will discredit him, or get him out of our hair. He was his usual charming self in telling me to back off, but he's going to find out soon enough that someone else is paying the bill.'

Alan's eyes closed tightly. His head felt as though it were about to explode. This was that bastard Grafton's doing, meddling about in affairs that didn't concern him.

'I think you need to get yourself up there pronto,' Ken advised, 'because if anyone's going to tell an investigator about your experiences with that family, it really ought to be you.'

The rain was continuing to fall, clattering over the trailer rooftops, slamming into windows, beating leaves from the trees and bouncing from the ground like a cascade of stones. The night shoot had been called off an hour ago, and the warning had already gone out that they were rescheduling to Saturday, which meant that the weekend break was effectively cancelled.

'I'm really sorry,' Susannah said to Lola on the phone as she let herself back into the lodge. 'I know it's your birthday and we were all going out for dinner, but I'm in every scene, so there's no way I can get out of it.'

'Oh, don't you worry about me,' Lola clucked. 'I've had enough birthdays to last me a lifetime, I don't need any more.'

With a smile Susannah shook off her raincoat, saying, 'I trust that's not exactly what you mean.'

After a beat Lola chuckled. 'I don't suppose it is, now you come to mention it. Anyway, I shall be all right. I expect Neve'll be here, and Pats. Alan might be back by then too.'

Susannah frowned, until remembering he was intending to come up to Derbyshire the following day, she said, 'Yes, I'm sure he will be, and he's bound to want to take you out, so you'll be royally spoiled. I'll let him know where your presents are so he can bring them along. Is Neve with you tonight? Or at Sasha's?'

'She was supposed to be here. Alan was dropping her off, but then he rang her to say something had come up, so she went home with Sasha.'

'Have you spoken to her?'

'Only when she called to let me know what was happening. Oh, and she sent a text about half an hour ago asking me to record your programme, because she was going out for something to eat with Sasha and her parents.'

'OK,' Susannah said, deeply moved by the fact

that Neve was still watching the programme in spite of how adrift they seemed.

She and Lola chatted on for a while longer, until picking up on how tired Lola was sounding, Susannah rang off and tried calling Alan. After being diverted through to messages she explained about the weekend, and ended by saying, 'Perhaps it's not such a good idea for you to drive all the way up here tomorrow. With the schedule falling apart I'm not sure what time I'll wrap, and when I do I expect I'll be fairly exhausted, so not much company I'm afraid. Anyway, call me when you get this and we can talk about it then.'

By the following morning she still hadn't heard back from him, which, if the truth were told, made her feel more relieved than concerned. She knew he wasn't going to be happy about her having to work at the weekend, so he was probably sulking, or hoping to punish her with silence, and she really didn't want to try and placate him, any more than she wanted to have a row. So, deciding to let him stew for the moment, she checked to see if there were any messages or texts from Neve. Finding none, not even a brief goodnight, or good morning, she glanced at the time, and seeing it was after nine, she scrolled through her numbers and pressed to connect to Sasha's mother at her office in Mayfair.

'Susannah,' Frances said, sounding as crisp and forthright as her lawyerly position required. 'You must be telepathic. I was about to call you. I'll come straight to the point, because I don't have much time. I'm worried about Neve. She's not been herself lately and a few minutes ago Sasha rang to tell me that Neve's thinking of running away.'

'Oh my God,' Susannah murmured, panic flaring.

'I've made Sasha promise to call me, or her father, the minute Neve mentions anything like it again,' Frances went on, 'but I think you should try to get to the bottom of what's going on, and alert the school so they're aware of the situation.'

'Of course, I'll do it right away,' Susannah assured her. 'Would you mind if I spoke to Sasha? If Neve's confiding in anyone . . .'

'By all means give it a try. We'll talk to her ourselves, this evening, but whether we'll be able to prise anything out of her is anyone's guess, what with sorority pacts and friendship vows, but she's obviously worried, or she wouldn't have rung me just now. Maybe you'll have more luck.'

'I'll call her when I know Neve's at Lola's,' Susannah told her. 'And Frances, I know I've said this a thousand times before . . .'

'Then don't say it again. Neve's a pleasure to have around when she's on form, and I know if our positions were reversed you'd be doing the same for Sasha. Incidentally, while you're on, I should tell you, your programme's much better than I expected. Well done. Now I'm afraid I must go, I'm due in a meeting.'

As the line went dead Susannah couldn't help smiling at the grudging compliment, but it quickly faded as she thought of how tormented Neve must be if she was considering running away. More panic and desperation swept through her, making her want to jump on a train to get to Neve now.

There was no way she could do that though, when she was due at the Centre in half an hour. It would probably have been an overreaction anyway, because lots of children spoke that way when they were unhappy and trying to get back at their parents. She wondered if Neve had ever said anything like it to Alan. Whether she had, or hadn't, she must call Alan right away and let him know what Frances had told her. Then she absolutely had to think of a way to start bridging the gap that seemed to be widening all the time between her and Neve.

After leaving Alan a message and asking him to ring as soon as he could, she spoke to Neve's housemistress, who, to Susannah's alarm, expressed her own concern about Neve's behaviour.

'We have a letter ready to go in the post to you today,' Mrs Dott told her. 'I'll send it anyway, but in a nutshell, she's still doing very well in lessons, so we have no concerns there. It's the fact that her usual spark seems to have gone that is worrying us. She's become withdrawn and uncommunicative, which isn't like her at all. She's usually one of the liveliest in her class, and very popular. I'm afraid we can't help linking this downturn in her spirits with your absence during the week.'

Admitting to herself how right Mrs Dott might be, Susannah assured her she'd be doing everything in her power to get to the root of the problem, and after thanking her for her concern and warning her about Neve's threat to run away, she checked the time before ringing Pats at her London office.

'Hi, you just caught me,' Pats told her when she

573

got through. 'I'm about to go into a meeting. What's up?'

'Neve has been talking to Sasha about running away,' Susannah said, coming straight to the point. 'It might be just talk, but after she asked Lola for Duncan's number . . . I don't want to take any risks.'

Pats didn't even hesitate. 'What can I do?'

'I'm going to try to get home this weekend, but it won't be easy when it'll mean leaving Marlene with an unfinished episode on her hands. So, in case I don't make it, I'd like you and Lola to sit Neve down and try to coax her to talk about how she's feeling. I know she's discussing it with Alan, but I think she needs to start confiding in one of us.'

'Absolutely,' Pats agreed. 'I'm going over to Lola's later to take her to bingo, so we can discuss strategy then and report back to you this evening.'

Feeling a slight unravelling of the tension inside her, Susannah said, 'Great. Thank you.' Her hand went to her head. 'It's all a mess, Pats,' she said raggedly. 'I've only just started here, and already it's falling apart around me, what with the baby, and Alan . . . But actually none of it matters. Nothing does, as long as Neve's all right.'

'She will be,' Pats said firmly. 'All you have to do is stay focused, trust in us, and I promise everything will come good.'

With those comforting words resonating in her ears Susannah rang off, and grabbing her script bag and umbrella started along the drive to the Centre.

In spite of knowing she didn't stand a hope in

hell of getting a change in the schedule, she called into the production office anyway to see if Marlene was around.

'She's in a script meeting over in the recreation barn,' her assistant told her. 'They've only just gone in, and they're having lunch served to them there, so I don't think she'll be out for a while. Can I pass on a message?'

Susannah was checking an incoming text, hoping it was from Neve, but seeing it was from Michael she opened it right away. 'Uh, yes,' she replied, a little distractedly. 'Maybe she could call me when she's free. My mobile will be turned off if we're shooting, but if she contacts one of the assistants, or my dresser, I'll get back to her as soon as I can.'

'No problem.'

As she walked away Susannah was reading Michael's text again. He was asking if the name Carl Pace meant anything to her. It didn't, but rather than text back she dialled his number.

To her frustration his phone was switched off.

Opening his message again she tapped in a reply saying she'd never heard the name before, and was about to add that she'd like to speak to him, when Lindon, the director, called her over, so quickly pressing send she went to find out what he wanted.

Michael found Susannah's text an hour later, when he popped out of a weekly meeting with his development team. After passing the information to Naomi to send on to the lawyers he made a couple of quick calls, then went back to the meeting, thinking no more about the text until a call came through just as he was returning from lunch.

'Grant,' he said, after Naomi had announced who was on the line and what it was about, 'you got the message. Apparently the name's a mystery to Susannah too.'

'Are you sitting down?' Grant asked. 'This isn't going to be the most edifying of tales I'm about to unfold, but it's one you need to hear.'

Surprised, Michael took the call off speakerphone and put the receiver to his ear. 'I'm listening,' he said, sitting back in his chair.

'Apparently Carl Pace has a sister, who used his name when she registered at the Internet cafe. Her name is Helen Cunningham.' Grant paused. 'Is this going anywhere for you yet?'

Michael frowned. 'I don't think so. Should it be?'

'Helen Cunningham is the estranged wife of Susannah's live-in partner, Alan.'

Michael swivelled his chair to stare out of the window, turning his back to the door. 'Go on,' he prompted.

'The investigators haven't spoken to Helen Cunningham yet, but they've had a long chat with Carl Pace, who's a very angry man on his sister's behalf. Apparently Cunningham left the family home under the very darkest of clouds. If I say there are two teenage daughters – Cunningham's stepdaughters – maybe you'll start getting the picture?'

'Jesus Christ,' Michael murmured, thinking immediately of Neve, and how the emails had cautioned Susannah to take care of her. *I wouldn't want the same happening to her as happened to mine.*

'The eldest is fifteen now,' Grant went on, 'but was still only fourteen when, according to Pace, Cunningham repeatedly raped her. Apparently the girl was a willing party, but she was still underage, so if it did happen – and that's a big if – Pace is right, in the eyes of the law it would be rape. She was completely besotted with him, apparently, and still is, but her mother won't allow her to have any contact. She's never reported Cunningham, because the girl refuses to speak out against him. In fact, she still seems to think he'll come back for her when she's sixteen.'

'So it's the ex-wife who's been trying to warn Susannah about Cunningham without getting her daughter's name, or her own, in the public domain?' Michael was turning the situation over in his mind as he spoke.

'It would seem so, at least on the face of it, but there's another side to the story, that, wait for this, has come from Cunningham himself. Apparently he turned up in Dewsbury yesterday, which is where Helen and her children have been living, with her brother, since Cunningham left. He was tipped off by his lawyer that some kind of investigation was under way, so he made it his business to contact the investigators and gave a full, and very plausible I'm told, explanation of what happened before he left his wife.'

Michael was already sceptical, but since he was hardly without prejudice, he simply said, 'Which was?'

'He says the older daughter developed a crush on him which was so intense that it became virtually unmanageable. He tried to warn his wife, he claims, but instead of taking the girl in hand she became jealous and started accusing him of things he wasn't doing, until finally he had no choice but to leave. Ever since, he's been plagued by threats from Carl Pace, who tries to extort money from him by saying he'll go to the police with allegations that are – according to Cunningham – outrageous and untrue. He says that the only reason he hasn't gone to the police himself over the – in quotes – blackmail attempts, is because he's concerned about the emotional damage it could inflict on the daughter. Lately, apparently, he's tried calling Pace's bluff by telling him to do his worst. As yet Pace has not gone to the authorities, which may, or may not, speak for itself.'

Michael's face was taut as he assessed what needed to be done next.

'I think the worst we're looking at here,' the lawyer went on, 'I'm talking about the programme now, is that Susannah will become embroiled in a pretty unsavoury scandal . . .'

'I want to talk to Carl Pace,' Michael interrupted. 'If you can, get him to come to London. I'll pay his expenses. Meantime, instruct the investigators to back off the wife, because if there is any truth to this, she's frightened enough already. We don't need to be making it any worse by letting her think we might take action against her over the emails.'

'OK, got it,' Grant replied. 'Anything else?'

Michael shook his head. 'No,' he answered, staring at the next four episodes of *Larkspur* that had turned up on his desk that morning. 'Unless you can tell me where Cunningham is now.'

'The last I heard he was still in Dewsbury, but I'll check and get back to you.'

As he rang off Michael was trying to decide whether or not to call Susannah right away. In the end, he decided to hold fire for the moment. Had Susannah ever expressed any concerns about her partner, or, more importantly, Neve, he might be taking a different view, but she hadn't. So, before making a rush to judgement and accusing a man of a crime that would ruin him for life if it got into the public arena, guilty or not, he needed all the information on the table. Then he'd decide how and when to break it to Susannah – presuming her partner's marital history was something she didn't already know about. The fact that he felt certain she didn't wasn't boding at all well for Cunningham. However, he knew he must keep reminding himself that he was not coming at this from an objective, or even a particularly professional, point of view.

Chapter Twenty-Eight

'Lola! Are you in there?' Patsy was calling through the letter box. 'I've come to take you to bingo. Remember, we arranged it on Sunday?' She peered down the hall, but there was no sign of anyone, and nothing but a distant radio to hear.

Telling herself that Lola must have dozed off, or had maybe forgotten and allowed someone else to wheel her to the community centre, she straightened up and looked around the estate. Dozens of windows were boarded up and covered in ugly graffiti, but others were glistening in a flood of afternoon sunshine. The sound of a baby screaming filtered down from one of the tower blocks, while a pile of rubbish from an upturned bin scudded across the ground in a flurry of wind. Otherwise the place was like a ghost town, which wasn't especially surprising when it was Wednesday afternoon and most people were probably at school or work.

She knocked again. 'Lola!' she shouted. 'It's me. Patsy. Wakey, wakey.'

Still receiving no reply, she let the flap snap shut and walked over to the sitting-room window. The nets were too dense to see through, and the glass panel next to the front door was bubbled and frosted. There was no way to get in through the back, nor could she go to Nora's for a key, since Nora and Stan's trip to Eastbourne was the reason she was here.

'Hello. Can I help?' a voice said behind her.

Starting, she turned round to see an Indian man in traditional garb standing outside the flat next door. With him was a diminutive woman, dressed in a colourful sari.

'Hi,' Patsy said. 'I was just . . . I don't suppose you've seen Lola today. I've knocked, but I can't seem to make her hear. We had an arrangement, you see. I'm here to take her to bingo.'

'Yes, she usually goes on Wednesdays,' the man confirmed.

'You wouldn't happen to have a key, I suppose?' Patsy said doubtfully.

'Yes. We keep it for emergencies,' he told her. 'She has ours too.' He turned and called something to his wife in a language Patsy didn't know, and the wife immediately disappeared back indoors.

Minutes later the front door was open and Patsy was stepping ahead of the man into the hall. 'Lola,' she called, trying to keep the concern from her voice. 'Are you in here?'

Still no reply, but she could hear the radio in the kitchen more clearly now, probably to deter burglars, and there was some kind of faint hissing sound. Then she registered the smell, and suddenly terrified of what she was going to find, she moved swiftly along the hall and came to an abrupt stop as she reached the kitchen door.

'Lola!' she gulped in panic. 'Oh my God,' and throwing herself down beside the old lady she quickly rolled her on to her back. 'Oh Lola,' she gasped, seeing blood on Lola's forehead. 'What happened? Where are you hurt?'

Lola's watery eyes were dazed and droopy and one side of her face seemed oddly scrunched.

'Oh no,' Patsy murmured, hugging her close. 'Call an ambulance,' she shouted to the neighbour, who was turning off the gas under the kettle. 'We need one right away.'

Not wasting a moment, he snatched up Lola's phone and dialled 999.

'Lola, can you hear me?' Patsy cried, ignoring how badly she was shaking. 'Can you lift your arms?' Even as she asked the questions she knew it was useless, there was no way Lola could respond. She wasn't even entirely sure she could see.

'It's all right,' Patsy whispered, clasping her gnarled old hands to her chest. 'The ambulance is on its way. You're going to be fine. I promise.'

The wait seemed interminable, but it was no more than ten minutes before the sound of sirens stopped at the edge of the estate and Mr Pavi, as he'd introduced himself, hurried outside to let the paramedics know where to come.

Soon the kitchen was full of people and Patsy was being edged aside as the experts took control. She barely registered what they were saying as she stood with her fists bunched at her throat, watching them perform a series of emergency checks before easing Lola on to a stretcher to carry her outside.

'We're taking her to the Chelsea and Westminster,' a kindly-looking man informed her.

'Can I come with you?'

'Are you family?'

'Not exactly, but . . .'

He smiled regretfully. 'Perhaps you could contact her relatives and let them know what's happened.'

'Yes, of course.' She was suddenly shaking so hard that she had to clench her hands tightly to try and force some steadiness into her limbs. 'Sorry. I need to pull myself together.'

'Here,' Mrs Pavi said, putting a glass of water into her hand, 'drink this.'

Patsy took a few sips, then as soon as the paramedics had gone she began hunting for her bag. Finding it under the table she pulled out her phone. 'I need to call Susannah,' she mumbled distractedly.

The Pavis watched as she dialled, looking anxious and ready to do anything to help. She gave them a quick look, then, as her call was diverted through to messages, she promptly rang off. This wasn't the kind of news to receive by voicemail. Someone needed to break it to Susannah in person, but Pats had no numbers for anyone at the Centre. Alan would, though, and he had to be told anyway, so she rapidly scrolled through her contacts, found his mobile number and pressed to connect.

To her frustration he wasn't answering either.

This time she left a message telling him what had happened, then she tried Susannah again. Her phone was still switched off, presumably because she was filming.

583

Patsy thought about Neve, unsure whether she should call her or not. In the end she decided she had to in case she was coming here straight from school. This time she got through straight away.

'Sweetheart, it's Pats,' she said when Neve answered. 'I need to get hold of your mother, but her phone's turned off. Would you happen to have anyone's number at the Centre?'

'No, I don't think so,' Neve replied. 'Why? Is something wrong?'

Before telling her Patsy said, 'Where are you?'

'Just coming out of school.'

'Is Alan picking you up by any chance?'

Neve's voice was clipped as she said, 'No. Sasha's housekeeper is. What's happening? Why do you need to get hold of Mum?'

Taking a breath, Patsy said, 'Lola's just been taken to hospital. She . . .'

'*What?*' Neve broke in. 'Oh my God. Is she all right? What happened?'

'She's possibly had some kind of stroke. I'm not sure how serious . . .'

'She has to be all right,' Neve cried in a panic. 'I won't let anything be wrong.'

'It's OK, they're taking care of her. Just get Sasha's housekeeper to drive you straight to the Chelsea and Westminster, and I'll meet you there.'

Susannah was standing at the top of an elaborate, sweeping staircase, a bronze statue of Mercury behind her, and a beautifully crafted limestone arch framing her. Below was the Painted Hall, Chatsworth's most impressive gallery. Currently it was playing host to the pre-three-day-event cocktail party that Susannah, as Marianne, had sneaked out of during the previous day's shoot, to play another kind of scene altogether in an anteroom. Now, she was about to stage her entrance to the party, in wide shot, since the close-ups had already been covered.

'Don't forget,' the director was saying from the bottom of the red-carpeted stairs, 'leave a beat after action, then look around at the paintings and up at the ceiling, before you take in the party below.'

Understanding that was how they would cut from her to the magnificent Laguerres that dominated the room, Susannah gestured with a hand to say she'd heard, since a make-up artist was applying a final coating of gloss to her lips.

As soon as they were ready to roll Susannah cleared the arch and waited in the corridor beside it for her cue to step back in again. A few seconds passed during which she was aware of a small commotion down in the hall, but since she could no longer see from where she was, she had no idea what was happening. Then she heard the first assistant shout 'Action!' and slipping instantly into character, she sauntered into position at the top of the stairs where she stood, hand on hip, gazing imperiously around the hall and ceiling, before allowing her sphinx-like eyes to fall like a predator's to the room below.

There was a second or two before the order to cut was given, and as she waited she noticed that Marlene had turned up. Surely she hadn't come in person to respond to Susannah's message earlier?

'OK, that's a wrap for Susannah,' the director announced.

As everyone started moving around, derigging tracks and lights, Marlene came to the foot of the stairs. The look on her face caused Susannah a momentary unease.

'Before you go,' Marlene said, 'I need to have a word.'

Susannah waited for her to climb the steps, then felt uneasy again as Marlene took her by the arm and drew her back into the corridor. 'Is everything all right?' she asked.

'I'm afraid I have some news you're going to find a little upsetting,' Marlene told her quietly.

Panic collided with the thud in Susannah's heart. 'Oh my God! Neve! Has she run away?'

Marlene frowned, but all she said was, 'No, it's not your daughter. We've just heard from your agent that your aunt has been taken to hospital.'

Susannah's eyes rounded with horror. 'What's happened?' she breathed.

'It seems she's probably had some kind of stroke.'

Susannah's hand flew to her mouth. 'I have to go to her,' she declared, starting to turn away. 'I have to go now.'

Marlene grabbed her. 'Of course, and it's all been taken care of . . .'

'Where is she? When did it happen?'

'I believe it was earlier this afternoon. We received the call about half an hour ago . . .'

'Half an hour!' Susannah shouted. 'You waited half an hour . . .'

'We needed to get this scene in the can . . .'

586

'Do you think I care about that? My aunt could be dying and you put your bloody schedule first.'

'I have to take these things into consideration, but the time hasn't been wasted. A production assistant has been to the lodge to pack a bag for you, which is already in the car that's waiting outside to take you to London. I thought you'd prefer to be driven than to fuss about with trains.'

Confused and slightly chastened, Susannah said, 'Yes, of course. Thank you. I have to go now. I need my phone . . .'

'Here.' A dresser was right behind her, handing over her location bag.

Taking it, Susannah said, 'It was my agent who called?'

'As I understand it a friend found your aunt and rang the emergency services. She couldn't get through to you, so she contacted your agent to get a number here.'

Still not able to think straight, Susannah thanked her again and began running down the steps into the hall. A path opened up as she swept across the room to where a barrier of ropes and screens had been assembled to keep out the crowds.

'See her outside,' Marlene shouted to a security guard.

Immediately Susannah felt a strong hand on her arm that began steering her through the throng of tourists who'd got wind of the fact that she was there. She barely heard them calling her name and demanding autographs, but as though on autopilot she managed to smile and be polite as she apologised for being unable to stop.

Minutes later she was in the back of a unit car,

speeding out of the grounds, and trying to contact Pats. Getting no reply, she left a message saying she was on her way, then tried her agent.

'Yes, it was Patsy who found her,' Dorothy confirmed. 'She's with her at the hospital now.'

'Did she say how serious it is?'

'I don't think she knows yet. She just asked me to contact you to tell you to come.'

Susannah's heart turned over. 'I need to call her again,' she murmured, and clicking off the line she was about to press in the number when Pats rang.

'Did you get my message? I'm on my way,' Susannah told her hurriedly. 'How is she?'

'I'm still not sure. No one's come to speak to us yet, but Neve's here, so as soon as there's some news hopefully they'll tell us.'

'Was it a stroke?'

'It hasn't been confirmed, but that was definitely how it looked.'

'Oh my God,' Susannah murmured, her mind already spinning with the horror of losing Lola. Then, thinking of Neve, she asked Patsy to put her on.

'Mum?' Neve's voice was tremulous and nasal. 'Oh, Mum, they won't let us see her.'

'It's OK, sweetheart. They will as soon as they've done what they have to.'

'How long before you get here?'

'A couple of hours, sooner if I can.'

'What if she doesn't get better? Oh Mum, I don't want her to die.'

'She won't,' Susannah said forcefully, as much to convince herself as to bolster Neve. 'We need to be strong for her now.'

'What if she can't speak, or walk?'

'Neve, darling, let's try not to frighten ourselves. We need to hear what the doctor has to say, then we can work out what has to be done.'

'I don't know where I'm going to live if Lola's . . .'

'Sssh,' Susannah soothed. 'It's going to be all right. Now can I speak to Patsy again?'

A moment later Patsy came back on the line.

'Tell me what happened,' Susannah said. 'What was she like when you found her?'

As she listened to the details, she was finding it all too easy to envisage the scenario Pats was describing, Lola lying helplessly on the floor, maybe knowing what had happened to her but unable to communicate, or even move, and perhaps feeling as afraid as Susannah was now.

When Patsy had finished she brushed away her tears, saying, 'Do you think she might have been dazed by the blow to her head, rather than anything more serious?'

'It's always possible,' Patsy said comfortingly. 'It's what we're hoping.'

Unable to think about the chaos this could throw her life into if Lola didn't come round, and not really caring either since Lola was all that mattered, Susannah said, 'Someone's trying to get through. I'll call you back.'

After checking and seeing it was Michael Grafton, she clicked on, saying 'Hello, I . . .'

'Marlene just called me,' he told her, 'so I wanted to let you know that if there's anything you need, or anything I can do . . . I'm in London for the rest of the week.'

'Thank you. That's very kind.' Her throat was tightening again.

'It's OK, she's in the right place,' he said gently. 'The Chelsea and Westminster has one of the country's best stroke units, so if that's what it is, she'll be taken good care of.'

'Yes, of course.' Tears were starting to spill from her eyes. 'I'm sure it'll all be fine.'

In a voice that sounded reassuringly certain, he said, 'I'm sure it will too.'

Just over three hours later Susannah was standing outside the Intensive Care Unit of the Chelsea and Westminster with Neve and Patsy, staring at a very young-looking doctor as he told them what had happened to Lola.

'In simple language,' he explained, 'a transient ischaemic attack means that she suffered a brief interruption to the brain's blood supply. It's a kind of mini-stroke. Nothing to be unduly alarmed about, but it is a warning that a much more serious attack could occur if the right precautions aren't taken.'

'So what you're saying,' Susannah said, hanging on to his every word, 'is that she's going to be all right?'

He nodded, and smiled as Neve turned into her mother's arms, sobbing with relief. 'She still seems to be experiencing some numbness in her face and right arm,' he told them, 'but this should disappear within the next twenty-four to forty-eight hours. After that, I'd like to keep an eye on her for a couple of days while we assess her condition. She suffered a nasty concussion when she fell, and I'd like to run more tests before we make the final decision on whether surgery, or drug treatment, is the best course from here. If it's the latter, she could be home again by Monday or Tuesday.'

Susannah turned to look through the glass wall to where Lola was lying on a narrow bed, her frail chest and limbs attached to all kinds of devices that gurgled and bleeped and hissed in a grisly kind of rap rhythm. 'How long will she be like that?' she asked.

'We'll transfer her to the stroke unit in the morning,' he answered. 'Right now she's quite heavily sedated, so if I were you I'd go home, get some rest, and come back again in the morning.'

Susannah was still looking at Lola.

'Why don't I stay?' Patsy suggested. 'If anything changes I'll call right away.'

'No Mum, let's stay,' Neve pleaded, her face as bloodless as Susannah's.

'She's unlikely to come round,' the doctor told them, 'and if you do stay, I'm afraid you'll have to wait out here, or in the cafeteria.'

Susannah's gaze still hadn't moved from Lola. 'I can't leave her,' she said, afraid that if she did the bond between them might start to fray.

'Then that's decided,' Patsy announced to the doctor, 'wherever we have to wait, we'll wait.'

He smiled kindly, and after assuring them once again that Lola's condition was not life-threatening, he returned to the ICU where a nurse was waiting to consult him about another patient.

'There's a Starbucks downstairs,' Patsy reminded

them a few minutes later. 'Does anyone feel like a coffee?'

Susannah nodded, and going to Lola's bedside she pressed a kiss to her fingers, then touched them gently to Lola's papery old cheek. There was no outward response, but she was sure that on some level her aunt would know she was there and feel as dearly loved as she was.

A few minutes later, as they rode down in the lift, Susannah turned her phone back on and saw, to her surprise, that there was still no message from Alan. 'That's odd,' she said, too numb to wonder for long about why he hadn't been in touch.

'When did you last speak to him?' Patsy asked.

Susannah thought. 'This morning, I guess. Or it might have been yesterday. I'm starting to lose track of time.'

As they stepped out of the lift into the lobby Neve muttered something that the others didn't catch. Her own mobile was clutched tightly in her hand, but she made no attempt to turn it on. She didn't want to speak to anyone tonight, or ever again, except her mother and Pats and Lola.

For most of the past hour the sun had been blinding, making the drive even more hazardous than the speeding maniacs and centre-lane huggers that were clogging up the M1. Now twilight was falling and, having pulled into a service area, Alan turned off the engine and sat with his eyes closed for a while, listening to the distant roar of traffic and occasional burble of voices as people walked by.

In the end, as the throbbing in his head started

to subside, he turned on his mobile and pressed in his lawyer's home number.

'Where are you?' Ken asked as soon as he answered.

'On my way back to London.'

'How did it go?'

Letting out a turbulent sigh, Alan said, 'The girl's still delusional, her mother's hysterical and that damned brother of hers should be locked up.'

'I wouldn't argue with that, but I have more news for you. Apparently Mr Grafton, Susannah's boss, is keen to speak to you.'

Alan's eyes were closed again. His skull seemed to be pressing in around his brain as though to crush it. He was trying to make himself think, but a terrible, black fear was tangling all the threads of his thoughts. 'I can fight this,' he said weakly. 'They're lying and they know it, but the position it puts me in . . .'

'Did they threaten to go to the police while you were there?'

'Of course. They always do, but they won't because they don't have a case. I never touched the girl, Ken. It's all in her head.'

'Don't worry, I believe you, and if they were serious about reporting anything they'd have done it a long time ago. Nevertheless, you can't take any risks. That kind of mud sticks to a man for life, whether or not the accusations are true.'

Alan winced as the truth shot through his head like a pain. 'Tell me something I don't already know,' he growled. 'It'll finish me.'

'Then we have to make sure it doesn't happen. How have you left it with Pace and his sister?'

'The same way I always do – I told them if they don't stop hounding me I'll have to go to the police myself, then they'll have to deal with the social stigma and trauma they're so desperate to avoid.'

'I'm beginning to wonder if you shouldn't make good on your word. You've got nothing to hide. As you say, you've never touched the girl, and if you get in first, a man with your training and . . .'

'It's not going to happen,' Alan cut in.

'But it can't go on like this. As an innocent man you shouldn't be made to suffer . . .'

'Listen, what should, or shouldn't, happen has no bearing on what will happen if I have to face charges of this sort.'

'Maybe we should talk to a barrister.'

'Maybe, but I can't think about it now. I've got more calls to make and there's still a long drive ahead.'

'So what do you want me to tell Grafton's lawyer if he calls again?'

'To mind his own goddamned business.'

'With pleasure, but a man in Grafton's position isn't someone to antagonise, and think of it this way, if he wants to talk to you, it's presumably because he's prepared to give you the benefit of the doubt.'

With a bitter snarl, Alan said, 'Well isn't that good of him?' Then, after another protracted sigh, he said, 'Let me think about it. There are other things going on right now that I have to deal with, so hold fire on everything until we speak again tomorrow.'

After ringing off, he sat staring blindly at nothing, hearing the thud of his heart through the drone of fear that was clogging his ears. When he finally felt able he connected to Susannah, who answered on the third ring.

'Darling, hi, I've just got your messages,' he said. 'Before we go any further, just tell me, how's Lola?'

'Stable,' Susannah answered. Her tone was flat, she sounded tired. 'They're keeping her in for a few days.'

'Where are you now?'

'In a coffee shop with Patsy and Neve. Where are you?'

'On my way home. I'm sorry I've been out of contact. I'll explain everything when I get there.'

'We're staying at the hospital tonight,' she told him.

'Do you want me to come?'

'You don't have to. It's best there aren't too many of us here.'

'Of course. What about Neve? Should I come and collect her? I'm sure you're both exhausted and one of you at least should get some sleep.'

As Susannah put the question to Neve he felt himself tense hard enough to crack his bones. 'She wants to stay here,' she told him, coming back on the line.

'OK. Before you go, have you had any unusual calls in the last, say, twenty-four hours? I mean, apart from the one about Lola.'

'What do you mean? Unusual in what way?'

'If you'd received any, you'd know, so I'll take it you haven't.'

'Alan, you're not making any sense.'

'Don't worry. It's just a disturbed client who's

been . . . Listen, we'll talk about it tomorrow. When are you going back to Derbyshire?'

'I'm not sure yet. I want to see how she is in the morning.'

'OK. Try, if you can, to get some sleep. Remember, it's not only you you have to think about now.'

As he rang off his eyes closed briefly, then steeling himself again, he connected to Neve's mobile, not sure how he was going to get her away from her mother tonight, just knowing he had to.

Finding himself diverted to messages, he bit down on his frustration and assumed a kindly, measured tone as he said, 'I wish you'd answer so we could talk. You know we need to, and remember, you're an adult now so you shouldn't be running away from your fears.' He took a breath. 'I want you to think about how much it would hurt your mother if she knew the kind of thoughts you have about me. Fantasies aren't harmful in themselves, but they can be misconstrued, particularly when you're getting them mixed up with reality. Remember, your mother's carrying a baby now, and I know that deep down, you won't want to be responsible for bringing anything bad into her world, or spoiling her dreams, especially when you helped make one of them come true. She's always loved me, Neve, you understood that, it's why you came to find me. And I love her. I love you too, but if you start saying things to upset her, if you try to pretend that what's in your head is real, then you'll leave me with no choice but to put you into the hands of another doctor. Believe me, I don't want to do

596

that, any more than I want you to be taken away. Your mother won't want it either. It'll probably break her heart, so don't let that happen, Neve. Just make sure our secrets stay tucked up in your mind, safe from the rest of the world, and call me back as soon as you can. I really want to help you, but you have to make it possible.'

Chapter Twenty-Nine

Michael Grafton was impressed by how swiftly Carl Pace had responded to his invitation to come to London. He'd received a call from Grant Mason the night before, informing him that Pace would be at the Soho offices by eight the next morning, and true to his word Pace was waiting in reception when Michael arrived, hands bunched between his stocky thighs, one foot juddering up and down with impatience, or nerves.

It was still early enough in the morning for Naomi not yet to be at her desk, so Michael took Pace up to his office where he made them both a coffee before settling down to listen to Pace's story. All the time Pace spoke Michael was watching him closely, determined not to let the man's appearance, or thick Mancunian accent, hold any sway. If he came across like a stereotypical football hooligan with his greying stubble, balding head, tattoos and earrings, that didn't make either him, or his family, any less vulnerable to crime than anyone else, or guilty of criminal behaviour. And certainly, if the resonance of sincerity in his tone was anything to go by, this man truly believed that a terrible offence had been committed against his niece, for which his brother-in-law Alan Cunningham should be made to pay.

'It makes me sick to my gut,' he spat as he banged a fist on Michael's desk. 'I keep telling our Helen that she can't let him get away with it. He should be castrated for what he did to our Julia, that's what should happen, and I know just the people to do it. And I'm telling you this, Mr Grafton, if I weren't a civilised man I'd have got them on it a long time ago, so that bastard's lucky to be walking around with his equipment intact, if you catch my meaning.'

Michael nodded briefly.

'He kept telling our Julia that it was all up here.' He was jabbing a stubby finger to the side of his head; spittle was spraying from his lips. 'He said she was imagining it, that it was all a fantasy, but she's not stupid. She knew what he were doing, and God help her, she wanted it, the stupid cow. She was mad for him, but she's a kid. What does she know? She still thinks he's going to come back for her, that it's only me and her mother who're stopping him. She's got a fucking – pardon my language – suitcase packed ready to take off on her sixteenth birthday. She won't hear anything bad about him, and she swears if we go to the police she'll say she made it all up and that he never laid a finger on her.'

Feeling for the man's frustration, but still trying to remain as impartial as possible, Michael said, 'So how do you actually know that he did?'

Pace's face darkened. 'You might want to stick up for the asshole, but I'm . . .'

'That's not my intention,' Michael interrupted.

'I'm just pointing out that this sort of thing is extremely hard to prove, and if she does have a vivid imagination . . .'

'I'm telling you that man raped her,' Pace growled. 'She might want to call it something else, but in the eyes of the law that's what it amounts to.'

'Did anyone ever see them together?'

'Aye. Her sister, Kim, but she's afraid to speak up because our Julia keeps calling her a liar. You see, the trouble is, Mr Grafton, our Julia's changing her story all the time, one day it's real, the next it's not, but she's no virgin, I can tell you that, because her mother had her checked out. OK, I know she could have lost it to someone else, but it were Cunningham who broke her in, and he were after doing the same to our Kim, I wouldn't be surprised. He's not safe around young girls. He uses, *abuses*, his position as a head doctor, when it's him what needs one if you ask me. He can't be right in his bonce doing what he does. That's not how any decent bloke would carry on, pushing himself on teenage girls who don't know any better. He got our Julia all suckered in, so she didn't know right from wrong any more. That's why our Helen took it into her head to try and warn Susannah Cates about the kind of man she was involved with. As soon as she saw it on the telly, Susannah talking about her girl, then heard who Susannah's childhood sweetheart was, she said to me, "Carl, we've got to do something. We can't just sit back and let him do it again, when we know what he's capable of." So I told her, "For Christ's sake woman, I've been saying all along that we have to go to the police," but she wouldn't hear any more about that. She won't put her girls through it. Not that I blame her. Jesus Christ, do you think I want them to suffer any more than they already have? Especially our Kim. She's that shook up about it, but the man has to be stopped.'

'So your sister tried by sending the emails?'

'That's right. The first I knew about them was when your people turned up the other day asking if it were me, otherwise I'd still be on her case trying to make her see sense. You've got to talk to Susannah Cates, Mr Grafton. You've got to make her understand that growing up with that scum doesn't make him any less of a pervert. A paedophile, that's what he is. A fucking nonce. He might be as clever as fuck with the mind games, and those girls might look older than what they are with all their fashion and make-up, but they're still kids, and he should be banged up out of harm's way where he can't mess with anyone's head except his own. They'll know how to deal with him on the inside, and good fucking luck to him, because he'll need it once those lads get hold of him.'

Leaning forward, Michael pressed a button on his desk to find out if Naomi had arrived yet.

'Good morning,' she said, coming on to the speaker. 'I could hear you had someone with you, so I didn't interrupt. Would you like more coffee?'

Michael glanced at Pace, who nodded.

'Two cups,' Michael said. 'Then get Marlene Wyndham on the line, and while I'm speaking to her call Grant Mason and ask if he has Alan Cunningham's mobile number.'

'I can give you that,' Pace told him, and taking out his phone he began scrolling through his address book. 'There,' he said, tossing the Nokia across the desk. 'You want to speak to him, I'm happy to pay for the call.'

Michael jotted down the number, then said, 'If you don't mind, I'm going to ask you to wait outside with my PA while I try to get hold of him. I think it'll be in everyone's best interests . . .'

'Marlene's on the line,' Naomi interrupted over the intercom.

Picking up the receiver, Michael put a hand over the mouthpiece as he said to Pace, 'I'm sure that coffee will be ready by now. I'll come and find you as soon as I'm done here.' After Pace had gone, he said to Marlene, 'Have you spoken to Susannah yet this morning?'

'About ten minutes ago. It turns out the aunt's condition isn't as serious as we feared, so she's going to try and get back up here late this afternoon.'

'Do you happen to know where she is now?'

'She was still at the hospital when we spoke, where she's been all night apparently.'

Michael was looking pensive. 'OK,' he said. 'I'll get back to you.' After disconnecting, he dialled Alan Cunningham's mobile number.

Cunningham picked up on the third ring with a gruff 'Hello.'

'Mr Cunningham, it's Michael Grafton here. I hope this is a convenient time.'

Sounding polite, but wary, Alan said, 'My lawyer passed on your message. I believe you want to talk about the emails my estranged wife sent to Susannah.'

'Amongst other things,' Michael confirmed. 'You're probably aware that we had them traced by a private investigator, who's since spoken to your brother-in-law, Carl Pace.'

'I am.'

'I've just been speaking to Mr Pace myself,' Michael continued, 'so I've heard, first-hand, his version of what's supposed to have happened between you and his niece.'

'Really? Well, if you've met him, you'll have seen for yourself what kind of man he is, but frankly, Mr Grafton, what you do or don't think of *his version of what's supposed to have happened* is of no interest to me. The man's a liar, his niece is a fantasist, and I'm sick to death of the way they keep hounding me.'

'Just tell me something,' Michael said, 'does Susannah know anything about this?'

'What do you think?'

'That she probably doesn't.'

'And it would suit you very well indeed, wouldn't it, if you could prove that Carl Pace's story was genuine, because we all know you've been dying to get your hands on Susannah ever since she came for an audition. Before probably, it'll be why you called her in.'

'I don't know why you're adopting such an aggressive tone, Mr Cunningham, but I can tell you this, as far as I'm concerned Susannah has a right to know who those emails came from and why they were sent. Whose version of events she chooses to believe will be up to her. Good day,' and before Cunningham could reply he cut the line dead.

* * *

Susannah had just flagged down a taxi when her mobile started to ring. Seeing it was Michael she clicked on right away, saying, 'Can I call you back in a few minutes?'

'No problem,' he responded. 'Use this number.'

After disconnecting she hugged Patsy tightly. 'Thanks for staying with us,' she said. 'We needed the moral support, and Lola was glad to see you were there when she woke up.'

With a smile Patsy said, 'It took us a while to understand what she was saying, but obviously her sense of humour's still intact.'

Susannah laughed. 'The joke of it is, I don't think she has any life insurance, but it was a funny moment anyway. Are you going to work now?'

'After I've been home to shower and change. Let me know what you're doing. If you go up to Derbyshire, Neve's more than welcome to come and stay with me.'

Embracing her hard, Neve said, 'Thanks. If Mum does go, then I'll definitely take you up on it.'

Patsy gazed curiously into her young eyes, feeling as though there was more to be seen if she could only find the right way to look. Then giving Susannah another quick hug, she jumped into her own cab, leaving Neve and Susannah to climb into theirs.

'Are you OK?' Susannah murmured, as Neve snuggled up to her in the back seat. 'Tired, I expect.'

'Yes, a bit. I don't have to go to school today, do I?'

'No. We'll spend the morning catching up on

some sleep, then come back to see Lola before I go on to Derbyshire.'

'So you are going to go?'

'I think I have to. Do you mind?'

'Not as long as I can stay with Pats,' and turning her face into Susannah's shoulder she tightened her hold on her arm.

Lifting up her mobile Susannah connected to the last call, and a moment later she was through to Michael.

'Hi,' he said. 'Marlene told me the news about your aunt. I'm glad it's not serious. How is she this morning?'

'Trying to be lively, but she's still weak in one arm and her speech is slightly slurred. She should be fine by the end of the day apparently, at least as far as that's concerned. She's got a horrible cut on her head with five stitches in it, and they still haven't decided whether or not she should have surgery to try and prevent a more serious stroke. They'll let us know in the next forty-eight hours.'

'Then I'll hope for her sake that the news is good. Marlene says you're going back to the set today.'

An ironic light flickered in Susannah's eyes. 'You were there when she made herself clear at the outset, no time off or changes to the schedule unless it involves death, disaster or some dastardly disease. As we managed to avoid all three I'm all out of excuses, so back to work I go.'

There was a smile in his voice as he said, 'What about Neve?'

'She'll stay with my friend, Pats, who'll probably bring her up to Derbyshire at the weekend, seeing as I have to shoot then.'

'Good. I'm glad things are sorting themselves out. You sound exhausted.'

'Actually, all I really feel right now is relieved that Lola's pulling through,' *and more moved by your concern than I can allow myself to tell you*, she added in her mind.

'You know if you need anything, you only have to call.'

'Thank you,' she whispered, and rested her head on Neve's.

'Actually, there's another reason I'm calling,' he told her. 'I have someone here I think you should meet. Where are you now?'

'On my way home in a taxi. Who is it?'

'It's probably best if he introduces himself. If you're feeling up to it maybe you could come here, to my office.'

Perplexed, and tired, Susannah said, 'Does it have to be today? I've been up most of the night, and I was hoping to go back to the hospital before I get the train.'

'I understand, but I think it should be today.'

'How about I speak to him on the phone? Or perhaps he could come to the house, if it's not too much trouble.'

'I'm sure it wouldn't be, but if your partner's there . . .'

'He won't be. When I spoke to him earlier he said he had appointments this morning, so he'll probably have left already.'

'In that case I'll give your address to . . . Actually, I'll bring him myself. We should be there within the hour.'

As Susannah rang off she felt Neve's head loll

forward, so put her phone away in order to hold on to her more tightly. Though she was curious to find out who Michael was bringing, uppermost in her mind now was Neve. This was the closest they'd been in weeks, and though it felt indescribably good, she couldn't help wishing it hadn't taken a crisis with Lola to bring them together. She inhaled the wonderfully familiar scent of Neve's hair and skin, and listened to the whisper of her breath as she slept. She could feel their bond tightening almost as though it could meld them into one. Then her eyes filled with tears as she reflected on how wrapped up in herself and the programme she'd been, because though she'd worried about Neve almost incessantly, the truth was, she hadn't taken enough time to fully consider how difficult life had become for her, struggling with the pain of the first break to her heart, feeling abandoned by both her mother and father, and believing that no one else would understand even if she tried to tell them. Apart from Alan, of course, but as Susannah held her precious daughter in her arms, she had to wonder, with almost more guilt in her heart than she could bear, how she could have been so selfish, and so insensitive to Neve's needs, to rely on someone else to help her deal with her angst when the only person who could really do that was her mother.

When finally the taxi drew up outside the house, Susannah saw, to her dismay, that Alan's car was still there. From their earlier conversation she'd expected him to be gone by now, but maybe he was on the point of leaving. She hoped he was, because no matter what excuse he might have for being out of contact for the last thirty-six hours, she really didn't want to hear it right now.

Feeling Neve come awake, she pressed a kiss to her head, and stroked the hair back from her face. 'We're home,' she whispered.

Bleary-eyed, Neve looked around, then realising where she was she buried her head back in Susannah's neck. 'Can't we go to Lola's?' she murmured. 'I'd rather go there.'

'But we're here now, darling, and . . .'

'So's he. I thought you said he was going to work. I don't want to see him, Mum. Please, don't make me.'

Holding her reassuringly, Susannah said, 'It's all right, he's probably just about to leave, and you can go straight up to your room.' When Neve didn't respond Susannah tilted her face up to look at her. 'Oh, my love,' she said, her heart contracting when she saw the tears, 'it'll be all right, I promise you.'

'No it won't, it never will be again . . .'

'I know it seems that way now, but come on, we can talk about this inside. The driver's waiting to be paid.'

Doing as she was told Neve got out of the car, and as they walked to the front door she took hold of Susannah's arm. 'I don't want to speak to him,' she said, as Susannah slipped the key in the lock. 'I don't care what you say . . .'

'Ssh, it's all right. You just go on up to your room.'

As they stepped into the hall Alan was coming out of the kitchen.

'At last,' he said, sounding relieved. 'Are you

OK? You must be exhausted . . .' He broke off as Neve dashed up the stairs, then looked at Susannah curiously.

Simply shaking her head, Susannah shrugged off her jacket, saying, 'I thought you were going to the office.'

'I decided to change my appointments so I could be here when you got back. How was Lola when you left?'

'Not too bad. The doctor's seeing her later, so we'll find out more then about how they're going to treat her.' She knew she should ask how he was, and where he'd been, but right now she either didn't care enough, or she was simply too tired to get into it. 'I'd better go up and see Neve,' she said. 'She's taken it pretty hard, and coming on top of everything else . . .'

'Would you like me to talk to her?' he offered. 'We'd started getting somewhere . . .'

'No, it's OK,' she broke in firmly. 'At the moment I don't think she really wants to talk to anyone, but I'd like to make sure she's all right. Actually, you might as well go on to work, if . . .'

'There's no reason for me to rush. I'll make some coffee and go and run you a bath, if you like.'

Wishing she could summon some warmth to her feelings as she thanked him, she started up the stairs. Something would have to change, she was thinking, they couldn't go on like this, but she couldn't cope with it all at present.

'By the way,' he said, as she reached the first landing, 'I've picked up a schedule of local ante-natal classes we can attend together while you're in London . . .'

'Not now,' she interrupted. Then, concerned about how crushed he might feel, 'Let's look at it later, when my head's a bit clearer.'

He smiled. 'Of course. Sorry. I keep getting carried away . . . Are you feeling OK? Apart from tired, I mean?'

'I'm fine, we both are, but coffee and a bath sounds wonderful.'

Finding Neve's door closed when she reached the top of the stairs, she knocked gently, and tried to push it open. 'It's me,' she called softly. 'Can I come in?'

Hearing a chair being dragged from under the handle, she frowned curiously, wondering why Neve would barricade herself in. 'What was that about?' she asked, as she closed the door behind her.

'I don't want *him* coming up here,' Neve said angrily.

Startled by the vehemence, but understanding that trying to hurt and reject the person who'd done the same to you was a normal part of a break-up, Susannah went to sit next to her on the bed, and slipped an arm around her. 'It won't always be like this,' she said gently. 'I know that's hard to believe when you're feeling the way you do now . . .'

'I hate him,' Neve seethed. 'I wish he was dead.'

'Ssh, you know you don't mean that . . .'

'Yes I do! I don't want to live here any more. Please don't make me, Mum. I know you're having a baby, and that you have to stay, but please can I live with Lola, or even with Dad? Anywhere, I just don't want to be here.'

Cupping Neve's face between her hands Susannah gazed deeply into her eyes, feeling her pain and confusion as though it were her own. 'I don't want to be without you,' she told her. 'You mean everything in the world to me . . .'

'I don't care,' Neve cried, starting to sob. 'You've got him now, and the baby, so you don't need me . . .'

'That isn't true. I'll always need you. I love you, Neve, more than my own life . . .'

'Then don't make me stay here. *Please*, let me go and live somewhere else.'

'But I thought you liked it here. You have your room . . .'

'I hate this room. I wish I never had to come here again.'

'Darling,' Susannah said, trying to draw her into her arms, 'I know how painful it is when someone doesn't feel the same way as you do, but Alan's so much older than you, and you'll meet someone else . . .'

'*Stop it!*' Neve raged, banging her fists into her mother. 'You don't understand. He makes me do things, Mum. He says it's what I want, but I don't. I hate it when he touches me, and when he makes me touch him . . .'

Susannah froze as the words hit her like a smack in the face. 'Neve, stop, calm down,' she broke in, so thrown by this new slant on Neve's pain that she was already rejecting it. 'Are you telling me . . . Are you saying . . .' *No, she couldn't be. Please God, no.* She wanted to grab Neve to her, but she needed to be sure she was understanding this correctly.

'I know it's my fault,' Neve choked, desperately.

'It wouldn't be happening if I hadn't let him see me one time . . .' Her face was ravaged with confusion as she looked at her mother. 'I want him to stop now, Mum,' she said brokenly, 'but he won't and he says if I tell anyone I'll have to be taken away for making things up and telling lies, because really it's all in my head. But I know it isn't . . . *Mum*, don't look like that. I'm sorry, I know you love him and that this is spoiling things for you, and if any of it gets out it'll be in the papers and you'll . . .' She broke off as, white-faced and shaking with horror, Susannah grabbed her roughly by the shoulders.

'Don't even think about any of that,' Susannah said fiercely. 'Just tell me what he did to you.'

Neve still seemed to be shrinking away with fear.

'I need to know,' Susannah urged. 'You said he touched you. Where?'

'Here, and here,' Neve said, putting a hand to her chest, then to the join of her legs.

Susannah's horror was growing to such a pitch it was almost unhinging her. 'Did he . . . Did he ever force himself on you?'

Neve's eyes went down.

'Neve, you have to tell me. Did he . . .'

'He made me put his thing in my mouth.'

'Oh my God,' Susannah gasped, gagging on the mere thought of it. Squeezing Neve's hands hard, she said, 'Did he ever . . . ? I'm sorry, darling, but I have to ask you this . . . Did he ever make you go all the way? You know what I'm talking about . . . *Oh Jesus Christ*,' she sobbed as Neve nodded. 'He took your virginity?'

'No,' Neve wailed, 'but he tried. He said I was

too small, but we could try again. I don't want to though, Mum . . . *Mum*, what are you doing?'

Susannah was on her feet. Her eyes were blazing with a deadly fury. 'Stay here and start packing,' she said. 'Don't come out until I tell you to.'

She went down to the first landing so fast she almost fell. Hearing him in the bedroom she turned from the stairs and flung open the door, so crazed with hate and violence that her fists were already flying as she reached him. 'You laid hands on my daughter!' she shrieked, banging a punch straight into his face, then another and another. 'You tried to rape my child, you filthy, perverted, monster . . .'

'Susannah, listen, wait,' he cried, trying to hold her off. 'I knew this would happen. It's what adolescent girls do . . .' He grunted as her knee smashed into his groin.

'I trusted you, you maniac,' she yelled, grabbing his hair and shaking his head as though to pull out every strand by the root. 'I thought you were helping her and all the time . . .'

'She's lying!' he gasped, cupping his groin with one hand while trying to fight her off with the other. 'She kept coming on to me . . .'

'Don't you dare blame her!' she screamed. 'She's a child! So help me God, I'm going to kill you for this.' Her fists and feet were flailing wildly, crashing into him with more force than she'd ever used in her life. She wouldn't stop, she couldn't. He had to suffer, he was going to pay . . .

'For Christ's sake, listen to me,' he shouted, attempting to seize her arms. 'Girls her age are fantasists. They make things up . . .'

'I'm not making it up!' Neve cried from the landing. 'You did all those things . . . *No!*' she screamed as Susannah turned round and he grabbed her from behind.

Susannah kicked out, used her elbows and feet and turned her head to bite him, but his grip was too strong.

'Let her go!' Neve yelled. 'You're hurting her.'

'Tell her you're lying,' Alan shouted. 'You know you are. You're jealous of her fame and all the attention she's getting, so you're trying to get some for yourself.'

'That's not true,' Neve screamed, her face contorting with pain.

'Don't listen to him!' Susannah was frantic, still struggling to break free.

'You've wanted to ruin things from the start,' Alan cried. 'You came on to me to try and steal me from her, and now you're . . .' He yelped as Susannah's foot slammed down so hard on his own that a bone snapped.

Springing away from him, Susannah ran on to the landing to Neve. 'Leave everything, we can come back for it,' she gasped.

As they started down the stairs, Alan reached over the banisters and clutched Susannah's hair, tugging her back.

'Keep going,' Susannah shouted to Neve as pain seared through her head, and swinging round she struck out with her nails to try to free herself. The burn was excruciating as her hair began tearing from her scalp. He was at the top of the stairs now, dragging her up. She rammed a fist into his gut and he doubled over, but still he didn't let go.

Grabbing him between the legs she squeezed with all her might.

With a roar he pushed her away. She staggered against the rail. Her feet slipped and suddenly she was plunging head first down the stairs.

'Mum!' Neve screamed, as Susannah ploughed into her, and as she lost her balance too, they both crashed to the floor at the bottom.

'Susannah!' Alan gasped, staring down to the hall in horror. 'Oh my God!'

In an instant he was beside them.

'Don't *touch* me,' Susannah hissed. 'Or her. Keep your hands away . . .'

'Mum, are you all right?' Neve gasped. Her legs were under Susannah, her shoulders slumped awkwardly against the wall.

'I'm fine,' Susannah said breathlessly. She tried to roll on to her knees, but a sharp pain dug into her side, making her groan.

'Let me help you,' Alan insisted.

'*Don't come near me,*' Susannah seethed. Neve's arms were around her now, and with a little more effort she was able to move herself off Neve's legs.

'Get out of here,' she managed to pant to Alan. 'This is my . . .'

'*Get out!*' she screamed.

Neve began helping her up, but they were both shaking so hard their legs were barely able to take their weight.

'Do you need an ambulance?' Alan said. 'Let me . . .'

'We don't need you. Just fuck off,' Neve spat, easing her mother down on the bottom stair.

'It's OK, I'm fine,' Susannah told her. Then to

Alan, 'Open that door, walk through it and don't come back until we've taken what's ours.'

'Susannah, you can't . . .'

'Just do it!' she screamed.

'I'm not leaving you like this. You might have broken something . . .'

'If I have, it's no business of yours.'

'You're carrying my child.'

Her eyes were so full of loathing as they blazed into his that his face turned ashen. 'You'll never have any rights to this child after what you've done,' she told him savagely. 'Paedophiles don't even get visits, so disabuse yourself of . . .' She gasped as another pain shot through her side.

'Mum, you're hurt,' Neve cried.

'I'm fine,' Susannah insisted. 'Just get him out of here.'

Limping to the door, Neve flung it open so hard that one of the panes cracked. 'Do as she told you,' she snarled. 'Get out, fuck off, drop dead. Don't ever come near us again.'

Alan was staring helplessly at Susannah, then clasping his hands to his head he started outside. 'You'll regret this,' he was saying. 'I'll leave now, but you'll have to face the truth. I'm only . . .' As he reached the front step he came to a sudden halt. 'What the . . . ? How did you . . . ?' He took a pace back and collided with Neve, who was staring at the short, balding man advancing purposefully through the gate.

Suddenly Alan turned and fled along the hall into the kitchen. Entering the house, the stranger lunged after him, but stopped abruptly as he spotted Susannah crouched at the foot of the stairs.

'What happened?' he barked. 'Are you all right?'

Susannah looked up, wondering who on earth he was. Then Michael appeared in the doorway behind him.

Immediately he was on his knees next to Susannah. 'Are you hurt?' he asked, putting an arm around her. 'What happened?'

'He pushed her,' Neve shouted.

Growling savagely, the balding man sprinted off down the hall.

'Can you stand?' Michael asked gently. 'Do you think anything's broken?'

'I'm not sure. I don't think so.'

Turning to Neve, he said, 'Go and call an ambulance, we'll take her . . .'

'No, I don't need one,' Susannah protested, trying to stand up.

Holding on to her he eased her to her feet, then felt her lean into him as dizziness swooped over her.

'I need to sit down again,' she said faintly. 'Let's go in there.'

'I think we should get you checked over,' Michael insisted.

Neve was regarding him warily. 'Excuse me,' she said, 'but who are you?'

'Darling, this is Michael Grafton,' Susannah told her.

Neve's eyes rounded. 'You mean *the* Michael Grafton?'

'That would be me,' he responded drily. 'And that, through there, I'm presuming, is the sitting room?'

Neve nodded. Then suddenly realising she was

expected to lead the way, she limped over to the door.

'You're hurt,' Susannah cried.

'I think I twisted my ankle,' Neve answered.

Moments later they were all sinking on to the sofas when the balding man came back, panting and wiping his hands on his jeans.

'He got over the wall,' he announced. 'Chickenshit bastard, but I'll be here when he gets back.' Registering the way they were all staring at him, he started to redden. 'Sorry about the language . . .'

'This is Carl Pace,' Michael told them.

Neve and Susannah looked at the man, clearly still none the wiser.

'I'm that bastard's brother-in-law,' Pace informed them gruffly. 'He's married to my sister.'

It took no more than a few moments for an awful understanding to dawn on Susannah. This man clearly detested Alan, and he had two nieces who had lived with Alan; two girls whom Alan was no longer allowed to see . . . 'Do you mind if I ask what you're doing here?' she said carefully.

Pace glanced at Michael, then at Neve.

'Maybe the explanation should wait until we're sure you're OK,' Michael said.

'I'm fine,' she told him. Then to Pace, 'Your nieces . . . Is that why . . . ?'

Pace's face hardened as he nodded, but softened again as he looked at Neve. 'Helen tried to warn you with the emails,' he said.

Susannah's eyes filled with tears as Neve came to sit beside her.

Sensing it was too little too late, Pace's voice

was ragged as he said, 'I tried to make her go to the police. I told her it would happen again, and as soon as we knew about . . .' His eyes were on Neve and for a moment Susannah thought he was going to cry. 'He can't get away with it again,' he said savagely.

'He won't,' Michael assured him.

Understanding already what had made Helen reluctant to report the crime, Susannah said, 'Neve and I will need to discuss what we're going to do.'

Though Pace looked on the brink of protesting, in the end he seemed to realise that once again a mother was protecting her child from the added ordeal of having to prove she was telling the truth.

'Carl, can we have a word outside?' Michael said. Then to Susannah as Pace started from the room, 'I'm going to flag down a cab to take you to hospital.'

'It was Neve who took the brunt of the fall,' Susannah told him.

'Then you can both be checked over.'

'I'm fine,' Neve said, even though she clearly wasn't.

Michael threw out his hands in mock despair, but the look he gave them brooked no more arguments. They were doing as they were told whether they liked it or not.

As soon as they were alone Susannah gathered Neve into her arms and held her so tightly that Neve could hardly breathe. 'We're going to work everything out, sweetheart, so don't worry,' she said, trying hard not to cry as she held Neve's face in her hands. 'You won't ever have to see him again.'

'No, I don't want to,' Neve said faintly. 'Not ever. I just want to be with you from now on.'

'You will be. The summer holidays are just around the corner, so you can finish early and come with me . . .' Her voice faltered as another quick pain caught her. 'I'll talk to your housemistress . . .'

'Don't tell her what happened,' Neve cried. 'I don't want anyone to know.'

'It's OK, I won't, but we'll probably need to talk to someone.' Her eyes closed as a terrible ache clawed at her belly. 'We don't have to think about that now though,' she said, weakly. 'As soon as we can we'll go up to Derbyshire and you can stay with me . . . If you like you can go and spend some time with Pats in Paris . . . Actually, I should call her. Can you pass me the phone?'

Taking it from the table behind them, Neve sat watching as Susannah connected to Patsy's mobile.

'Hi, it's me,' she said when Pats answered. 'Neve and I are on our way back to the hospital.'

'Already? Has something happened to Lola?'

'Not to Lola, to me and Neve,' Susannah told her. 'I'll explain when I see you. Is there any chance you can meet us there?'

'Of course. Are you all right?'

'I think so, but we'll both be a lot better once we're out of this house.'

Chapter Thirty

Leaving Carl Pace to wait for Alan's return, Susannah and Neve climbed into the taxi Michael had hailed, and sat huddled together as the driver responded to Michael's instructions.

By the time they arrived at the hospital it was clear to Susannah that she was losing the baby, but she said nothing, only rested her head against Neve, and felt the comfort of Michael's arm around her as he helped them from the back seat and led them into A & E. Hardest to bear at the moment was the guilt, knowing how terribly she'd let Neve down. What kind of mother was she? It felt as though the tiny life inside her, so completely dependent on her, was now responding to her rejection. She wanted desperately to hold on to it, to reassure it that she loved it with all her heart, but the blood she could feel trickling away from her was enough to tell her that its little spirit had already flown. For the moment, not even the fact that it had avoided having Alan as a father was providing any comfort.

The next half-hour passed in a blur of tears and discomfort as doctors and nurses came and went, carrying out checks and making various pronouncements that she barely took in. Neve was treated too, and found to have nothing more serious than contusions and a lightly sprained ankle. They were both incredibly lucky that nothing had been broken, at least nothing physical.

When Patsy arrived she stayed with Neve while Susannah was taken off for an ultrasound, where her miscarriage was confirmed and she was informed that they were going to perform a D & C right away.

As she waited to go into theatre more tears rolled on to her cheeks. Her heart felt as though it was fracturing in two. She'd failed both her children and had no idea how she was ever going to make anything right.

'Hey,' Patsy whispered, coming into the cubicle. 'You're going to be OK.'

'I know,' Susannah said. 'It's just . . .' but she didn't want to put her pain into words. It might seem as though she was trying to lessen it, and that wasn't something she deserved. 'How's Neve?' she asked.

'I've just taken her upstairs to see Lola. The doctor says she's fine to go home when she's ready.'

'Did you stay with her for the internal?' Susannah asked.

'Of course. She was very brave, and everything's fine, physically. One of the nurses gave me some leaflets about who we can contact for counselling. Neve doesn't want to talk about that right now, though. Considering Alan's profession it might be difficult to get her to see anyone.'

'We'll have to make sure it's a woman.'

'Of course.' Then, after a pause, 'What do you think we should do about him? Actually, don't answer that. Now isn't the time to discuss it.'

'It'll be up to Neve,' Susannah said. 'If it weren't for all the publicity it's likely to attract, thanks to me, I'd try to persuade her to talk to the police, but she won't want all that attention. It'd be horrible, and probably end up making things even worse, especially if he starts accusing her of lying.'

Patsy's expression was sour as she said, 'If it's the last thing we do, we're going to make that man pay for what he's done. We'll begin by getting him struck off whatever professional list or charter he's on, because the way he abused his position will be enough to guarantee he never practises any kind of psychology again.'

Wanting to change the subject, Susannah said, 'How's Lola? Has a decision been made about surgery, do you know?'

Pats brightened. 'Apparently they don't think it's necessary.'

Susannah's eyes closed with relief. At least some news was good. 'Is Michael still here?' she asked faintly.

'I'm not sure. He went outside to make some calls a while ago and I haven't seen him since. He wanted you to know, though, that he's already spoken to Marlene and you're not even to think about going back to work until the weekend at the earliest.'

Susannah nodded. 'I'll be fine by tomorrow,' she said. 'More than anything right now, I need to sleep.'

Patsy turned as the curtains opened, then stood aside as the orderlies came in to take Susannah to theatre. 'I'll be here when you come round,' she whispered, and blowing a kiss she left them to it.

Wandering back upstairs to check on Neve and Lola and finding them both asleep on Lola's bed, she stood staring down at them fondly. Neve was such a good and beautiful girl – she really didn't deserve what had happened to her, especially when her only motive for bringing Alan into their lives was to make her mother happy. It had to be a cruel and perverse god who'd allow a child's kindness to backfire on her in such a brutal and devastating way. She couldn't help feeling ashamed and riven with guilt herself, for being so busy with her own life that she hadn't paid proper attention to what was going on with Neve. She was going to be there for her now though, in any way she could.

When finally she tiptoed away and took the lift down to the lobby she ran into Michael Grafton on his way back in.

'Susannah's in surgery,' she told him. 'Neve's out for the count.'

'Actually, it's you I was looking for her,' he informed her. 'Would you like some coffee?'

'I'd love some,' she replied.

A few minutes later they were seated at a window table in Starbucks, Pats with a large china mug of latte, Michael with a small espresso.

'We've let Neve down so badly these past few weeks,' Pats said with a sigh. 'I should have realised what was happening. It seems so obvious now . . .'

'Things often do, with the benefit of hindsight,' he reminded her. 'And blaming yourself won't help anyone. The important thing is to make sure it doesn't happen to anyone else, which is why he has to be reported.'

She nodded soberly. 'Of course, but I can understand why Susannah's reluctant to put Neve through it.'

'So can I, but I've just spoken to Carl Pace who thinks there's a chance his niece might have second thoughts about going to the police, once she finds out she has a rival for Cunningham's affections.'

Patsy's lip curled in disgust. 'Then let's hope she does,' she retorted. 'Do you happen to know where he is now?'

He shook his head. 'Pace is still at the house, waiting, but there's been no sign of him yet. Anyway, what we need to focus on is where Susannah and Neve go from here. In the short term they can probably stay at her aunt's?'

Patsy nodded. 'Or with me. Susannah's talking about taking Neve up to Derbyshire for the summer.'

'I thought she might, and I've been doing some thinking that I'd like to run past you.'

'Shoot,' Patsy invited.

By the time she'd finished hearing him out she couldn't say whether she was more impressed or relieved by his suggestions. 'I think it's a perfect solution,' she told him eagerly.

Apparently heartened by her response, he said, 'The question is, do you think Susannah will?'

Though Pats was fairly confident Susannah would, she decided it might be wiser to let her speak for herself. So with a smile she said, 'I guess we won't know that until you ask her.'

That night Patsy took Susannah and Neve back to her rented flat in Knightsbridge. After serving them generous helpings of scrambled eggs with smoked salmon, which neither of them managed much of, she tucked them both up in her bed and left them alone to talk.

As the door closed behind her Neve's head fell against Susannah's shoulder and, feeling a harrowing mix of grief and love, Susannah gathered her in tightly and pressed a kiss to her hair. 'How are you feeling?' she whispered softly.

'OK,' Neve answered. Her voice was thin and shaky. 'I just feel really bad about you and the baby . . .' She faltered on a sob. 'Are you very upset about, you know, losing it?'

Pulling her in even closer, Susannah swallowed her own tears as she said, 'Yes, of course, but right now I'm more concerned about you, and how badly I've let you down. I'm so sorry, my darling. I should have realised what was happening. I . . . It just never occurred to me that he'd . . . Oh Neve,' she choked as tears spilled on to her cheeks. 'I wish you'd told me. You should never have had to go through anything like that.'

As more sobs shook Neve's body Susannah wept with her, wrapping her up so closely it was as though she might merge them into one. 'I'll never let anyone hurt you again,' she whispered fiercely and raggedly. 'I swear, I'll always be there for you. You mean everything in the world to me.

Oh God, I can't bear to think of what you've been through . . . My poor, poor darling . . .'

'He's out of our lives now, isn't he?' Neve said, lifting her head. 'Please say we're never going back to that house again.'

'Of course we aren't. Not ever.' Taking Neve's face between her hands, she gazed far into her puffy, bloodshot eyes, so full of uncertainty and dread that it was as though the fear stabbed straight to the depths of Susannah's heart. Merely to think of what had been done to her daughter was tearing her apart in ways that made her want to scream and lash out violently again and again. It was so much worse than if something terrible had been done to her: she only wished to God it had, so that she could be the one to deal with it now. She didn't want Neve to have to suffer for another minute, she wanted to take it all on herself so that Neve could be as pure and innocent as she'd been before that monster had laid his hands on her. But it wasn't possible. She couldn't turn back the clock, or erase memories, all she could do was try somehow to get Neve through this, and though she really didn't want to know the details, she wasn't going to allow her own revulsion and cowardice to back her away from the atrocity now. Neve had to be helped to find the road to recovery.

She started to speak, but the words dissolved before they were formed, as though afraid of what they might provoke. She swallowed and tried again. 'Do you want to tell me what happened?' she asked softly.

Neve immediately shook her head. 'No,' she

said. 'I just . . . I never want . . . He . . .' She choked and began to break down. 'It was horrible, Mum,' she gasped. 'He kept touching me . . . I knew it was wrong. I told him he had to stop, but he said it wasn't real, that I was imagining it, but I'm not stupid. I knew it was happening . . . He said if I ever told anyone I'd ruin everything for you with my lies and fantasies . . .'

As Susannah's heart ached with Neve's torment and confusion, she felt such a murderous rage that she had to bury Neve's face back in her shoulder so as not to frighten her. 'You know what he did is a crime, don't you?' she said, trying to keep the savagery from her voice. 'He could go to prison . . .'

'I don't want to tell the police,' Neve cut in desperately. 'I'll have to talk about what he did, and I don't want to, Mum. Not to strangers, or to anyone. He'll only say I was lying. I just want it to go away. Please make it go away.'

'Sssh, it's OK,' Susannah whispered, stroking her hair and feeling the terrible impotence of not being able to put everything right for Neve. 'Don't worry, no one's going to make you do anything you don't want to,' she told her, knowing it was still too soon to be having this conversation. They should try again in a few days, when the shock of it all had had some time to wear off, and perhaps they could do so with some professional guidance, if Neve would allow it.

Seeming satisfied with her mother's reassurance, Neve continued to lie against her, pressing in as close as she could get. After a while her head came up again. 'What are we going to do if he tries to come after us?' she asked, starting to sound panicked.

'He won't,' Susannah said firmly.

'But how do you know that? He could be outside now, waiting for us . . .'

'He'll be too afraid that we've spoken to the police,' Susannah assured her. 'He'll keep away from us now, I promise.'

'So can it be just me and you again, like it always used to be? And Lola when she gets better. She is getting better, isn't she? Please say she is, Mum, I don't want her to die . . .'

'Sssh, you saw for yourself that she's doing fine. She'll be home again any time now.'

'But what if she can't manage on her own? We'll have to live with her, because she needs us, and anyway, we've rented our house to someone so we don't have anywhere else to go.'

'We'll work everything out, so stop worrying yourself now . . .'

'When are you going back to Derbyshire? Can I come with you? I don't want to stay in London . . .' Her agitation was suddenly arrested by the phone ringing in the next room. 'What if it's him?' she cried, her fingers digging into Susannah's arm. 'He might be . . .'

'It won't be,' Susannah soothed, 'and even if it were, Pats would never allow him to talk to you.'

'Or you?'

'Or me, but I promise you it won't be him. It's probably Frank, or someone from Patsy's office. This is her apartment, remember? He won't even have the number.'

Seeming to relax again, Neve rested her head

back on Susannah's shoulder and closed her eyes. A moment later she was crying again. 'Are you really sad about the baby?' she asked huskily.

Susannah's heart twisted. The answer was yes, but she was trying not to think about it, because she was feeling much worse about it than she'd ever want to admit to Neve. In the end all she said was, 'It's probably for the best that it doesn't have him as a father.'

Neve nodded. 'That's what I think, but *we* would have loved it, wouldn't we? It would have been ours and we'd have taken care of it and never let him have anything to do with it.' She swallowed hard as her voice started to tremble again. 'I wonder if it was a boy or a girl,' she said weakly.

Susannah's eyes closed against the heartache. There was so much to deal with, emotionally and practically, and tonight she simply didn't have the energy to begin even trying to find answers. 'You should get some sleep,' she said softly. 'The doctor gave us something to take, so I'm going to get it from my bag, OK?'

After a moment Neve rolled on to her back, allowing Susannah to get up from the bed.

'Would you like anything else to eat or drink?' Susannah offered, looking down at her tender, blotchy face and tousled hair.

'No thanks.'

Offering a smile of encouragement, Susannah stooped over her and kissed her gently on the forehead. 'Won't be long,' she promised.

She found Pats in the sitting room with a pile of paperwork on the arm of the sofa next to her, and her laptop open on the coffee table.

'Hi,' Pats said, looking up, 'how are you feeling?'

Susannah's expression turned faintly ironic. 'I'm not sure I know how to describe it,' she answered. Then, after rubbing her hands over her face, and back through her hair, 'Neve's got so much going round in her head . . . She needs to sleep, so I'm going to give her the sedative we brought home with us. Do you know where I left my bag?'

'It's in the kitchen,' Pats answered, getting to her feet. 'Perhaps you should take something too.'

Susannah didn't protest, only followed Pats into the kitchen where she dug into her bag for the small envelope containing four Temazepam. 'I'll just give her half,' she said, shaking one into her hand.

'Here.' Pats was passing a glass of water. 'Is there anything else you need?'

Susannah shook her head. 'No thanks. I'll come back when she's asleep.'

To her surprise, and relief, when she returned to the bedroom she found Neve had already drifted off, so after sitting with her for a while in case she woke up again, she took the sedative away and went back to the kitchen where Pats was making tea.

'Who was that on the phone just now?' Susannah asked, as she put the glass on the draining board.

Once she'd finished laying out cups and saucers Pats turned to lean against the counter top. 'It was Michael Grafton,' she answered, folding her arms. 'He's coming here tomorrow to talk to you, if you're up to it.'

At the mention of his name the awfulness of the day came flooding back to Susannah, making her feel restless and sick, and both relieved and embarrassed that he'd been there.

'I said I'd call to let him know if you weren't,' Pats told her.

'I'll be fine,' Susannah said. 'I don't know how we'd have got through today without him.'

Pats nodded agreement. 'He had a call from Carl Pace about an hour ago,' she said. 'He didn't go into any detail, but apparently Pace was still waiting when Alan got back to the house. To quote Michael, Alan got at least some of what he had coming.'

Susannah looked away.

'Don't think about him now,' Patsy cautioned.

'I can still hardly believe . . .' Susannah began in a whisper. 'To think of him . . .' Her mind reeled away from the images. 'I'd like to kill him,' she said through her teeth. 'I would have if I'd been able to. Look at my hands.' She held them out, showing the broken nails, bruises and swellings. 'I trusted him,' she went on, her voice rising with incredulity and anger. 'I believed everything he told me about Neve. When I think of how he used his position, his training, to convince me he was helping her, when all the time . . .' Her eyes closed as fury and disgust engulfed her. 'He's a monster, Pats. He's not the person we used to know. He's someone else now and he has to pay for what he's done.'

'He will,' Pats assured her. 'Once the police have been informed . . .'

'I'm not sure we can do that. Neve doesn't want to talk to them.'

'That's understandable right now. She might change her mind in a few days, but even if she doesn't apparently Carl Pace is confident his niece will stop protecting him once she knows about Neve.'

The reminder of Carl Pace's niece made Susannah shake her head in mute dismay as she thought of the lies Alan had told about his wife and why she'd stopped him seeing her daughters. She should have realised straight away that something wasn't right. How could she have been so blinded by her need for love, and Neve's for a father?

'We were all taken in,' Pats said gently after Susannah had voiced the anger she felt with herself. 'He was very clever. He knew exactly how to use your past relationship and his professional status, and we had no reason not to trust him.'

Susannah was shaking her head in abject dismay. 'Even if Neve does end up agreeing to talk to the police,' she said, 'we can't have her name being bandied about in the press.'

'We'll make sure that doesn't happen. The authorities know how to handle these things . . . Are you OK?' she asked, as Susannah put a hand across her waist.

'Just a twinge,' Susannah replied. 'It'll be fine.'

Patsy's eyes came up to hers. 'How are you feeling about that?' she asked softly.

Susannah shook her head. 'I'm trying not to,' she answered, but tears were already welling in her eyes and began to fall as Pats came to embrace her. 'It was just a poor, innocent little soul,' Susannah sobbed. 'It wasn't to blame for anything . . .'

'Of course it wasn't,' Pats soothed. 'And I know this is harsh, but if it had survived it would have kept him in your life and I don't think you'd want that, would you?'

'No of course not, but it seems so awful to think it's for the best. I was its mother. I'd have loved it and cared for it. So would Neve.'

'We all would, but try to think that it's gone to a better place now. Someone once told me that there's a special place for children and animals in this great big universe of ours, where only good things happen and they're always happy.'

Susannah smiled weakly. 'It's a nice thought,' she whispered.

'Isn't it?' Pats agreed. 'Now here you are,' she said, passing some kitchen towel, 'dry your eyes while I pour the tea.'

Doing as she was told, Susannah sat down at the table and reached for her bag. 'Did Michael say what he wants to talk about tomorrow?' she asked, taking out her phone and turning it on. 'I guess it'll be about when I can go back to Derbyshire. Physically I should be fine by tomorrow, but I can't leave Neve. I'll have to take her with me . . .'

'Or she can stay here with me, and I'll bring her up at the . . . What is it?' Patsy asked, seeing the blood draining from Susannah's face as she listened to a voicemail. 'Oh God, don't tell me it's him.'

Susannah's eyes came to hers as she listened.

'So please call me back,' Alan was saying. 'We

634

need to talk. I have to explain what happened and why Neve believes what she's saying. She can be helped and I know, as her mother, that you'll want to make sure she gets the very best care. OK, it can't be me, I accept that. I've tried, and now, God help me, I seem to have made things worse, when all I ever wanted was to be a father to her, and to our own baby when it comes along. Susannah, please don't give up on us. We can get through this. You just have to trust me and . . .'

'I can't listen to any more,' Susannah snapped, cutting it short. 'The bastard! He's still trying to say she made it up. He seems to think . . .' A blaze of fury suddenly fired in her head. 'I'm calling him right now,' she seethed. 'I'm going to tell him . . .'

'Susannah, you're in too vulnerable a state at the moment. Let the police, or Carl Pace and his family deal with him.'

Susannah was already connected, her eyes dark with rage, her lips pale with exhaustion and anger. 'It's me,' she said tightly when he answered. 'I'm calling to let you know that you are going to pay for what you've done to Neve. Whatever it takes I'll make sure you suffer every bit of the disgrace you deserve, and all the . . .'

'Susannah, listen!' he cried. 'We need to talk . . .'

'That is never going to happen,' she broke in furiously. 'I don't want you near me, or my daughter ever again . . .'

'But the baby . . .'

'There is no baby! You killed it, Alan, when you pushed me down the stairs.'

'Oh my God. Susannah . . .'

'That's where your punishment begins,' she said savagely. 'Don't call me again, ever.' As she ended the call she was shaking so hard that she dropped the phone on the table, and as great huge sobs began racking her body Pats quickly wrapped her in her arms as though to hold her together.

'It's all right,' Pats soothed, stroking her hair. 'Just let it out. Everything's going to be fine. It'll take some time, but we're going to get through this. It'll be as though he was never a part of our lives. You have my word on that.'

It was almost eleven o'clock the following morning when a bleary-eyed Neve hobbled into the kitchen, to find Pats working from home.

'OK?' Pats said, smiling fondly as she looked up. Neve nodded.

'How's the ankle?' Patsy asked, looking down at the bandaged joint and finding herself unable not to notice how beautiful Neve's legs were. It sickened her to think of Alan even glancing at them, never mind doing what he had, but her eyes showed only tenderness as they came back to Neve's.

'It still hurts a bit,' Neve answered, 'but it's OK.' Then, after a pause, 'Mum's in the bathroom.'

Seeing she was about to cry, Pats got up to gather her into her arms.

'It's all my fault,' Neve sniffed. 'I didn't want her to have the baby and now . . .'

'Ssh, that's nonsense,' Patsy soothed. 'It wasn't anyone's fault, apart from Alan's, and if you look at it that way, he doesn't deserve to have children anyway.'

'But what about Mum? It was her baby too . . .'

'She's got you, and nothing in the world matters more to her than that.'

'Thank you, Pats,' Susannah said, coming into the kitchen behind them. 'That's what I've been trying to tell her,' and joining in the embrace she kissed Neve's head firmly.

'OK, so who's for breakfast?' Patsy offered, sensing the need to move on with something mundane and normal. 'I went out early to get croissants and *pain au chocolat*, and there's a great coffee machine here.'

'I hope you're going to eat,' Susannah said softly to Neve. Her eyes started to tease, 'I know you're hungry, your stomach's been going like "Pomp and Circumstance" this past half an hour.'

With a smile Neve leaned in to her mother and rested her head on her shoulder. 'I'll have a *pain au chocolat*,' she said.

'How did you sleep?' Patsy asked Susannah as she started to make fresh coffee.

'OK, I think,' Susannah replied. 'I'm certainly feeling better this morning than I did last night. How are you?'

Patsy laughed. 'I'm fine, and I've managed to get out of a meeting this afternoon, so if Neve's ankle is up to it, I thought I'd take her for a little retail therapy around Knightsbridge.'

Neve's eyes widened. 'Knightsbridge is like major,' she murmured, 'but what about Mum?'

'She can always meet us somewhere, if she likes,' Patsy answered, 'but Michael Grafton's due here at midday, so I thought we should make ourselves scarce before that so they can have a chat.'

Neve turned to Susannah in alarm. 'Does that mean you'll have to go back to Derbyshire today?' she asked.

'Probably not today,' Susannah answered, 'but when I do go, you'll be coming with me.'

Neve still seemed worried. 'What about Lola?' she said. 'We can't leave her here on her own. She'll get all lonely, and what if she has another fall?'

'She's going to be in hospital until early next week,' Susannah reminded her, 'so we don't have to worry too much over the weekend. Pats will go to visit her, perhaps.'

'Of course I will,' Pats assured them, 'and Frank's going to try to get over, so he'll no doubt dazzle her with more of his atrocious charm. And as for what happens when she comes out . . .' She looked around. 'Whose phone is that?'

'Sounds like mine,' Susannah answered, turning cold in case it was Alan trying to get hold of her again. 'It's probably Marlene,' she said, as much for her own benefit as Neve's. And seeing when she dug it from her bag that it was indeed Marlene, or someone from the Centre, she said, 'I'll take it in there.'

After she'd gone into the sitting room Pats gently eased Neve into a chair and put a *pain au chocolat* in front of her. 'I don't want you to worry about anything, OK,' she said in a whisper, 'including Lola. It's all being taken care of . . . I'll explain more when we go out. For now, all you have to do is come with me to get yourself all kitted out for the next few days in Derbyshire, then we'll go back to the office to sort out a whole new stash of make-up for you to take with you. Frank and I will collect your other stuff from Clapham, so don't even think about that.'

'And Mum's?'

'Of course, hers too.'

Neve looked down at her breakfast as Pats turned to pour some coffee. When she picked it up, she didn't attempt to take a bite, she only went on staring at it. 'It *is* my fault, Pats,' she said quietly. 'If I hadn't gone on to that website . . .'

'Darling, you have to stop this,' Pats said, gently but firmly. 'Remember, I backed you all the way, and I'm the adult here, so if anyone should be bearing the responsibility, it's me. But how can I, when neither of us had any idea what kind of person he'd turned into?'

'I know, but if . . .'

'No buts. What you did by going on to the website was out of love for Mum, and it's a cruel, cruel fate that made it turn on you the way it did. I just wish you'd told one of us sooner, but thank God you did in the end, and now, you'll never have to see him again.'

Neve's eyes looked haunted. 'What about if we go to the police?' she said. 'Will I have to see him then?'

Taking a breath, Patsy said, 'Only if it ends up going to court.'

Neve paled. 'Then the papers will find out and

everyone will know, and it'll be really horrible for Mum . . .'

'All she'll care about is *you*,' Patsy broke in. 'We'll all fully understand if you don't want the world finding out what happened, but you mustn't hold back because of Mum.'

'He shouldn't get away with it though, should he?'

Patsy shook her head. 'No, he shouldn't, but there's something you don't know, about his stepdaughters . . . He did the same to one of them, and it's possible she might report him once she finds out that he's done it again.'

Neve's gaze seemed to lose focus as her eyes drifted away.

'Listen, it's too soon for you to be trying to make any decisions,' Patsy said, coming to sit next to her. 'Let's just get ourselves through the next few days for now. There's no rush. You can be with Mum, or in Paris with me when I go back, and you'll be able to talk about things with either of us any time you want to. You know we'll be right behind you, no matter what, don't you?'

Neve nodded, and rested her head on Patsy's shoulder.

'It was Marlene,' Susannah announced, coming back into the kitchen. 'I've told her I'll be back tomorrow in time for the night shoot. You'll be coming too,' she told Neve. 'We're almost at the end of term, so I'll talk to your housemistress about releasing you early.'

Neve nodded bleakly.

Susannah's eyes went to Patsy's. They could only take this one step at a time, and to expect

Neve to be bouncing back already would be asking too much. However, they both took a little heart as she finally bit into her *pain au chocolat*.

'So do you think you might come shopping with us later?' Neve asked. 'I mean after Michael's gone.'

Susannah smiled. 'I expect so,' she said. 'But before that, I have to work out what I'm going to wear today.'

With mock weariness Patsy said, 'I guess it'll have to be something of mine, but please try not to do me the disservice of looking better in it than I do, because that just wouldn't be kind.'

Neve giggled, and the sound of it was so magical for Susannah that she could have hugged Pats to within an inch of her life for making it happen.

An hour later, wearing a cream linen shift dress and no shoes, Susannah was blinking in astonishment as she looked at Michael Grafton. 'Are you serious?' she asked, hardly daring to hope he was.

Laughing, he said, 'Did it sound like a joke? It wasn't meant to.'

'No, but . . .' She shook her head, not sure whether to object on the grounds of the offer being too generous, or simply to throw her arms around him in a bruising display of gratitude.

'Actually, something I forgot to add,' he said, 'is that Ellie, my daughter, who's the same age as Neve, if you recall, is going to be around for the summer, so that's another reason why it could work.'

Susannah was so still so stunned, and moved,

that all she could manage was, 'Are you sure? I mean, you hardly know us and . . .'

'Listen, the Long House is there, standing empty,' he repeated. 'It has three bedrooms, all on ground level, which is going to be important for Lola. One of them is pretty tiny, but you'll probably be over at the lodge most of the time, so that's hardly going to matter. What's more, Binkie's in the cottage next door, so Lola will have company, and Neve can either have Ellie for company, or you can take her to the set with you. I know it's only a solution for the summer, but at least it'll give you some breathing space to think about what's to be done when it comes time for Neve to go back to school.'

Susannah pressed her hands to her cheeks, wanting to cry, she felt so relieved. 'If you're absolutely sure we won't be in the way,' she said. 'I mean . . .' Her eyes came uncertainly to his. 'Perhaps you're not going to be there, so it won't . . .'

'I think my daughter would have something to say about it if I weren't,' he interrupted wryly. 'But I will need to be in London from time to time.'

Susannah started to smile as her eyes filled with tears. 'Then provided it's OK with Neve,' she said, 'and Lola, and I'm sure it will be, how could we possibly refuse?'

'I'm sure I don't know,' he replied ironically. 'And now, I'm afraid I must leave you. I have an appointment in Covent Garden at one thirty. Marlene tells me you're going back to Derbyshire tomorrow, so I'll be happy to drive you if you can

be ready to leave by midday. We'll send a driver
for Lola when she's fit enough to come,' and after
a quick glance at his watch he gave her an ironic
sort of smile and was gone.

Chapter Thirty-One

Six weeks later Patsy was sitting at her desk in Paris when a shadow fell across the doorway and Frank said, in a long-suffering sort of way, 'Patreesha, looking at you now, I feel my inner tiger starting to roar.'

'Will you please go away,' she said, turning to her computer screen. 'I'm very busy and you are a distraction.'

Coming up behind her, he tilted her head back and growled.

'Frank, you can't keep doing this,' she muttered, quite serious in spite of how much she loved his playfulness. 'People can see, and as the two most senior members of the company, it isn't acceptable for us to bring our personal relationship into the office.'

'You are correct,' he agreed, all contrition. 'Which is why I am here to propose . . .'

She waited, expecting him to finish the sentence. When he didn't she pretended she hadn't heard and continued studying the spreadsheet on her screen.

'You do not wish to know what I wish to propose?' he challenged, perching on the edge of her desk.

Debating whether or not she should rise to this, she ended up saying, 'As long as it's not marriage, I'm all ears.'

'Ah, now that is something I might consider when I am free to do so,' he admitted. 'Until then, my little cabbage, you are safe.'

'Phew!' she retorted, and turned round to look at him. 'So, what are you about to wow me with?' she challenged, folding her arms.

'As a matter of fact, I have a small list of things,' he replied, and glanced at his watch. 'My first proposal is that perhaps I must allow myself to be 'ead 'unted.'

'To be what?' she said, screwing up her nose.

'Let me see, we have not the same expression for this in French – we say . . .'

'Headhunted!' she cut in. 'Are you seriously . . . ?'

'Ssh,' he said quickly, 'we must not let all the world know, but yes, I have been made an offer by Lancôme to join with them, and maybe I think I must say yes.'

'Maybe I think you must not,' she told him, hotly. 'We need you here, and where's your loyalty? Claudia's a wonderful employer . . .'

'*Je sais, je sais* and it is not that I wish to leave, but I think it is very difficult for us to continue as we are, *non*?'

'*Non*, I mean, *oui*, I mean, yes, but to decamp, Frank . . . That's taking it too far. We can find a way . . .'

'No, we cannot. I have made up my mind, and when a man makes up his mind, you understand, the word is final. I must accept the offer from Lancôme . . .'

'But you don't want to.'

'This is true, but you are not going to leave, and one of us must, so I am willing to do the honourable thing for the sake of our future.'

Patsy opened her mouth to protest again, but found no words coming out. 'What if our relationship doesn't end up going anywhere?' she finally managed. 'You'll have thrown away . . .'

'I am throwing nothing away, because our relationship will go somewhere,' he informed her, as though he had some kind of inside knowledge. 'So this is my number one proposal proposed and accepted. I shall go to Lancôme. My number two proposal comes from our meeting yesterday concerning the face for the new teenage range, and it came to me this morning that perhaps we can open the search up from France to include other countries, and if we do this, we can, perhaps, put Neve forward for consideration. She is very beautiful, *oui*? And now we are at the end of July and she is in Dobbyshere with her mother, I was thinking that when we go to visit them in August, we can take some photographs of her and show them to the rest of the team on our return. What do you say?'

Patsy was staring at him, dumbfounded. It wasn't that the idea of suggesting Neve hadn't occurred to her, because it had, but she was biased, and it would smack of nepotism, so no way could she entertain it. Coming from Frank, however . . . and if it were turned into a Europe-wide search, and if she removed herself from the final selection panel . . . 'I'll need to give it some thought, and talk to Claudia,' she said in the end. '*And* Susannah.'

'Of course,' he agreed affably. 'Next on my list of proposals is that you will meet my son, and if you like him we can take him with us to England. My wife is to go on a yacht in Greece for the summer, so he is now going to be with me for all of the time. I do not want to miss our holiday together, so I will be very happy if he can come too.'

Patsy's heart melted as she laughed. 'Frank, he's five years old and your son, how could I possibly not love him and want him to come with us?'

'You have not met him yet,' he warned. 'He is very like me, this is true, so of course you will love him, but I am afraid he is like his mother too.'

Her eyes narrowed. 'What does that mean?' she asked warily.

'It mean that he is very good-looking, so you will not only love him, you will adore him and maybe fall in love with me just because of him, and I would like you to fall in love with me because of me.'

Wishing she could get up and put her arms around him, she said, 'Don't worry, the falling's all done.'

'This is true?' he said, looking surprised.

'*C'est vrai*,' she replied.

'You love me?'

She nodded.

'Then maybe you will say so?'

'*Je t'aime*,' she whispered.

He started to grin. 'Now I come to my last proposal,' he said mischievously.

'*Frank*, if you dare . . .'

'You do not know what is it.'

'I can guess.'

He scowled discouragingly.

'I'm warning you, the answer will be no.'

'Are you sure?'

'I'm sure.'

'Completely?'

'Absolutely.'

'Then this is very sad,' he said mournfully, 'because now it means you do not have the pleasure of me for lunch.'

Susannah was speeding along the country lanes of Derbyshire as fast as her little G Wiz would allow, which was around forty miles an hour at a push, but that was fine. She wasn't in any particular hurry. It was simply that she was keen to get back to the Long House where she, Neve and Lola were hosting a party that evening to welcome Pats and Frank, and Frank's son, Jean-Luc, who were due to arrive in a couple of hours. Since Michael's housekeeper had insisted on taking over the catering, and Michael himself was providing the wine, there wasn't much for Susannah to do other than shower off the delightful smell of horses after a day in the saddle, dress in something light and summery, and pin up her hair because its weight, in this heat, made her hotter than ever.

Doing her level best to overtake a tractor, she waved out to the driver as she finally steamed past, and received a friendly honk for her trouble. This daft little car that ran on electricity and looked like something Noddy drove, had been a gift from the manufacturer in exchange for her being photographed behind the wheel. At the last minute Neve had agreed to take part in the shoot, which had resulted in a happy boost for the publicity as one of the tabloids ran it on their front page alongside the headline *G Wiz it's the Blonde Bombshells*.

Ever since, she and Neve had become something of a local attraction as they chugged merrily around the countryside in it, mainly between the Centre and the Long House, and once even as far as the supermarket in Matlock. Unfortunately, they'd run out of power while there, so Michael and Ellie had had to come and rescue them, leaving a handful of unit drivers to load the car into a horsebox and whisk it off to the nearest plug.

Watching Neve and Ellie together had become a source of great joy to Susannah over the past seven weeks. Almost from the start they'd been virtually inseparable, and now Neve was spending more nights at the manor than she did at the lodge or the Long House. During the day the two girls were either to be found mucking out stables, or learning to ride in Neve's case, Ellie lending moral support, as she'd owned a horse since she was old enough to walk; or helping out in some capacity at the Centre. In looks they could hardly have been more contrasting, since Ellie might easily have passed for an Italian, her hair and complexion were so dark and exotic, while Neve was becoming blonder by the day now that summer was upon them. In fact, there were times when she looked so radiant that no one would ever have guessed she'd been through a trauma so recently, much less one so horrible. However, there were still nights when she crept into Susannah's bed, needing comfort and reassurance, and any mention of Alan in her hearing seemed to deaden everything inside her.

Since his arrest, after Helen and Julia had reported him to the police, he'd been released on bail, then promptly driven into hiding by the press. The tabloids were having a field day, thanks to his involvement with Susannah, though Neve's name had never yet been mentioned as a victim, only as someone who'd been lucky to escape 'the psycho predator', mainly because Susannah had respected Neve's wishes and not added her own accusations to Helen's. However, she'd privately contacted Helen to let her know that if she needed any support she'd be willing to talk to Neve again. So far Helen's only reply had been to say that while she appreciated the offer, she saw no reason to subject Neve to the kind of media circus that would make her suffering even greater than it was already, just because she had a famous mum.

With the programme's security being so tight Susannah was generally safe from prying lenses while shooting, and ever since Michael's lawyer had requested, and won, a court order to stop photojournalists from hounding her during her journeys between the set and the manor, the going had become much easier. Of course, it hadn't prevented the inevitable speculation about the nature of her relationship with Michael, but neither of them had ever commented on it publicly, nor, in fact, had they mentioned it to one another. They simply behaved like the good friends and neighbours they were, occasionally enjoying a drink, or perhaps a meal, together in the evenings, but never alone, always with the girls and Lola, and Lola's new best friend, Binkie.

Now, as Susannah urged the G Wiz in through the estate's back gates, she ignored her ringing mobile because she was certain it would be Neve, asking how much longer she was going to be. Instead, she drove up to the front of the Long House and gave a cheery little toot on the horn as she came to a stop, to let those inside know she was back. It was a picture-book dwelling, constructed of Derbyshire sandstone and long-straw thatch, and fronted by sprightly clusters of hollyhocks mingling with a tumbling riot of colours from Lola's lovingly tended hanging baskets.

To her surprise, no one came out to greet her. Apart from a couple of horses regarding her in their usual desultory fashion from their stables across the way, and the twitter and bustle of swallows swooping about the cobbled yard, there wasn't much sign of life. Even Binkie's rose-covered cottage next door seemed to be shut up, which wasn't usual for Binkie, since her windows and front door were generally wide open.

Curious, and even a little concerned, since the party tables should be set up by now, and the buckets of flowers she'd ordered were nowhere in evidence, she took her script bag from the back seat and carried it into the cluttered dining room just inside the front door.

'Neve!' she shouted. 'Lola! I'm back. Where are you?'

Her voice echoed through the rooms and came back to her with a doubtful sort of resonance. Where was everyone?

Opening up her phone, she was about to call Neve when it rang to let her know there was a message. Connecting to it, she dragged an elastic from her hair and had started to shake it out when another call came in, so switching to it, she said, 'Hi, is that you Neve? Where are you?'

'Actually, it's me,' the voice at the other end said, and she instantly froze.

'How did you get this number?' she spat.

'Susannah, before you ring off, please just listen to me,' he cried desperately. 'Even if we never speak again, I need you to know . . .'

'I'm not interested in anything you have to say,' she told him savagely. 'Now leave us alone, or I swear we'll add our case to Helen's.'

'But Helen's dropped hers,' he told her. 'As soon as she realised . . .'

'You're lying.'

'Ask her. My lawyer got a call yesterday. The police aren't pressing charges, because they know Julia's lying. She's been assessed by other professionals. It's why I'm calling, because Neve needs to do the same. I never touched her, Susannah. It's all in her head. Since her father left . . .'

'I'm not listening to this,' Susannah snarled. 'Neve's no fantasist.'

'I know you don't want to believe it, but for God's sake, the rest of my life is at stake . . .'

'Why, if Helen's not pressing charges? What do you have to fear?'

'Susannah, listen . . .'

'No, you listen. One way or another you're going to pay for what you did to my daughter. Now don't ever ring me again,' and before he could say any more she cut the line dead.

For several minutes she stayed where she was, feeling breathless and disoriented and as though the sun had shrunk behind a cloud, even though it continued to dazzle just as brightly. Merely speaking to him had left her feeling soiled, and so angry she was starting to shake.

Opening up her mobile again, she was about to call Michael when she spotted a note pinned to an apple in the fruit bowl, written in Neve's familiar hand.

Hey! Decided to hold party at manor. Wear blue dress we bought in Fenwicks, with sparkly bodice and no straps. I've got blue sandals, but have left silver ones for you. Lola's in her retro hotpants (joke)! Pats rang to say on way from airport and Frank's driving so they might end up in Cornwall. love me xxx PS: Silver's being driven over tomorrow for weekend. PPS: Please can I ride her? PPPS: love you. PPPSS: so does Lola. PPPSSS: Can't think of anything else but knew it would make you laugh!

Indeed Susannah was smiling, and, wondering how it was possible to love one human being so much, she put the note down and rang Michael.

'Hi, we're all waiting for you,' he said when he answered. 'Or we will be in about half an hour.'

As she told him about Alan's call, she walked back through the dining room and into the snug little alcove that she used as a bedroom on the nights she spent here. Neve's and Lola's were further along the narrow passageway that ran the length of the house, and the bathroom was the other side of the kitchen.

When she'd finished he said calmly, but very firmly, 'Put it out of your mind now. I'll have spoken to the lawyers by the time you get here, so everything will be taken care of.'

'But if Helen has dropped the charges . . .'

'If she had, we'd have been told by now. He's a desperate man who's playing desperate games, so don't rise to it. Now, don't be late, we're all looking forward to seeing you.'

After thanking him Susannah rang off, wondering how she'd ever have got through any of this without him.

Minutes later her phone rang again, and seeing it was Neve she put on a sunny smile as she answered. 'Hi darling. Everything OK?'

'Yeah, cool,' Neve assured her. 'Can you bring my stuff with you when you come? I'm going to stay here tonight. You know what I need. It's all in the bathroom, apart from my nightie.'

'Of course, your ladyship. Anything else?'

'I don't think so. You got my note? Did it make you laugh?'

'It did.'

'Actually, there is something else, but I'll tell you when I get here, because it's really major.'

Since her tone was playful Susannah wasn't worried, only intrigued. 'Do I get a clue?' she prompted.

'Um, let me see . . . No, I don't think so. You'll just have to wait. Oh, but I can tell you this, Lola and Binkie have joined a bridge club.'

'But Lola can't play.'

'Nor can Binkie, but Tom Court, you know, the man who comes to do whatever to the trees? He's been teaching them, and they're making up a four next Thursday with some other dude Tom knows. They keep insisting it's all about cards, but I know it's just a cover for a seriously hot date. Do you think we should get Lola some new undies?'

Susannah laughed, and laughed again as she heard Lola say, 'Don't waste your money, I won't be wearing any.'

'She's such a tart!' Neve shrieked. 'Actually, she's been on the sherry, which I keep telling her isn't allowed with her blood pressure.'

'One or two won't hurt,' Susannah told her. 'Just make sure she doesn't get out of hand, we don't want her attempting the cancan later if she's not wearing any knicks. Now, I'm getting in the shower. I'll see you in about half an hour.'

'*Chérie,* you need to wake up now,' Frank said softly, giving Pats a gentle shake. Patsy blinked open her eyes and took a moment to remember where she was.

'How are you feeling now?' he asked, glancing over at her worriedly.

It took another moment for her to register that. 'Better, I think,' she said, and sitting up straighter she reached for the mineral water she'd propped behind the handbrake. 'Are we there yet?' she asked, taking in the undulating patchwork of countryside spreading out around them in every shade of green.

'Very soon, so I need you to read me the final directions.'

Turning to look in the back seat, Patsy smiled to see Jean-Luc still sleeping, his feathery dark lashes fanned over his swarthy cheeks, his thick dark hair matted to his head in the heat. He looked so adorable, all tucked up in his car seat with his favourite teddy on his lap and several other toys around him, that she ferreted out her camera to add yet another shot to the dozen or so she'd already taken.

Though he'd been a little shy at their first meeting, a couple of days ago, he'd come out of himself enough by now to insist that she should be the one to sit in the back seat of the car with him, not Papa. This was why Frank was driving, and Pats was feeling so grim, having never been a good traveller in the back, so as soon as Jean-Luc was asleep Frank had stopped the car for her to return to the front.

Now, as she unfolded the printout of directions Susannah had emailed, Patsy yawned, then groaned. Her stomach was still in protest and the water didn't seem to be helping too much.

'I don't know about a party, I think I'll end up going straight to the bathroom, or bed, when we get there,' she commented. 'Where are we now?'

'We have just pass through Matlock,' he informed her. 'I know I must keep straight for three miles, but I would like you to watch out for the sign, because Susannah says it is *un peu caché.*'

A few minutes later, spotting the signpost tilted awkwardly into a hedge, Patsy cried, 'There it is! Turn left now!'

Frank hit the brakes, Pats jerked forward and

the driver behind swerved dangerously close to a ditch.

Neither of them spoke as Frank steered the car slowly into a narrow lane and continued to motor on at a leisurely pace.

Patsy turned to check on Jean-Luc, and was amazed to find that he was not only still in his chair, but still sleeping, though his head was lolling to the other side now and his teddy had fallen out of his lap. Reaching back to pick it up, she held it in her own lap and started to laugh. 'I swear, out of a nation of crazy drivers, you are the absolute worst,' she told Frank.

'*Merci, chérie,*' he replied modestly, as though she'd just paid him the greatest compliment. 'And you are the most beautiful passenger, full of calm and encouragement and excellent timing with your directions. I think maybe soon I need some more.'

Knowing if she kept her head down for more than thirty seconds Frank would be pulling over for her to swerve into a ditch, she scanned the rest of the directions as fast as she could. 'At the end of this lane there's a T-junction where we turn right,' she gabbled, 'then we go over a humpback bridge and turn immediately left. After that we follow the road for about a mile, with a high stone wall on one side and a stream on the other until we come to a set of huge black iron gates at which point we will have arrived. She says to call when we reach the T and this must be it, coming up. That's a stop sign, Frank! *Frank! Stop!*'

'I am stopping.'

'Use the brake!'

'Ah, I knew I was forgetting something.' Bringing the car to a nice smooth standstill, he said, 'It is a very good thing you are 'ere, because I would not know how to stop otherwise.'

Stifling a laugh, she turned to look out of the window, taking in the picturesque setting of an old Roman bridge and a narrow stony brook bubbling along beneath a sun-dappled canopy of leaves. Moments later she'd connected to Susannah. 'I think we're about two minutes away,' she told her.

'Fantastic. I've just arrived myself, so I'll make sure the gates are open when you get here. Drive straight up to the house and we'll meet you out front. Is everything OK? How's Jean-Luc?'

'Asleep at the moment, but he's very excited about the horses.'

'Excellent. There's a little Shetland stabled here that belongs to a neighbour, so he can probably ride her. The champagne's on ice and the guest wing's ready, so see you in a . . .'

'We're here! *We're here!*' Patsy shouted, as a set of black gates slid across her peripheral vision. 'We've gone straight past,' she informed Frank hotly, hearing Susannah laugh as she rang off.

Bringing the car to a halt, Frank slipped it into reverse and started to back up. By the time they'd returned to the gates they were gliding open.

'Oh. My. God,' Patsy murmured as they turned into the drive, hardly able to believe her eyes. 'This is something else, isn't it?'

'*C'est magnifique,*' Frank agreed. 'If this is where we spend the next two weeks I might not want to go 'ome again.'

'Me neither,' she smiled, wondering if there really was a sense of peace and tranquillity emanating from the sun-soaked gardens, or if it was simply her need that was creating it. The whole place seemed to ooze an air of romance and elegance, and she could so easily picture Susannah here, moving like a sylph amongst the fountains and statues, a willowy sensuous figure with shining blonde hair, dressed all in white.

As they reached the forecourt Jean-Luc started to stir. *'Papa,'* he said sleepily, *'j'ai perdu mon teddy.'*

'Le voilà,' Pats said, passing it back to him. *'Nous sommes arrivés, chéri. Est-ce que tu voudrais du jus et une grande tranche de gâteau?'* We've arrived now, sweetheart. Are you ready for some juice and a nice big piece of cake?

His large eyes rounded as he nodded.

Hardly able to wait to hug him again, she was out of the car as soon as Frank stopped, and was just lifting him from his car seat when Susannah and Neve erupted out of the house, followed by Michael and an extremely striking young girl, who had to be Ellie.

'Oh my God,' Neve cried as soon as she saw Jean-Luc. 'He's absolutely gorgeous. *Bonjour mon petit,'* she said, holding out a hand to shake his. *'Je m'appelle Neve, et tu es tres beau.'*

Jean-Luc looked uncertainly at Pats, then buried his face in her neck.

'Don't worry, he won't take long to break out of it,' Pats assured Neve, and hugging her with her free arm, she treated her to a hearty kiss on the cheek. 'This place is awesome, isn't it?' she muttered.

'Wait till you see inside,' Neve muttered back, then turning to Michael and Ellie she said, 'El, this is my godmother, Pats, who I've told you all about. Pats, this is Ellie. She's my absolute best friend. Actually, we're more like sisters – and maybe we would be if Mum and Michael could get their act together,' she added under her breath.

'I think he heard,' Pats told her as Michael's eyes started to shine. 'Hi,' she said, embracing him. 'And Ellie, you're not only beautiful, *chérie*, you're stunning, and you also have impeccable taste in best friends.'

Though Ellie blushed slightly, she was clearly thrilled with the compliment, and hardly even hesitated when Pats enveloped her in a hug. 'This is Frank,' she told her, as he came round the car with Susannah. 'And this here is Jean-Luc,' she added, as he peeped up to get another look at what was going on.

'*Est-ce que tu peux nager, Jean-Luc?*' Ellie asked kindly.

'There's a swimming pool here?' Patsy said, looking as though she were about to swoon.

Laughing, Susannah nodded. 'But come on, I'm sure you all want to freshen up before the party, and Lola's dying to see you. She's round the other side on the terrace with Binkie, too hot to move.'

'You mean too squiffy,' Neve corrected. Then, squeezing Patsy's arm as they started towards the house, 'It's so wonderful that you're here,' she said, excitedly. 'Ellie and I have this thing that we're going to tell Mum and Michael about later. It's like the best idea, and I really think everyone's going to love it.'

'I can hardly wait,' Patsy said, glancing at Susannah, who simply shrugged as though to say she had no idea what it could be.

Pats was about to tell Neve that she had some news for her too, but realised she couldn't until she'd run it past Susannah first.

'You are right not to say anything yet,' Frank told her, when they were in the guest-wing sitting room – which was in addition to the guest-wing library, guest-wing TV room and two guest-wing bed-rooms – 'because I 'ave 'ad another thought that per'aps we should discuss. It might change things a little. It is *un peu* wild, but where would we be without wild?'

'I can't imagine,' Patsy laughed, looking up from Jean-Luc's little suitcase, where she was rummaging for trunks. Jean-Luc himself had chosen to stay on the terrace with Neve and Ellie who were jointly doting on him, and feeding him all kinds of treats he probably wasn't allowed, but he was on holiday, so it wouldn't hurt just this once.

'This is right off the top of my 'ead,' Frank said, skidding a palm off his shiny pate, 'but seeing those two girls together just now give me an idea. Maybe, and I stress maybe, they can both be nominated as the face for the teenage range. Ellie is how you say, *trés foncée*?'

'Dark complexion?' Pats provided.

'*Oui*. And Neve is very blonde, so per'aps it is a way to promote all the different colours of the range and maybe we can call it Nevelle, or Nevelly, or something like that. Or nothing like that. Anyway, what do you say, *en principe*?'

661

Patsy was regarding him incredulously. *En principe* it was completely mad, and would change the dynamic of everything they'd already set in motion, but he obviously knew that and it didn't seem to be fazing him at all. Dropping the clothes she was holding, she went to put her arms around him. 'What I say is that you're a genius,' she murmured, with her lips touching his.

'This I know,' he replied with a bat of his eyelashes.

'It won't fly,' she told him, 'but what was it that American guy said, nothing can ever happen without an idea? Or something like that. Actually, I think it was without a dream, but hell, who cares? Everything's worth a shot, so why not your insane . . .' She had to break off as a lingering wave of nausea swept over her. 'Oh, God, I'm sorry,' she said weakly, resting her head on his shoulder. 'It'll pass in a minute.'

'I'm sure it will, but I know, *chérie,* that it is all a part of your plan to make sure you are the one to drive back, not the crazy Frenchman.'

She managed a smile as she said, 'How come I'm so transparent to you, when I'm such a mystery to myself?'

Chapter Thirty-Two

As soon as they were all gathered on the water-garden terrace with glasses in their hands and the evening sun turning everything golden around them, Michael called for quiet and proposed a toast to welcome the guests. 'Please treat the place as your own,' he told them warmly. 'The girls will show you where everything is, such as the pool, tennis courts and stables, and I think you've already met Sheila, my housekeeper, whose every wish will be your command, and no, I don't have that round the wrong way.'

As everyone laughed, Patsy tilted her glass to the fluffy-haired Sheila and received an impish wink in return.

'So now it's only left for me to say drink up, help yourselves to food and may your stay with us be as memorable – in a good way – as we're all hoping for.'

As Susannah sipped her champagne, her eyes were on his, watching him and the way he was watching her. Though she could feel the current of a silent communication running between them, she couldn't be sure what he was saying, only knew that it had been like this for weeks, and still she hadn't summoned the courage to take it any further. She wasn't entirely sure she ever would, since he'd made no move to, either.

'You have to take the initiative,' Lola kept telling her. 'I can't see why he'd have a problem with that.'

'He's a man who knows his own mind,' Susannah argued. 'If he wants something, he goes out to get it. I'm here, we see each other all the time, and he's doing nothing, so I'd say that speaks for itself. Besides, Neve is my priority, and I really don't want to go rushing into anything again.'

'Pffft,' was Lola's usual reply, an expressive little sound that she was making right now as Sheila failed to refill her glass up to the brim.

Aware of Michael coming to stand beside her, Susannah continued to smile at the way everyone was becoming involved in Jean-Luc's cute attempts to speak English. He was doing so well for someone so young, and not only with the language, because he didn't appear in the least bit tired after travelling all the way from Paris. In fact, he was decidedly lively, and apparently not at all daunted by being the centre of attention.

'Shall we go inside for a moment?' Michael said quietly.

Trying to ignore the jolt in her heart, since he was almost certainly intending to report back about Alan, she kept hold of her glass and followed him through the kitchen into the conservatory, where the overhead fans were rotating at speed, and the first crimson rays of sunset were bathing the plants in a vivid fiery light.

After opening the outside door to let in more

air, he said, 'Helen Cunningham has not dropped the charges. The trial is still scheduled to go ahead in October. So nothing's changed.'

Feeling even more relief than she'd expected, she sounded slightly shaky as she said, 'Thank you for going to the trouble of finding out. I wish I knew how he got my number. Maybe I should change it again.'

'It's probably not a bad idea,' he agreed. Then, after sipping his champagne, 'Actually, that's not all.'

She became very still, hoping against hope that whatever else there was, it wouldn't be bad.

He smiled, as though to relax her. 'I've instructed the lawyers to write to your husband again, assuring him that Neve is perfectly safe here, so he doesn't have to worry about what he's reading in the press. It might be a good idea for you to speak to him yourself, though. Or Neve, if she feels up to it.'

'I will,' Susannah promised, horribly aware of how small-time, and probably sordid, her life must seem to someone like him whose own existence was so far removed from the world of junkies, money-grubbers and worst-imaginable offenders. Knowing she'd brought it to his doorstep was making her feel more ashamed than ever. 'If I offer him some rent from the house, I'm sure he'll stop making a fuss and go away,' she said, knowing her humiliation was showing in the colour of her cheeks. 'I'm not sure about Neve,' she went on awkwardly, 'but I'll put it to her.' She took a sip of champagne to bolster herself, then forced a smile.

'That's better,' he told her softly.

She looked up into his eyes.

His gaze was intense and knowing and making her heart beat faster.

Lifting his glass, he said, 'So, Pats is here at last. I know how much you've been looking forward to seeing her. It's a pity you couldn't get more time off, but the rest of us will do our best to keep them entertained.'

'She won't want you to go to any trouble,' Susannah assured him, 'and at least I'll be here for the first week.' Then, feeling self-conscious and oddly at a loss, she found herself bringing up a subject she'd intended to leave until tomorrow. 'I'm not sure what you're going to make of this,' she said, 'I have to admit, I'm quite flummoxed by it myself, but I was talking to Pats before the party and, well . . . She and Frank would like to know what *we* think of the girls being put forward as possible faces for a new range of cosmetics designed for teens.'

He blinked in confusion and frowned. 'You mean, like . . .' He was searching for a word. 'Models?' he said, clearly unable to come up with a more agreeable term, at least as far as he was concerned.

'I suppose like that, yes,' she answered, hiding a smile. 'If we're not opposed to it, they'd like to take some photographs while they're here to show to the Bryce board when they get back to Paris.'

Still obviously thrown, he took a breath and blew it out slowly.

Realising he was trying to find a polite way of saying no, she decided to speak up for the cause, guardedly, in spite of her own reservations. 'You'll need to discuss it with Rita, of course,' she said, 'and we'll want to know a lot more about what it entails before we can give the go-ahead, such as whether they'd be required to take time off school. If they are, personally, I don't think I can agree to it.'

'Me neither,' he said, evidently glad to be offered at least one objection.

'This is every young girl's dream,' she reminded him gently, 'and if you don't mind me saying so, you're starting to look a little curmudgeonly.'

He immediately laughed. 'OK, let's keep it to ourselves for now,' he said, 'because I'm sure once the star babes get hold of it there'll be no turning it down.'

'To be frank, I'm not sure we can anyway. Think about it, how's your conscience going to cope with knowing you've prevented your daughter having a chance at a once-in-a-lifetime opportunity of fame and fortune?'

He looked defeated. 'Put like that, not at all well,' he admitted.

She started to smile.

Meeting her eyes, he was on the verge of saying more, when the door swung open and Neve burst in, all puffed up ready to speak. Coming to an abrupt halt as she suddenly realised she was spoiling her own plans, she quickly backed out again, saying, 'Sorry, ignore me. I didn't happen. Gone. Bye.'

As the door closed Susannah turned back to Michael, amused and embarrassed. 'I apologise for my daughter,' she said. 'I'm not quite sure what that was about . . . Anyway, you were about to say?'

'I only wish I had the chance,' he replied, 'because I do believe my own daughter is about to . . . Yes, here she is,' and once again the door swung open, this time with Ellie surging in its wake.

'Dad, I'm really, really sorry,' she began with feeling, 'but Neve and I have an announcement we have to make, and it won't work if you and Susannah aren't there.'

'Can't it wait?' Michael asked reasonably.

'No, it can't. We've been building up to this, and we rehearsed it so's we'd say it right at the start of the party, then you go and disappear . . . *Don't* look at me like that!'

'Like what?' he laughed.

'Like that.'

Susannah glanced up him, but saw only innocence where a moment ago there had been a terrible scowl.

'OK, let's get it over with,' Michael sighed, 'or I can see we'll never have any peace.'

'*Yes!*' Ellie cheered, and spun round to go out again.

Once they were back on the terrace, Michael obediently followed Ellie's instructions by refilling everyone's glasses and standing next to Susannah as Neve linked an arm through Ellie's, and waited for everyone to be quiet.

'What's going on?' Binkie grunted from her deckchair, only half awake.

'I'll tell you tomorrow,' Lola whispered.

'OK,' Neve began, starting to go up and down

on her toes, 'this is our announcement. Well, actually, it's more of a suggestion really, but it's really cool and I know you're going to love it, Mum, because it's the answer to everything, and I mean everything. Well, almost everything . . . Anyway, I hope you'll love it, because I really do.' She took a quick breath and said, 'I've been thinking about this, and I was wondering if, in September, instead of going back to my old school I could go to Lady Jane's, with Ellie.' She pressed her lips together in an anxious smile and looked at her mother pleadingly.

Susannah only blinked.

Neve continued to watch her, hopefully, encouragingly.

Still at a loss, Susannah turned to Michael, whose expression told her that this was the first he'd heard of the scheme, too. However, Lola, she noticed, was beaming happily and nodding, making it clear she was fully aware of the plan and heartily approved.

'But it's a *boarding* school,' Susannah finally managed, with a meaningful glare at Lola.

'Yes, but I'd be coming home at weekends,' Neve told her, 'so it wouldn't really be any different to before, except you won't have to worry about who's picking me up, or dropping me off, or where I'm staying each night, because I'll be at school.'

Susannah could hardly refute that, but was still confounded as she looked at Patsy.

'Sounds a pretty good solution to me,' Pats told her.

'It *is*,' Neve insisted. 'It's only about twenty

miles from here, so you could even come and pick me up in the G Wiz without running out of power. Well, it might be a bit far, but Ellie gets the train, so I can always come with her, except when she goes to her mum's, because she has to go in another direction then. Anyway, I think it's a really good idea and it's what I want to do, so . . .'

'Neve, hang on, hang on,' Susannah interrupted. 'We need to discuss this in private . . .'

'Why?' Neve cried, starting to redden with frustration.

'You know very well why.'

'No, I don't.'

'OK, then I'll say it now. You seem to be assuming that we'll still be at the Long House after the summer, but this is only temporary. We'll be going back to . . .' She looked down as Michael put a hand on her arm.

'Personally, I think it's worth considering,' he declared, 'but before anyone starts getting carried away, it might be a good idea to find out if there's a place available.'

'We already know that there *is*,' Ellie jumped in. 'Gemma Gibson left at the end of last term, so . . .'

'And the place might already be taken,' he interrupted. 'No, listen,' he said, as she made to go on, 'I've already told you that in principle it's worth considering, but Susannah obviously needs some time to get used to it, and . . .'

'We can definitely afford the fees now, Mum,' Neve told her plaintively.

Susannah started to answer, but suddenly found herself wanting to laugh. 'OK, let's do as Michael says and take one step at a time,' she said. 'Right now, I think we need to ask Pats if she's feeling all right. You've gone very pale,' she told her, as everyone turned to look at Pats.

'Oh, I'm fine,' Pats assured her. Then, 'Actually, on second thoughts . . .'

Frank took away her glass, saying, 'I think maybe you need . . .' He whispered in her ear and she nodded.

'Need what?' Susannah prompted.

'If you will excuse us, ladies and gentlemen,' Frank said, slipping an arm round Pats, and a moment later they were hurrying in through the kitchen.

Neve's eyes were wide as she looked at Susannah.

Susannah laughed and threw out her hands.

'*Où il va, Papa?*' Jean-Luc asked Neve.

'Oh, sweetie,' she said, scooping him up. 'He's just popped inside. He'll be back any minute.'

His big eyes filled with worry.

'Say it in French,' Susannah reminded her, and putting down her glass she went off to find out what was going on.

'She is in the bathroom at the end,' Frank told her, as she came upon him in the hall. 'And please take care, because she is kicking the bookette.'

'She's what?' Susannah laughed, knowing he couldn't mean how it had sounded.

'This is the right expression, *non*, when someone vomit?'

'No,' she told him, highly amused. 'I'll go and see how she is.'

671

Finding the bathroom door unlocked, Susannah let herself in and closed it behind her.

'Frank, I swear I'm going to brain you if you offer me . . .'

'It's me,' Susannah told her.

Pats lifted her head, and after deciding she could probably stand upright, she turned away from the loo, dabbing a towel to her mouth. 'What brought this on?' Susannah asked suspiciously.

'It's travel sickness,' Pats answered.

'Are you sure?'

'Of course I am.' Then, seeming to realise what Susannah was thinking, 'I'm on the Pill.'

'Maybe you forgot to take one.'

Patsy regarded her with menace.

Susannah started to grin. 'You'd make a wonderful mother,' she told her.

'I'm telling you, I'm not pregnant. Apart from being on the Pill, it's the time of the month.'

Susannah looked dejected.

'Will you behave!' Patsy protested. 'We've hardly been an item for five minutes, so it would be a bit rash to be having a baby now.'

Sighing, Susannah said, 'As someone who's just learned the hard way what it can mean to jump in too soon, I guess I have to agree. I was just thinking . . . No, you're right. It's way too early for anything like that, but I know you want children, so . . .'

'I'm still only thirty-six,' Pats cried, 'so don't write me off yet. It'll happen when the time's right, just not yet. Now come on, tell me, what's going on with you and Michael? You've been in this dreamy place for weeks and still no action?'

Susannah had to laugh. 'Does the romantic poets' society know what they're missing in you?' she wondered.

Patsy grinned. 'Seriously, what's really going on? I saw the two of you slip away just now, so what was that about?'

Susannah's eyebrows arched. 'As it happens, it was about Alan, but don't worry, it's not serious,' she added when Patsy's expression darkened. 'We won't go into it now, it's not worth it. What I can tell you, though, is that I mentioned your proposal for the girls, and he's not *entirely* opposed to it, but he's not exactly wild about it either. My guess is it'll get a more sympathetic hearing from Rita.'

'Well, it's a long way from being set in stone,' Pats reminded her, 'and it might never happen, but I think Frank's right, it's worth exploring. Now, to haul us back on track – what is going on between you and Michael? Anyone with eyes in their head, or romance in their soul, can sense the chemistry between you, so . . . ?' She spread out her hands in encouragement.

'I don't know,' Susannah said with a sigh. 'He never actually says anything. We just seem to dance around one another, a little flirtation here, the odd look or suggestion there . . . I keep thinking maybe he likes me, but doesn't want to get involved, and maybe I don't either after everything . . .'

'Oh for heaven's sake,' Patsy huffed impatiently. 'How can he not want to be involved with *you*? Look at you. Unless the man's gay, or celibate, or gaga, which he clearly isn't, he's got to be mad for you, so *you* have to stop holding back, because I suspect that's what's really going on here. He's just being sensitive to what you've been through . . . No, don't argue with me. I'm sure I'm right, not that I blame you, because having got it so spectacularly wrong before, I can see that you might be afraid to trust yourself again.'

Susannah swallowed. 'So what do I do?'

Patsy took a breath to answer, before realising she didn't have one. 'I think,' she said in the end, 'you have to start trusting *him* – and that shouldn't be too difficult when we consider everything he's done for you. I mean, just letting you be here should be enough to kill off all your self-doubt . . .'

'Yes, but . . .'

'No buts. Think about it this way. He hasn't pushed himself on you at all while you've been here – he's seemed to understand very well that you need time and space after what you've been through. In my book that proves he's really valuing you and the chance of a future relationship. Actually, the more I talk about him, the more I'm falling for him myself, except Frank's a pretty worthy individual with his heart in the right place . . . Not a lot else, it has to be said, but that's another story. Back to Michael. You have to admit that he's really been there for you since everything blew up. Even before that, because he's the one who changed your life, who really believed in you, and made your dreams come true. Oh God, someone please give me a violin.'

Susannah bubbled with laughter.

'He really cares for you, my darling,' Patsy told

her with feeling. 'Anyone can see it. He just needs to know that you're ready for him to come into your life the way he wants to be in it.'

As a wild surge of nerves coasted through her, Susannah said, 'Come on, let's go and rejoin the party. We'll have plenty of time to talk over the next two weeks.'

A while later, as Pats and Frank strolled amongst the reflecting ponds with Jean-Luc, and Neve and Ellie sat making a fuss of Lola and Binkie, Michael emptied the last of a bottle of champagne into Susannah's glass, saying, 'Well, I think the welcome party was a success, do you?'

'Very much so,' she told him warmly. 'It's incredibly kind of you to have invited them, and to let them stay here, at the manor.'

His eyebrows arched humorously. 'It's not as if we're short of space,' he said drily. Then, after finishing his drink, 'I hear Silver's coming over tomorrow.'

She nodded. 'Just for the weekend. It'll be wonderful to ride him more freely, without a crew around us, and the usual stop-start of the action.'

'Maybe I could join you on one of our horses,' he suggested.

Her eyes went up to his. 'I'd love that,' she replied, probably too eagerly, but the idea of galloping through the dales with him was lighting up every romantic thought in her soul.

He smiled, then went to help Lola into her wheelchair so Binkie could take her back to the Long House.

After kissing both old ladies goodnight, Susannah stood with Michael, watching them weaving a little unsteadily along the path that led over to the stables. She could feel his presence as warmly as the evening sun on her skin. He could almost be touching her, and she was almost leaning back against him. Catching her breath, she gazed out at the surrounding hills, glowing like molten honey at the end of a blisteringly hot day. All her senses were aware of him. It felt as though something invisible was fusing them. She thought his eyes might be on her, but she didn't look, only continued to drink in the beautiful scenery.

'I imagine the sunsets here are even more spectacular in winter,' she said, hardly aware of what she was saying. Then, afraid that might sound as though she was angling to stay on to find out, she said, 'I'm just thinking about how the mist changes colours and shades and . . . This is beautiful, but it's pristine and clear, and sometimes more depth and shadow add so many other dimensions . . .' With a hiccup of laughter she said, 'I wish I knew what I was talking about. It must be the champagne.' She wanted to turn and look into his eyes, but was afraid to in case her own were too full of feeling.

In the end she felt his hand on her arm, and as he eased her round to face him her breath stopped and her heartbeat started to slow.

He waited for her to look up, and as their eyes met he said, very softly, 'Will you spend the night here with me?'

As a wave of desire rushed through her, she began to smile at the humour that came into his eyes. Clearly he'd registered their silent audience too, though no one could have heard what had been said. 'You realise everyone will know?' she said quietly.

Leaning in a little closer, he said, 'I've a suspicion they're expecting it.'

She gave a gurgle of laughter, and as he touched the backs of his fingers to her cheek she could only wish that they were already alone.

When finally they were, he drew her into his arms, and as his mouth came to hers, tenderly and brutally, she knew then that all the dreams she'd had of him holding her like this, peeling away her clothes and pressing his body to hers, were going to pale in the dazzling light of reality.

Missing

Susan Lewis

It's an early autumn day like any other as Miles Avery drives his wife, Jacqueline, to the station. Nothing remarkable crops up in conversation, nor do either of them appear anything other than their normal selves. At the station, Jacqueline gets out, takes an overnight bag from the back seat, then turns towards the platforms. This is the last anyone sees of her.

Three weeks later, Miles calls the police. Enquiries are made, but there is no evidence of her boarding a train, or even entering the station. Very soon the finger of suspicion starts to turn towards Miles, and as dark secrets from the past begin to merge with those of the present, the great love he has been trying to protect is not only revealed but thrown into terrible jeopardy . . .

'A multi-faceted tear jerker' *heat*

'An irresistible blend of intrigue and passion, and the consequences of secrets and betrayal' *Woman*

arrow books

A French Affair

Susan Lewis

When Natalie Moore is killed in a freak accident in France her mother – the very poised and elegant Jessica – knows instinctively there is more to it. However, Natalie's father – the glamorous, high-flying Charlie – is so paralysed by the horror of losing his daughter, that he refuses even to discuss his wife's suspicions.

In the end, when their marriage is rocked by yet another terrible shock, Jessica decides to go back to France alone in search of some answers. When she gets to the idyllic vineyard in the heart of Burgundy she soon finds a great deal more than she was expecting in a love that is totally forbidden and a truth that will almost certainly devastate her life . . .

'One of the best around' *Independent on Sunday*

'Spellbinding! . . . you just keep turning the pages, with the atmosphere growing more and more intense as the story leads to its dramatic climax' *Daily Mail*

arrow books

THE POWER OF READING

Visit the Random House website and get connected with information on all our books and authors

EXTRACTS from our recently published books and selected backlist titles

COMPETITIONS AND PRIZE DRAWS Win signed books, audiobooks and more

AUTHOR EVENTS Find out which of our authors are on tour and where you can meet them

LATEST NEWS on bestsellers, awards and new publications

MINISITES with exclusive special features dedicated to our authors and their titles

READING GROUPS Reading guides, special features and all the information you need for your reading group

LISTEN to extracts from the latest audiobook publications

WATCH video clips of interviews and readings with our authors

RANDOM HOUSE INFORMATION including advice for writers, job vacancies and all your general queries answered

Come home to Random House

www.rbooks.co.uk